FAST DEATH OF A SHORTSTOP

Lofton found Franklin Street. He identified the house more easily than he thought he would, the name ROSA in pink letters on the mailbox. He knocked on the door, but no one answered. He tried to see through the gauze curtains hanging on the inside of the door's window. He knocked again, tried the handle, and stepped inside. He called Gutierrez's name. He hesitated. Maybe Gutierrez was sick, or asleep. Maybe he should forget it and go back to the park. No, he wanted this story. Lofton stepped around the corner into the kitchen and saw Gutierrez lying on the floor, dressed in his baseball uniform, his body twisted at a bad angle between the table and the refrigerator.

"The theme of the lone heroic reporter in a town full of enemies is rendered with some authentic newsroom touches."
—*Publishers Weekly*

"The haunting landscape Stansberry paints stays with you in a way that baseball books and mysteries often can't."
—*The Spokesman-Review/Spokane Chronicle*

"The character portraits here—and most of the sturdy baseball sequences—are quietly absorbing." —*Kirkus Reviews*

QUANTITY SALES

Most Dell books are available at special quantity discounts when purchased in bulk by corporations, organizations, and special-interest groups. Custom imprinting or excerpting can also be done to fit special needs. For details write: Dell Publishing, 666 Fifth Avenue, New York, NY 10103. Attn.: Special Sales Department.

INDIVIDUAL SALES

Are there any Dell books you want but cannot find in your local stores? If so, you can order them directly from us. You can get any Dell book in print. Simply include the book's title, author, and ISBN number if you have it, along with a check or money order (no cash can be accepted) for the full retail price plus $2.00 to cover shipping and handling. Mail to: Dell Readers Service, P.O. Box 5057, Des Plaines, IL 60017.

THE SPOILER

Domenic Stansberry

A DELL BOOK

Published by
Dell Publishing
a division of
Bantam Doubleday Dell Publishing Group, Inc.
666 Fifth Avenue
New York, New York 10103

ISBN: 0-440-20304-X

Reprinted by arrangement with Atlantic Monthly Press

Printed in the United States of America

Published simultaneously in Cananda

April 1990

10 9 8 7 6 5 4 3 2 1

OPM

I would like to thank Joyce Johnson, Jay Neugeboren, and David Lyon—each of whom helped tremendously with the writing of this book.

This book is a work of fiction. All the characters who play a part in the story are creations of the author's imagination. Even the city of Holyoke differs in some respects from the real Holyoke, Massachusetts.

for Adam Hammer

THE
SPOILER

1

Below him, in the dirt beneath the third base bleachers, a gang of kids played flip for quarters. When the game got slow, Lofton looked down past his feet, through the planks, and watched them. They played two at a time, first scratching a cross in the dirt, then sketching a circle around it. They flipped their knives through the air, seeing who could come closest, point first, to dead center.

When a fire truck took a nearby corner, its siren lilting and whirling, echoing through all the neighboring streets at once, the kids stopped playing and pushed toward the left field gate. Frank Lofton watched them jump on their bicycles and give chase. He imagined the warm, damp air rushing by their faces, the sweat on their arms, as they pedaled after the siren, into the old immigrant neighborhood. Closer by, other teenagers leaped over a wire fence, then ran to catch up with the engine.

Lofton couldn't blame the kids for wanting more action. The game was slow; the Holyoke Redwings were losing. The Redwings' pitcher wiped his brow, stared at the batter, then wiped his brow again. The catcher, his iron mask yanked back over his head, walked out to talk to his battery mate. More fans were moving to the top of the bleachers. They craned to see the fire, but there seemed to be nothing to see. Although fires were a familiar sight in this part of town, this time there were no flames, only the usual smoke rising from the blackened stacks of Holyoke's paper mills.

The truck had parked nearby on Beech Street, its siren off, its lights still flashing. Two men climbed from the truck and walked to one of the wooden row houses. Lofton pulled out a cigarette. He took a couple of puffs, then felt—or imagined he felt—the familiar ache in his chest. He held the cigarette a little farther from him but did not put it out.

The two firemen, small and distant in their yellow slickers, walked back to the truck, unable to find the fire. On the field the Redwings' pitcher went into his windup. Lofton stared at the siren lights blinking off and on, red and yellow, over and over. He heard the rumble of traffic. He felt the summer heat on his skin. Hypnotized, as people sometimes are by summer and baseball and evening lights, he let his mind empty. He tried to think about nothing at all. He touched his chest. He let out a deep breath. *The doctor was playing games with me. A real joker. A fraud.* Even so, Lofton supposed the doctor, despite his unfathomable manner, might be well intentioned.

Wood snapped against rawhide, like the cracking of bone. The Glens Falls runner rounded third, put his head down, and kept going. A second later he spiked his toe into the heart of home plate, and the Holyoke Redwings trailed by four. Across the way the fire engine switched off its flashing lights and pulled into traffic, headed up the hill toward the freeway and the Old Soldiers' Home, with the kids pedaling behind.

"False alarm," said a woman in the stands near Lofton, her voice soft and gruff, like that of an unhappy lover. Lofton shared her disappointment. Like the others, he would have liked to see a fire. He took a drag off his cigarette, then put it out against the bleachers.

Lofton had learned from Marvin Tenace, the team scorer, that the Holyoke Redwings had never had a winning team here in Massachusetts. The Redwings were a minor league club, operated by the California Blues and franchised out to Massachusetts owners. The names of the local owners changed every few years, but the results were always the same: The Redwings lost a lot of games, and the crowds were small. The problem was not here in Holyoke, Massachusetts, Tenace told Lofton, but on the West Coast. Lofton heard the same from the players, the fans, and the crew in the press box. The California brass spent its money on its big-league talent, buying established stars from other big-league teams. It let its minor league club in Holyoke go its own way, a break-even affair for the local owners, maybe, and a write-off for the California organization, as well as a place for the players to mature.

"Mature, hell," the center fielder Elvin Banks had told Lofton. "I'm an old man." Banks was twenty-six.

Lofton, a free-lance writer for the *Holyoke Dispatch,* had been in town for only a month, since early in July. He had been a reporter for thirteen years, and it had not been too hard talking the *Dispatch* editors into giving him a few features, though the editors tried to steer him away from ballpark stories and into the city. Still, he spent much of his time at the ballpark. Lofton had played a few years of college ball—a good freshman season, a fair sophomore, a bad junior—but never, except in pure idleness, had he considered going professional. Even so, he was curious about the players. Most of those here were out of California, brought up from the Single A club in Redwood City. Now they found themselves at the other end of the country, in a struggling mill town where the unemployment rate was high and many of the downtown buildings had been burned and gutted by fire. The unmarried players roomed together in pairs. The lucky ones lived in redesigned convenience apartments not far from the ballpark, at the edge of the Puerto Rican neighborhood. The married men, at least those who could afford to bring their wives, lived farther out in places like Chicopee and Westfield and Springfield—anyplace that was not Holyoke.

Though few players admitted it, most knew they did not have the talent to make the big leagues. In a way, it was worse for those who had talent, or thought they did. Lofton had heard the players gripe. There were no openings at the top, they said, not in sunny California. The big boss, Cowboy, a retired Hollywood singer, liked to hold on to his organization's minor league talent until it was overripe and rotting on the vine. Bruised bones. Broken ribs. Torn cartilage. It was not until you were useless that Cowboy put you on the block.

The other clubs had gotten wise. Nobody touched dead meat.
They let anyone with Cowboy's brand float off the waiver list
and out into the street.

Lofton did not know how long he would stay in Holyoke.
A short, balding man in his late thirties, he had driven out
from Colorado in a rusted Plymouth that threw clouds of
smoke from its exhaust. While behind the wheel, he'd often
looked at himself in the rearview mirror. He did not look like
a man who had just left his wife. He did not look like a man
who, concerned he might be dying, had slammed out of the
doctor's office before getting a diagnosis. (Thinking back, he
suspected his behavior that day with the doctor had been a
sham; he had other reasons for wanting to run away from his
life, from Maureen.) Every time he glanced in the rearview
mirror, he looked fine. The police, however, did not care how
he looked. They stopped him twice for the Plymouth's black
exhaust, once in Nebraska, the other time just outside New
York City. The car was in his wife's name, and the tickets
would go to her address. Maureen had always written the
checks. If she were not thinking—or caught in a moment of
tenderness—Maureen might pay for the tickets. *She should
tear the tickets up,* he thought, but he knew that she wouldn't.
Maureen had always been generous with him, generous to a
fault, and though Lofton hated to admit it, to treat her badly
gave him pleasure.

On the mound the Redwings' pitcher was losing control.
After giving up the run, he had walked the next man and was
about to do the same with this batter.

Closer by, in the stands near Lofton, the small crowd yelled
encouragement and stomped on the bleachers. A large,
drunken man in a blue T-shirt beat on an overturned garbage
can with a kitchen spoon. That man and the others who made
the most noise, including the small contingent from the halfway house across from MacKenzie Field—these were the
regulars.

Lofton eyed the young pitcher, a tall blond kid by the name
of Rickey Sparks. Down from a bad year with the Triple A
club in Salt Lake, Sparks had been the Redwings' only decent
hurler through the first half of the season; he pitched every
fourth, sometimes every third game in the rotation. It was a
lot of work, some said too much, for a pitcher at this level.

Nonetheless, Sparks had thrown well during the first half of the season, bluffing the Eastern League batters with a bad curve, then firing the ball past them. But Salt Lake did not call him back, Coach Barker overworked him, his only real pitch was the fastball, and now his arm was getting sore. Between games, and sometimes even between innings, Sparks sat with his arm immersed in a barrel of ice. He was determined to get back to Salt Lake, then up to the majors before the end of the season, so he could be with the big club for the play-offs, warming up in the bullpen while Cowboy watched from behind his glass booth and smoked his Hollywood cigar, smiling benignly whenever the TV cameras zoomed by.

Sparks was sweating on the mound. He bore down hard, trying to ignore the men on base. The runners broke with the pitch, and Sparks threw wild to the plate. The catcher, a lumpy Polish boy whose last name Lofton could never remember, was unable to field the ball. The runners advanced, walking the last few feet and mocking the crowd.

Coach Barker went out to talk to Sparks. He touched the youngster on the shoulder to calm him, in a fatherly manner, Lofton noticed, though he must have known he was ruining Sparks's arm by pitching him so often. Now that Lofton thought about it, he realized that Sparks, who had signed out of high school, probably was not that much older than his own boy, from his first marriage. Maybe five years. He had seen the boy once: a small, wrinkled, and ugly infant.

Barker left Sparks in. The Glens Falls batter cracked the next pitch, a weak fastball, back harder than it came. The ball, hit knee-high, backspinning and whiffling through the humid air, bounced off the infield grass, past the diving shortstop—Randy Gutierrez—and out into left field. Both runners scored. Coach Barker called time and headed out again. When Sparks saw him, he threw his glove into the dirt and stomped off the field. The crowd stood and hissed. They were mean, tired of losing.

Go soak that flamethrower, Sparks. . . . That's right, soak that flaming asshole. . . . Loser, loser, loser . . . Soak her up good, Sparks. . . . Go on, go back to your mother. . . .

While the new pitcher warmed up, Lofton stepped behind the press box, a beaten yellow stand with plywood benches and a door that would neither close nor open completely.

Teenagers, walking by with hot dogs and Cokes, beat on the back of the box with their fists, enjoying the sound of the thumping, shaking wood. The reporters inside did not bother to chase the kids away.

Lofton was working on a story for the *Dispatch,* a quick color piece about tonight's game. The regular sportswriter was on vacation. The *Dispatch*'s editor paid Lofton by the piece. Not a good way for a reporter to make money, but he was not too concerned. He still had some money left over from his days in California as a regular reporter—from those long years between his two marriages—and he had money coming from a piece on street crime he had sold in Denver. Anyway, he did not mind being broke. He hustled more; he felt more alive on the streets.

He had been headed for Boston when he left Denver. He wanted an eastern city, he told himself, something different, something far away. Holyoke had been an overnight stop. He remembered it from his college days at the University of Massachusetts, a dozen or so miles over the hill in Amherst. He had intended to drive the next morning into Boston, about two hours away; but instead, he'd stumbled across the Redwings playing ball in this dusty park. Now, several weeks and a half dozen stories later, he was still here, still in town, still wandering the streets. Sometimes he thought about his first wife, Nancy, who lived not too far away—along with his son and her husband—over the border in Vermont. Though the notion had crossed his mind, he did not intend to visit her.

Lofton leaned against the press box and watched the new pitcher warm up. He decided to wait to get his story, partly because Sparks needed time to calm down but also because he himself was in no real hurry. He did not like doing interviews, and he enjoyed leaning against the press box. He could lean there and let his thoughts spin lazily, disappearing like a fly ball into the haze over right field.

"I get men your age doing this all the time. They have trouble at home, trouble being happy. And instead of admitting what's going on, they decide it's something else. Something physical," the doctor said. He toyed with a paper clip as he spoke. *"And some of them are right about themselves. Some of them are dying. But most of you,"* the doctor went on, smiling

cryptically, "you're just bored. You're just looking for something to flirt with."

Lofton thought about it. He looked out the window at the blue sky.

"Listen, I'll level with you. I can give you a lot of tests, and they'll cost a lot of money, and if they come up positive, there's nothing I can do. You want my advice?" the doctor asked, pointing at Lofton's shirt pocket.

"No," said Lofton.

When he looked at the field, he could not remember the name of Sparks's replacement on the mound. He had seen the reliever before, grew up in Bakersfield or some forsaken part of the Golden State. The reliever threw high fastballs and slow curves, always over the plate. His pitching was beautiful to watch. Unfortunately it was also easy to hit. The Glens Falls batters would love him. It was going to be a long game. Lofton ducked into the press box to get the reliever's name.

Inside, Marvin Tenace, the scorer, was complaining. Tenace always complained. He liked to run down the new local owners, Jack Brunner and Tony Liuzza, a businessman and a lawyer who had bought the Holyoke franchise together during the off-season. The California organization still controlled player development, of course; Brunner and Liuzza rented the park and collected the gate.

"Those jokers don't care anything about increasing attendance," Tenace said, shaking his head. "They're too busy touching each other's cocks."

Tenace, of course, did not say such things when the owners were around. An ungainly man, as overweight as he was rude, Tenace was uneasy when the reporters and the owners happened to be around at the same time.

There had been a general uneasiness in the press box, about a week back, on the day Lofton had first met Jack Brunner and Tony Liuzza. Lofton hadn't been on assignment that night; he had just been killing time in the press box. It was a promotion night; the team was giving away decals at the gate. Brunner and Liuzza had walked up to the box so the local writers could get a story and the team could get publicity. A young woman had walked up with them. A dark-haired woman, wearing a stark white blouse, she hung back while the reporters asked the owners questions. She had a way of standing, with her head to the side and one foot turned out, pointing away, that made it seem as if she were watching for something coming up behind her. Twenty-seven, twenty-eight years old, Lofton guessed. Despite her distracted air, Lofton could see the young woman was listening. She eyed the reporters as they asked Brunner and Liuzza the usual things, good-natured stuff intended to help the new owners get their publicity: How do you feel about your partnership now, more than halfway into the season? What are you going to do to improve attendance? What do you think the Redwings can do to get out of their slump?

Tony Liuzza, the lawyer, a neatly dressed man in his early forties, answered most of the questions. He smiled often, but his smile lingered awkwardly and gave the impression—inherent in his overly delicate, thin lips—that the smile itself was somehow painful. Even though he answered all the questions the right way, his manner was a little too studied, and he did not seem at ease talking to the reporters.

The older of the two owners, Jack Brunner, was tall and big-boned, with high cheekbones, graying temples, and sharp iron-gray eyes. He was in his middle fifties. At first Brunner said little during the interview. A businessman, he owned some buildings in downtown Holyoke and some welfare housing in the mill area. While Tony Liuzza answered the questions from the press, Brunner watched. The dark-haired woman watched, too. Lofton caught her eyes once, then a second time. He wondered what she had to do with the owners.

Toward the end of the interview there was one of those silences in which the reporters seemed to run out of questions. It happened often enough, particularly on promotion pieces like this one where you ended up with a little content and a lot of fluff. Then the Springfield reporter, a young kid named Rhiner, came up with another question, off the wall, it seemed at first, at least to Lofton.

"How are you two getting along now, with the election heating up?"

There was an awkward silence. The thin smile was fixed painfully on Liuzza's face. Brunner made no attempt to answer. The young reporter pushed the question further, directing it toward Brunner now. "What's going on in the legislature? What's Senator Kelley up to with your project?"

Lofton was curious despite himself. He had heard Senator Kelley's name batted around the press box before. Kelley was Holyoke's representative to the State Senate, a rising politician. ("The women voted him in," Tenace had said one day. "They voted for the bulge in his pants.") Lofton wondered what connection Senator Kelley might have to the Redwings and their owners, but the silence went on, Liuzza staring shyly at the ground, Brunner beside him as quiet and helpful as a bull whose pasture you had just strayed into. At the mention of Kelley's name, however, the young woman had lost her distracted air. She studied the young reporter who had asked the question.

"Yes, why don't you tell us about Kelley?" Lofton said, a bit surprised at himself. He hadn't intended to do anything but listen, but asking questions was something he did instinctively, grabbing at information, at names. Also, he realized, he had wanted to see if he could get the young woman's attention. He did. She studied him now as she had studied the other reporter.

"Come on, guys," Tenace said. "This is baseball. Don't ask questions like that. You know what Jack Brunner is doing for downtown, now, don't you?"

Brunner gave Tenace a quick, hard look, then unexpectedly turned to the reporters and smiled. He had the sort of charm that large men sometimes have, despite their size, or maybe because of it; his voice was deep, seductive in its self-confidence.

"Come on, I'm a businessman," Brunner said. "Of course I want a profit on my buildings downtown. The renovations on my property are an investment. I'd be doing that no matter what. If it's good for the town, if it builds things up, that's what business is supposed to do."

There was another pause. Lofton didn't quite understand; Brunner was talking not about Senator Kelley but about local business, about real estate development and downtown property.

"Sure," Brunner went on, "Tony Liuzza and I, we have our differences off the field, but it's nothing; when you get down to it, we're both still Democrats." Brunner put a hand on Tony

Liuzza's shoulder. "Don't let anybody fool you about that. . . . Come on, let's enjoy the ball game."

As a way of ending the interview, Brunner shook hands with the reporters. He would have passed over Lofton if Tenace hadn't intervened.

"Don't forget our new man. He's a real reporter. From out of town," Tenace said, trying to be funny. "He's with the *Dispatch* now—showing the rest of these guys how it's supposed to be done."

"Down from the big leagues, huh?" Brunner said as he shook Lofton's hand. His grip was firm, and he held the handshake longer than most men, long enough to make you want to let go. The young woman was still watching, taking in this interchange.

After the owners had left, Lofton listened to the reporters' banter. He learned that Brunner and Liuzza were both active in the Democratic party. Brunner supported the current governor. Liuzza, on the other hand, had decided to support the liberal challenger in the upcoming Democratic primaries. Liuzza had political ambition as well as family money, and it was rumored that the combination would fetch him a good-size plum—maybe a secretaryship in the Massachusetts Department of Education—if his man won the governorship.

"So there's bad blood between Brunner and Liuzza?"

Rhiner, the young Springfield reporter, shrugged.

"No," said Tenace. "No bad blood. Brunner and Liuzza are still buddies. Weren't you listening?"

"And what about that renovation project? What's that about?"

Nobody responded, at least not right away. The reporters were watching the game, and it took a while before Rhiner decided to talk.

"Brunner owns some buildings downtown. He's hoping for some federal seed money to help with renovation, but the state has to act first. Massachusetts has to cough up some funding; then the feds will follow suit. Senator Kelley heads up the committee that decides how much money, if any, the state's going to give. So Brunner's at his mercy. . . . And Kelley's the one who talked Liuzza into switching sides in the governor's race."

Lofton got the general idea. It was the usual tangled busi-

ness of local politics, but when you got beneath the surface—
ignored the committee meetings, the press conferences, the
mounds of documents and legal abstracts—it was really
pretty simple. One man controlled something the other
wanted. In this case Kelley controlled the state renovation
funds that Brunner needed, and the two men were on opposite
sides of the political fence.

"Why doesn't Brunner just switch sides, too?" Lofton
asked.

"Who knows?" the reporter said, cocking his shoulders and
smirking, the same wise-guy look Lofton had seen a hundred
times, on a hundred different reporters, and even once or
twice in the mirror.

As the game wore on, most of the other reporters cleared
out, mumbling that they'd gotten their story, if you wanted to
call it that, and there was no sense in hanging around any
longer tonight, no use in milking a cow that had been dead as
long as the Redwings, the sorry birds. The owners and the
dark-haired woman stuck the game out together down below
in the first base stands. A curious triangle, Lofton thought; he
couldn't quite figure them out. Tenace noticed him watching.

"The woman's name is Regina Amanti. She's Tony Liuzza's cousin," the scorer said, "and Brunner, he's giving her a
little piece of pork on the side."

When neither Lofton nor Rhiner responded, Tenace repeated himself and nudged Lofton, just to be sure, it seemed,
that the reporter had caught his meaning. When Tenace still
got no response, he shook his head sadly. "You guys are really
something, you know that," he said, then called down to one
of the hawkers to bring him something to eat.

Since the day he'd met Jack Brunner and Tony Liuzza,
Lofton had been back to the field often. The reporters in the
box knew him. They nodded to him, in the way that reporters
did, quick and noncommittal, giving him a fast up-and-down,
sizing him up—as if he were a woman, or an athlete on an
opposing squad—then turning their attention back to the
game. He knew they still regarded him as an outsider. He had
not gone through the ritual with them: getting drunk; talking
the gossip you could not print; bitching about local editors;
complimenting their work.

He saw one of his own recent pieces on a folded page of the *Dispatch,* on the metal chair next to the Springfield reporter. If he'd wanted to, he could have recited the piece out loud.

EVEN DEAD MUST PAY

For more than three hours yesterday the corpse of a 48-year-old Hispanic woman sat slumped over a table in a Ward 3 housing project while neighbors and a county examiner tried to hire an undertaker.

In the course of writing the story, he had wandered door to door with the dead woman's sister-in-law. He'd watched from the curb while she tried to collect money from neighbors and friends to bury her brother's wife. She collected the money in twenty-four hours and gave it to the mortician, who, though he would not speak to Lofton, told the woman he would not bury welfare people anymore, not without cash up front. That whole time, and now as well, reliving the memory, Lofton thought of the dead woman slumped over the kitchen table. Her image disturbed him; he could not get it out of his mind.

He had told the reporters here that he was a correspondent for the *Globe* and that he was only doing features for the local papers. In fact, he had contacted Steve Warner, an old college friend who now worked the city desk at the Boston paper.

"How's your new wife?" Warner had asked over the telephone. Lofton had not talked to Warner for some time, since before his own second marriage, but news of weddings—like news of births and deaths—had a way of traveling.

"Maureen? She's fine."

"Where are you two staying?"

"The cemetery," Lofton said. It took a second for Warner to laugh. Then there was a hesitation, Warner waiting for the real answer. Lofton told him Maureen was still in Colorado; she would be here soon. He asked if the *Globe* would be interested in a story about Holyoke, a color piece. Warner was encouraging but vague. When Lofton called again, Warner was not at his desk. Lofton guessed the problem was that he'd been living too far west, out of range. He was not ready, at least not yet, to move into the city and compete with the Boston hacks on their own turf.

"Working on another special for the *Globe?*" Tenace asked

the question from the side of his mouth. He wore an idiot grin, but Lofton could tell he meant no harm by what he said. Rhiner, the Springfield reporter, let out a brief, unconcealed laugh.

When the game resumed, the regulars fell back into complaining, a slow slur of complaints muttered between pitches and dropped balls. Tenace complained he was not getting paid enough for scoring. The games went on too long, too fucking long. The Springfield reporter said the new owners weren't handling the press right. They weren't baseball men, they didn't understand much of anything. They'd bought the team so they could showboat to their friends. The concessioners and the hawkers, who sat in the press box during their breaks, complained the most bitterly. The crowds were rotten, and the new owners had cut their commissions. Things were better, they said, before the old owner sold out to Brunner and Liuzza. And the team—no one could remember one this bad.

"Lover girl's here again. She was asking for you a little while ago," Tenace said, pointing a fat finger at Lofton.

"Who?"

"The Amanti whore, over there." Tenace nodded in the direction of the first base stands, where Amanti and Brunner always sat, behind the dugout of the opposing club. "Yeah, she sent a kid over. Said she wanted to talk to the guy from the *Globe*. The one who did all the specials." Tenace smiled.

The Springfield reporter laughed again, harder this time. Lofton paused at the broken door, propped full open with Tenace's cooler.

"What's the reliever's name?"

Tenace told him, and Lofton left. He headed toward the top of the stands. He was irritated with Tenace, or maybe with himself. Sometimes he did not like being laughed at. But the Springfield reporter, Rhiner, was still young, baby-faced. Maybe when he looked at Lofton, he knew he was looking at himself in fifteen years. Lofton lit a cigarette, drawing on it fiercely now, and smoked it all the way down.

Lofton sat high in the bleachers, in a place where he could study both the field and the Amanti woman. Though Tenace had said she was looking for him, Amanti hadn't approached him, at least not yet. She had walked up to the concession once, then stood around as if waiting, but Lofton had stayed in his seat. He was not quite sure he believed Tenace; the scorer liked to play games. Besides, if she really had something to tell him, it would be best to let her make the first move. Meanwhile, he made notes, questions he should ask Sparks, obvious stuff he did not even need to think about. The idea of a more wide-ranging story, something that would capture the flavor of the team and the town, intrigued him.

As he sat, he jotted down names. Brunner. Liuzza. Amanti. Tenace. He wrote the names as they came to him, trying to visualize the faces, marking down bits and scraps of their histories, whatever he knew. It was an old journalist's habit, partly, but it was something he had done as a child, too, writing down the names of his teachers, of girls in the neighborhood, of major league ballplayers, imagining their faces, their lives. The names, the people would come alive in his dreams, the faces changing, until by the time he woke up the faces no longer went with the names, and he didn't know whom he had been dreaming about. The same type of thing still happened to him sometimes. The street corner he stood on would suddenly look, except for some small, mysterious difference, like every other corner. He would not know where he was or whom he was going to see. A second later everything would occur to him at once, a tangle of names, of alleyways, in which he was immediately lost.

He added another name to his list. Dick Golden. Earlier that day he had talked to Golden, the Redwings' general manager. Golden had pitched with the California Blues for a season, then been drafted by the army. It had happened during the Vietnam War, and Golden had refused to go. Lofton remembered the *San Jose Star* carrying stories on the business. It wasn't a matter of principle, Golden had said. He didn't have an opinion on the war either way; he simply wanted to play ball. Lofton remembered a follow-up story, a few years later, about Golden's handicapped wife. Golden had aged since the time of the newspaper photos. The aging was surprising, distressing. Lofton remembered admiring Golden, rooting for him. Now, though the man was a few years younger than Lofton, he looked older. Though he still carried the same good looks, there was a hardness in his face, a hardness in his eyes—a gray look that was almost empty at times, as if he looked at you from someplace far away, or maybe did not even see you at all. Only occasionally, and then only for brief instants, could you catch a glimpse of the talented, innocent kid Golden had once been.

"I keep track of the paperwork, chase the kids off when they try to sneak in," Golden had said as they stood together during practice, watching the Redwings shag balls under the afternoon sun.

"Any good prospects?"

Golden scanned the field, as if evaluating the players. "Some of the California kids look pretty good," Golden said.

Lofton nodded. "Which ones?" Golden himself had gone straight from college ball to the majors. Lofton remembered his glamorous rookie year: how it had culminated, like a television movie, in Golden's marriage to a beautiful young woman who had admired him all summer from the third base bleachers. What he really wanted to ask, of course, was how Golden felt. Was he bitter? He held off asking, partly out of respect, but partly because of Golden's reputation for moodiness, his tendency to lose his temper suddenly and without warning.

"Tim Carpenter, if a place clears for him. Sparks, maybe. His arm looks good, sometimes," Golden said.

Because the West Coast papers had made a fuss over his resisting the draft—one labeled him the "California Dodger" —Golden and his wife headed for Canada. But the papers soon forgot; Golden's name dropped from the headlines. So Golden did his stint in obscurity, pitching semipro for the Alberta Stars, working part-time as a sportswriter, copying scores from the wire services. By the time Jimmy Carter had granted amnesty to draft resisters, Golden's pitching arm was gone, his wife confined to a wheelchair—multiple sclerosis— and the rookie bonus spent. After Golden failed at a comeback, Cowboy told him abut the Holyoke job. Now he counted the gate for Brunner and filed scouting reports to California.

"The players, they excited about being in the Blues' organization?" Lofton asked.

"Of course they're excited. They'd be foolish to be otherwise." Golden bent over, picked up some trash, and pitched it into a can. He walked away from Lofton, into the clubhouse.

* * *

Though the score did not change, and the Redwings were not threatening, the fans let out a cheer. Batting now, with two outs in the sixth, was Randy Gutierrez, the Nicaraguan shortstop whose wife and kids were waiting back in Managua until Randy had something firm with the Blues' organization. Gutierrez was popular with the local fans, particularly the Puerto Ricans. Good field, no hit—that was the line on Gutierrez. Unless he started hitting soon, Gutierrez might find himself back in Managua.

Gutierrez made the sign of the cross before stepping into the batter's box. He took a called strike, then backed away from the plate.

Lofton had assumed until a few days ago that Gutierrez's slump was just a slump. Maybe there was too much pressure on him to make the big leagues; maybe he felt too much uncertainty about his family back in Managua. Tenace, however, had another explanation. Gutierrez had gotten carried away in Holyoke. He spent his spare time getting coked up with the ballpark honeys. His seven hundred dollars a month —a double leaguer's salary—disappeared, Tenace said, quicker than a sneeze in the air, so now Gutierrez was in debt, playing worse and worse, digging himself one deep hole.

Gutierrez took another strike, moving his bat this time but coming around too late, after the pitch had hit the catcher's leather. Lofton hoped there weren't any Blues scouts in the stands.

Gutierrez's decline was a story he thought he could sell if he played the angles right, maybe to the *Globe* or a sports magazine, for more money than the *Dispatch* paid. He would have to interview him, get some quotes about the slump, label him a hot Blues prospect—true, in a way—and rely on Tenace's insinuations to get drugs and women into the story. Then, at the end, a thin ray of hope, maybe the religious angle, the sign of the cross.

Gutierrez stepped up to the plate and watched a pitch float over the outside corner. Ball one. His partisans yelled encouragement, a smattering of Spanish and English. He stepped out of the box, surveyed the stands behind the first base side— where Amanti and Brunner sat—and then crossed himself again.

The Glens Falls pitcher, a bullish man with a huge chaw of tobacco in one cheek, stepped off the mound, stared down Gutierrez, then spat in the infield dirt.

The pitcher went to his delivery. Gutierrez took a wide-sweeping swing at a sucker pitch. Strike three. A small, fat man cursed in Spanish and kicked at the bleachers.

I could write him up, Lofton thought, and Randy Gutierrez, whose career is going nowhere, probably would never know. Speaks English, but with an accent thick as mangoes are sweet, and sure as hell can't read it. But focusing on Gutierrez would be too narrow; the story would be trashy. He wanted something better.

From where he sat, Lofton could see the sweep of the field, the iridescent blue and black of the evening sky beyond the low, shattered skyline of Holyoke. He looked from the Amanti woman away to the recreational fields beyond. Another game, between two local American Legion teams, was being played in a field nearby. Often they received better coverage in the Holyoke paper than the Redwings.

MacKenzie Field, where the Redwings played, was next to Holyoke High, part of the city's recreation department. A high school track ran through the outfield. The outfielders complained about it. They had to field skidding balls off the crushed cinder. Rather than dive to catch a low liner, the fielders often let it fall in for a hit.

He made a few notes, but there was no way he could get it down, no way he could separate the cars moping along the dirty streets from the men jabbering in Spanish in the stands behind him from the players who struggled on the sparse, shabbily tended turf. No way he could separate himself from Tenace, from the bitter hard-core fans.

He went back to studying Amanti. She had a shadowy presence and did not seem quite real. Tony Liuzza, the younger of the two owners, the lawyer, was not at the park today. He seldom was except on promotion nights. Amanti sat close to the other man, Jack Brunner, but not so close as to touch him. There was a small space on the gray bench between the two. Occasionally Brunner leaned forward, touching her on the knee and calling attention to something on the field. She would respond, nodding her head as if she did not quite hear him. She had the same preoccupied look while watching the action.

The crowd started to thin. The Glens Falls team, an aggressive Chicago franchise, hit the ball hard, stealing bases and making Holyoke look, if possible, worse than they were. Lofton watched Coach Barker. The man had lost his fatherly mood. He stormed onto the field, a showman's gesture, and waved the reliever off with his hand. He called over to the first baseman. To that player's surprise, Coach Barker handed him the ball, pointed to the mound, and went over to play first base himself. A good move, thought Lofton. The game was lost. Might as well entertain the fans.

During the break the Amanti woman suddenly left Brunner. She touched Brunner on the shoulder first. Brunner glanced back, nodded his thick head, and she left. She walked up the stands toward Lofton. Though he had been wondering when she would come, he was still surprised when she stopped in front of him and introduced herself. He glanced to the press box, but Tenace and the others could not see him from this angle.

She did not seem as good-looking up close as she had from a distance. A dark woman with dark hair, she had unsettling blue eyes and a splotchy birthmark on her left cheek. She stood in front of him awkwardly, but even in her awkwardness there seemed something feigned, something rehearsed. Her eyes did not settle on him but skirted the crowd. He asked her to sit down. She shook her head.

"I saw you in the press box. You're a reporter?" she asked, though her inflection suggested she already knew the answer.

"Sure," Lofton said. "I'm a reporter."

She smiled, nothing flirtatious, just a smile. She told him she had a story, something he might be interested in. He shrugged and motioned for her to sit down. She refused again; instead, she handed him a slip of paper. He unfolded it, glanced at her name and address written in harsh black strokes on white paper, then tucked it into his shirt pocket.

"When should I come?"

She did not seem to be listening. She glanced from the concession stand to Brunner, then to the press box. Brunner had not looked back during this interchange. Lofton did not know why, but he did not want Brunner to see them talking.

He could think of nothing else to say to this woman; he almost wished she would go away. He watched the first baseman, who was warming up on the mound now, practicing his delivery to the catcher, pausing every once in a while to look over at Coach Barker, as if wondering how long before the ruse would be over and he could go back to his regular position. Amanti touched Lofton on the shoulder, arresting his attention.

"Tomorrow?" she asked, a note of anxiety in her voice. He nodded, and Amanti went back down the stands to Brunner.

Lofton felt nervous. He did not trust this woman. Though the stakes were small here, or seemed small to Lofton, people always tried to use the press in some way—to grind someone else's nose, to promote themselves. Still, he might wrestle something from her, some small scrap of color he could paste into the background of the story he wanted to write.

On the field, the first baseman had finished warming up in his new position. From the looks of him, he had probably pitched before. A lot of minor league talent had played pitcher at some point or the other, in high school or college. Aside from being good showmanship, Barker's move, transferring the first baseman to the mound, made a degree of sense. No point in dragging another good arm into a lost game.

The first baseman pitched surprisingly well. To the cheers of the crowd, half-drunk on ballpark beer, he struck out the opposing pitcher. The next batter hit the ball hard, but the Holyoke right fielder, caught up in the carnival atmosphere, made a daring dive and caught the ball before it hit the asphalt track.

When the inning was over, the first baseman walked off smiling, obviously pleased with himself. Lofton was amused, but he was not impressed. When you knew you were going to lose, when all the pressure was gone, then sometimes you outperformed yourself.

The rest of the game went quickly. Glens Falls scored once —a long, solo home run by the team's cleanup hitter—and Holyoke did not score at all. Afterward Lofton hurried down to the dugout. In contrast with the fans, who had enjoyed a good joke, the players were grim. They shuffled off the field

slowly. Even Elvin Banks, the center fielder who liked to flirt
with the teenage girls after the game, was subdued.

Lofton was struck, again, by how young the players were.
There was still a part of him, left over from when he was a
kid, that idolized ballplayers, that saw them as men engaged
in an important, epic struggle. To see them as just kids was
disillusioning.

He could not find Sparks. He saw the Springfield reporter,
Rhiner, interviewing the first baseman. He walked up close
and eavesdropped, writing down what the first baseman said.
Rhiner threw him a foul look, but Lofton did not care. He
wrote the quote down anyway, leaving blanks for the words,
the sentences he did not catch, figuring he could guess at
those if he needed them. Nobody expected you to be that
accurate. He had one question of his own for the first baseman, but Rhiner herded him away. Lofton asked Tim Carpenter, the second baseman, instead.

"Where's Sparks?"

Carpenter, another blue-eyed Southern Californian, did not
know. He shrugged his shoulders. Lofton spotted the first
baseman, free now from the Springfield reporter's questions.

"Where's Sparks?"

The first baseman shrugged also. "Split, I guess. Probably
in the showers."

He should have guessed. After leaving the dugout area, he
ran up the third base side toward the small brick building that
served as the Holyoke team's clubhouse, general office, and
meeting room. He ran by the players, scanning for Sparks.
Instead, he found Coach Barker.

"Where's Sparks?"

Lofton was out of breath. Barker did not answer.

"Can I ask you a question?"

"You just did," said Barker. Lofton ignored the crack.

"Just tell me, what are Sparks's chances of making it up to
the majors?"

"This year? I don't know about those things. The Blues
have—"

"I don't mean now. I mean ever."

"Sparks is a major league prospect."

Coach Barker looked at the dirt as he said it. It was just a
line. He would say the same about any player.

"Then how come you pitch him so often? His arm can't survive that."

Barker kept looking at the dirt as he walked toward the clubhouse. Lofton asked again.

"Because that's what he wants. Simple." Barker still did not look up. He grabbed the handle of the clubhouse door. Lofton stopped. Barker had a policy, no reporters inside. At least not until you had been around for a while.

Lofton waited outside. Lumpy, the catcher, came out dressed in street clothes, a pair of jeans and a white T-shirt. If he had showered, it did not look it.

"Where's Sparks?"

"Dunno."

"Inside?"

"Ain't seen him."

Lofton gave up and left the stadium.

Outside in the parking lot he saw him. Sparks, still dressed in his Holyoke whites, stood talking to a woman. Amanti. Sparks seemed animated, upset. Amanti, on the other hand, looked placid as a cat. Maureen's black cat, Lofton thought; then he instantly remembered Garcia was dead, run over by a car.

Soon the conversation ended. The Amanti woman walked away, and Sparks, his head down, remained staring at the asphalt.

"I miss that cat," Lofton whispered to himself, and left Sparks alone in the darkness.

He took the back way home, along the less well-lighted streets. A longer way, but he was in no hurry, even though he had to have his story ready for the *Dispatch* by early morning.

The streets were dark and dirty; they smelled of wet ash and rotting plywood. Many of the tenement buildings had been burned, their doors and windows covered with old wood and nailed shut. Men sat on their porch steps, their wives talking to one another in the shadows behind them. Kids straddled their banana-seat Sting Rays and laughed to one another. A Hispanic man in his early twenties, long black hair tied in a ponytail, cupped his hands and yelled out in Spanish. Lofton could not tell if the man was yelling at him, only that what the man yelled was an insult. The man stood on his porch step and glared. Lofton kept walking.

His old redbrick hotel stood on Cabot Street near a canal where the Connecticut River had been siphoned off into a green and unmoving stream between two old mills. He asked the night clerk if there had been any calls for him. No one had called, but there was a letter from his wife. He put the letter in his shirt pocket and went up the narrow stairs. He could smell the heavy odor of Puerto Rican cooking, tomatoes and grease, and could hear the thick Spanish of the family on the first floor.

When he lay down in his room, he could not get himself to read the letter in his pocket. He got up and took a cigarette from the pack of Viceroys on top of the old Crosley refrigerator—he had cigarettes everywhere—and opened the refrigerator door for a beer. Again he went back to the bed. He still did not open the letter.

He had met Maureen at his brother's house in Denver. He had just come out from California, where he'd been working on a story for the *San Jose Star,* about a city councilman hooked up with the gaming parlors and crack houses downtown—and with other things, too, that reached out in a complicated, tangled web to Las Vegas and to the state legislature in Sacramento. His editor at the *Star* had been resisting the story the whole way, every column inch. Then, and it had seemed a coincidence at the time, Lofton had gotten a call from Senator Hansen in Washington. The senator wanted Lofton to be his press secretary for the Sacramento office. Lofton was tired of fighting his editor; the story itself had become frightening, maybe dangerous; besides, he liked Senator Hansen, so he took the job. Things had been great for him at first, chumming with Hansen when the senator was in town, drinking with the governor's boys and their blond secretaries, but then the whole thing had gone sour in a way he didn't like to think about anymore. So Lofton had recouped his losses: He walked out of the office and drove to his brother's house in Colorado.

When he first saw Maureen, she sat at the kitchen table, her back to the door, while his brother, Joe, chopped salad greens at the counter in front of her.

"Frank," his brother said, "I have somebody for you."

A clumsy introduction, but Joe had always been clumsy. When they were kids, he could not even shag a fly ball. He was afraid and cringed at the last minute. Other times, like running track, he was beautiful.

At first he'd thought Joe and Maureen were together, considering the familiar way they talked and how, when standing up to help with the plates, Maureen touched his brother on the shoulder. She was the type his brother would dig up, a schoolteacher, never married, a plump, almost pretty woman with pale skin and black hair. Except there was something about her—a fierceness in her eyes, maybe, or a hollow in the cheeks, or a way of turning her head—that made her seem, from certain angles, beautiful and that told him she was not involved with his brother.

"So how do you know my brother?" he asked when Joe was off in the other room.

"He dates my cousin, Daisy," Maureen said. "She's a writer, too. And a bitch."

Lofton liked Maureen. She held her hand to her throat when she talked, and later that night, when she took him for a drive through the empty back streets of Denver, they stopped at a fashionable bar in the warehouse district and sat close to one another, touching and kissing in the gloomy, smoky air. The next morning he looked out the upstairs window of the old house she lived in, bought with the insurance money her father had left when he died. He could see over the rooftops toward the Colorado Rockies: the old brownstones, the tall buildings and steel towers, all converging at the base of the great mountains jutting out of the high plains. As she leaned over him, he noticed fine wrinkles in her face and a clear depth in her eyes. They got married with his brother watching, half smiling in the bright courthouse air.

After they were married, Lofton decided to stay away from the dailies and work free-lance instead. With Maureen working, and her house paid for except taxes, he had a chance to make the transition. When he did not have an article, which was more often than he cared to admit, he drove down to Mile High Stadium to watch the Bears, a hot Triple A club with players who were going places. Though he enjoyed watching the games, it bothered him that all he could pick up in town were nickel-and-dime features for the local papers. Part of the reason for his difficulty, he grew to suspect, had to do with that Hansen business back in California and the rumors that went along with his sudden departure. He did not tell Maureen about any of this; her goal, it seemed, was to be happy, to be fascinated with the life around her. She was as impressed with the view out an alley window as she was with the scent of the wind whipping through the vast farmlands. He remembered now lying in bed beside her and staring into the darkness. In Denver, when the smog lifted, you could sometimes smell the entire Midwest, the heart of the country, whipped up against the Rockies. He might have been able to stay in Denver. Then one night Maureen said she wanted to have a child. The darkness over the bed suddenly seemed infinite. He remembered when his first wife, Nancy, had gotten pregnant. Instead of cementing their marriage, the pregnancy had ended it. For a while he'd wanted her back; he wanted the child, his son, he'd told himself. Lying beside Maureen, staring into the darkness, he tried to imagine his son. Denver was an impossible city, he told himself; he couldn't stay there any longer.

One day, while Maureen was at school and the Bears were out of town, he went into the garage to look for a mower. The backyard was overgrown with high grass. Before he could find the machine, his leg went numb and the numbness seemed to reach from his toes to his chest. He pitched onto the floor. His chest hurt. He coughed into his fist.

"Was there blood after you coughed?" the doctor asked. The doctor was young but moved slowly, speaking through a western American accent, as if the wind were blowing in his face.

"Yes," Lofton said, but wondered if it was true. Had he seen blood? His mother had died of cancer, but he did not really believe it could happen to him.

"Have you ever hurt that leg before?"

"No," he said. Then he remembered yes, of course, he had hurt the leg, when he was coming down, years ago, from retarring a roof, and his ankle twisted on a lower rung of the ladder. He was answering everything wrong, backwards. He avoided the doctor's eyes.

"Did the blood leave any stains? On your shirt, your handkerchief?"

He shook his head. He hadn't checked, he said. The doctor held a stethoscope to Lofton's chest. The man's face was inscrutable. "I had a man in here yesterday who insisted that faith heals, that medicine kills, that men only die when, deep down, they want to die."

"What was he doing here?"

"Dying," the doctor said.

Eventually Lofton slammed out of the office. The doctor watched placidly. A few days later, while sitting at his desk, a cigarette in his hand, Lofton felt his chest tighten. He got angry, no explanation in the world, and smashed his fist, first into the keys of his typewriter, then into the windows of the lower part of the house. By the time he had finished, the tightness had passed.

Maureen looked around in disbelief. "Why have you done this?"

"To relieve my tension," he said. He grinned. Maureen ran upstairs, and he chased her. She would not let him into the bedroom.

Lying in his bed, Lofton kept thinking of Maureen. He remembered places he had been, most of them alone, so that while he thought of her, he also thought of the humid fields of Iowa, of a gas station somewhere in the California desert, of the ragged sweep of brownstones in polluted Denver. She was everywhere, even here in this sagging bed, listening with him to the street noises coming through the window. He touched the letter in his pocket again. He wished she would not write.

He set the half-finished beer can on the nightstand. He was drowsy. Forcing himself up, he sat at the Formica table and opened the letter. It was brief, written in her strange, angular handwriting. It did not seem like the handwriting of a schoolteacher. She said simply that she was selling the house, filing the papers for divorce.

He went to the refrigerator and opened a new beer, forgetting about the half-finished one by the bed. He thought about the story he had to work on, how he should focus on Sparks, but in a way that would not humiliate the pitcher. He lay down and played with the first line in his head: "After a

frustrating evening, Rickey Sparks threw his pitching glove
into the dirt," but before he could get it right, he began to
doze.

He woke up in the early morning, before light. Standing in
the clothes he had slept in, he typed out the story and drove
to the *Dispatch*. He made deadline without any problem.

Later that day he drove the back way out of Holyoke, past
the tenements where laundry hung drying in the humid Massachusetts summer air. In another minute he was over the
bridge, across the Connecticut River, driving past the rich
colonial homes of South Hadley, a town that took its tone
from Mount Holyoke College, a women's school of stern
brick buildings covered with dense ivy.

He followed the road up over the Notch, past the gravel
mill at the peak of the Holyoke Range. His car had trouble
making the low, steeply sloping hill, but the downhill coast
into Amherst was easy.

When he reached Amherst, he was early for his meeting
with Amanti, so he parked his car near the Commons, a large
block of trees and grass nestled in the center of town. The
University of Massachusetts, where both Lofton and Nancy
had gone to school, was just a few blocks away. She had been
a thin, sandy-haired Irish girl with a striking profile and the
ability, when she wanted, to draw attention to herself. Only,
when she received the attention, she seemed to withdraw. Under close scrutiny she became remote. When he courted her,
she was elusive. He was stubborn. Maureen, now that he
thought about it, had been more fun.

It had been a long time since he'd been in Amherst. He felt
unreasonably afraid someone might recognize him. The town
had not changed much. Hastings Newsstand still stood in the
middle of the block of buildings owned by old man Hastings,
though, Lofton guessed, it must be his son who ran the business now. The tobacco store was still there, and the skid row
bar, or the closest Amherst would ever have to such a thing,
still existed under the same name: the Mongoose. Some of the
other places had changed ownership, the bars had changed
decor—polished butcher-block wood instead of Formica, men
waiting tables instead of women. But Amherst had always
been essentially a polished town, where the young people kept

their hair in place even when they drank and had an innocent look about them, the attractive and soft air of polite, insecure children being groomed for the offices of New York and Boston. Lofton, who grew up in California, had never felt at home here. He was glad it was summer and the town given over to the locals.

Amanti lived down a side street. He decided to walk. He did not want to drive up in his rusted car. Her place was an anomaly on this quiet street of older houses. She had the lower apartment in a wood-grained fourplex, a dwelling more like one in a West Coast suburb than a New England town.

He knocked, but no one answered. He stood on her porch step, in the bright, muggy air, feeling conspicuous in his rolled-up shirtsleeves. He remembered feeling this way in college, once, when he had knocked on a coed's door. He had suspected the girl was inside, refusing to answer. But there was no reason now for him to feel like an intruder or an unwanted suitor. He was only working on a story, tracing a lead, doing his job.

He knocked again, but there was still no answer. He swore to himself, then turned to find Amanti coming up the walkway behind him.

"Sorry to make you wait. I just took a walk to the grocery."

"It's all right. I enjoyed standing here." He tried to say the words as if they were true. If she had heard him cursing, she did not let on.

Inside, the apartment was spacious, sparsely furnished. A wood-block table. A white rug. A couch with chrome armrests. And a high, arching roof, wide beams stretching from end to end. Several paintings hung on the wall, all contemporary, all similar: light-hearted colors patterned in elusive, meaningless designs.

He followed her into the kitchen. She did not speak to him as she put the groceries on the counter.

"So what's up?" Lofton asked. The question sounded awkward, foolish. Amanti let it hang in the air unanswered.

She put the groceries away with brusque movements, ignoring him, as if he were a neighbor who had stopped by uninvited. When she had finished, she glanced about the room, avoiding his eyes. She seemed confused, as if trying to remember something she had forgotten. Then she took a step toward him, placed her fingers on the kitchen counter, and let out a quick sigh. Lofton studied her fingers. She held them very still on the countertop.

"I know I told you I had a story, but now that I've had time to think about it, I'm not sure, really, that it would be the best thing. . . ."

Lofton said nothing. Some people, when they told you something—whether you were a reporter, or a lifelong friend, or the slob next door—blurted the thing out to you, giving it up all at once. Others wanted you to ask questions, to work the information free, while they pretended they didn't want to let go. Either way, whether you were quiet or asked questions, once they had decided to tell something, they usually told it. People knew, mostly by instinct, that the only way for a person to remain objective was to remain ignorant, and once they had told you what they had to say, you were no longer outside the situation, but inside it. You were involved, and that's what they wanted.

"The reason I hesitate is that it has to do with one of the owners of the Redwings. Jack Brunner."

She mentioned Brunner's name so casually—in the same way she might tell him she had forgotten to buy something at the store—that he wondered if what she had to tell him would be important, or even interesting. Then he saw her seriousness: the tenseness in the way she stood, in the way she turned her head when he tried to look at her directly. There was an incongruity in her manner he could not place. Maybe it lay in her features: the high cheekbones of a German woman, the blue and crystalline eyes, yet the dark skin of a Mediterranean. And there was that birthmark, or scar, a place on her cheek where the skin was white and mottled, as if she had stayed out in the sun too long and her skin were peeling. She lit a cigarette, its acrid, unhappy smoke filling the air around them. Without asking, he reached to the pack and pulled one for himself. For a second he imagined that moment of stillness on the ballfield, that infinitesimal pause in which the pitcher, already wound up and ready to throw, stood balanced on one foot, his weight hung back, the other foot in the air, and the batter stood waiting, his bat cocked—a moment as quiet, and as brief, as the moment between heartbeats.

"You don't have to tell me anything," he said. "I can just turn around and walk out the door. It's up to you."

"No, why don't you sit down?" She blew out smoke as she said it and gave him an unsure glance he found seductive. He nodded but remained standing. Amanti still held her fingertips pressed against the counter. The tips were turning white.

"Brunner's burning Holyoke. He's doing it for the insurance money."

"So?" Lofton heard the edge in his voice. The sudden revelation bothered him. Why was she telling him this?

"I found out by accident. I don't want Brunner to know."

Amanti's face seemed suddenly old. He lit the cigarette he had taken, looked at the smoke curl from its end, then put it out without smoking any.

"Why don't you go to the police?"

"I don't have any proof. Besides, he owns Holyoke. They all love him there. And other reasons. I just can't go to them myself. I'm too close to the whole thing."

He was about to ask her what difference it made, why didn't she just keep quiet and let Brunner go about his business? He thought back to the interview with Jack Brunner and Tony Liuzza that he'd witnessed in the press box. There had definitely been some tension between the two men. If what the boys in the press box said was true, Liuzza's jump from one side of the Democratic party to the other was not pure principle. Meanwhile, Jack Brunner had his business interests to look after. If the state was balking on providing funds for his Holyoke buildings, then maybe Brunner was recouping his losses in other ways. Burning the buildings, collecting the insurance—that would be one way out of a bad investment. Maybe Amanti was right.

"How do you know all this?" he asked.

She didn't answer right away, and when she did answer, it wasn't to the point, or didn't seem to be. "I don't want anyone to get hurt," she said. Still, he could understand her being afraid of Brunner. The man reminded him of a bulldog. And if Brunner was capable of hiring arsonists, he was probably capable of hiring other characters as well.

"No, I don't want *anyone* to get hurt," she said again. He suddenly realized, by the way she turned and looked at him, by the tone of her voice, that she was about to give him some-

body's name, that of the person who would be hurt. He remembered a woman he had interviewed once, a burglary victim, who had suddenly spat out her nephew's name.

"You have to promise to keep me out of it. I can get you in
touch with someone who knows more than I do, but you'll
have to be careful. You'll have to approach him right. He's
frightened."

"I'm a reporter, not a psychiatrist," Lofton said. The edge
in his voice grew sharper. "I can't worry about your friend's
feelings. I really don't know if there's anything I can do anyway. What's your idea, for me to write a story that puts Brunner away? That's not the way things happen. And why me?
There are a hundred other reporters in this town."

"You're new. Brunner, well, he controls a lot of people."

Amanti went to the window. He was angry. He liked this
less and less. Most journalists stayed away from anything that
looked dangerous. A lot of stuff went on that the law termed
crime, but it was the way the world worked, legal or not. To
try to make your reputation by nailing someone to the wall,
that was foolish business. If you wanted to write something
like that, you'd be best off changing the names and calling it
fiction. That way readers could draw their own conclusions,
and there would be no lawsuits, no angry politicians, no angry
men in organized crime. At least not usually.

He got up from the table. Amanti followed him to the front
room, where he hesitated in front of the colorful, cheerless
paintings. She touched him gently on the arm. He liked the
contact but mistrusted her at the same time. Yet he had to
admit she might be leading him into a good story: the Redwings struggling while the team's owner burned the city
around them.

"Randy Gutierrez . . ." she said. That was the name, the
person she did not want to see hurt.

"Gutierrez? The Nicaraguan?"

Amanti looked at the painting. She pressed her fingers
against his arm in the same stiff way she had pressed them
against the counter. He looked at the scar on her cheek and
wanted to touch it.

"Gutierrez. Well . . ." Lofton sighed. He had been thinking of interviewing Randy Gutierrez, the Redwings' shortstop. He might as well go ahead.

"I'll feel him out and let you know." Lofton suddenly saw himself dead, lying on the garage floor in Colorado, blood dried on his mouth.

Amanti withdrew her hand. "Good, but please don't come up to me in front of Brunner, not at the field. Call me here."

Lofton followed her to the door. He watched the way she pressed her fingers against her thigh—a nervous, absent gesture.

"Tell me," he said, pausing at the open door. "Why bother? Why not just keep it to yourself?"

She gave him a startled look. "I don't know, maybe I'm bored," she said. "Maybe I just want to do the right thing."

She touched his arm again, not avoiding his eyes this time but staring straight into them, as if trying to decide whether or not she had made a mistake talking to him. He thought of asking her about the business with Sparks in the parking lot but decided to keep it to himself, at least for now.

After Lofton had left, Amanti went to the phone and dialed Senator Kelley's office in Boston. Just as she heard the ringing on the other end of the line, however, she hung up. No, not this time, she thought; he can call me. She went over her conversation with the reporter. He was a disheveled man, who had an odd habit of not seeming to look at you while you spoke, except occasionally, and then very directly, in a way that was disarming and made you wonder if you had said something you hadn't intended. At such moments, despite his loose, ill-fitting clothes and sloppy manner, he was not bad-looking: dirt-colored olive brown skin, dark eyes, and a nose that looked as if it had been broken, maybe, when he was a kid.

"We can use him," Kelley had said, sitting on the edge of her bed. "And he'll get lost when we want him to—with a little incentive. He's done the same sort of thing before."

She lost her patience and called Kelley's office again. This time she let it ring through. Amanti had talked to the secretary a hundred times over the last four years, left a thousand messages, but she had never seen the woman; she had never been to Kelley's office. Still, the secretary knows me, Amanti thought; she recognizes my voice, too. "No," the woman said, "the senator is out of the office. He won't be back till tomorrow."

"Where will he be tonight?"

"He has an engagement."

"With his wife?" Amanti asked. The catch in her voice was barely noticeable.

The secretary hesitated. "No," she said at last, "his wife's at their cottage on the shore."

When Kelley called, it was late, past midnight. He asked her about Lofton but only enough to see that everything had gone the way they'd planned. His voice was that of a slightly drunk, happy man, gruff and pleasant, like the sound of a stream rolling over a bed of rough stones. She tried to imagine his face as he spoke, but she couldn't. It was just his voice, the stream in the darkness: I'll be out to see you soon, any day now. Amanti wondered where he was at the moment and whom he had been with. He went on talking, the same melodious sound, and finally she saw his face—his black hair and blue eyes—reflected back at her in the running stream.

2

Early the next morning, before dawn, the fire sirens caterwauled, loud, mournful, insistent, and raised Lofton from his bed. He ran to his window. The roof of the neighboring building was flat, and he could see over it into the street. Down there the cars slowed in the blue air, pulling to the curb, while, for an instant, the engine raced by, its lights flashing red and angry down the alley. Lofton climbed down the fire escape. By the time he reached the street, the engine was gone, but he could still hear it, moving somewhere deeper into the neighborhood. He tried to follow the siren, but suddenly its wailing stopped; the truck parked on some corner he could not find. Up one long, narrow street he saw the glare of a fire, he thought, high in the windows of an apartment building, but closer up he saw the glare was only the reflection of neon from across the street. He stood on the corner, trying to catch his breath. A couple of boys, bandannas around their heads, stood nearby, watching him. They wore T-shirts torn at the sleeves, pants torn about the knees and split upward, exposing the dark skin of their thighs. Three or four more boys stepped out of an alleyway, and the groups called to each other in Spanish. Lofton stood between them. He saw the dark passageways of the city spreading out in front of him, saw himself lost in the city, and he knew he would not be able to find the fire. He put his head down, like a bull, so no one would bother him, and headed back toward the hotel.

The next afternoon Lofton sat at the Formica table in his room, puzzling over an assignment his editors at the *Dispatch* had given him, puzzling and sweating. A radio outside was blasting. The temperature was in the nineties. *A Caribbean pressure cooker,* said the radio weatherman. *A heat wave from hurricane country.* Lofton did not know if it was the heat—thickening like fog in his head—but he could not, after hustling over the hot streets all day, figure out how to play the story they wanted him to write. Everyone he had talked to, even his editors, seemed double-handed, manipulating the information for reasons of their own. The names in his notebook were becoming difficult to keep straight. He wrote them down with an old tarnished silver fountain pen, something his brother had given him years back. It was one of the few possessions that he had kept over the years; he did not take the pen out into the streets with him but left it in a drawer in his room, knowing he would lose it otherwise, leaving it behind on a bar counter or on someone else's desk.

Earlier that morning, when he had gone to the *Dispatch,* the sports editor had sent him over to the city desk, to McCullough. McCullough was the one who had sent Lofton on the funeral parlor story, to follow the woman looking for money to bury her dead sister-in-law. "I want tough, meaningful stories," McCullough had said. Today, since the Redwings were gone on the road, McCullough wanted Lofton to talk to a man who had been assaulted on the street. When police responded to the call, McCullough told him, they had ended up arresting the victim, a man named Lou Mendoza. The cops took Mendoza on a vandalism charge, and the assailants got away.

While McCullough gave Lofton the story, Kirpatzke walked up. Kirpatzke was a thin, nervous man with a bad complexion and long yellowish hands he seemed unable to control. Technically Kirpatzke was the night editor, but he seemed to be around all the time. Smiling slightly, as if he were half-amused but mostly weary, he walked over, as he always did, to find out what McCullough was assigning.

Kirpatzke often said nothing, just stood and listened and watched, though sometimes he cut in to change the story's direction or to suggest killing it altogether. He irritated Mc-Cullough, Lofton could tell, but McCullough, a serious bruiser of a man, played along anyway. Press box rumor said Kirpatzke used to have a better job, more prestige, more money, up at the *Springfield Post*. There was a hint of scandal —something Kirpatzke had done wrong or bungled—which made Lofton curious, of course, but he did not know for sure why Kirpatzke had left the bigger Springfield paper to work at the *Dispatch*.

"What story you giving him?" Kirpatzke asked.

McCullough told him, and Kirpatzke shook his head. He waved his long yellow hands in the air, then settled them near McCullough and drummed the fingers on the desktop. "Where did you get that idea for this business, Einstein's notes?"

"Einstein?" Kirpatzke repeated.

The second time Lofton heard the name, he remembered where else he had heard it recently. It had been in the press box on the night Jack Brunner and Tony Liuzza were interviewed. After the others had left, Lofton had asked some more questions about the Redwings' owners' involvement in Democratic politics, and about Brunner's building investments downtown.

"Who do you think you are, the new Einstein?" Tenace had said, and laughed. One of the remaining reporters laughed, too, though not so loudly or so long. At the time Lofton had thought it was nothing but another one of Tenace's bad jokes.

Now the two editors stared at each other. They were at odds: Kirpatzke wry and bemused, his tie loose around his neck; McCullough frowning, comically, like a short, fat boy in a cartoon strip.

"There's no sense chasing that stuff," said Kirpatzke. Mc-Cullough didn't agree.

"Listen, I'd rather do sports anyway," Lofton said.

"Wouldn't everybody?" Kirpatzke turned to Mac. "Did you get it from Einstein?"

"Einstein was a reporter here?" Lofton asked.

McCullough nodded.

"Where is he now?"

"He's not with us anymore."

"Where is he?"

Neither editor answered. They were more concerned with each other than with Lofton's questions. "I'd like to do something on Randy Gutierrez, the shortstop," Lofton said.

"Another baseball story, hell. We've given Brunner and that bunch all the publicity I can stand. Everybody else in this state might be working for the Democratic party, but we're not. Or at least I'm not," McCullough said, shooting a look in Kirpatzke's direction.

Lofton mentioned the scene at the ballpark and repeated what he'd learned: how the younger owner, Liuzza, had joined up with Kelley, and how both men were backing the liberal candidate, Richard Sarafis, for governor. "That leaves Brunner the odd man out, and I don't think he's too pleased about it."

Again the two editors paid little attention to Lofton. They each remained in their respective places, saying nothing for a long time, each man tugging at his lips and avoiding the other's eyes—as if trying to avoid the fact that when you got down underneath the skin, there was not really very much difference between the two of them.

"That's old news," Kirpatzke said suddenly, as if that somehow settled something. "Besides, we've already got a political reporter."

"I'm not interested in writing politics; I just can't help wondering if anything's changed in Massachusetts since the last time I was here."

The truth, Lofton had already guessed, was that nothing had changed. Aside from a few people dying and some younger ones taking their places, the political machinery was pretty much the same. The party regulars plastered the telephone poles and signboards with names in the summer heat, and the names stayed there to whiten in the sun, then to dampen in the snow and the wet. Eventually either the names faded or the paper that carried the names yellowed and frayed in the wind; then someone came along with more names to plaster over the ones that had disappeared. No, the names had not changed, at least not in any way that mattered, and the machinery had not changed either. Whoever won the Democratic primary, it was the same thing as winning the governorship. The Republicans were gray men in gray suits with gray ties in a party permanently out of power. So in the end it was only the Democrats, and for the last twelve years that had meant either Richard Sarafis or Ed Wells. Wells had won the governorship last time around, Sarafis before that, and now they were plastering their names up all over again. "How does this new senator, this guy Kelley—how does he fit in?"

"He's preening himself for bigger things, you ask me," Kirpatzke said. "Maybe he thinks he can be governor someday. Anyway, he wants to prove he can deliver the vote out here. He's got ambition."

There was another pause, more lip pulling and a general silence that suggested the editors had been through this conversation before, and even their mutual dislike for each other couldn't get them excited, at least not at the moment. Lofton asked where the *Dispatch* stood on the election.

"Nowhere," Mac said.

"That's right," Kirpatzke agreed, brightening up in a way that was obviously and deliberately false, like a Christmas tree in a department store window. "We're taking no sides, holding up the lantern of objective truth. That's why Mac wants you chasing two-bit thugs around town. Keeps the heat off. Makes us look impartial and socially conscious at the same time. . . . Why don't you cut it out, Mac, and let the guy do his lousy baseball story?"

"Crime's an issue here," Mac said curtly. Kirpatzke sighed and shook his head. He started to say one last thing, it looked like, making ready a final pitch to can the story. But then he changed his mind and just walked away.

"I knew a man who had a breakdown writing crime." Lofton smiled.

"Lots of people have breakdowns," said McCullough. "You're free-lance, so do as you please."

After stopping at payroll, while walking down the hall, Lofton had caught a glimpse of Kirpatzke and McCullough, haggling apparently. They stood in one of the side offices, the door open. McCullough had his back to Lofton. Kirpatzke was shaking his head over and over and waving his yellow hands in the air.

The business between the editors hadn't bothered him much until he saw Lou Mendoza's apartment building. Why send a reporter to interview a man arrested for small-time vandalism? He would have walked away from the story except the Redwings were out of town, and he could not talk to the shortstop Randy Gutierrez—the man Amanti had directed him to—until the team came back.

Inside, the place was dirty, the hallways scrawled with graffiti. He found Lou Mendoza upstairs, in a four-room apartment with tattered wallpaper, peeled away in spots, each layer a brighter color than the one before. A young woman cooked in the kitchen, stirring sweet red Goya paste into the rice. Mendoza sat on the couch; he didn't wear a shirt. Playing with a pencil, touching the point delicately, as if it were a knife, he told Lofton he wanted nothing to do with the press, that the papers never got anything right because they were on the take from the police. Even so, it was obvious he enjoyed being interviewed and seemed to think he could somehow use the attention to his advantage.

"You make heroes out of the Latinos, and they are the ones who tried to kill me. Why should I trust you now?"

"Who are the Latinos?"

"The police report said they were trying to rob me, but it wasn't robbery. The Latinos didn't want my money. They want me. They want to kill *me* on the street." Mendoza pointed at himself with a peculiar pride. He spoke with an accent, but it was the accent of a native, someone who had grown up on the streets and could speak both English and Spanish well enough, but each with the inflections of the other. The right side of his face was swollen, but he smiled as he spoke to Lofton, a smile that was somehow both menacing and friendly at the same time.

"There were too many for me to fight back. They held my arms and beat me in the face. Pretty soon there was blood in my eyes, and I couldn't see. I couldn't feel either. I didn't even know when the police came. They took me in their car, but pretty soon the radio said they want me for burglary, robbing, something like that. So the police take me to the station. But that vandalism they talk about—it's nothing. Nobody lives there; the place is burned out by fire, just windows on an empty shell. Who cares if I smash the glass out?" Mendoza paused, realizing his mistake. "But I didn't break any glass, don't write that down. I just want people to know that the police, instead of helping me, of chasing murderers, they put me in jail." Mendoza paused. He clenched his fist and raised it, melodramatically, to his chest. "Meanwhile, the people in Holyoke—everybody starves."

"Who are the Latinos?" Lofton asked again.

Mendoza shook his head, as if amazed by Lofton's ignorance. Then he told Lofton that the Latinos were a street gang. Mendoza himself had belonged to a rival gang, the Wanderers, but his gang had broken up, thrown off its colors, and decided to go legitimate. At least that was Mendoza's story.

"They're trying to kill all the old Wanderers. They're hunting us out, one by one. We want to be like the rest of the community. That's why the Latinos hate us. We're not hoodlums; they are."

After the interview Lofton had gone to the Holyoke police station and found one of the arresting officers, a man named James Lopez, who was half Puerto Rican, half Anglo.

"Listen, I can't tell you anything. The case is headed for court. Off the record . . ." Lopez raised his dark eyebrows.

"No, not off the record."

"Off the record," Lopez said, ignoring him, "that mugging business is nonsense."

"What about his face?"

"Fuck his face."

Lopez walked away. He did not seem to care what Lofton put in the paper. Lofton dogged him down the police station steps to his cruiser.

"Don't let him fool you with that starving Puerto Rican routine. We've heard it before. If the Latinos hit him in the street, it's what he deserves. They would've taken care of him if we hadn't stumbled along at the wrong time."

"What do you mean?"

"We been after him for a long time. Finally, we get him, not much, just this vandalism, breaking and entering, and the landlord drops it. Can't believe it. The bastard landlord's been complaining for years. 'Get the punks that trash my buildings!' We get the kingpin of trash, and he drops the charges."

Now Lofton sat at his Formica table, shirtsleeves twisted up, notebook in front of him, a half-typed sheet rolled into the typewriter: "Lou Mendoza, who claims he was beaten and robbed late Friday, has threatened to bring suit against Holyoke police for harassment and neglect of duty."

Lofton was not sure what to do with the story. Officer Lopez did not want to be quoted. Mendoza, on the other hand, seemed to have an ax to grind—against the Latinos and the police—but how much of what the man said was true? Still, there seemed to be something under the surface, something neither man was saying. Now that he thought about it, Lofton wondered about the way McCullough had gotten the story idea. Why was the editor poking around in Einstein's notebook? A reporter's notes were supposed to be left alone, especially at his own paper. Why had Einstein left the paper, and where was he now?

He was still puzzling over the story when the knock came, timid at first, then a quick, staccato rapping, loud enough to break through the music of the radio in the alley. He opened the door, and the hotel clerk gave him a message. It was from Amanti. She wanted him to call. Just as well, he thought, it was too hot in the apartment, and he could finish the story later, after he had eaten, when his room had had a chance to cool in the evening air.

He walked to Barena's, not far from the ballpark, a cafeteria-style Italian restaurant owned and operated by a family of Greeks. The food wasn't wonderful, he told Amanti from the phone booth in the corner, and the air-conditioning didn't work as well as it might, but Barena's let you sit there as long as you wanted. Amanti was silent on the other end, but he went on talking, friendly, wondering what she'd wanted. For an instant, his own voice sounded far away to him, as if someone else were doing the talking. There's also an old color TV, he said, plugged into the cable from Boston, that shows Red Sox games. The color's bad, but the picture's clear as cake.

"Not tonight," Amanti said, "but I can meet you Friday." She gave him the name of the Little Puerto Rico, a café down on Commercial Street.

The conversation confused him; Amanti almost acted as if his call were a surprise. First his editors, then Mendoza, Lopez, and now Amanti—nobody approached him directly; they all came from angles. Maybe it's the heat, Lofton thought. Maybe people just aren't thinking clearly in the heat.

* * *

Lofton wanted to get a look at MacKenzie Field in the dark when the stadium was empty. A high green fence surrounded the field, but he knew a place around back where the neighborhood kids had kicked a hole large enough to crawl through. Brunner had ordered the hole boarded several times, but the kids kept kicking it open. Lofton found the hole and crawled through on his hands and knees.

Standing inside the park, his shirt soaked through with sweat, he no longer heard the sounds he took for granted while walking the streets: the beer-gutted laughter, drunken shouts, and loud Hispanic music that seemed always to spill from the tenements. Only one sound got through to him as he stepped into the Redwings' dugout: the long skid of tires on asphalt, followed by the brief, heartbeat blaring of a horn. He shrugged and sat down in the dugout. The accident, if that's what it was he had heard, seemed far away, maybe nothing, maybe just a noise beyond the center field wall.

There had been times like this in Denver, when he had stayed up in the bleachers after the Bears' games, reluctant to go home. He remembered the papers back in the hotel that he needed to sign for Maureen, something to do with the house; she had suddenly decided she wanted to sell it. The papers sat in a pile of other papers along with Maureen's first letter to him in Holyoke, the one that told him never to come back in one line, and in the next said she could not take the sound of her own footsteps pacing the empty house. He had not given her any reason for his leaving; he had mentioned neither his trip to the doctor nor his own misgivings about having another kid. She would make herself happy soon enough, he told himself.

He got up to leave, to walk around the base paths, maybe, or to take a long stroll down the right field line. He spotted a baseball bat leaning in the far corner of the dugout, and he picked it up, running his fingers over the smooth, polished grain. He felt a hairline crack near the trademark. Probably happened on a ground ball, bad enough to make the bat worthless, so the equipment man would not bother to cart it back. Lofton carried the bat with him onto the field.

He kicked the dust from home plate, which glowed white in the darkness, almost phosphorescent. He stared out at the deserted field toward the ghostly wall in left center. He imagined the players, the pitcher standing on the mound and the team in position behind him. He took several swings, trying to make the swings smooth and level, putting all the force of his thirty-seven-year-old body into hard chops at the elusive moon half-hidden in the damp mist over Holyoke.

Backing off from the plate, he flexed the muscles in his back, placing the bat between his knees and rubbing his palms together, a ritual he had seen many men go through over the years—no, not men; boys, children ten, fifteen, even twenty years younger than he—and a ritual, of course, he had gone through himself. And he remembered how his mother, dead twenty-five years now, had come to watch him play sandlot ball in the bitter-bright streets of San Jose, California. It was the summer she died, and she came not with his father but with some other man.

His mother had been a small dark woman who spoke with an acerbic tongue and always wore sunglasses, as if she were in the movies. She and his father fought long and bitterly, always, up to the minute she left him for that stranger who came to the games, a thin man with a frightening presence, or so Lofton remembered him, though he had never seen the stranger close enough to know his face. He knew only the smoky haze that seemed to surround the man and envelop his mother.

Mrs. Lofton died of cancer, a malevolent growth that spread from her lymph glands through her body like a small, angry fire. She knew she had the disease when she left her husband, Lofton found out later, and the stranger knew as well. What bitterness inspired her leaving Lofton did not know. He had given up wondering. He remembered his father crying—drunk, Lofton guessed now—when he thought his sons asleep. And he remembered lying awake, the transistor radio on the bed beside him broadcasting the ballgame, and trying to imagine the land of the dead. He would close his eyes and try to talk with the people there. At first, nothing. No shadows. No whispers. He would keep his eyes closed until, eventually, he saw himself on the street, following the back roads through the city, under the freeway, past the railyards, the cracked porch stoops, and into the ballpark. He saw himself standing alone on the soft outfield, listening to the outfield grass whispering his name over and over.

Now he stepped back to the plate. He crouched at the knees, flexed his wrists, and stared at the mound. The moon hung over center field, fat and silver. He cocked the bat tight, saw the imaginary pitcher rear back, his foot kicking high. Lofton kept his eye on the moon. When the pitcher let loose, Lofton swung hard, hard as he could. He imagined the smooth crack of his bat against the ball and saw the moon high over the park. He ran to first, rounded the corner, and kept running. *I can't tell if it will clear the fence, a double at least.* The stands were full, the Amanti woman and Brunner and his brother and Maureen and Nancy, all the people he knew, watching silently from the bleachers as he ran. *A gathering of the dead.*

He rounded second, digging toward third. *Off the center field wall, a triple.* He wanted more. He ran faster now, faster than he knew he should be able, effortlessly, as if fifteen years of cigarettes and beer were nothing. His invisible opponents scurried after the ball in the dark, trying to nail him before he reached home.

The catcher waited in a crouch. *The relay's coming from center; I'll have to slide.* Lofton imagined the play as he'd seen it unfold on television, the camera replaying it from every possible angle, the runner diving headfirst to the plate, stretching out with one hand while the ball rifled in, bouncing hard off the infield grass, a perfect shot into the catcher's glove, which whisked down to tag the sliding player, but too late, the umpire's arms already outstretched, palms down: Safe at home!

But that was not what happened. He did not get a chance to go into his slide, to evade the imaginary tag. Headed down the third base line, he slipped, almost as if an invisible hand had pushed him face forward into the dirt. He lay with his cheek against the ground, his hand outstretched toward the plate. He was out, the game was over, the winning run did not score, and the park was empty. The fans had left, forgotten his name as they piled into their cars and drove home to sleep.

Lofton got up slowly. His body hurt. His arms were abraded, small bits of gravel stuck in his palms. His cheek was scratched and bleeding, his slacks torn at the knees. But when he walked back to the street, his body sore and aching, Lofton felt good, better than he had felt for a long time.

The heat did not break. Lofton waited on his meeting with Amanti, on the return of the Redwings to MacKenzie Field, and stayed away from the *Dispatch,* where they would pester him about Mendoza. He worked in the Holyoke Public Library, a fading white building with Corinthian columns. The building stood in the center of town, next to a park where teenagers idled beneath the trees, listening to their boom boxes. An old, sun-pocked man sold shaved ice from a wooden cart on the sidewalk nearby.

Lofton wanted to know more about the fires in town. He hoped he could find out from old newspaper stories; at least they would give him a starting point. He could do better research at the *Dispatch,* or at the larger Springfield paper, for that matter, where part-time librarians clipped, sorted, and pasted the stories into books by subject matter, but he did not want anyone at the papers to know what he was researching.

Besides, he preferred the pale anonymity of the public stacks, the heavy wooden tables, and the dim, cool whirring of the electric fans. Also, though it was sometimes distracting, he liked the fact that there were people in the library. He liked the old men who came every day to read the papers from Boston and New York, the children who drifted through the stacks piling up books on dragons and war heroes and ballplayers. He even recognized one of the boys, a pale-haired teenager who sat with the halfway house gang at MacKenzie Field, his baseball cap twisted backward on his head. The kid walked with a limp and had loose, sagging features. At first he thought the boy might be retarded, but hearing the kid talk to the librarian and seeing the books he hoarded changed Lofton's mind. Still, there was something wrong with the kid. He had a hurt look on his face that made Lofton think again of his own son, who was normal enough, as far as he knew, but whom he thought of as somehow damaged, or scarred, or maybe just unhappy. More than once he looked up to see the boy staring at him, but emptily, as if he were not really there.

Lofton scanned both papers, the *Holyoke Dispatch* and the *Springfield Post.* There was a recurring story that worked its way through the years—the back and forth in the state legislature on Holyoke's downtown renovation project. One season it was on, the next off, and the money never got out of committee. This year, with the election coming, the issue was alive again.

Starting with the issues from April, when the minor league season began, he studied the papers more closely. He found an opening day story which pictured the Redwings' owners, Jack Brunner and Tony Liuzza, standing with the mayor of Holyoke at MacKenzie Field. The three men smiled for the camera. Liuzza told the reporter that he and Brunner had gotten to know each other through meetings of the local Democratic party.

"Jack just came up to me one day and told me the Redwings were up for sale. Being a frustrated ballplayer myself, I couldn't resist. I liked the idea of free tickets to the games."

The story told him little he didn't already know. It mentioned how Brunner's construction company, Bruconn, planned on renovating an abandoned mill downtown: American Paper. The more Lofton thought about it, the more buying the team seemed a good move for Brunner, something to endear him, and his business interests, to the local politicians. Only, with his partner, Tony Liuzza, flip-flopping in the Democratic party, the situation might be going sour. No wonder, Lofton thought, there had been tension between Brunner and Liuzza that night in the press box.

Lofton found some business on Kelley, too, a story announcing how the state senator had endorsed Richard Sarafis for governor. "I support Richard Sarafis because he's the candidate who cares about the disenfranchised, the people away from the power centers, and that includes not only the citizens of Holyoke but all of western Massachusetts."

Lofton had seen Richard Sarafis speak once, back when Sarafis was a young liberal—as Senator Kelley was now—the candidate with the clean record and clear eyes who worked the college campuses, the immigrant wards of Boston, the parlor halls of the wealthy, all with the same deft skill. Though Sarafis had aged more than a dozen years from the time Lofton had seen him, you couldn't tell time had touched the man at all from the looks of the picture at the top of the newspaper page. The makeup men, the hair dye specialists, and the tailors conspired to keep him forever young.

The real focus of the picture, though, was Senator Kelley. He moved with his hand extended—a small man, slightly burly, with his hair vaguely mussed. The camera had caught him in motion, just as his head turned away from Sarafis, so that his expression was disarming. It was Kelley's eyes. They seemed almost black in the photograph, as if contemplating some inner depths. If you did not know the circumstance of the picture, you would have guessed that the smaller man was the one with the power and that Sarafis, stiff, smiling, practiced, was some kind of plaster dummy set up for show.

The article said little else of substance, just the usual campaign rhetoric, but there was again brief mention of the renovation project planned for downtown Holyoke. The funding issue was currently being swatted around a committee that Kelley headed: "The Wells people are trying to foul the Holyoke money by attaching unacceptable stipulations. They don't want it to go through, not unless we award the contracts to their cronies. They're just daring me to kill it, knowing how much the people in my district need that project. The truth is, their stipulations are unacceptable, and I'll kill the whole thing before we let them have their way, even if it is an election year. I'm not playing partisan politics."

All told, the articles on Brunner and Kelley told Lofton little he had not already learned. Senator Kelley supported the challenger Sarafis. So did Liuzza. Brunner was on the other side with the incumbent Wells. Both groups seemed to want the Holyoke project to go through; they just wanted to make sure their side got the credit and their supporters got the cream.

As it turned out, the reporter who wrote about the fires in Holyoke was Einstein, the same reporter whose name Tenace had mentioned and who, according to the boys at the *Dispatch,* had left town without so much as blowing them a kiss good-bye. Lofton came across Einstein's work often in the paper: "Maria Ramirez, mother of six, her dress torn and soot-smeared, watched as rescuers searched the debris Tuesday for the body of her sister, believed dead in the recent blaze." In his stories Einstein made a practice of listing the owners of the buildings that burned; not one of the buildings had belonged to Brunner. One anonymous man who'd been burned out of his apartment said all the fires in Holyoke were arson, part of an insurance fraud scheme. A lieutenant on the arson squad said no, the buildings were old, they were fire traps. Sure, some of them were torched, but most went up through carelessness, just like anywhere else.

Einstein's most interesting stories, however, were his pieces about the Latinos, the street gang Lofton had learned about from Lou Mendoza. Over the course of several months Einstein had tracked the career of one of the gang's leaders, and eventually he had written about the young leader's death.

The leader of the Latinos had been named Angelo. The pictures showed him to be in his late twenties: a good-looking, dark-skinned man, with thick, full lips and wild black hair. When he talked, he mixed the language of the street with the slogans of the sixties' left wing, which Angelo was too young to have been part of but which he may have remembered or read about in books. He had been mobilizing the Puerto Rican community in an unusual way, at least for the leader of a street gang: giving speeches on street corners; criticizing the police and the drug dealers all in one breath. Angelo's popularity grew, and as it did, so did the size of the Latinos. He set up Latino patrols to protect storekeepers, to watch the streets at night, to try to stop the fires that, despite everything, still burned. In the process a street war broke out between the Latinos and a rival gang, the Wanderers.

Angelo's credibility became tarnished, however, after a street battle that left three young men dead on the street. Afterward Holyoke's mayor called the incident "tragic, barbaric" and made a public appeal—directed mostly at Angelo —for both street gangs to disband, to join the community, to let the police patrol the streets.

In full battle gear, scarves flying, chains hanging from their belts, knives sheathed at their sides, Angelo and a half dozen Latinos stormed into the next City Council meeting. Angelo took the platform and addressed the people in the auditorium. His people would not disband, he said, not ever.

"If you lived in our houses, in our streets, in our tenements —in our city that is burning—then you know why we can't disband. People like Mayor Rafferty say that it's all accident, all vandalism, simply our own people destroying ourselves and our homes. Would you burn your own homes? . . . The police, the white businessmen, the neighborhood crooks and thieves—like the Wanderers—they're the ones who gain. It's a system."

Lofton looked at the newspaper photo Einstein had taken of Angelo at the meeting. The gang leader stood on the platform, legs straddled wide, his finger pointing at the audience.

"We know who's burning our city, and we won't stop our war until they've been stopped. And those who think they're too powerful to be punished—we'll drag them down, too. That's why the politicians want us to disband and why the police are afraid of us."

Afterward the mayor had dismissed Angelo as "a fringe lunatic—a low-rent Al Capone trying to pass himself off as Che Guevera. We can't let him terrorize us." Then he announced that the Wanderers, the rival street gang, had agreed to throw off their colors and disband. He called on the Latinos to ignore their leader and do the same.

A few nights later, after walking out of a corner grocery store, Angelo had been shot twice in the head. He'd taken a bodyguard along with him to the store, but the Latinos did not carry guns, only knives. Both Angelo and his guard died at the scene. The store owner hadn't seen the murderer, he said; he didn't know anything about it. The two Latinos bought cigarettes, walked outside; then they were dead. "That's all I know," said the owner, "and all I want to know."

After Angelo's death Einstein did a story on the gang leader's funeral, and then that was it. Einstein's by-line disappeared from the *Dispatch* in early July, just before Lofton had got to town. Since then the paper had run little else about the Latinos or the Wanderers. Lofton now realized, thinking back on what Mendoza had said about taking off his colors, that he should go back and press Mendoza harder on the status of the rivalry, try to get to the bottom of what had happened between the two gangs, and see how it related to the fires.

Late one afternoon Lofton left the library for a while, taking a walk to clear his head. When he returned, the librarian approached him.

"Did your friend catch up to you?" asked the librarian, a shy, thin woman who tired hard to smile when she spoke.

"Friend?" Lofton said. He did not understand what she meant.

"Yes, he asked how you were coming along with the project. And he asked what papers you were looking at." The woman's smile faltered.

"Oh, yes," he said. "Right." He still had no idea what she meant.

"Good," the woman said, her smile firm now, satisfied.

Lofton sat awhile longer at the table. He could no longer concentrate. Who could be looking for him? No one could know he was here—except, now that he thought about it, he had mentioned, during an idle moment in the press box, that he needed to do some research in the library. But who would be following him? One of the reporters? Tenace? It didn't make any sense. He went up to the librarian's desk and called out to the young woman. "My friend?" he asked. "What did he look like?"

The woman seemed embarrassed.

"What did he look like?" Lofton repeated. He began to wonder if she had made a mistake, confusing him with someone else.

"About this high." The librarian raised her hand a few inches over her head. "Brownish hair." Her smile was gone; her cheeks were red. "I'm sorry, sir, I don't really remember."

On Friday he headed for his lunch with Amanti at the Little Puerto Rico Café. He left his hotel early, thinking maybe he could stop along the way at Mendoza's, get a few last details for that story McCullough wanted, and at the same time maybe learn something more about the Wanderers and the fires.

As he walked through the Flats, where Einstein had gone for his stories and where the fires were the most serious, he saw kids picking through the debris of a recently burned building. Perhaps they were even the same kids he had seen in some of Einstein's newspaper photographs. In the full-color glare of midday the young boys, wearing cutoff shorts, T-shirts, crucifix chains hanging around their necks, seemed less real, more frightening than a newspaper photo.

When he reached Mendoza's building, three young Puerto Rican men, teenagers really, were standing at the top of the steps. They did not move from the door as Lofton approached. The tallest of the three wore a brightly colored scarf around his head, silver and gold: the colors of the Latinos street gang. He shot a question at Lofton, speaking in rapid, clipped Spanish. Lofton did not understand. He thought it best, however, to pretend that he did.

"I'm looking for Lou Mendoza."

One of the other two took a quick stutter step toward Lofton. The tall kid with the head scarf extended his arm outright, across his friend's chest, signaling him to stop.

Lofton stood still, his heart pounding in his head. Now he noticed all three of them were wearing scarves. The angry one who'd been intercepted by his friends wore his colors tied around his arm. The third man, who leaned against the doorframe as if bored, had his scarf hanging from his belt, near a knife in a leather sheath.

"No está," said the one with the headband.

"Okay, *gracias."*

Lofton blinked up at the gang members. He tried a ridiculous, friendly wave and then—turning his back—headed down the stairs. Halfway up the street he braved a look over his shoulder. They were gone.

Just machismo, bravado, Lofton thought. The kid had no plans to come after me. Mendoza's name, though, had sure set him off.

The Little Puerto Rico Café was on a partially renovated block below the city's business section. It was hot and crowded, full of men and women talking loudly, mostly in Spanish. A quick-footed counterman yelled out orders over the din and paused, every fourth or fifth step, to wipe his hands on his dirty apron. A solitary waitress hurried back and forth between the customers and the kitchen.

Amanti was waiting in an upholstered booth in the back. She wore a black skirt and red blouse, so at first he did not recognize her, her clothes were so like those of the women in this district.

"Have you talked to Randy Gutierrez yet—the shortstop?" she asked.

"No, the team's out of town."

She smiled. Up close he noticed the faint white gloss on her lips and her red stone earrings—garnet maybe, he couldn't be sure; he only knew the stones looked like nothing women here could afford.

"I've been doing a lot of reading down at the library, looking into the fires."

She stared at him, her eyes a distant blue, as if she were staring at the ocean. She seemed to enjoy sitting here. He could feel himself sweating. The five-blade fan whirring overhead did little to cool the place. The waitress set down some water and hurried away. The water was warm, without ice. He wondered when Amanti would say why she had called him. Did she have some new information?

"A man named Einstein used to do the fire writing, a good job really." Lofton paused. She did not seem to be listening to him, but glancing about the place, studying it. She enjoyed it, the slumming.

"What happened to your face?" she asked.

Lofton scowled, touched his cheek; he had forgotten about the other night in the park.

"I slipped."

She nodded, smiling, and he got the impression that, improbable as it was, she somehow knew of his adventure alone at MacKenzie Field.

"Anyway," he said, wanting to see how she'd react when he contradicted the story she'd told him the other day, "according to Einstein, a lot of the locals feel someone's behind the burning, for insurance. But all the buildings are owned by different men, no pattern at all. And Brunner doesn't own any of them."

She looked at him, her eyes no longer clear blue but smoggy, like the sky over Holyoke. When the waitress came, Amanti ordered without even looking at the menu card. Apparently she had eaten here before.

"So that's what the papers say about the owners." She tried to say it with confidence, as if of course the papers were wrong; but her tone was quirky, quavering, and it occurred to Lofton that the way she had breezed in here, her apparent self-confidence, was a sham. He was so pleased with his observation, with her weakness, that he forgot to ask her how she knew the papers were wrong about the owners. In another moment the weakness was gone, and she held her fingertips against the tabletop in the same stiff way she had held them against the counter at her apartment.

"How long have you known Brunner?"

She laughed. "I've known him awhile. He's a friend of the family. Not my family exactly—the Liuzza family. Tony Liuzza's my cousin."

"I know. I heard that in the press box."

Lofton felt, he thought—it was one of those fleeting sensations that afterward seem to have been imagination—her shoe brushing against his leg. The restaurant was unbearably hot. He could smell the scent of her perfume. He saw Amanti was hot, too, a faint trace of sweat where her hair swept over her brow.

The food came, a thick mix of rice and tomatoes and vegetables and pork, not very good, or at least not what he had expected. He was used to the spicier Mexican food of California and, because the people were Hispanic, had thought this would be the same. They ate quietly, and he studied the turn of her cheek, the slight blush of rouge on her dark skin, near the scar. On one hand, he wanted the meal over as soon as possible—it was too hot here and he had little appetite—but on the other hand, he wanted to stretch it out. He did not look forward to spending the evening in his impossibly warm hotel. He asked her how Randy Gutierrez had come to tell her about the fires. She passed over the question. She leaned back in the booth, putting her hands underneath her legs and rocking herself, incongruously, in a way that reminded you of a teenage girl. She told him the neighborhood they were in had not always been Puerto Rican. Ten, fifteen years ago, it had been inhabited by Irish, Polish, a few Portuguese.

"My father would walk us down here sometimes, me and my brother, back when this place belonged to some Poles. My father was in the restaurant business, too, and my brother and I would sit here, drinking Cokes, while the owner and my father talked."

"Is your brother still in town?"

"No, he's dead. A car accident."

Though her face grew serious for a second, she didn't stop rocking, swinging her feet like a child. Ironically, when Lofton tried to imagine her as a child, he saw her—small, dark-skinned, quiet, standing by her father's side—as one of those young girls who seemed to carry adult secrets inside without realizing, not yet, what the secrets were, the type of girl grown men, even decent ones, would look at and see in a way different from the way they saw their own daughters. Though her shoe brushed him again, there was nothing in her face betraying she had touched him. It was still the girlish look. Lofton moved away, avoiding the swinging foot. She didn't talk to him about the arsons, the way she had the first time he talked to her, but instead, she told him about her family. People sometimes did that when you interviewed them, talking about anything but the matter at hand, sometimes because they were nervous and sometimes just because they wanted you to like them. With Amanti, it was hard to see what her reasons were. She told him how her parents had moved to Holyoke at the time of the Korean War. They'd left their old immigrant neighborhood in New Haven, she said, not because they were suddenly prosperous, like some of their neighbors, but because the Italians were moving out and the blacks moving in. So her father opened a restaurant on Locust Street in Holyoke. A small place, as much a tavern as a place to eat. Her brother had been born before the move, but Amanti had been born in Holyoke.

"On weekends, when I was little, we used to drive over the river to the Liuzzas' house. They had a big house, modern, that sprawled all around. My mother wanted a house like that, like her sister's, but my uncle was more clever than my father. You see, Uncle Liuzza was born into a rich family."

Amanti told him about the weekends at her uncle's house and about Tony Liuzza, her cousin. Her mother always doted on Tony Liuzza. The doting went back to the time before she'd been married, when she'd thought she would never have children of her own, but the doting continued after she had found her husband, after she had a son of her own, and after Amanti herself was born. It was always Cousin Tony in her lap, Cousin Tony being blessed with small kisses behind the ear, Cousin Tony whose collar she straightened with long fingers.

"If you want to know the truth, I think my mother had a thing for my uncle. She never did anything about it, of course, but that's why my parents moved up this way in the first place, because the Liuzzas were here. My uncle was going to help my father out with the restaurant; they talked all the time about moving it up to the highway, where my father could catch the tourists on the way to the Berkshires. Uncle Liuzza kept promising money, but it never came."

"How did the Liuzza family get their money?" Lofton asked.

"Munitions. Cannons for battleships, something like that. They made a fortune during World War II. But after Korea, Uncle Liuzza went into real estate. . . . He pushed Tony, from the time he was little, to be a lawyer. On weekends, when their house would be full of people, Uncle Liuzza would take Tony and show him around like he was some kind of prize. My brother always hated Tony. Maybe it wasn't fair, but I didn't like him much either."

It probably wasn't fair, but Lofton could understand. He could imagine Tony Liuzza as a teenager, standing just outside the adult conversation—a fresh, well-scrubbed boy, gangly despite his good manners. Of course his cousins would hate him. Lofton guessed he could hate Tony Liuzza, too, if he wanted, just for the guy's advantages. Liuzza's thin, painful smile was probably because he knew how people hated him, and he probably hated himself, at least a little bit anyway. Tony Liuzza had attended private school, Amanti explained between sips from her water glass, and Amanti's mother had wanted to send her children, particularly her son, to such schools. The best Amanti's father could afford was the local Catholic schools, so the boy went there. He went wild anyway. He hung around with the kids from the tenements. Then one day her brother got too drunk, took out the family car, and lost control on an ice-slick curve; the car hit the guardrail once, then a second time, and flipped over into the ravine below. Six months later Amanti's father died, too, a heart attack. "After that Uncle Liuzza loosened up with his money—enough so my mother could close down the restaurant and send me off to college in Boston. But that stopped a couple years back. My uncle doesn't approve of the way I live these days. Neither does my mother." Amanti gave him a shy, evocative look that seemed to hide some deeper embarrassment. "My mother has what she wants, though. My uncle and aunt let her move into their house, gave her a bedroom all her own—Cousin Tony's old room."

Amanti had stopped rocking. She did not look like a little girl anymore. Neither of them spoke for a while. Lofton listened to the slow whirring of the ceiling fan overhead. He still needed to know why she was sending him to talk to Randy Gutierrez. Had the shortstop confided in Amanti? He also needed to know more about her relationship to Brunner. Tenace had made plenty of insinuations, but the scorer, Lofton knew, had a mind that ran down a one-track road to the garbage dump. Lofton was about to ask her some questions, but Amanti broke the silence first. Her voice had a whole new tone.

"What do you want in Holyoke?"

Lofton was taken aback. He had no answer ready.

"This is where my car ran out of gas," he said, and felt a thin, clever smile crease his face. It wasn't a pleasant feeling.

"That's baloney."

She was right, of course. He could try to tell her the truth, he supposed. He could tell her that he had been on the verge of the good, happy life when something that resembled the big black shadow of death had fallen across his bed one night. (He might be dying, he might not, but that wasn't the point; even the doctor had been clever enough to see that.) The shadow had whispered to him in a voice that was seductive all right, sweet as failure, and he had gotten in the car so he wouldn't have to listen, so he could go for a long drive in which he was nobody, just a pair of headlights in a great big fog. The only trouble was that sooner or later you had to stop, and then you were somebody again, and the voice started up all over. He could have told Amanti this, he guessed, if he could find the words, but there's no way to tell people such things. Instead, he got clever again. "I'd been driving all night, and I saw a sign that read: 'Journalist wanted. Fame and fortune next three exits.' I thought there might be something to it. . . . So you tell me. What do you want?"

She regarded him for a long moment. Her eyes were darkened with some sort of liner. Behind the darkness, though, the eyes glittered. The glittering eyes admired his cleverness but at the same time told him she knew it was still baloney.

"Been married?" he asked.

"No," she said. "I haven't had that pleasure." He heard irony in her last remark, and—though she tried to keep it out

—some resentment. He could not say why, but he felt a sudden surge of affection for Amanti.

After the meal he walked Amanti to her car, parked in a municipal lot off High Street. Outside, a man on the sidewalk behind them let out a high whistle and a shout. Lofton turned, but the man was not concerned with him or Amanti. He was just calling a greeting to a friend who stood outside the abandoned Sunoco station across the street. Two young boys on bicycles pedaled up next to Amanti; on the sidewalk ahead, a woman and her children stopped to press their noses against the display windows of a bridal store. Aside from this small cluster of people, the street was pretty well deserted in the afternoon heat. Lofton remembered how the people in Mexico, noisy and active on the streets, always crowded close together, it seemed, no matter the empty spaces around them, and how the city women dressed the way Amanti dressed now, in hot dark colors, no matter the heat.

They took a footbridge across the canal. "Let's cut this way," he said, touching her lightly on the arm, then pointing toward a row of stone tenements tucked between the factory canal and Holyoke's main street. They stopped at the corner, hesitating at the sight of the crumbling, cramped buildings. He remembered the gang members at Mendoza's, and it suddenly seemed stupid to go on. There was noise and clutter everywhere, graffiti and torn bits of plaster, and the impossible feeling that there were thousands of people living on this short, narrow block. An old woman turned a dull, resentful eye toward them, and he and Amanti stood caught in their hesitation. Then, as if the entire scene had been staged for them, Lofton heard the cry of a fire engine. The slow eyes of the Hispanic woman turned away, and people rushed toward the plume of smoke the next block over.

"Incendio! Hay un incendio!" the children cried, running, excited, down the block. Without thinking, he and Amanti hurried, almost trotted, toward the smoke, Amanti clutching at his elbow as they went.

Ahead, the engine turned the corner. They arrived a moment later, in time to see the firemen hurling their axes into the windshield of a Ford van. The smoke had been deceptive. It was only a car going up in smoke, spilled gasoline, maybe, or the vain attempt to collect insurance on a junker, or maybe just done for fun, because burning things was the way the poor expressed themselves in this town.

"Why did you do it? Why did you do it?" A young man yelled and grabbed a small boy in the crowd. Lofton was alarmed at first, then saw the man was joking. The little boy ran, laughing and screaming, back to the tenements.

Slowly the crowd broke up: Amanti taking her hand away from his arm; a white teenager in dirty clothes running to catch up with his friends, a black Carib scolding his wife; and the Hispanic girls, wearing tight clothes and bright earrings, gathering their younger brothers and sisters.

He walked Amanti to her car in the parking lot behind City Hall. On the way he asked her again about Brunner. She had told him that Brunner was friends with the Liuzza family, but that didn't explain everything. She hesitated, then looked at him directly.

"I'm his mistress," she said.

Her eyes widened a little, but they also got very dark. If there was any light in them, it was way back somewhere he couldn't see. Then she resumed the posture she'd had back in the restaurant, that of woman acting like a girl, or of a girl acting like a woman, he wasn't sure which anymore.

"Why didn't you tell me sooner?"

"I figured you'd find out on your own. It isn't exactly a secret. I think even his wife knows."

"Is that why you want me to write this story—to help you get rid of him?"

"I could do that on my own."

Amanti started the engine. Lofton reached through the window and touched her shoulder. There were a lot of things he still needed to know.

"I've heard some stuff in the press box. About some renovation project Brunner's mixed up with; only the government part of the money seems to be tied up in the state legislature. What about this Senator Kelley?" Lofton asked. "What's his connection to all this?"

"I don't know anything about politics." Amanti's voice was sharp, distressed. Without looking at Lofton, she slid the car into gear. All right, Lofton thought, I'll check into Kelley myself. Watching her back into traffic, giving her a quick wave that she returned at the last minute, he guessed that her sudden anger was more at herself than at him. She hadn't liked admitting her affair with Brunner.

Amanti was tired of the heat. Even though summers were always hot in Massachusetts, no one seemed, especially in the small towns, to take air-conditioning seriously. The local man Brunner had gotten to install the central air in her apartment had done it incorrectly. Not one in a long line of repairmen had been able to make the system work the way it was supposed to. So the shower was the best way to cool down. She turned the water on as cold as she could stand it.

She wondered why Lofton had asked about Kelley, if it was just coincidence or if the reporter had some idea what had gone on between them for the last four years. The latter didn't seem likely. The few people who knew there had been anything between herself and Kelley—the Liuzza family, her mother, Brunner—weren't likely to say anything. She was Brunner's mistress now, yes, and he got what he paid for, and in a certain way she enjoyed the touch of his rough hands; but the man with whom she struggled in her thoughts had always been Kelley, and still was Kelley, at least most of the time. And Brunner knew that.

Amanti turned off the shower. She didn't towel herself dry, not completely. She put on a thin, loose robe and went to the living room. She sat down between two fans and let the breeze cool her. Though she was still conscious of the oppressive, dreamy heat around her, she could avoid it so long as the fans blew across her damp skin and she didn't move too much or too quickly. It was curious, she thought, how she'd had trouble picturing Kelley's face the other night. The truth was, though, she had learned the trick of keeping her mind empty. It hadn't always been that way; she had once dwelt infinitely over everything that happened to her, every conversation with Kelley, every fragment of her childhood. She had just found out it was easier not to think things over, a kind of escape when escape was impossible. You could keep everything way back in your head—your past, your lovers, your present, your future—and pretend none of it existed, which was nonsense, of course. Because then those things controlled you without your knowing. Or you could do it the other way: You could study the details of your life intently, the way as a kid she had

studied her face in the mirror—and later, as an adult, she had
studied Kelley's face on the bed beside her—but then you
knew the details too well, and it was impossible to change
anything. So, both ways, it was the same. Once something was
in motion, it was in motion. Your life went in its own direction. You could watch or not, do it as you pleased, but you
shouldn't expect the simple act of flipping your eyelids up and
down to change anything.

Still, her talk with Lofton had gotten her thinking. She
went to her trunk, took out an old photo album, and started
looking through the pictures: her parents' old house in
Holyoke, gray and weatherbeaten; the restaurant with its big
yellow sign and her father standing beneath it; her brother
leaning against the car, jet black hair, black jacket, cigarette
between his lips, imitating some actor he'd seen in the movies.
There was only one picture of herself as a girl, thin-legged,
smiling toothily, wearing a dress that fell all the way to her
shoes, but there were several that had been taken when she
was older, a college student posing in cashmere sweaters beneath old trees, in front of old buildings, all of which seemed
to be covered with ivy. Oddly, she hadn't dressed and posed
like that when she first entered college, the way many of the
other girls had, but toward the end, when in fact she had
stopped attending classes, though she was still enrolled. While
the pictures showed she was conscious of the irony, she
remembered being dead serious at the time. In the album,
scattered among the clear snapshots, were ones that had not
developed properly. Several years ago she had tucked the un-
recognizable shots in with the others, dark prints in which the
underlying image was so faint that she had to struggle to pick
her face, or that of some forgotten friend's, out of the blackness. At the time these prints had made the other photographs seem more poignant.

She came to a photograph of Kelley. The sky behind him
was gray, the clouds darkening, but the light must have been
right because it had caught him well. His hair was black as a
stallion's, and his eyes a deep dark blue. They were the sort of
eyes that changed color with the light. What she had always
liked about the photograph was the way it showed the color
of his skin, a pure, startling white that might have seemed
unhealthy, or effeminate, on another man—and sometimes

seemed that way on Kelley—but on that day, she remembered, his skin had had a soft, beautiful luster. She remembered that day at the beach. As they walked along, and the
water wrens skittered to be out of their path, Kelley had told
her that the one thing he had liked about being a lawyer was
talking to the jury, and the one thing he liked about being a
politician was talking to the crowd. (Kelley was a good
speaker, Amanti had known at the time; she now knew that
there were men better, but that didn't matter.) Talking to a
crowd, Kelley told her, was better than talking to one person
because it wrenched you in the gut, it made the blood pound
in your ears even when you were speaking as softly as you
could. Everything fell in line in front of a crowd; everything
was simple and pure, and the things you had done, no matter
what—those things were right. The rest of your life you
sloshed through the mire and the muck, you did things which
no God-fearing bastard would do—but which everybody did,
he was learning—and you knew you would go to hell except
for the fact that there was no hell and for the fact that the
second you stepped onto the platform you knew everything
had a reason.

Amanti had first met Kelley not in Boston but at the
Liuzza house. It was on a weekend, more than four years ago,
after the time of the cashmere sweaters but before she had
dropped completely out of school. Her mother had insisted
she go with her to one of Uncle Liuzza's get-togethers. "Your
uncle's paying for your college," her mother had said, "he
invited us over, and I don't want you to insult him."

When they reached her uncle's house, a group of men sat
around the living room table. Uncle Liuzza was there, and
Tony sat beside him, looking as he always looked in his father's presence, anxious to please but slightly beleaguered,
smiling continually. Her uncle introduced her to the other
two men. One was Jack Brunner. He took her hand a little
roughly and held it a bit longer than you might expect. When
Brunner let go, he smiled and gave her an indiscreet once-
over, his best smile. Then her uncle introduced Kelley.

"David Kelley here is running for the state legislature; he's
a fine young man," her uncle said. At the time Kelley did not
seem young to her; he was in his middle thirties, more than
ten years older than herself. Kelley took her hand when they

were introduced. His was a lighter touch than Brunner's. She
liked his touch. She could feel Brunner, and the others,
watching as her hand lingered. Her mother made a motion
that it was time to leave, to go back into the kitchen with the
other women, but Amanti sat down with the men. Uncle
Liuzza frowned, but rather than trouble himself with asking
her to leave, he simply went on as if she weren't there.

The men talked about Kelley's campaign. Kelley was running in the district that encompassed a small triangle of towns
including Holyoke, Chicopee, and the rural, wealthier area of
South Hadley. Kelley had grown up in Chicopee, the son of a
hardware store clerk, and gone to law school on a scholarship.

"The working class will go for you," Uncle Liuzza said,
"and I'll get the rich son of a bitches to fall in line. It's just a
matter of promising a few zoning changes."

Uncle Liuzza looked significantly over at Brunner, then at
Kelley. Kelley smiled wryly, ingratiating and defiant simultaneously, and the defiance made you like him all the more.
Uncle Liuzza liked Kelley, too, she thought. Or at least her
uncle hoped he could use him to help get some of his green-
belt property rezoned; it had been a concern of her uncle's for
years. It didn't take much to see that Brunner didn't share her
uncle's attitude toward Kelley. Though Brunner was in construction himself and wanted the same zoning changes, he
was hesitant to throw his support behind the younger man.

"It comes down to the big picture," Brunner said, throwing
a glance in Amanti's direction, as if she were the arbiter.
"There's a governorship at stake now, too, you know, and I'm
afraid Kelley here's supporting the wrong man."

It was an old conflict, this argument over which Democrat
—Sarafis or Wells—should be governor. Amanti had realized
instinctively, even at that first meeting, that Brunner and Kelley's disagreement had more to do with the clashing of their
personalities than it had to do with politics or even self-inter-
est. There was a natural antipathy between the two men. Uncle Liuzza worked to patch it over. "You don't have to agree
on the governorship issue to support him as our local representative. I don't agree with him either, but he's going to
make some changes that'll never be made otherwise. . . . After all, you're in construction yourself, aren't you?"

Brunner agreed, though somewhat reluctantly. During dinner the issue was dropped. A red-haired woman with features as fine and fragile as porcelain sat next to Kelley. She wore very bright, colorful clothes; she smiled constantly, nervously, though at no one in particular. She hardly spoke and her hand fluttered nervously over her soup. She was Kelley's fiancée, Amanti learned, the daughter of a powerful politician. There was a tenuousness about her, a sort of loose hysteria under the surface that seemed as if it might actually break her apart, and Amanti noticed the way Kelley occasionally reached out to touch the woman, as if to see that she was still in one piece.

Amanti found herself sitting next to Brunner. She ignored him at first, until she saw Kelley was watching. Then she changed her behavior. She talked to Brunner throughout dinner in a way she thought to be both flattering and clever, occasionally grazing the man's shoulder with her hand and cutting her eyes toward Kelley, to see if he was watching. He was. For a second Brunner rested his hand in her lap. Though it was gone just as quickly, she still wondered why she hadn't moved to take it away.

After dinner, when everyone else was in the front room drinking, Kelley caught Amanti alone in the kitchen. He leaned up against the counter beside her. Amanti could still remember the moment in great detail: Kelley's aggressive slouch; the calm way his hands rested against the counter; his clear voice as he asked her where she lived, where she went to school, how old she was.

As they stood there like that, Brunner walked in. Though Brunner was married himself, you could see the jealousy in his eyes, not necessarily because he wanted her, she realized, but because he did not want Kelley to have his way in everything; Kelley leaned back and smiled. The air was charged with an exotic excitement that she could not put a name to but that she still remembered.

"That night, when your uncle first introduced me to Brunner," Kelley told her later, "I could tell it bothered him how easy I sat there in Liuzza's house. He didn't like it. And he didn't like the way I smiled when I shook his hand."

She got together with Kelley that very next weekend in Boston. That's when the affair started. For a while it had seemed Kelley would break off with his fiancée, but he never did. Perhaps it was because he loved the woman. Kelley had said that himself several times. Or perhaps it was because he needed the political support of her powerful father. Kelley had said that, too. Either way he went ahead with the marriage, and went on seeing Amanti.

The times when she had been with Kelley were intense, and the times when she was not with him—which were sometimes brief and sometimes long, depending on his social schedule and political commitments—she carried that same intensity within her, so that it gave special drama to the simplest moments, to the mere fact of walking down the Boston streets and feeling the wind in her face. She felt as if her life were propelled in a way that the strangers on the street around her could never know. Other times she felt as if the core of her life had rotted away and all she had left were the individual moments, instants when she almost hated Kelley, when the gap between her everyday life and her secret life was accentuated too painfully. Despite herself, she enjoyed the tumult of her emotion and did nothing to change the way things were.

Then the affair was discovered. Uncle Liuzza found out. So did the red-haired woman's powerful father. Uncle Liuzza put pressure on her, the father-in-law put pressure on Kelley, and the whole thing was complicated by the fact that Kelley was up for reelection, and complicated further, twisted into knots, by a foolish, unnecessary kickback scheme the only intention of which, it seemed, had been to irritate his father-in-law, who in turn promised to forget the whole thing, to wash it away and help Kelley with his reelection, so long as Kelley didn't do anything to hurt his daughter. Kelley agreed. He promised not to see Amanti. So she started up with Brunner, to rile Kelley's jealousy. Though that had worked for a while, it had not worked quite well enough, and gradually—in a way that sometimes confounded her and sometimes seemed inevitable —she had become enmeshed with Brunner.

Kelley came back, of course. Lately she had seen him as much as ever. The changes that took place, in herself and in Brunner and in Kelley, took place slowly, so in some ways she didn't even notice them. Several months ago she had found out about the arsons. Brunner had told her himself, in an incident that still bewildered her. Even so, the fact of the arsons hadn't seemed particularly important to her at first, just old buildings burning and the transfer of money from one account to the next, the sort of thing men talked about around tables, the air stale with cigarette smoke and liquor while they debated the legality of some plan, or how to disguise the illegality, then smiled to themselves when the lines seemed sufficiently blurred. Later she read in the paper how some people had died in one of the buildings; then, by coincidence, it seemed, she ended up in the same room with Randy Gutierrez, the Redwings' shortstop, who told her more about the fires.

When she mentioned what was going on to Kelley, he seized upon it. Kelley came up with a plan to leak the information to the press. They would find a reporter they could control, and they would get him started on the fires. Then Kelley would go to Brunner himself. He would say that he knew about the arsons, that this reporter had told him. He would offer to help Brunner, to put a rag in the reporter's mouth, so long as Brunner switched sides in the gubernatorial race. Switching sides meant, of course, contributing money. If Sarafis could win, then Kelley would be in good shape to buck his father-in-law, to do as he pleased. The whole scheme depended on finding the right reporter. Someone not already in Brunner's camp, someone who—when the folding money was on the table—would take a few dollars and keep his mouth shut. Lofton's arrival in town seemed like perfect timing, though there was always someone like that guy around, Kelley told her, with his kind of history, who had been involved with something just like that business with Senator Hansen in California. Still, it was perfect. "All you have to do is keep the reporter interested, push him in the right direction. I'll arrange the rest."

Now Amanti shook her head and wiped her brow. The heat was too much. She found herself staring at one of the black, indecipherable photographs. She went back into the shower to cool herself down.

Last winter she had been in the shower on a day as cold as this one was hot, trying to escape the winter cold as she now tried to escape the heat. Brunner was visiting. He had come across her photo album while she was in the shower. When she got out of the shower, he had been standing in the hall outside the bathroom, holding the book in his hand.

"A lot of pictures in here of Kelley," he'd said, and then

added with a certain pleasure, "From what I hear, he's got himself another mistress now."

Amanti had brushed past him into the bedroom, trying to ignore the sudden draft of cold, the sharpness of the air. Now, turning the shower on a little harder, she wondered if what Brunner had said that day was true and figured it probably was.

On Saturday morning Lofton called McCullough to ask him if he would like a story on Randy Gutierrez's slump for Monday sports, since the Redwings would be back soon. He got Kirpatzke instead, and Kirpatzke agreed so quickly, so easily, it made Lofton wonder. Kirpatzke did not even ask about the story on Lou Mendoza, but then he hadn't wanted him to write it in the first place.

"I was thinking . . ." Lofton paused.

"You were?"

Lofton ignored Kirpatzke's tone.

"What happened to Einstein?"

"Einstein?"

"Yeah, Einstein, the writer who did the fire stories, the features on the Puerto Rican wards, that stuff."

"What about him?"

"Have you heard from him yet?"

Kirpatzke was silent.

"No news?" Lofton said.

"He hasn't been sending me any postcards, if that's what you mean."

Now it was Lofton's turn to be quiet.

"All right?" Kirpatzke asked.

"All right."

The following day Lofton called Golden to arrange an interview with Randy Gutierrez.

"Gutierrez?" Golden asked. Lofton was weary of people responding to him with one-word questions. Even so, he guessed Golden sounded brusque because he thought such formalities unnecessary. It was common practice for sportswriters, especially in the minors, to wander onto the field and talk to the players.

"Will you tell him to hold some time for me?"

Golden said he would. Lofton hoped so. He wanted Randy
Gutierrez to know he was coming, to feel the interview was
official, something sanctioned by the club.

Of course, there was another side to it, one that said he
should just catch Gutierrez by surprise. The shortstop's situation in Holyoke was precarious. He was having a bad season.
His contract died at the end of the summer. He wanted to
immigrate, to bring his wife and children up from Managua.
He might be superstitious about talking to the press, too, the
same way he was superstitious about dressing out in the clubhouse before a game, figuring it would bring him bad luck on
the field. If he was concerned about the Immigration and
Naturalization Service—with the Sandinista trouble, the INS
was looking at all Nicaraguans, even ballplayers, with a suspicious eye—then that might also make him reluctant to talk.
Gutierrez might avoid him, say he had to work with the
trainer in the locker room, some damned excuse, or, better
yet, pretend he spoke no English whatsoever. And if Gutierrez were tied up with Brunner, as Amanti had indicated, then
he might disappear from the lineup completely.

But no, Gutierrez couldn't run, especially if he had something to hide. That would be the worst thing, the most obvious thing he could do. Finally, Lofton felt he had made the
right decision. By giving Gutierrez advance warning, he gave
him time to think things over, time to get nervous. It was
Lofton's experience that it was best to catch politicians off
guard with a quick, direct question at an unexpected time,
usually after a defeat. But others, those not used to the press,
got more nervous, more apt to stumble, the more time you
gave them to think things over.

He expected Gutierrez, like all ballplayers, would talk in
clichés: Keep my eye on the ball, do what I can for the club
and things will come around, been down before, motivate myself, concentration, control. Somewhere in there, interrupting
that steady predictable stream, Lofton would ask how he
liked Holyoke—*The fans here are good to me*—and then, after
asking Gutierrez something about the owners, mentioning
Amanti's name, he would slide toward the question of the
fires. If Gutierrez wanted to talk, as Amanti said, it should
not be that hard. He would assure him that he wouldn't print
anything sensitive. At least not now. As far as the *Dispatch*

went, he knew what he would give it: Gutierrez's background, his nervous eye, his slump, his determination.

When Lofton arrived at the park, the Redwings were taking practice. A few diehard fans stood by the sidelines, watching and talking among themselves. Gutierrez was not on the field, nor was he in the locker room. Lofton could not find Golden either, so he asked Coach Barker, the manager, who was gruff and brief as always.

"Gutierrez'll be here. At least he better be."

Game time approached, but still Gutierrez did not show up. Lofton talked to Tim Carpenter, the second baseman. He knew Gutierrez as well as anyone. The pair had roomed together for a while. The Redwings' program compared them to Luis Aparicio and Nellie Fox, the double-play infielders for the old Chicago White Sox.

"Randy had a bad road trip. Lots of errors and no hits. He has some trouble concentrating."

Tim Carpenter avoided Lofton's eyes; something in his voice suggested there was more to the matter than a simple slump or some problem in concentration.

"Drugs?" Lofton blundered out with it, regretting it instantly, though he knew such blundering, such clumsiness in interviews, was his strength as a reporter.

Carpenter shot him a dirty look. A moment later, when the national anthem—a scratchy tape played over the public-address system—started, he placed his cap over his heart and turned to the flag. Lofton turned with him. He tried to apologize, but Carpenter did not let him.

"Save it," Carpenter said. "You guys are all assholes."

The anthem ended, and Carpenter trotted off to his defensive position.

Lofton felt bad. Tim Carpenter was one of the hustlers on the team, one of the few with real spirit; his position was solid all the way up through the California organization, and it was too bad no other teams had expressed interest in him. Second base had been Lofton's own position in college, back when he was light on his feet and could pivot quickly. He liked watching Carpenter play. Lofton told himself he would write a story that made Gutierrez look good for the *Dispatch*, to prove that Carpenter's opinion was unfair. He had just been doing his job; surely Carpenter could understand that. Still, he wished the interview hadn't gone sour. If nothing else, he had hoped to get Gutierrez's Holyoke address from Carpenter. Tenace, over in the press box, might know the name of the family Gutierrez lived with.

Just then, however, Lofton spotted Dick Golden. The general manager was coming in from the street with the young, retarded-looking kid Lofton had seen at the library. The boy still wore a Redwings' cap, twisted backward on his head. When the kid got Golden's attention, he fidgeted in front of him, his eyes downward, his feet jittering, his hand moving up and down as if it belonged to another person. The kid had a habit of following the players around, and recently he'd taken to Golden. Lofton guessed that the kid knew Dick Golden had been a star once, a big-league pitcher in California. As Lofton approached, Golden handed the kid some money, and the kid ran off.

"Paying him off?" Lofton asked.

Golden gave Lofton a sharp look. "No. He's getting me a Coke. The kid's always around. He likes to do things for us. Better he's here than out on the street somewhere."

"Sure," Lofton said. "Small crowd tonight, isn't it?"

"Sure is," Golden said. Then he added impatiently, "You want something?"

"Gutierrez's address."

"It's against policy," Golden said, and turned his back on Lofton.

"If I find him, I'll send him out to the park."

"Just mind your business." Golden was suddenly angry, his voice sharp and bitter. "I don't need you people pestering me."

Lofton headed to the press box. He wasn't having much luck. What he had heard about Golden was true. The man was moody, even nasty. Settling down between the other reporters, he mentioned it to Tenace.

"Oh, Golden, he's always like that," said Tenace, entering a mark on his scorecard. "One minute he's an angel. Paint wings on him, and he'd float to heaven. Next minute he's a son of a bitch. Can't blame him, though. His wife's stuck in that wheelchair."

When the field changed hands, Holyoke coming to bat,

Lofton tried to edge Tenace into telling him what he needed to know. Tenace always loved to talk.

"The family Gutierrez rooms with, haven't they put up players before?"

Tenace squinted up at him, then away. For once he seemed at a loss for words. After waiting for a few minutes, Lofton repeated his question. Tenace turned nervously and squinted up at him again.

"Hey," he said, "what happened to your face?"

Lofton reached a hand to his cheek and remembered the other night, how he slipped while running the bases. "I slipped in the parking lot." Lofton shrugged awkwardly.

"Chasing that Puerto Rican pussy again, huh, boy?"

Down on the field Carpenter, the leadoff batter, singled sharply to right. Tenace made a mark on his scorecard and turned back to Lofton. He could not leave the joke alone. "Our star reporter here, he fell drunk on his face last night while trying to stick it to some Puerto Rican gash."

Lofton laughed, trying to go along with the joke. Again he asked Tenace where Gutierrez lived. This time Tenace acted as if he hadn't heard the question.

Suddenly Lofton thought of something. "Hey, did you come looking for me at the library the other day? Was that you?"

"No, not me. I don't go anywhere near those places. Not my style, not ever." The scorer shook his head and turned back to the field.

Annoyed, Lofton watched Tim Carpenter increase his lead off first. Carpenter jumped with the pitch, stirred up some dust, and slid headfirst into second, the throw coming in high and late behind him. The crowd stood and cheered.

"You doing a feature?" asked Rhiner, sounding amused.

"Yes," said Lofton. "That's what I'm doing."

Carpenter was advancing to third on a slow grounder; he scored on the next play, on Banks's deep fly. With two outs Lofton figured the scoring was over for the inning. Sitting in the press box—still trying to think of a way to coax the information from Tenace—he watched the Glens Falls pitcher, a jittery youngster just up from Single A, throw four balls in a row to Lumpy, the Redwings' catcher. As the pitcher waited for a new batter, Lofton felt someone tap him on the shoulder. It was Rhiner.

"The family Gutierrez stays with, their name's Rosa," the reporter told him. "They live off Beech on some side street, Franklin, I think. She rents out a walled-in porch out back."

Lofton said thanks. It was a first from Rhiner, an effort to be friendly, to help him out on a story even though they were on competing papers.

When he reached the grassy area behind the first base bleachers, the crowd was cheering. Another walk, this one to the Redwings' first baseman, Lynch. The jittery youngster loaded the bases, and up came Singleton, Gutierrez's replacement, a short, bulky man, surprisingly fast on his feet but a little clumsy with the glove. He hit the first pitch hard. The ball rose off the bat, traveling just this side of the left field line and clearing the fence. A home run. Lofton headed to the exit. Five to nothing, Holyoke. A good lead, but the Redwings had let games like this get away before.

He found Franklin Street, a small avenue on the border between two neighborhoods, one white working class, the other Puerto Rican. He identified the house more easily than he thought he would, the name Rosa in pink letters on the mailbox. He walked around the back, following a narrow concrete walkway, cracked in places so the grass grew through. He ducked under a low-hanging willow and found a door off to the side of the house. A small shrine to the Blessed Virgin stood at the bottom of the steps that led to the door. He knocked on the door, but no one answered. He tried to see through the gauze curtains hanging on the inside of the door's window. He could see nothing distinctly, only hear a radio inside playing Hispanic music. He knocked again, tried the handle, and stepped inside. He called Gutierrez's name and knocked on the wall framing. He hesitated. Maybe Gutierrez was sick, or asleep. Maybe he should forget it and go back to the park. No, he wanted this story. He needed to feel out Gutierrez before returning to Amanti. Lofton stepped around the corner into the kitchen and saw Gutierrez lying on the floor, dressed in his baseball uniform, his body twisted at a bad angle between the table and the refrigerator.

3

Gutierrez was dead. By the angle at which he lay, it looked almost as if he'd died before hitting the floor. His shoulder jutted into the air, his head was bent back, bleeding through a large wound in the skull, and his cheek was pressed against the table leg. The body was twisted too violently, and there was too much blood, to imagine he had lived long after being shot. A good-size gun, Lofton guessed, maybe even a rifle, fired from close range. Inches.

Years ago, when Lofton's mother died, his father had kept both Lofton and his brother away from the funeral. The deaths he had seen since were those of strangers: a kid buried under a bus; a woman pulled from a river; a heart attack in an airport lobby. When such events happened, they did not seem real, but rather like something from television or the movies. This was like that, too: the death of a stranger, his blood smeared in a bright, cinematic puddle on the linoleum. Unlike the movies, however, there was no camera to fade to another scene. Lofton had to turn his head away, take a deep, unconscious breath—the brief image of the Amanti woman flickered through his mind—but when he turned back, Gutierrez was still there. Lofton felt he should do something; what, he wasn't sure. He could not escape the feeling that someone was watching, that he was somehow guilty. He had the urge to run, but instead, he stood and stared at Gutierrez's blood. Out the kitchen window he caught a glimpse of the evening sky. It was the same sky as always. No difference in the world.

Finally, he bent over to feel the shortstop's pulse. As he did so, he imagined himself sitting in his room, staring into the ghost light of the television, into the land of violence and shadows, the seductive world of black revolvers and red lips. Then there was the *No* in his mind, the denial. *I am not responsible. I did not do this.*

He dropped Gutierrez's wrist and lit a cigarette as he walked away from the body. He reached for the telephone, then stopped. No fingerprints, no trace of involvement. A stack of papers and unopened mail was scattered on the table. He picked the papers up, started to sort through, then changed his mind. He could do that later. He grabbed a dish towel. Using it as a glove, he searched the apartment: the kitchen cabinets, the bathroom, the dresser drawers. He found some letters with Nicaraguan postmarks, a bank statement, a vial of pills, a thin chain with a medallion of Jesus. He added them to the papers on the table and then went over every place he might have touched, wiping it clean with the towel. He gathered the pile of Gutierrez's things and left. As he wiped the door handle outside, he noticed again the shrine of the Virgin at the base of the steps outside; her plaster base was cracked and crumbling, as if she had been a long time out in the weather. He hurried away. A young couple walked hand in hand on the street, but they did not notice him.

A few blocks from MacKenzie Field he stopped at a gas station. He called the police from the phone booth and told them there had been a murder at Gutierrez's address. The police operator tried to keep him on the line, but Lofton hung up. He would not give his name.

As he approached MacKenzie, the kitchen towel and bundle of papers still under his arm, a pair of squad cars drove by with their sirens off. They turned the corner quickly, one after the other, in the direction of Gutierrez's neighborhood. He was surprised they'd responded so soon.

The game was over. The stadium lights were still on; but the entrance was chained, and Lofton could not see the scoreboard from this angle. He paced nervously back and forth, wondering what to do. A small group of teenagers stood not far away. The boys stared at him, their eyes dull, glittering pools, as if they were high on drugs. He asked them who had won the game.

"Holyoke," one of them said. "We beat 'em good."

A few minutes later an ambulance rushed by the ballpark. The kids grabbed their bicycles, and Lofton followed, too, with the vague idea that he was somehow safer close to the crime. On the way he stashed the towel and papers beneath a hedge.

The ambulance stopped on Gutierrez's street. By the time Lofton arrived, a neighborhood crowd had already gathered. The kids from the ballpark were there, too, joking and laughing, standing with their bicycles in the revolving ambulance light: red and blue, blue and yellow, yellow and red. The ambulance driver stood by the wagon's rear door, talking to a paramedic. The paramedic lit a cigarette. Apparently the police were in no hurry to get Gutierrez to the morgue.

A patrolman guarding the driveway held a long-handled flashlight, and the air around him was electric with voices. Some voices came from downtown, operators relaying trouble and its code names over the squad car intercom. Other voices came from the walkie-talkie at the cop's belt, chatter from inside the house.

Lofton walked up to the policeman, thinking—it seemed natural enough—that he should turn himself in. The cop shone the flashlight beam in Lofton's face, a bright, intense light that forced him to close his eyes and turn his head. Instinctively he raised his hands in a gesture of surrender.

"I'm the man who called in," he said quickly. "I found the body." He listened to himself speak the words as if he said nothing unusual.

The flashlight dropped slightly. The policeman scanned him up and down but would not meet his eyes. Lofton had noticed that about policemen before. When they were dealing with the public, when they had a job to do, they often did not look you in the face. They could not take the chance of succumbing to individual entreaties. The cop kept his eye on Lofton's hands.

"I have a witness here." The cop spoke into his walkie-

talkie. There was a scuttle of static, some conversation back
and forth—he could make out the officers' voices inside the
house—and finally, one of them told the patrolman to hold
Lofton inside the squad car.

Though he was beginning to have second thoughts, he did
not resist. He walked in front of the cop to the passenger side
and waited while the man opened the rear door. After Lofton
was inside, the cop reached through the front window and
pulled a switch. The door locks clicked. A sliding metal
screen, closed shut in the center, divided the front seat from
the back.

"Sit tight," the cop said, laughing a little, then moving
down the walk to take up his old position. When the cop was
gone, Lofton tested the rear doors. They were locked solid.

From where Lofton sat, he could still hear the voices of the
men inside the house coming over the patrolman's walkie-
talkie. He could see a man stationed outside the apartment
door, another man roaming the backyard, and he could hear
them talking to each other over the static, joking and exchanging information with the men inside. He heard continued references to the plaster Virgin and some grim remarks
about Gutierrez's body on the floor. He imagined the men
rummaging through Gutierrez's apartment, the rooms lit with
bright strobes. Over the crackle of the walkie-talkie, he heard
them say it looked as if someone had gone over the place
already.

"I guess whoever was here before us, they didn't look up
inside the Virgin." Someone laughed. "Too bad, because the
fellow missed himself a bonus."

Lofton grimaced. He wondered what he had missed. And
why the hell he had turned himself in. He had learned better
years ago. Once, as a young reporter, he had spent three hours
in the station detailing a holdup he had witnessed to the police, then promised he would not write it up until the man had
been apprehended. His editor had had him transferred back to
obituaries. This could be a lot worse. Not only would the
police try to tie up the story, but they might figure out he had
lifted Gutierrez's papers. Even if they couldn't prove he had
taken anything, they would accuse him, make him go down to
the station. They would swagger, threaten—play it just like
TV. Lofton wanted none of that.

He looked down the street. The cop was busy with his flashlight. Lofton tried the sliding door on the metal screen that separated the front seat from the back. It wouldn't budge. A man dressed in street clothes—a detective, he guessed—came down from the house. After looking at Lofton in the back seat, he tried to open the car door. When this new cop found the back door was locked, he cursed. He got in the front of the car, then reached under the dash to trigger the switch. The detective paused to relay some technical information to the operator. He gossiped with the operator about the murder.

"Some Puerto Rican in a baseball uniform. No identification around anywhere, no papers, only the name across the back of his shirt. Gutierrez. Looks like a drug thing, maybe. Found some coke stashed up inside a plaster Virgin on the porch. We got a witness here."

"Is he the one that called in?" the operator asked.

The detective glanced through the screen at Lofton. "You the one that called in?"

Lofton nodded.

"Why didn't you give your name?"

"I was scared."

The cop turned back to the microphone. "Yeah, he's the one that called in. Says he was scared. Should I hold him here for O'Neill? All right."

After hanging up the mike, the cop came around to the back of the car. He opened the door and slid in next to Lofton. He showed his wallet and his badge.

"I'm Detective Ryan. You're going to have to wait a minute or two. Our homicide chief wants to talk to you."

Lofton could smell whiskey on the man's breath.

"You a friend of the deceased?" Ryan asked.

"No, I was here by coincidence."

Ryan nodded wearily. "Yeah, I was just off duty when this happened, sitting with a couple of the guys. Now it looks like we're in for a whole night of shit." His face was pale, deeply creased, although he was probably only in his early fifties.

There was some more noise over the intercom; in the static Lofton heard a voice asking Ryan to come back up to the house.

"I've got to get back in there. You just hang on."

Detective Ryan started up for the house without shutting the cruiser's door. He would have left the door open if the cop with the flashlight hadn't called, "Hey, lock 'em up!"

Shaking his head, Ryan walked back. He slammed the cruiser door, then hesitated for a second. Looking back at Lofton, he reached under the dash and threw the lock.

Lofton mumbled to himself. They hadn't let him go, but they hadn't questioned him either. Ryan hadn't even asked him his name. The detective had talked about the case in front of him, giving away information casually. True, Ryan did not know he was a reporter, but it still seemed like sloppy police work.

He sat for a few minutes more, growing restless the whole time. The homicide chief Ryan had mentioned did not show up. He wondered if this homicide chief was inside the house, or down at the station, or at home watching "Kojak."

Someone else from the crowd approached the cop who guarded the driveway with the flashlight. The cop went through the same routine he had gone through with Lofton. He shone the light in the man's face. Though Lofton recognized the man, he couldn't remember his name: a beat reporter from the *Springfield Post*. Must have been hanging around late when the murder came over the CB. He guessed the other reporter could not know much. No name for the victim. Nothing about the drugs. No sense of the story. Still, he cursed himself. This story should be his. He tried the door again, but of course it was still locked.

After a while Detective Ryan came back down from the house. He reached into the cruiser and took some cigarettes off the dash.

"I can't believe this," he said. "I want to go home and get some goddamn sleep."

"How much longer is your chief going to be?"

"Forever," said Ryan. Then he said it again, apparently liking the sound of the word. "Goddamn *forever.*"

"Can I go over to those bushes?" Lofton asked.

"What for?"

"What do you think?"

"I'm not supposed to think," Ryan said, looking up at the house, shaking his head in irritation. "I'm not supposed to be here. I'm supposed to be off tonight. These people are full of all kinds of silliness. You seen one body, you seen them all. They got half the city in there; I don't know what they need me for."

Lofton asked him again if he could go over to the bushes.

"Go ahead. If you want to piss, I'm not stopping you."

"I can't. Remember, you got me locked in here."

"Right. I forgot about that."

Ryan reached beneath the dash. As Lofton got out of the car, he noticed the *Post* reporter was busy again with the cop at the driveway. The reporter was persistent. The policeman had his back to Lofton. Some more voices came over the static of the cruiser's intercom, asking again for Ryan.

"Those bushes, over there," Ryan yelled out. He pointed at the house next door.

Lofton stepped behind the bushes. He could see Ryan. The detective was not watching him at all; he was standing up, barking into the microphone and scowling up at the house, one elbow leaning against the roof of the car. The detective started to swear into the mike. Lofton stepped out of the bushes and walked into the darkness, trying to be as calm as he had been next to Gutierrez's body. Cutting across a corner lawn, he waited for the cops' cries. He imagined the shots breaking out, himself collapsing, the grass against his face as he died. He broke out running. After a while he stopped. He made it to his car, in the lot next to his hotel. As he drove over to the *Dispatch,* his hands were unsteady. He had probably made a mistake leaving the squad car. He should never have gone back to the crime to begin with. He had made a simple thing into a mess.

From outside, the *Dispatch* looked shut down. There were no lights and only a single car stood in the parking lot. Inside, the building was dark and hot. He found Kirpatzke at the night desk, his tie loose around an unbuttoned collar, sitting alone in the green glow of the computer terminals. Kirpatzke told him the electricity had gone, the air-conditioning didn't work, and the only power was the backup generator to the computer. Kirpatzke's shirt was damp, and so was his brow.

"I just stumbled into a murder."

Kirpatzke tilted his head. He held a paper clip between his teeth and thumbed at it with his nervous hands.

"Remember that ballplayer I was going to interview? Randy Gutierrez? The Redwings' shortstop? Well, I went over to his place and found him dead on the floor. A bullet in the skull."

Kirpatzke raised an eyebrow. "Thrilling."

Despite himself, Lofton smiled. "They found some drugs stuffed up inside one of those plaster Virgins, at the bottom of his steps as you walk in. I was there with the cops for a while, but they don't know I was the one who found the body. I think I can write it up pretty well."

"Yeah, well, you know," Kirpatzke said, smiling slightly, ironic, "we don't play murders here. It's poor taste."

Lofton was about to protest when he realized Kirpatzke was toying with him. There was no way the paper would pass up the story of a dead ballplayer. The editor's smile deepened, but it lingered too long. His amusement now seemed forced, weary, his features lined with exhaustion. "A murder, huh?"

"Why don't you get a day job?" Lofton said. "Or try another business?"

"It's my commitment to the truth. I can't let it go." Kirpatzke laughed, self-deprecating. Even in the darkness the editor's skin seemed jaundice-colored, tinged by nicotine; that was odd, Lofton thought, since as far as he knew, the editor didn't smoke. Lofton glanced around the empty building.

"Always like this at night?"

"Depends. Usually we get a few people in and out. I weed through the wires, listen to the citizen band. Maybe write a story."

"Not too many small-town papers even bother to keep the place open at night. Why here?"

"The *Post* does it, so we do it."

Lofton nodded, but it still didn't make sense. He knew that Kirpatzke used to work at the *Post*. That paper, he knew, was part of the Klondike Syndicate, a newspaper chain that knew how to make money, moving into weak markets and dominating the smaller papers with its money and its size. Here the Klondike people put out a morning paper and an evening. The basic core of each was the same; only the evening paper was more sensational. Small papers like the *Dispatch* competed by hiring men like McCullough, who could glance at a police log and see a front-page grabber. And they also, Lofton knew, needed reporters, writers willing to stay in town for love or lack of imagination. None of that, however, explained Kirpatzke's presence here in Holyoke. He had had a better job, more money, more prestige, up the road. Why had he left the Springfield paper? Maybe the rumors—the hints of scandal Lofton had heard in the press box (the reporters gave no details)—held some truth. Still, you could tell Kirpatzke had been in the business for a while; he had worked hard.

"Actually," Kirpatzke went on, "I'm up all night anyway, I prefer it, so I keep the place open. That's all. And sometimes someone else comes in with a story."

Lofton glanced around the building, dark except for the faint glow of the computer screens. He could hear the computer's hum as well and imagined Kirpatzke sitting here alone, night after night, in the deserted building.

"You better get working on that story if you don't want to be here forever," Kirpatzke said finally. "Grab a terminal. The computer man's not here, the system's junk, but I think it'll hold."

Lofton went to the area known as the ghetto, where proofreaders corrected copy on the green computer screens. The proofreaders, of course, were not in at this hour, and Lofton sat alone. He painted the story in bright, sordid colors, describing the angle of Gutierrez's body on the floor, the plaster Virgin with the cocaine, the crackling static, and the neighborhood crowd in the street outside. He described Gutierrez's last at bat during the previous home stand, how he had crossed himself over and over between each pitch. He did not mention, of course, the letters he himself had taken from Gutierrez's apartment, and he left out what Amanti had told him about Brunner and the arson downtown. When the police saw the story, they might come after him, asking where he found his information. There was a chance one of the cops would recognize him, and they would want to know why he had left the scene. He would say he had given his name to the detective; he could not help it if they were too goddamned incompetent to write it down. If that did not work, well, he would think of something else.

He was still working early in the morning when the proofreaders came in. Kirpatzke wandered by to read over his shoulder. The proofreaders, women mostly, fell silent and hunched their shoulders when Kirpatzke approached.

"I want you to do another story on Gutierrez, a follow-up," Kirpatzke said. "A feature piece, color, not hard news."

Lofton nodded, keeping his eyes on the screen. Kirpatzke touched him on the arm. "I don't want you trying to solve the murder, nothing like that. Let the cops take the risks. You do the people stuff, talk to the man's friends. You know, human interest."

Kirpatzke gave him a weepy smile that was only partly ironic. "You know, touch their hearts."

When Lofton finished the story, his body itched. Too much coffee, too many cigarettes. Back in the hotel, he had trouble sleeping. His sheets were dirty, the night was hot, and there was noise in the apartment below. He floated on the surface, not quite awake, not quite asleep. He dreamed of his wives, and he dreamed of the Amanti woman. They watched from the left field bleachers while he ran the bases. Something pursued him, he didn't know what. He woke in the morning so hot and feverish, so drenched with sweat, that he thought he must be dying. *The doctor knew something he wouldn't say.* But no, the desk clerk and the men in the lobby were drenched in the same sweat, their faces red and puffy. It was simply the heat wave. If it was killing him, it was killing everyone else as well.

He tried calling Senator Kelley's office in the morning, then again in the afternoon. He didn't know how Kelley fitted in to things, or if he fitted in at all, but for the moment it didn't much matter. The senator wasn't coming to the phone. "He's out of the office," the secretary said. "He's tied up in a meeting. Could you please hold?"

The Redwings would start practice at four. Lofton decided to go to the park early to start his follow-up, although he did not relish the prospect of talking to Gutierrez's roommates. He was sure they would be reading his story, and the police had probably seen it as well. The *Dispatch* had given the story good play, running it alongside a news file photo of Gutierrez, dark-eyed and handsome.

Before he left his hotel, as he stood sweating in the lobby, the clerk handed him a telegram. It was from Maureen. "AM GOING AHEAD WITH PROCEEDINGS."

Lofton felt bitter, though he knew he had done nothing to prompt his wife to act otherwise. Here I am dying, he thought —*am I dying?*—and Maureen was going ahead with the proceedings.

In the midst of his anger he dialed Amanti from a phone booth in the lobby. A man answered, a harsh, possessive voice dirty with sleep. Lofton hung up without saying a word. Brunner?

He left the hotel, circled the block, and dialed again from a booth on the street. This time Amanti answered.

"You've heard Gutierrez is dead." Lofton was impressed with his brutal tone, then ashamed of himself. He saw the body on the floor, the skull splintered and bleeding. The air in the phone booth seemed too thick to breathe, too hot, and the light outside too bright.

"Yes."

She sounded composed. Lofton wanted to shout at her. He waited a long minute. He imagined the man with the insidious voice standing behind her.

"Can't you talk?"

The same stillborn silence followed, a pause he could not interpret. Was she trying to get rid of him? Who was the man who'd answered?

"Yes, that's fine. Do you think you could deliver it sometime later in the week?"

"Deliver what?"

There was another pause. Then he realized his mistake. "All right, I understand. Should I call back later, after the game?"

"Yes, that would be fine. I'll be here."

Lofton was glad when the conversation ended. Outside the booth the air was a little easier to breathe.

Before Lofton's phone call Kelley had been lying on Amanti's couch, drowzing uneasily in the afternoon heat. He and Amanti had learned of Gutierrez's death earlier that morning, and the death had made Kelley rethink his plans. He had thought he could use Lofton, as well as his own power in the legislature, to make Brunner switch sides in the primary campaign. He still thought so. Only he had not expected so quick, so violent a reaction, not so soon after the wheels had been set in motion.

"We don't know that Brunner's behind the shortstop's death," he said, without any real conviction. "It could be coincidence. Gutierrez hung around on the street a lot with those cocaine people. He could have brought it on himself."

"Maybe it's our fault," Amanti said. "We brought attention to him, and that's why he's dead. Brunner, or someone, didn't want him talking."

Kelley nodded. He had thought about that. The shortstop's death was a hard responsibility, one that made his own stake in what happened seem more important, more real. Still, the death had made him very tired. He leaned back and closed his eyes. One event followed another, down a very long line, and at the end of the line was himself. He saw himself falling over, tumbling, shattered into pieces, the faces of a crowd. The crowd looked up at him. There was a reason for everything, he knew, and it was there on the platform, dressed in his own best clothes.

Amanti knelt on the floor beside Kelley, one of her hands resting on his stomach, her finger toying with the ribbing of his blue shirt, skirting an undone button. She studied his face, the closed eyes, the partly open lips, the black tassel of hair. When she moved closer to him, she smelled the sharp, familiar pungence of his body, the mix of men's soap and cologne and sweat. As in the past, the smell triggered the image of the dark-paneled corridors of the building where he worked, the smile of the secretary she had never seen. She imagined him walking into his office, his slight swagger, a gait that was childlike and cocky, like a boy's strut on the day he leaves high school. She reached her hand toward his shirt collar, ready to kiss him. It was a familiar action; she had done it a hundred times, and it always reminded her of the first time they had kissed, when she had reached up and touched his collar, seen for a second the vulnerability in his face, and then pulled him closer.

Now the phone on the table behind them rang. Kelley got to it before she did. He had been in contact with his office, worrying about a committee meeting on the Holyoke project, and he expected a call back. He answered in a voice not quite his own, as if waking from a deep sleep. In another second he laid the phone back down. His expression was puzzled.

"Whoever it was, they hung up," he said. "Not a word."

"Brunner," Amanti whispered. She felt a quick chill at the possibility. Brunner called her regularly, and maybe he'd hung up at the sound of Kelley's voice. Still, she doubted it. Brunner would be more likely to ask for her anyway, to bludgeon his way through Kelley. The senator smiled. He seemed to derive pleasure from the possibility that it had been Brunner on the other end.

A moment later the phone rang again. This time she answered it herself. The voice was Lofton's. She glanced over at Kelley, saw his wry, confident smile, his eyes—almost black now, it seemed, unreadable—and she turned away from him. Lofton seemed upset, a little crazy. She talked to him without letting Kelley know who it was. When she got off, she told him it had been a deliveryman with a new part for the air conditioner, a pump or a filter or some damn thing, she wasn't exactly sure.

"Why did he hang up the first time?"

"I didn't ask," she said. "Maybe it was a bad connection."

She enjoyed the lie. There weren't many opportunities for her to lie to Kelley in the way he lied to her. While she watched, Kelley called his office in Boston. The secretary gave him his messages. There was one he hadn't expected: The reporter, Lofton, had been calling his office. Persistently. Suddenly Lofton seemed to be everywhere.

"Did you mention my name to him?" Kelley asked Amanti.

"No," she said.

"I don't like him calling my office. He's getting too close."

For a moment Amanti hoped Kelley might abandon his whole scheme. Gutierrez's death, Brunner's potential for violence, Lofton's persistence—things were happening in a way he hadn't planned. If he were patient and let it all pass, then his career, his power, would develop regardless, she told him. "Your father-in-law will see to that," she added, somewhat bitterly. "By pushing too hard, you're risking what you already have."

"You sound like my wife," Kelley said. His face twisted

into a smile. "I'm not afraid of Brunner, and you shouldn't be either. He might be behind the shortstop's death, but Brunner wouldn't do anything to hurt me—or you. . . . I'll just have to get some other things moving sooner than I planned."

Kelley paced. His movements were a little wilder than usual, like a horse jittering in the pasture before a thunderstorm, but his voice was the opposite, very low, very calm—as if he were somehow the horse's master, too, soothing the animal—saying how before he confronted Brunner with the arsons, he needed to line up his committee vote on the Holyoke project. Pressure Brunner from that angle, too. Brunner should worry about the reporter, he should feel pressure, but we don't want Lofton to actually write the story. No, that would foul everything. No money, no nothing, the fruit knocked from the trees before it was ripe.

"It's going to take a little time to get everything set up. In the meanwhile, I want you to stay away from the reporter. At least until I tell you. Let him turn in circles for a while."

"You're using me," she said. She heard the wildness in her voice. It hadn't been what she intended to say. "You've got another woman in Boston."

"You know I'm married. You've known it all along. When all this is over and Sarafis is in office, I won't need her anymore, or her father. I'll have my own power base. A good one. But we need Brunner's support, his money, and he'll kick back a lot to keep his arson ring going. After this is finished, no one will be able to hurt me—to hurt us."

His voice had the quality it had onstage, as if he were talking to a group of people. At the moment she did not believe anything he said. "It's not your wife I'm talking about. You have another woman—a mistress."

"As soon as we've gotten rid of the reporter, you and I'll get out of here for a few days. We'll go rest. Just hold on a little while longer. And don't talk to Lofton again until I tell you."

Kelley touched her on the cheek, lifted a strand of her hair. She closed her eyes. For a brief second they were just two people anywhere. The things they had been discussing were no more important than the daily conversations of newscasters, the analysis of intrigues in remote nations, events that occurred on back-alley streets in cities you would never see.

When she opened her eyes, Kelley's face seemed unbelievably delicate, as if she were looking at it through glass. She had an undeniable urge to reach through, to break the glass.

"I don't know if any of this is fair to Brunner," she said, knowing the effect the remark would have. "After all, Jack has helped me a lot. It doesn't feel right."

Kelley's face blanched; the red rose fiercely to his cheeks. He pulled away from her. As she watched him turn away, the satisfaction the remark had given her, his small pain, started to fade. "I won't talk to the reporter until you tell me," she promised. "I'll stay away from him."

From his place high in the stands Lofton watched the players drift in. They came alone or in pairs, dressed in their street clothes: crew-neck T-shirts or light button-down short sleeves; thin chains—tokens from lovers or family—around their necks. As Tim Carpenter walked in, he glanced up at where Lofton was sitting. Elvin Banks, the center fielder, walked beside him, carrying a portable cassette that played a tinny, melancholy Stevie Wonder.

You are the sunshine of my life. . . .

Even after the pair had gone inside the clubhouse, Lofton continued to hear the song, an echo in the hot, breezeless afternoon. It reminded him of that day in his junior year at college when he had fallen from the roof: the sun hot on his back; the tar vapor rising from the shingles; the radio playing on the porch. It had been a bad season, his body thickening, maturing. He had lost a step on the long run to first base and spent a lot of games riding the bench. He had been climbing down the ladder from the roof, looking down at the grass as he did so. Maybe it was the angle, or maybe the heat, or the tar vapors, but the lawn below him had seemed to stretch luxuriantly away, infinitely almost, like a golf course or a cemetery. Then he had slipped, falling to the grass, landing crookedly, twisting. The first thing he thought was, there it goes, my pivot, no more second base. And with the thought he had been relieved.

* * *

It was a long time, longer than usual, before the players
came out of the clubhouse. Lofton guessed they were having a
team meeting, Coach Barker talking to them in his gruff, impossible manner, telling them to win this one for Gutierrez.
Finally the men filed out, not in haphazard groups as they
usually did but in a continuous, determined stream, one
player after another, each with a black armband over the blue
sleeve of his practice jersey. A few glanced up at Lofton—the
same steely dislike—but there was no whispering, no talking
among themselves.

The players started their warm-up, wandering off in groups
or alone now, stretching on the outfield grass, running laps
and wind sprints, whipping baseballs to one another through
the heavy air. He needed to talk to a few of them, to get
quotes for Kirpatzke, but instead, he stared at the playing
field, watching the slow, clocklike motions of the players, listening to the over-and-over slap of the ball against leather.
The air was thick, almost palpably so, as it had been in the
phone booth earlier. The players moved through it as if they
were underwater. Below him, Tim Carpenter pulled a bat
from the rack near the dugout. His face was red and flushed,
as if he were angry, conscious of Lofton looking down at him.
But that could be the heat. Carpenter's jersey was already
streaked through with sweat.

"Randy has been down, really down." Lofton had quoted
Carpenter in the story. He had mentioned the drugs in the
Virgin, insinuated that Gutierrez was having trouble with
money. All true.

One of the papers Lofton had lifted from Gutierrez's apartment was his bank statement, an almost empty savings, an
overdrawn checking, not too much different from Lofton's
own.

He had not lied in the article. There had been sympathy in
his portrait of Gutierrez, he told himself, and compassion.
But it was not just the article that bothered him. *If I hadn't
taken on the story, if I hadn't started poking around, then
Gutierrez would still be alive.* Gutierrez had died, it seemed,
because someone was afraid of what he might say. Either that,
or his death was sheer coincidence. Who else knew about the
interview Lofton had planned with Gutierrez? Amanti, that

was certain. Now that he thought about it, lots of other people had known as well. He had mentioned the upcoming interview with Gutierrez to Kirpatzke and McCullough, that day at the *Dispatch*. And to Carpenter, Tenace, Barker, Golden. They all had known he was looking for Gutierrez. But none of them, as far as he could tell, had any reason to murder the shortstop. Not unless they were involved with Brunner and his arsons.

If Amanti had not placed her fingers on his arm, he thought, he would never have seen Gutierrez's dead body on the floor. Somebody else, Einstein maybe *(what the hell had happened to him?)*, would be writing this story.

Tim Carpenter took a batting tee and set it up near the fence beyond home plate. He placed one ball after another on the tee, driving each one into the steel mesh of the backstop, his bat a vicious blur in the thick air.

Finally Coach Barker came onto the field. He unlatched the gate behind home, and some of the fans who came early to watch—including the weird kid Lofton had seen at the library, the kid who seemed to be everywhere—helped push the batting cage onto the field. A few of the players came into the dugout, grabbing helmets and sorting through the bats; others took positions around the field; while still others drifted farther away, continuing their warm-ups. Carpenter kept hammering at the tee while the batters lined up. Coach Barker pitched, and fielders began to call out, their chatter like the scattered crying of insects, a distant rising and falling in the high grass along the roadside. Lofton stood up. He was hot and dizzy; his shirt, like the players', was soaked through with sweat. He walked down the bleachers slowly, pausing at each step. He had his interviews to do.

The batters smashed Barker's pitches back onto the field, driving the ball into the ground sometimes, sending it in low, bouncing trajectories over the infield dirt; other times knocking it farther, so the ball hit in the outfield, skimmed, and disappeared into the grass, like a rock thrown over the surface of a pond; and occasionally connecting so well that the ball flew over the outfielders' heads, hitting against the stadium wall or leaving the park altogether, landing in the street and ricocheting in the rush-hour traffic. The fielders chased the balls, sometimes straining and diving, more often letting them fall in and die, then walking over casually and throwing the scattered hits, one by one, back to a young pitcher who stood behind second base and tossed the retrieved balls into a bucket. Sparks, tonight's starter, paced the warning track in left field.

Lofton worked his way down the bleachers, leaned awhile against the low cyclone fence, then climbed over. Barker did not like reporters on the field, but at this moment Lofton was not conscious of boundaries. The field was as much his as theirs. He had stood at home plate the other night, run the bases, and fallen down as hard as any real player in any real game. He had lain awake as a child, long after the house had quieted and his brother slept in the other bed, and listened on his transistor to the Giants at Candlestick Park, the static and hum of cracked bats, leather against leather, announcers saying the names of Mays and McCovey and Marichal.

Lofton stepped over third base, the sweat streaming down his forehead, as Coach Barker went into his windup again.

"A lot of the players, they're at the age where if you're good—not great, not excellent—just good, then baseball's going to break your heart. They'd be better off going home," Barker had told Lofton once during an interview. Lofton, looking across Barker's desk into his crusty eyes, had not expected him to say that. Then he realized the manager, with his twenty-five-odd years coaching the minor league circuit, was talking about himself. He should have quit a long time ago.

Now the batter at the plate connected, and someone from the outfield cried out, "Hey, you, heads up!"

Lofton did not have time to react, which, when he thought about it later, may have been fortunate. The ball shot by, inches from his head, so close that he could hear it. He took a step forward, threw his hands back, lost his balance, and fell onto the ground.

Lofton sat in the dirt. Several players, including the man who had been in the batting cage, rushed forward. "It's okay. It didn't hit him," yelled someone, Carpenter, he guessed. Then he saw the second baseman standing nearby, smiling grimly.

Lofton grinned up at the players around him. They stared dumbly back. He caught Barker's eye. *Barker knows,* he thought suddenly, but what did he think Barker knew? That, sometimes, it was just impossible to leave, that you always yearned to make the great catch, to feel your cleats in the velvet grass, to hear the crowd whispering your name? It was silly. Barker looked him over, shook his head, and turned away. Someone came running with a bag of ice.

"No, I'm fine. Scared me but didn't touch."

Lofton hurried away, breaking through the circle of broad-chested uniformed players. He felt the players watching as he headed toward the bleachers. Why do I do such things? he wondered as he climbed the bleachers, feeling himself gasp, short of breath. He had deliberately walked into the middle of the field, just as last night he had almost given himself away to the police. "Fuck," he whispered, his breath suddenly gone, replaced by a pain, like a gnarled fist, rising in his chest. The air went gray, and he reached through the fog, making it to the long grandstand seat, then rolling over onto his back. He lay that way a long second, then remembered the players were still watching. He sat up.

"Just catching a suntan," he yelled. "Go on without me."

He was surprised at their laughter and more surprised, a second later, when he realized his pain was gone.

Holyoke retook the field at game time, the black armbands crisp against the bright white of their game uniforms. The crowd was a little bigger than usual, more people from the Puerto Rican neighborhood, fans of Randy Gutierrez. Before the national anthem the public-address man asked for a moment of silence in memory of the shortstop. That silence would be Gutierrez's only public eulogy, aside from Lofton's work in the paper, but Lofton felt a current of emotion run through the crowd. After the anthem the fans gave the Red-wings a strong, bitter round of applause.

The game turned into a pitchers' duel. Sparks had a wild, nervous look about him, as if he were afraid the murderer was in the ballpark, his gun trained on the mound. Sparks tugged at his jersey and scanned the stands between every pitch. Lofton remembered the scene he'd witnessed between Sparks and Amanti in the parking lot. Was the pitcher scanning the stands, looking for her? Either way, the tension served Sparks well because he had an edge on his fastball that had been missing since early in the season.

The West Haven pitcher was a black from the Caribbean, Jose Hernandez, who had grown up in Springfield and had pitched on this field before, when Springfield High School played Holyoke High. West Haven had picked him up out of the Yankees' organization just the week before. The Carib had a sidearm delivery, a pistol-whipping motion that Lofton had not seen before and that baffled the Holyoke batters. Neither team scored through the first four innings. In the fifth Sparks weakened, as he always seemed to in the middle going, and gave up a two-run homer. Lofton winced. The fans swore. But in the sixth and seventh Sparks, though struggling, held West Haven scoreless.

Lofton kept expecting Holyoke to come back. There was just that feeling in the air. The team was playing too crisply, with too much determination to lose. In the eighth Elvin Banks got to the Carib, pulling an inside fastball over the left field fence. Holyoke had cut the margin to 2–1. Sparks held West Haven again in the ninth. The crowd stood and clapped. Sparks ran from the field, head down, looking harried and uncomfortable.

In the ninth the Carib seemed to lose control. The fans started in on him, loud and mean. He walked the catcher Lumpy and the first baseman Lynch, perhaps the two weakest hitters in the lineup, and with one out and Singleton at the plate, he wild-pitched the runners along.

The West Haven manager came out. From the quick, brisk way he moved, Lofton guessed the manager meant to pull the Carib from the game. The Carib shook his head. He did not want to go. The infielders gathered in a semicircle around the mound. The discussion continued until the manager relented, turning the ball back over to the Carib and letting him have his game, win or lose. The Carib struck Singleton out swinging.

That left Holyoke with runners at second and third, two gone, and Tim Carpenter coming up. Lofton joined in yelling encouragement. He doubted Carpenter could hear him.

Before stepping into the box, Tim Carpenter leveled his bat at the Carib and took several practice swings. In three at bats so far, Carpenter had struck out, fouled out, grounded weakly to second.

This time, when the Carib went to his windup, Carpenter stepped out of the batter's box. The Carib stepped off the pitching rubber and waited. After Carpenter reentered the box and cocked his bat, the Carib stared at him a long time. He finally went to his delivery, but just as he did, Carpenter stepped out. The umpire, raising both arms high, ordered Carpenter back to the plate. Lofton liked the way Carpenter was playing it, back and forth, teasing the Carib.

At last the first pitch came, a wicked, breaking curve thrown with the velocity of a fastball. The pitch broke inside for a strike. Carpenter had not even swung. The next pitch was the same, only Carpenter swung this time, and missed. He backed from the plate again. The umpire, raising his hands again, commanded Carpenter back to the box. Carpenter snarled, and the fans cheered him on.

Carpenter fouled off the next pitch, hitting a weak grounder to the right side. It had been the same pitch, the fast curve. Though Lofton expected the Carib would come in with something different now, the pitcher stuck with his pitch. And Carpenter fouled the curve again. Surely the Carib would throw a straight fastball, or a change-up, something to catch Carpenter off guard. But no, a third time he came in with the curve, and a third time Carpenter fouled it away, only harder this time, again down the first base line. A few feet farther to the left, and the ball would have been fair, bouncing over the base at first. The two runners would have scored. Holyoke would have won. Carpenter's tenacity is paying off, Lofton thought; the Carib is getting impatient, coming over and over with the same pitch.

The crowd was on its feet now, all of them yelling at Carpenter to hit the ball, to whack it back at the Carib, to knock it down his throat, to do it for Gutierrez. It was a shabby crowd, and Lofton was moved by its vehemence. The Carib looked the crowd over, grinned, and lifted his cap. They hooted and hollered as he went to his windup.

Here it comes, thought Lofton; here comes the change-up. He was wrong. It was the same pitch, the mean-hooking curve. Carpenter swung and missed. The game was over.

Lofton hurried to catch the players before they reached the

clubhouse. He needed some quotes for Kirpatzke, anything. Some of the fans leaned over the low sideline fence, reaching out to the players, trying to shake their hands. A band of kids followed the West Haven team, yelling insults. A small police guard formed near the West Haven team bus.

He spotted Singleton, Gutierrez's replacement. Walking up to him, his reporter's brashness returning, he asked Singleton, as sympathetically as he could, how he felt.

"Not too good," said Singleton, a short, sulking man who stared guiltily at the dirt. "It's a hell of a way to get into the starting lineup."

4

Among Gutierrez's papers, Lofton had found three letters, two from Gutierrez's wife, and another letter, half-finished, that Gutierrez had been writing to her. He laid them out on the table and tried to translate, to remember his high school Spanish. He did not know whom he could trust to translate the letters for him. Worse, he felt guilty handling the dead man's papers; it was like digging around in the grave. He motioned to the waitress to fill his coffee cup—only here, in this air-conditioned restaurant above the expressway, was it cool enough to drink coffee—and he looked toward the phone. He had tried calling Amanti last night, after the game, and tried again this morning, standing in the parking lot booth across from the *Dispatch*. It was almost noon now. He was beginning to get worried.

Both Kirpatzke and McCullough had been behind their desks at the *Dispatch* when he had taken his story down this morning. He would have preferred to talk to Kirpatzke, but McCullough had sequestered him first. McCullough had read the first line of his story out loud.

"Wearing black armbands in honor of their lost compadre" —McCullough paused at *compadre*, gave Lofton a look, and went on—"the Redwings lost a bitter game devoted to the memory of Randy Gutierrez."

Kirpatzke, sitting a few desks away, looked over at Lofton and McCullough. He wore the same grimy shirt he had worn the night Lofton saw him in the darkened building, as if he'd never gone home.

"This a mood piece?" asked McCullough, puffing out his cheeks. Between the two editors, Lofton didn't know which was worse: the hard-nosed, one-track McCullough or the sardonic Kirpatzke. Though Kirpatzke was within earshot, he showed no signs of participating in the conversation. It could be that the editors had already had an argument once this morning, and Kirpatzke just didn't feel like haggling.

"All right, this looks good," McCullough said at last. "We can use it. It's fine. But what about the murderer? They got any idea who killed the shortstop? Or why? There's no hard, investigative work in this story."

"Kirpatzke said he wanted it this way."

"What's this supposed to be, a tea party?"

Lofton shrugged. Kirpatzke, across the way, had his head down, pretending not to be listening. McCullough frowned heavily at the top of his desk for a long moment, as if trying to decide something.

"What about the other story—Lou Mendoza, the assault victim? Did you ever talk to him?"

"Sure, I talked to him."

"Well, Mendoza called the paper. Said he wants to talk to you. I set up a meeting."

"He called here? Why?" Lofton remembered his second visit to Mendoza's house, when the Latinos had chased him away. He wasn't so sure he wanted to step into the middle of that conflict again, even though it might lead to more information about the fires.

"I think there's a story there," said McCullough, and slid him a piece of paper. "This is where you're supposed to meet."

"A church," said Lofton. "You're kidding?"

"Check it out," McCullough said, his face widening into a sudden smile. "You're doing a good job."

Outside, Lofton shook his head. McCullough was like a lot of small-town editors: unreasonable one minute, your best friend the next—so long as you were doing what he wanted and not asking for much money. Lofton headed across the parking lot to a phone booth on the street. He still wanted to get in touch with Amanti. Before he could reach the phone, however, he heard someone behind him. Kirpatzke. The editor hurried to catch up.

"He sending you on that Mendoza stuff?"

"Sure."

"I'd stay away from it if I were you. Mendoza's hooked up with those street gangs, you know, knives and chains."

"I had that figured out. But why tell me now? You've known all along. You published Einstein's stories; you've seen his notes."

"Just making sure you know what you're getting into. It's your choice. McCullough won't care if you don't do that story. A lot of our regulars won't deal with those people."

"Einstein did, didn't he?"

"That's something you might want to think about," said Kirpatzke. "And this, too: Einstein never picked up his last paycheck."

"So?"

"Maybe Einstein loved truth and justice, but he didn't love the *Dispatch*. That check isn't the kind of thing he'd leave behind. . . . Anyway, I've got another story I want you to do on that dead shortstop."

Kirpatzke outlined the new feature he wanted on Randy Gutierrez, more interviews with the team, the atmosphere of grief.

"Why didn't you give me this in front of Mac?"

"I thought I'd do us both a favor and save some arguing."

When Kirpatzke was gone, Lofton tried the phone booth. Still no Amanti. He tried all morning, then got in his car and drove to her apartment to see if he could find her. As his car mounted the Notch, he thought things over, trying to keep everything straight. He knew Brunner and other businessmen owned property downtown, buildings that would cost a lot to renovate, particularly if the federal money didn't come through. A lot of people in town said even the most honest landlords hoped their buildings burned now, before the renovation funding was canceled and while insurance paybacks were still high.

Angelo, the Latinos' leader, had said he knew who was behind Holyoke's fires. Then, a few days later, Angelo had died. According to Amanti, Randy Gutierrez had known something linking Brunner to the arsons. Now Gutierrez was dead, too. Einstein was missing. Amanti didn't answer her phone. Glancing in the rearview mirror, Lofton wondered again who had been looking for him that first day at the library, when he had begun researching the fires. The road behind him was empty. He was tracing two story lines, one starting with the dead shortstop, the other with the warring street gangs. As he accelerated his old station wagon into the curve, he had the hunch that the two lines were going to intersect sooner or later, as almost always happened.

Approaching Amanti's house, Lofton heard light jazz coming through the open window. She did not come to the door right away, and he grew frightened. He did not want to walk in and find Amanti as he had found Gutierrez. He knocked again, the music lowered, and a little while later Amanti came to the door.

"I've been calling you since last night," he said.

Amanti let out an uneasy sigh, touched his arm, and led him to the living room. He sat on the sofa, and she sat in one of the low-slung modern chairs. He bent over, nervous despite himself, clasping his hands together between his knees.

"Would you like a drink?" Amanti asked. She picked up her own glass, half-empty on the table beside her, and made drinks for them both. He had to hold himself from taking his down too quickly, from losing himself in the coolness of the ice.

"Why haven't you been answering the phone?"

"I was afraid," she said.

"Afraid of who?"

Amanti did not answer. Lofton listened to the pause, to the sound of the insects in the grass. "Who was that man who answered the phone yesterday?"

"No one," she said. "A friend."

Amanti ran her finger around the rim of her glass. She wore a thin cotton blouse and summer slacks. Gutierrez, Brunner, the Redwings, the dust and ash of Holyoke—all seemed remote, a distant setting. Lofton felt himself slip into the moment. The banter. The starts and stammers. The averted eyes. The cigarettes. The tonic spiked with gin.

"Did you know what was going to happen to Randy Gutierrez?" he asked.

"No, of course not." She said it briskly, offended. She held her finger still on the cool lip of the glass.

Lofton rubbed his hand through his hair. The alcohol had gone to his head in the heat. "Why did you bring me into this?"

"I thought somebody should know."

"Right, so now Gutierrez is dead, and I'm the one who had to find the body. I don't like looking at dead people." His vehemence surprised him. Lofton glanced at the bad paintings and swirled the ice in his glass. He imagined Gutierrez again. He saw the cramped kitchen, the body on the floor. He smelled the blood on the linoleum.

Amanti would not look him in the eyes. She lit a cigarette, and the smoke curled back around her head. She hid herself in the smoke. He reached over and took a cigarette from her pack.

"You have to tell me what Gutierrez told you. There's no other way for me to know." Lofton's voice was calm now; he could hear the calmness as he had felt it the night he found the body. Glancing down the hallway, he saw the door to Amanti's bedroom stood open. He heard his words as if he stood in that bedroom listening to himself, as if he were in a movie and the camera were focused on somebody listening in the other room. Suddenly he became afraid that there really was somebody in that other room.

"Sparks, does he know about the fires?" It was a guess, wild as the wind from left field, based only on the fact that he'd seen Amanti and the pitcher talking together out in the parking lot. Amanti shifted in her seat, enough so that Lofton thought his guess had been right. He walked down the hall and glanced into the bedroom, then came back. There was no one there, not unless he was crouched somewhere Lofton couldn't see. He chided his imagination.

"What are you doing?" asked Amanti.

"Nothing," he said, embarrassed. "Tell me what Gutierrez told you. And tell me about Sparks. Start from the beginning."

* * *

She was not sure how much she wanted to tell Lofton, if she should tell him anything at all. Kelley had told her to avoid the reporter. She had done so, she told herself. Despite her charade with Lofton that day on the telephone, she hadn't answered the phone since. But when she'd seen him coming up the walk, she'd let him in. He had heard the music in her apartment, she guessed, and not to let him in, to pretend that there was nothing at all that she knew would be worse than to walk the line between saying just enough and too much. Besides, she wasn't worried about Sparks; the pitcher was interested in only one thing, and that was the movement on his fastball. It was all he ever talked about.

"Sparks used to search Brunner out after he pitched," she said. "Brunner takes an interest in the players, and I guess Rickey thought he might get some help when it comes down to whether the Blues decide to pull him up at the end of the season. The times he talked to me, it was always about his career. He's worried about it. It worries him to death."

"I thought Golden filled out the scouting reports. Why should Sparks bother with you and Brunner?"

"I guess he's just playing every angle he can think of. He's obsessive. But underneath it all, he loves playing baseball, I guess. At least that's what he says."

Amanti did not know much more about Sparks than she was saying. Her only close contact with him had been several weeks back. That particular night Brunner had left the game early, and Amanti had remained alone in the stands. Earlier in the season she probably would not have stayed. She had started coming to the games because Brunner had asked; it was better than staying at home. Brunner watched the game ferociously. He would tighten his fist when the team fell behind, whispering heatedly to himself, a running commentary on the game, and he would stand up to cheer and swear, but only for an instant, when something good happened on the field. (Her cousin Tony Liuzza watched the games with far more detachment. He seemed bored, like a child with a toy he'd never really wanted.) Though baseball itself did not interest her, and she could have made excuses to Brunner, she had continued to come to the games. There was something about sitting in the sparse crowd that she enjoyed, the quality of light as it struck the field, the movements of the young players, their determination, and how that determination could be frustrated, or rewarded, simply by the angle at which the ball hit the turf. She paid little attention to the score; she often left the game without knowing who had won, though she knew it was true that Holyoke usually lost.

This particular game, however, Holyoke had won. She left the field alone, and by coincidence, it seemed, she ran into Rickey Sparks.

"Where's Jack?" he said. Though he often sought Brunner out after he had pitched, he did not seem to enjoy the conversations themselves. Sparks had a look of perpetual scorn. "Did he see the movement on my fastball?"

"Brunner's gone, but I'll tell him. I'll make sure he knows."

Sparks nodded. He seemed amused. Then he asked her, with as much challenge in his voice as anything, if she would like to come over to a small party at the apartment he shared with Tim Carpenter. "The team's got tomorrow off, and I have trouble sleeping after I pitch anyway." His voice was strong with innuendo, enough so that she knew that the challenge was a bluff; he did not expect her to come over.

"Sure," she said.

Once there, she felt a little awkward—and Tim Carpenter had felt that way, too, she thought—because Sparks and Randy Gutierrez had brought along a couple of the ballpark girls, obviously their dates, and that made it appear that she and Carpenter were a pair, an idea neither of them was too comfortable with. Carpenter stuck it out for a while, until one of the girls took out her mirror and laid it out on the table. Then Randy Gutierrez took out a plastic Ziploc and drew some lines on the glass. Carpenter excused himself and went back into his room. He had roomed for a while with Gutierrez, she knew, but apparently he didn't want anything to do with coke. Sparks gave her a look, as if to see how she would react; it was plain he was worried what she would say to Brunner, but it was also plain that there was another side to Sparks: Part of him did not care what anyone thought. He would do as he pleased.

"How about you? Did you do the coke?" Lofton asked.

"Maybe I did," Amanti said. "I don't see what difference that makes. . . . But Gutierrez, he got himself wired, talking

half Spanish, half English. He started going on about buildings burning and people, sometimes, getting trapped inside.
At first I thought he was talking about Managua, where his
wife lives, he was so upset."

While Amanti spoke, Lofton imagined the scene in the ballplayers' apartment: the vinyl couch where the girls sat flirting
with the players; the white Formica tabletop; the stereo
against the wall; the spackled ceilings; and Gutierrez leaning
over, moving his hands as he talked. Lofton saw the echo of
those movements in Amanti's gestures. Amanti, seeing the
way Lofton studied her, moved her hand to her collar.

"How did Sparks react to this?"

"He didn't seem to like Gutierrez talking so much. It was a
little crazy. I think maybe he was worried that the whole
scene would get back to Coach Barker. Or to Brunner. But he
was pretty high himself, having a good time. To tell you the
truth, he didn't hear most of what Gutierrez told me. He went
off with the girls to a package store, to get something to drink,
some beer, and that's when Randy told me he knew who was
burning the buildings in Holyoke."

"Who?"

Amanti hesitated again. Her blue eyes seemed dark, the
light inside them once again remote, receding, the last light on
the last car of a train deep in a mountain tunnel.

"Did he mention Brunner's name?"

"No."

"Then why do you insist that it's Brunner?"

"He mentioned Golden . . ." Amanti said. "Gutierrez
liked to hang out on street corners, Puerto Rican bars, places
like that, and he heard things. At least that's what he told me,
and he said that he knew that Golden was delivering money
to the torch, to *un hombre del fuego*. I remember the phrase
because he kept saying it over and over. *Un hombre del
fuego.*"

A man of fire. It was a dramatic term, almost silly, thought
Lofton, except he could imagine Gutierrez speaking the
words, dead serious, pausing for effect. "Gutierrez was really
raving," she went on. "One minute he seemed proud of everything he knew, of the information about Golden; he would act
completely confident. The next minute he was afraid. He said
they were going to kill him."

"Who was going to kill him?"

"I don't know. If you want to know the truth, though, I got the idea that he was in trouble with the dealers, that maybe they had fronted drugs to him, and now he couldn't pay back."

Lofton wasn't sure what the story proved. Gutierrez's ravings could have been sheer nonsense, events scrambled in his mind by drugs and paranoia. Maybe, as Amanti said, he owed some street pushers some money. Maybe the pushers had threatened him. At the same time Gutierrez had to be worried about his status with the Redwings. Golden was a symbol of authority on the team. It could be that Gutierrez had taken all the things he was worried about and scrambled them together and come up, the way drug freaks often did, with this new explanation for his problems.

"What else did he tell you?"

"Nothing. He said, 'Randy Gutierrez is a good man.' That's all. He said all he wanted was to play baseball, to bring his wife and family to America. He didn't care about anything else."

"Could be," he said, "that Gutierrez was setting the fires. Maybe that's how he paid for his drugs."

"Do you believe that?" she asked. Her voice scolded, but she stood up to refill his drink.

He leaned back and closed his eyes. The insects seemed louder. Not crickets after all, not like the ones he remembered. He wondered what the insects were. Cicadas? Tree criers? He could not tell. Settling back, he tried to imagine Gutierrez lighting the fires. Instead, he saw Managua—or his vision of that place—the inner city in rubble, the small, narrow streets spiraling away from the center into the impoverished neighborhoods where electric cables ran to small shanties. In the center of the shanties, in a clearing: a baseball diamond. Jungle ferns by third base. Cheap wooden bleachers. Colorful streamers. The type of place Gutierrez would have played when he was a boy, when the politics of Holyoke streets—and of Nicaraguan revolution, for that matter—were nothing, not real yet, not even a nightmare.

"No, I don't see Randy Gutierrez setting fires. But why do you think Brunner had anything to do with this? Golden was the name Gutierrez mentioned, not Brunner."

"Golden works for Brunner. It's that simple. Golden wouldn't be involved in something like that on his own."

"Maybe so," Lofton said. "But Gutierrez's story, if he was as wired as you say, doesn't prove anything. Besides, it's secondhand information. It's just rumor, something overheard on a street corner by a cranked-up minor league ballplayer, who barely spoke English when he was alive. Now that he's dead, his story won't even translate. It doesn't mean a thing."

Amanti shrugged. Lofton still had the feeling there was something she wasn't saying, some information she was holding back. The story about Gutierrez wasn't everything.

"Who picked up the phone when I called here the other day? Brunner?"

"No." She crumpled her cigarette pack and dropped it on the table. She went to the bedroom. No, Lofton thought, don't go there. He imagined Brunner, his pig-thick face, coming out of the room with her. Lofton sat on the edge of the couch. He knew it could not be true.

She came back alone. She carried a fresh pack of cigarettes. She sat close to him, so there was only a small space between them on the white cushion.

"That night you first contacted me," he said, "when you came up to me in the stands. Afterward, when the game was over, I saw you talking to Sparks out in the parking lot." He looked down as he talked. The space between Amanti and him had all but disappeared. "What were you talking about?"

"He had a bad game, you remember, really awful, and he was worried that I'd mention that other evening to somebody, that his using the coke would get back to management. It's not exactly what a young player's supposed to do in his spare time. He avoids me now, doesn't come anywhere near me, or Brunner either, at least not when I'm around—just hoping I'll forget I ever saw him. But he doesn't have to worry because I've already forgotten him."

"There's nothing else between you and Sparks?"

Amanti laughed. "I'm not interested in Sparks, and Sparks isn't interested in me. Even if he were, he wouldn't do anything about it. The last thing he wants is to get Brunner mad at him."

Lofton was quiet. He guessed he believed her story. He

would talk to Carpenter and Sparks and find out if there was anything else.

"Looks like we're in this together," Amanti said. A line, and a bad one—she knew it, too, he could tell, because he saw her wince. She seemed uncomfortable beside him, weary, a little drunk, and he reached to touch her. His mouth—filled with the taste of cigarettes and gin—would taste to her like one of the open gutters in Holyoke, like burnt ash and stale alcohol. He did not care. She would taste the same. Between them, neither would notice.

Though she kissed back, closing her eyes and touching him at the same time, the moment was sloppy, the kiss awkward. The second time was better. Just as he was catching her rhythm, Lofton heard a rustling noise in the hall. He jumped to his feet.

"What is it?" she asked.

He went to the bedroom. He glanced under the bed, into the closet, opened the door to the room across the hall. There was nobody there, nothing at all.

Amanti lay in the dark, not in her usual room, but in the extra bedroom at the front of the apartment. She came here when she couldn't sleep, when her bedroom seemed too dark and she needed a place where sleep would sneak up on her. In the dresser drawer, wrapped in a blue towel, was a gun. Brunner had bought it for her back when he first moved her into this apartment. "Something to keep you safe from the college kids," he had said, with only the slightest trace of a smile.

Lofton was gone. He had gotten up in the middle of their embrace, started checking around her apartment, then told her he had to get back to the ballpark. She wondered why she had kissed the reporter. She hadn't meant for that to happen, she told herself, but then she knew it wasn't quite true. She liked Lofton, she was angry at Kelley, she was afraid of Brunner, and touching the reporter had brought all the emotions together at once.

Now she thought about Brunner. In some ways what she had told Kelley the other day was true: Brunner had been good to her. Though she had never intended for things to go on with Brunner as long as they had, it wasn't until recently that she'd started to fear the man, that the steel edge of his personality had seemed untempered, razor-sharp. Of course, that edge had always been there. It had been there on the first day she met him, at her uncle Liuzza's. It had been there two years later, when her affair with Kelley seemed to be collapsing and Brunner had shown up at her doorstop in Boston, unintentionally comical, clutching a bunch of flowers in front of him. Sometimes she wondered why she had let him in. Though she had told herself she had taken up with Brunner to inspire Kelley's jealousy—and that was true—she did enjoy Brunner's protective spirit, his thick charm, his way of watching over things important to him. He had a firm desire to control. Sometimes that desire collapsed into a wide smile that expressed the need for admiration and affection. It was that moment of collapse that she liked, though such moments had gotten rarer, and sometimes dangerous.

Brunner came from a neighborhood not too much different from Kelley's, or her own, but unlike Kelley, he had not gone to college. Instead, he had worked himself up in the construction trade. He now lived in a house that he had bought from the bankrupt son of a New England pulp merchant. It was an old house, finely kept, emblematic—at least to Brunner—of a class of society that he both envied and despised, a class that Kelley had walked into easily. Amanti understood the frustration in Brunner. Sometimes, particularly when Kelley appeared to be vacillating in his affection for her, she even shared Brunner's dislike for Kelley, his hatred. She had made love to Brunner, in those first days, with a fierce intensity that expressed that hatred.

That intensity had worn off, so their intimacy now was as simple and cold and startling as the wind over a winter lake. But intimacy wasn't the point anymore, at least not with Brunner. He was supporting her and had been doing so for several years now, ever since Uncle Liuzza had cut off her money.

Brunner had moved her out to Amherst. He took particular pleasure in the fact that he had a mistress in a university town; he enjoyed fucking her in the midst of the lives of professors and students. He also enjoyed the fact that he had gotten her farther away from Kelley, though his own interest in her waned with the senator's distance and increased if he knew the other man had visited. (Sometimes it seemed to her

that each man was only interested in her in direct proportion
to his rival's interest. Who they really want to fuck, she
thought, is not me but each other.)

Still, there had always been times with Brunner, as with
everyone, when you could see behind the mask and read the
thoughts there, knowing what he was feeling, even if a second
later you could read nothing, and you were no longer sure the
moment had even happened.

Last April, Brunner had picked her up early one morning,
then taken her around with him from construction site to
construction site. He had said little. There seemed no point in
the excursion, but she had gone along anyway. After lunch he
had started drinking, uncharacteristic of him, and he had told
her, as they drove around in the car, that the entire state was
corrupt, that the big politicians played ball with each other, in
their Ivy League suits, and pretended to be clean and pure
when they were not clean and pure. A man had to watch out
for himself. The government dallylagged on contracts and
federal money, and the men in the Ivy League suits got rich
from the dallylagging while your regular guy went poor. Well,
not this regular guy, he said, pointing at one building, then
another, as they drove down the street. They were government garbage, kindling, fire to warm your bones. Brunner's
voice was thick and he was drunk and he wanted her to know
that he was as important as Kelley or anyone else. He had
himself well protected. He had papers, and those papers
would make sure that no one could hurt him without hurting
everyone else, and that would never happen because the big
boys never got hurt. Though he hadn't said what was in those
papers, he had taken her to where they were. He had opened
the safe and added some more papers, and then turned to her
with a look in his eye that seemed close to crazy, the moment
of collapse gone awry. The next day he was the same as ever.
His expression admitted nothing of what had happened.

At first she had ignored the incident. Whatever Brunner
was doing took place in a world she had nothing to do with,
over which she had no control. Then there had been the night
at Sparks's apartment when she had talked to Gutierrez,
when the dark-skinned shortstop had sat Indian-style, cross-
legged on the floor across from her, the collar of his blue shirt
open several buttons, showing his hairless chest, his dark skin.

He had held the matchbook curled in one hand, and his voice, as it raced on telling her about Golden and the fires in Holyoke, had been full of excitement.

She had told Kelley what Gutierrez had said not so much because she thought something could be done as to convey the excitement she had felt, the danger. Now she was sorry that she had told him anything, but she knew that was pointless, that of course she would have told him, it wasn't a matter of volition, but of the way things happened, just as of course the phone would be ringing now, and of course it would be Kelley calling at the same moment she was thinking of him. He called almost every night lately.

"Have you talked to the reporter?"

"No," she lied.

"Good, but I want you to talk to him now. I want you to tell him to get off the case."

"What if he doesn't listen?"

"I'll talk to your cousin. We'll give him some extra incentive," he said, but Amanti was paying more attention to a voice she thought she heard in the background, behind Kelley's. It wasn't his wife's voice, she didn't think, and it was too late for him to be at his office.

That evening a new pitcher joined the Redwings, Ramon Kubachek, a big, burly man who wore his uniform so baggy it looked like pajamas. Kubachek was a veteran, one of the few in the Blues' farm system, particularly at this level of play. Cowboy had bought him from the Yankees last year to help the Blues with their late-season pennant drive, but Kubachek pitched poorly. The Blues' championship bid had failed.

This year Kubachek had started out with the Blues but had thrown nothing but junk in the early going. Cowboy had sent him to Salt Lake. Now Kubachek had slipped a notch farther down into Holyoke. For Kubachek, such slides into the minors were not unusual. Once, he had even disappeared altogether, quitting baseball for a year, then showing up with the Portland Mavericks, an unaffiliated club in the Pacific Coast League, a team filled with castoffs: Jim Bouton, Luis Tiant, Willie Horton—men perennially on the comeback trail. But then the team was bought by the Pirates, the old players scattered, and Kubachek showed up, miraculously, it seemed, with the Yankees.

Cowboy had bought him for a big price and was still paying Kubachek under that contract. Kubachek said he did not care where he played, majors or minors or on the moon, so long as he got his money. When his contract expired, he would play Puerto Rico, Mexico, Japan; it made no difference to him, he said.

"My arm's as good as ever," Kubachek told Lofton before the game, spitting tobacco juice and sneering at the dirt as he spoke. "My being here has nothing to do with that. The Blues are playing like shit, and Cowboy needs a scapegoat. That's me. But I don't give a goddamn. They'll call me up before the end of the year, when they need help. Just watch."

Kubachek drew a good crowd, the biggest Lofton remembered seeing in Holyoke. More important, the club seemed to come alive around the pitcher, to take the field with more excitement. The air seemed charged, as if Gutierrez's death had never happened, or had happened somewhere far away—as if it were a story that had come in over the wire, another dateline, another city.

He still needed more on Gutierrez. Kirpatzke was not quite ready to let the story drop. Kirpatzke wanted a composite—a "tribute" Kirpatzke had called it: an interview with Gutierrez's teammates, a description of the neighborhood he had lived in, a summary of his career. Kirpatzke also wanted, incredibly, to patch a call through to Gutierrez's widow in Managua. And he wanted it all for Sunday's paper. He planned to run a black-bordered picture of Gutierrez on the sports page.

Lofton told himself he would start the interviews after the game. The tribute, if he were careful, might provide a good excuse to ease in questions about the fires. On the basis of what Amanti had told him, Tim Carpenter and Rickey Sparks would be the most likely to know something helpful, though it might be difficult getting either of them to talk. Carpenter, the second baseman, had gotten angry with him earlier for writing the story that mentioned Gutierrez's use of drugs. And Sparks was so worried about the big leagues that he might not say anything at all.

In the press box Tenace and the reporters were chattering about Kubachek's sudden arrival at MacKenzie Field.

"Should pitch him every day," said Tenace.

"Yeah, wear him out like a cheap suit."

"Kubachek is too smart. He ain't Sparks."

"We'll see."

Holyoke edged ahead in the second inning on a couple of bloop singles and a Lynn error. The Lynn Sailors were a Seattle farm club that led the other division of the Eastern League. The Seattle farm system offered its players a real chance to move up, and the Lynn players usually showed enthusiasm. They had talent, too, more talent than Holyoke, but the Sailors did not look good tonight. They could not handle Kubachek's knuckleball. Few saw that pitch at this level of play.

"See you got yourself back on the front page, Lofton," Tenace said. Rhiner looked the other way.

"Rhiner here's worried you're gonna move over to the *Post* and take his job."

"Don't be ridiculous," Rhiner shot back, with a hint of malice that confused Lofton. "It won't be long before the *Dispatch*'s regular sportswriter comes back from vacation; then you'll have to get your stories somewhere else."

"Don't worry. I've got enough to keep me busy," Lofton said. It was true. He had forgotten that the *Dispatch* had a regular sportswriter. Rhiner leaned back, cooling off. Suddenly Lofton guessed the source of the reporter's anger: Rhiner had been the one who told him Gutierrez's address; then it had turned into a big story, murder. Rhiner had probably been kicking himself for giving it away. Maybe Rhiner's editor had been kicking him, too. Lofton gave up and settled in to watch the game.

Jack Brunner appeared behind the third base stands. Though no one had said a word, Brunner's sudden appearance, Lofton realized, had drawn the attention of the people in the press box. There had been no reason he could put his finger on, no noise, no fanfare, but it had happened anyway: everyone turning to look at the owner. Brunner was a big man, true; good-looking, maybe, with his high-boned face and well-muscled body (though there was something animalistic about him, too, something ugly); but there was nothing sensational to draw your eye toward him. He wore ordinary, comfortable clothes, a plaid shirt, thin khakis. Perhaps it was the way he carried himself, loose and calculating, convinced of his place in the world. Brunner walked toward the press box, headed to his usual seat in the first base bleachers. He seemed to look past Lofton, not to see him or consider him of particular importance, except at the last second, when Lofton saw a flicker in the steel-gray eyes, like the shutter of a camera. For a few moments Brunner stopped to survey the field, standing not two feet away. They all stared at his back through the wire-mesh fence the whole time he stood there, except for Tenace, who kept his eyes on his scorecard. When Brunner walked away, Tenace let out an unconscious sigh.

The chatter in the press box died down. Soon there was only the banter of Lynn's radiocaster to the fans back home. Lofton wondered why people would listen to Lynn on the radio when they could go down to Fenway or watch the Red Sox on television. He could ask himself the same question, he supposed. Why did he stay in Holyoke?

He sat in the box through most of the game and listened to the Lynn announcer speak in his peculiar accent, laying the stress—to Lofton's ears—on the wrong syllables of the Holyoke players' California names. Tenace said little. Rhiner wrote down, in painstaking detail Lofton found amusing, the exploits of the players on the field, keeping track on a scorecard and making notes in the margins. Another reporter, a man from a small paper upriver, stared into the heat and listened to the play-by-play, occasionally taking notes on what the Lynn announcer said. Either way, it was easy enough to catch what was going on in the field, obvious to everyone that Lynn batters floundered stupidly in front of Kubachek's knuckler but clobbered any other pitch he threw, no matter how much the hurler stomped around on the mound before delivering.

Kubachek made a mistake in the seventh, when Holyoke had built up a 4–0 lead. With two out he lost control and walked a pair of batters. The Lynn right fielder, a burly, unshaved kid with a low hitting average, knocked a fastball out onto Beech Street, a three-run homer that cut Holyoke's lead to one.

The score stayed the same into the ninth, when Lofton left

the press box to sit in the bleachers behind Holyoke's dugout. He needed some quotes, something to fill out his "tribute." Once, when he was Rhiner's age, he would have dreaded such a story, been uncomfortable asking people questions about a dead friend, but that wasn't true now. People, when you got down to it, enjoyed talking about the dead.

Throughout the game Lumpy had trouble fielding Kubachek's knuckler. It was, by its nature, a confusing, ugly pitch, difficult to hit, difficult to catch. Even the pitcher's grip, the fingertips pressed flat against the ball, knuckles protruding, looked painful, ugly. Lumpy, not an adroit catcher even by Eastern League standards, seemed mystified by the way the ball spun and sank, sometimes this way, sometimes that, as it came into the plate. Though he could not always stop the knuckler with his glove, he did stop it with his body, letting the ball bounce off his chest, his mask, his arms—anything to stop it.

In the ninth Kubachek got the first batter on an easy grounder to Carpenter at second. He crossed the second batter up with his knuckler, three quick strikes, but Lumpy boggled the last pitch and threw wild to Lynch at first. The Lynn runner went all the way to second, then to third when the next hitter sent one of Kubachek's dying fastballs to deep right. Why Kubachek had thrown it, Lofton could only guess: probably to prove to somebody—himself—that he still had the old smoke. He didn't.

Last up was the Lynn right fielder, who had hit a home run in the seventh. Kubachek looked to the dugout, but Barker made no move to bring in a reliever. The Holyoke fans cheered.

The Lynn right fielder was greedy, eager to connect. Kubachek got him to swing on the first pitch, a slider that broke to the outside. Lumpy had a hard time fielding the ball, and it rolled away. The crowd screeched as the runner headed home. But the Lynn Sailor only bluffed; the ball had not rolled far enough for a serious try.

Kubachek went into his antics on the mound, stomping and pacing in circles, hitching up his pants, peering in at the batter, then giving his shoulders a violent shrug and turning away. When the umpire lost patience, Kubachek stepped forward, threw up his long arms, and came in with his weakest pitch, the fastball. The Lynn right fielder hit the ball, and hit it hard, though a split second too late; the ball went foul. Kubachek strutted about the mound, as if he had planned the whole thing.

Kubachek played the corners the next two pitches, curves that broke away and hung outside the strike zone. The Lynn batter held off. Two balls, two strikes. Lofton scanned the crowd. Brunner stood up in the stands, staring down at the action.

On the next pitch Kubachek tried the corner again and missed. A full count now. Coach Barker stood in front of the dugout. He flashed a sign to Kubachek, holding up his hand with all five fingers spread apart—probably telling him to take the corner again, to risk the walk with first base open.

Kubachek went back into his stomping routine; it was what had made him famous, what brought the fans out. Finally, though, he came in with the throw, and the pitch was beautiful, so beautiful Lofton felt himself catch his breath: a slow-breaking knuckler the right fielder had to swing at, the ball hung so fat and tempting over the meat of the plate, a sure strike. At the last possible second, the ball spun lazily away, slowly, still tantalizing but out of the strike zone, too far away for the batter to hit. Too late. The batter swung and missed, fooled completely. Unfortunately the pitch fooled Lumpy, too. He batted at the ball with his glove, and the ball rolled back between his legs. The Lynn players shouted from the dugout, and the batter hurried for first.

The Lynn base runner at third, who had broken with the pitch, came hard for the plate. The fans screamed behind Lofton. Lofton, the players, the fans, Brunner—they all were on their feet. Lumpy fumbled for the ball.

The runner was almost home. Close, too close. Dully, in unbelievable slow motion—the crowd groaned with anxiety—Lumpy groped at the ball. Then, somehow, he got it into his glove and lunged heavily at the runner. The two men smashed into one another, a vicious thud. The runner went down, and Lumpy stood in front of the plate, the ball still in his glove. The umpire made a grand sweep with his right hand, thumb pointed down at the dust. The runner was out. Holyoke had won.

Lumpy held the ball over his head, and the crowd screamed

louder. A joyous rush such as Lofton had not felt since he was
in Denver and the Broncos beat Oakland in a National Football League play-off game. That day there had been nothing
more beautiful than the junk and debris of Denver, the sal-
vage yards that seemed to sprawl out at every freeway interchange, the lots and lots of trailer trucks, railroad cars, and
corrugated warehouses. Here, in Holyoke, as that day in Denver, he screamed with the rest of them, forgetting his role as
the writer and forgetting the gun-gray eyes of Brunner across
the field. He wanted to let go with the feeling, to be with the
crowd, to file out onto the street and pat some friend on the
back, to drive home together over the glass-shattered streets.

The Redwings mobbed Kubachek and Lumpy. Some fans
climbed the fence and joined the mob. The two hired police
guards made a halfhearted effort to herd them away. Lofton
jumped the fence and hurried toward the scene. Rhiner was
there, too, and the two reporters jostled against each other.

"The fastball, why did you throw it there, at the end of the
game?" Rhiner yelled out.

"Because I felt like it," Kubachek yelled back. That was
enough for Lofton. He could use that quote, work it in somehow. He looked for Coach Barker, for Tim Carpenter. He got
caught in the middle of a group of fans, smelled their sweat,
their beer-drunken breath. The boy from the library, his Redwings' cap tilted crazily over his eyes, grabbed Lofton's arm
and jumped up and down, hysterical with joy. Lofton pulled
away and caught hold of Carpenter.

"Tim, I need an interview." Lofton tried to put a note of
sincerity in his voice, a hint of apology. He recognized, instead, his own slurred, lazy-tongued California accent, still
not that much different from when he was a kid.

"Later," Carpenter said. "After I shower. Meet me by the
gate."

Lofton let him go. Barker was walking down the third base
line toward the dugout. Lofton started after him, but a cluster
of fans crushed around him, A policeman shouted. As Lofton
turned, breaking from the circle of people, he saw Brunner
holding open the clubhouse door, watching proprietarily as
the players filed in. Sparks was one of the players, but he did
not look up at Brunner, not now. Neither did any of the
others.

"Fun's over. Time to get moving."

It was a security guard, his voice high and nasal, not quite believing its own authority.

"I'm a reporter, goddammit." Lofton stepped away from the man and headed for the main gate. The Lynn team bus stood idling by the curb, and the Sailors filed on. Some Holyoke fans stood nearby and heckled them. A group of teenagers, Puerto Ricans mostly, but a few whites. The same kids Brunner tried to keep from kicking in his fence night after night.

"Nobody comes to Holyoke and lives. . . . *Muerate al equipo*. . . . Get out of here, *maricones*. . . . *Vamos,* Lynn faggots . . . *Viva Gutierrez!*"

When the Redwings played in Lynn, this would come back on the team. Lynn was a rough town; the fans would ride the Redwings hard. Even so, he enjoyed the way the Holyoke kids yelled at the visitors. He waited for Carpenter until the Lynn team bus pulled away, headed for the Motel 6 in Chicopee, where the team would stay until its Holyoke road stand was over. Then he knocked on the clubhouse door.

It was Golden who opened it. "What do you need?" His voice seemed friendly, but his eyes were empty, and he did not look Lofton in the face.

"Tim Carpenter said he would talk to me after the game, but I can't find him."

"He left, with some of the others." Golden gestured down the right field line, to the other exit. Though it was a simple gesture, in the way Golden's hand rose and fell, in the lowering and veiling of Golden's eyes, in the creases of his quick, hard smile—in the whole motion that was over in a second—Lofton tried to read Golden's guilt, to tell if it was true that Golden was dealing with arson, acting as Brunner's front man. The gestures gave him no clue; they were simply movements, nothing inherent in them, just as there was nothing inherently good and evil in any movement: swinging at a ball, lighting a match, pulling a trigger. He thought of confronting Golden now, but that would be rash, he told himself; it wasn't the time. In another quick motion Golden had closed the clubhouse door.

Lofton hurried after Carpenter and the others. He started to run, his breath rasped, there was a small soreness in his

lungs. When he reached the right field gate, he did not see
them. He walked the city streets, headed home, but with an
eye out for the players. Along the way he kept imagining he
saw them, always one block over, just rounding the corner of
some burned-out building, disappearing, just as he caught up,
into the thick-tongued alleys of fire and ash.

Lofton reached the church at midnight, the Iglesia de las
Flores Rojas. He looked through the dim air for Mendoza.
Life-size statues—the saints, he guessed—stood in alcoves at
the periphery of the church; Jesus, arms extended, stood at
the front; and behind the altar, arranged in tiers reaching to a
crude, golden sun, were clay statues of more saints, the apos-
tles, the Holy Family. He cursed McCullough for ever having
set up the meeting. He did not want to be here, and he
wouldn't have come if he hadn't thought the warring street
gangs somehow knew something about the fires.

"Señor Lofton."

Lofton turned. Mendoza stepped out from behind a statue.
Lofton thought he saw movement to the side, maybe just a
shadow, a statue flickering in the candlelight.

Mendoza walked slowly, one hand held behind him. He
came to within a few feet of Lofton, then slid into a pew.

"Join me," Mendoza said. Lofton slid into the same pew,
always keeping his hands in front of his body. After a while
Mendoza put both hands on the pew in front of him. Lofton
relaxed a little.

"I know this is a funny way to meet, but I can't take the
chance for anyone to see us. It isn't safe for me on the
streets." As Mendoza talked, he slipped down onto his knees.

"Excuse me," Mendoza said. "It's a habit in church."

"What do you want to tell me?"

Mendoza slid closer. He gave Lofton a funny, unreal smile.
"You're the one who wrote about the baseball player, the
shortstop?"

"Yes," said Lofton.

"Then you know."

"Know what?"

"You know how people can die," Mendoza said. Despite
Mendoza's apparent seriousness, the remark seemed humor-
ous; Mendoza, for a moment, seemed aware of the effect, and

to enjoy it. "The first time I saw you, I didn't tell you everything," Mendoza said, "or maybe you didn't understand. We're at war here, my people and the Latinos."

Mendoza had gone through this routine during their last conversation, telling him how his gang, the Wanderers, had supposedly taken off their colors, as the mayor had asked, and gone legitimate. He said the same thing with more fervor now.

"My people, we work hard. We feed each other; we take care of our own. We don't want attention, or to be called hoodlums. But the Latinos keep up the war, hunting us out when we walk alone, or when we sit eating in our houses. They kill us one by one, like some dogs, and the police—though they talk one thing in the newspapers—they let us die. They watch and smile. That's why I'm hiding now; the Latinos are after me. . . . They're going to search and hunt until they kill me."

Once again the fact that he was the object of the Latinos' search seemed to please Mendoza. "What do you want me to do?" Lofton asked.

"I want you to tell people what the Latinos are doing. Tell them in the papers. Like you told them about the dead ballplayer. I want to be safe in the streets."

Mendoza's story didn't quite jibe with the one Lofton had gathered from Einstein's newspaper work. The Latinos had lost their leader, Angelo, and they felt the Wanderers were responsible. Now Mendoza wanted Lofton to write it up from a new angle, favoring the Wanderers.

Mendoza looked toward the crucifix; his tongue darted over his lips.

"I need more proof," Lofton said. "I can't go on just what you say."

"What proof do you need? A dead body?"

Mendoza's eyes glimmered in the darkness. The words sounded—almost, Lofton could not be sure—like a threat. Mendoza bowed his head, muttering as if in prayer, "I don't want to die, but if I die, it will be brave. I do it for my people." His eyes closed, head still bowed, Mendoza seemed self-conscious, an exaggeration of some role he was trying to play. He wants me to write him up, to make him into a hero, Lofton realized, to dramatize their street war so that, when he

dies, at least someone will be watching. Though in some ways
the whole business was sheer melodrama, the war between the
two gangs was real enough, Lofton knew.

"The fires . . ." Lofton said, starting to ask Mendoza, but
at the mention of the word Mendoza grabbed his arm. The
man was lean and tense beside him, his face shiny in the
candlelight, his eyes fierce, unnatural. Then it hit Lofton, and
he wondered why it had not hit him before. Drugs. Coke,
maybe speed. Mendoza was cranked up, acting the way Gutierrez had been that night with Amanti, frightened one minute, boastful the next, veering back and forth. Only Mendoza
was a more violent man, more dangerous. Lofton imagined he
could smell the drugs, the white powder, the rush of electricity mixed with Mendoza's sweat in the steamy air of the
church.

"Maybe you will help us. Or maybe, if you can't help,
you'll just mind your business. That other reporter, he wasn't
as smart as you."

"No," said Lofton.

"No?" Mendoza laughed, a little crazily, as if deciding
what to do next. Finally he let go of Lofton's arm. He laughed
again and eased away, farther down the pew. He said nothing
more. He walked down the center aisle, turned at the last
moment back toward the altar, genuflected, and disappeared
into the statues.

Almost the first thing the next morning, as Lofton left his
hotel, he saw several of the Latinos standing on the corner
across the street. As soon as they spotted him, they came in
his direction. What he had feared would happen seemed to be
taking place: By contacting Mendoza, he had stepped into the
middle of the warring gangs. All he could do was watch the
Latinos approach, slouching lazily, lithely as cats, young,
muscular, only partially domesticated. One of the young men,
whom Lofton sized up as the most dangerous of the three,
stood a few steps behind the others. He wore a jeans vest over
his bare chest, a bandanna around his black hair, and stood,
not really looking at Lofton, one hand buried in a pocket that
probably held a switchblade, or some iron knuckles, or maybe
just one of those key chains with a spike at the end.

"Mendoza. Where is he?" asked the tallest of the three

Latinos, the leader apparently. At least he was the one who did the talking.

"You're asking the wrong man," Lofton said. Up close he thought he recognized these three now; they were the same ones who had greeted him out in front of Mendoza's apartment building. They hadn't done anything to him then, and they probably wouldn't do anything now. Still, the dangerous-seeming one moved imperceptibly closer, and Lofton caught a look at his face. Despite the early hour, the kid was already high, not with flashy, expensive stuff like Mendoza had been on last night, but with something slower, heavier, cheaper—some combination of alcohol and barbiturates, Lofton guessed.

"We know you were with Mendoza last night. Where is he?"

"I don't know. What makes you think I've seen him?"

"The Wanderers aren't all with Mendoza, not anymore. A lot of people don't like what he's doing, so they talk to us. We didn't miss him by much last night; if you don't want to get killed, you should keep to yourself."

"Killing him won't get you anywhere. It won't change a thing."

"That's what the other reporter said, too. Angelo listened to him, to the Jew. 'Build a movement,' the Jew said, 'get the attention of the people, of the community. Drive out the pushers. That's the way to get Mendoza.' The Jew was bullshit. So Angelo is dead from his bullshit. Now we want Mendoza."

"Good luck." Lofton turned, but the Latino grabbed him by the arm.

"What are you going to write in the paper?"

"Don't flatter yourself," Lofton said. "You people can kill each other all you want. I've got more important things to write about."

He was risking it, he knew. He could see the drugged one peering at him.

"Do you know why Angelo's dead?" the leader asked. "Do you know why they killed him?"

"Tell me."

"Angelo knew the Wanderers were behind the fires. Not all of the Wanderers, just some of them. Mendoza most of all. He got paid for setting the fires, and that's why he had the Wanderers kill Angelo: to protect his business."

"Who pays Mendoza to set the fires?"

The Latino said nothing. He didn't seem to know the answer. "Okay," Lofton said, "but if Angelo knew this, why didn't he tell the police, or the Jew, or someone who could do something? What proof did he have?"

The three Latinos looked at each other, and it was clear to Lofton that there was no proof. Or if there was any proof, it was some incident buried in the feud between the two gangs, a scene witnessed late at night, when some Latino caught the smell of kerosene, then turned to see a quick flare of light, perhaps even glimpsing the retreating backside of some kid he'd grown up with, a rival now, a member of the Wanderers. That was the closest thing to any kind of proof the Latinos might have, nothing that would stand up in court. The tallest of the three, seeming to sense Lofton's skepticism, spoke loudly. "Angelo listened to the Jew say just what you're saying now. He wanted proof, too. We aren't going to make that mistake."

"If Mendoza's burning the buildings, he's not doing it for himself, and he's not doing it for free. He's on a lot more expensive drugs than your friend back here." The drugged, dangerous-seeming one looked up, sensing he'd been insulted, but Lofton kept talking. "You kill Mendoza, they'll just find someone else to take his place. I want the big joker—the one behind the scenes."

The leader of the small group was quiet for a moment, contemplating not what Lofton had said so much as his face, his expression, the way he stood. He let go of Lofton's arm. The other two, though, were getting restless, bored with all the talk. The one who had been quiet the whole time, who seemed neither drugged nor dangerous, stepped forward. He took his hand from his pocket and pointed a short finger at Lofton. "If you know where Mendoza is, you better tell us."

"I don't know any more about where that bastard is than you do," Lofton said, and turned back to the leader. "Do me a favor, when you find him, don't kill him right away. I'd like to ask him a few more questions. If I'm not at my hotel, I'm at the ballpark—every time there's a game. You can find me there."

This time Lofton did not brave a backward glance until he was more than a block away. By then the corner was empty, the Latinos nowhere to be seen. His heart was beating faster than he would have liked, but he had to admit that the Latinos, if he could believe them, had helped color in another piece of the picture. Mendoza was the torch, the punk in the street with the crazy glare in his eye and a fondness for drugs, strong ones that knocked you higher and sweeter than you'd ever get with Mad Dog and marijuana. Golden was the go-between, the contact man who made sure Mendoza got his instructions and his money. And Brunner was the dog on top. Though it all made sense, and would look beautiful on the blue-and-white pages of his notebook, Lofton still knew he could not prove a word, at least not yet.

5

A half dozen or so Redwings were lining up at the batting cage. Others took positions in the field, then hurried down to catch their own practice when the line got thin.

They donned the blue, visored helmets, their batting gloves, and picked out their bats, hefting them over their shoulders, stretching and yawning while waiting their turns. Some nodded to Lofton, knowing, he suspected, that he wanted to talk about Randy Gutierrez.

Often this past month he had sat on the sidelines and listened to the players during practice. They talked to one another while selecting their bats, talked of players on the other teams, of each other, of old teammates now up in Triple A or others who had gone down the other way and were working some job back home. They talked of their fathers' businesses, of their degrees in accounting or in physical education, or worst of all, like Lynch, the first baseman, they worried over what jobs they might get in the off-season or what they would do when the Blues cut them for good. They joked over how drunk Lumpy had been the night before, or about Singleton's getting slapped by a dyke in a Northampton bar, or about the tight-jeaned girls who hung around after the games and went away with Elvin Banks, the center fielder. They talked about

things like this, or about nothing at all, instead standing silently under the hot summer sun, listening to the whipcrack
of the bat, the thrum of the traffic, and the slow drumming of
their thoughts until somebody said, "Hey, did you see that
piece in the paper?" and they would look sidelong at Lofton,
and the talking would begin again, somebody griping about
the California organization, about the miserable way Cowboy
used his farm leagues, and wondering why the man even bothered, if it wasn't just meanness and some weird spite. And all
the while, spinning in the secret wheels of their imaginations
—Lofton guessed—the players dreamed of how they would
escape this city, this singed town of Puerto Rican music and
dirty bars, and hit the glitter world, real fans, real teams, real
reporters. Real fame and real money, a town where the fans
thrilled and screamed while the ball wasped through the air of
a real city: a major league city.

Lofton stood by the dugout, watching the players wait their
turn. They exchanged dry looks, spat out the dark tobacco
juice, and walked up to the cage. He wondered if Dick
Golden, who had spent most of his life around baseball fields
—and who had fought the U.S. government when it had tried
to take him off the mound and into the army—could really be
helping Brunner with his arson schemes. Lofton held off approaching Golden, partly because it might be dangerous to
reveal his suspicions, but more because he wanted to believe
Golden was innocent. A lot of people had not liked it when
Golden had resisted the draft, but at least he'd been honest
about it, saying he did it for his own reasons and for no one
else's, and admitting his own reasons were as selfish as the
next man's. Lofton did not like to think that Golden had been
forced to buckle under, to play someone else's game.

As the players finished batting practice, he ventured closer,
talking to them, getting what he could for the hack story
Kirpatzke wanted, all the while hoping some other information might come up to help him close in on Brunner. He
asked the players how Randy Gutierrez's death had affected
their play on the field.

"I guess it's brought us around. I been playing good, but
it's hard to remember that he's dead. You start to forget, so
many guys come and go," said Lumpy, the catcher, his big
hands hanging awkwardly at his side.

"When Randy died, it left a hole in our team. Like part of us died. I feel like that sometimes, like it was me that died," said Lynch, the first baseman. "I keep thinking he's still here, sitting at the back of the bus. Sometimes, out of the corner of my eye, I see him."

"What they said wasn't true; he didn't take drugs," said Singleton, Gutierrez's replacement. He and the center fielder, Elvin Banks, talked to Lofton together. Elvin Banks told Lofton how Gutierrez always mumbled to himself in Spanish, especially after he had struck out or muffed a play in the field. Singleton told him that back in April, at the Redwings' home opener, Gutierrez had lost his way to the park, so he had had to play in his place. Lofton wrote it down. Good. Perfect. Kirpatzke would love it. Banks, a good-looking black man in his middle twenties, told Lofton about a snowstorm in Buffalo, back in the early season, on the Redwings' first road trip. Elvin Banks was from a middle-class family in New Orleans; his family didn't want him up here playing ball; they wanted him home.

"Randy woke up and there it was: a foot and a half of snow on the ground. I'd seen something similar before, once in northern Mississippi. Bad enough for me, but Randy shook his head all day long, pinching at himself and picking the snow up in his hands. The game was called, and I walked him around town. He kept saying this had to be some strange, cold heaven."

Afterward Lofton watched Banks go to the cage. His swing was muscular and compact. He slammed all of Coach Barker's pitches into the outfield and sent a few farther, into the Beech Street traffic. Lofton's mind went back to the powder inside the Virgin. Snow. Heaven. Cowboy and his big cigars. Salaries in six figures. Brunner and Amanti. Amanti and the white sheets rustling in her back bedroom. The air was hot; sweat trickled down his temple.

Tim Carpenter was in the cage now, one of the last batters. He had avoided Lofton, waiting for his turn on the other side of the cage. His style was different from Banks's—wide, shoulder-heavy swings that sent the ball spinning out on a line, then dropping halfway between the infielders and the outfielders, not far from that asphalt track. When he was

done, Carpenter walked toward Lofton, as if now he was
ready to talk. Lofton called out his name.

"Yeah," Carpenter said in his clumsy California slur. He
held the end of the bat in the dirt and balanced his weight
against it. Lofton asked him about the snowstorm in Buffalo.

"Yeah, I remember that. I was still asleep when Randy got
out of bed. We roomed together on the road, and the day
before, he'd been chewed bad by Barker. Too many muffs.
When he woke and saw the snow, he thought he was dreaming."

Lofton wrote it down. He decided not to ask Carpenter
why he had gone out the other gate, avoiding him after last
night's game. It was more important to see what he could find
out about Gutierrez.

"Anything else you remember?"

"No, just do it up good, Lofton, and keep that drug stuff
out of there. Randy had his problems, but he was no worse
than anybody else, no worse than you or me."

"Right." Lofton made a show of writing it down. *No worse
than you or me.*

Carpenter went on leaning against his bat, then spat into
the dirt. Lofton wiped the sweat from his face. This long
silence, this lingering, maybe, was Carpenter's way of telling
him something.

"You got any ideas?" Carpenter asked.

"Ideas?"

"Who killed him. You got any ideas?"

"None. Do you?"

Tim Carpenter twisted the bat, digging a small hole in the
dust. "No," he said, and pushed his bat back into the rack.

"Do you remember that night at the apartment? With you,
Amanti, Sparks. Gutierrez was there, talking. He was upset."

"What night do you mean?"

"After the game."

"We play lots of games. What are you after?"

Lofton paused. He knew he should be careful. If he said too
much to the wrong person—and if word got back the way it
had gotten back on Gutierrez. . . . Yet he had to ask questions to get answers; there was no other way.

"It was a night after Sparks had pitched. He had won, and
then you and Amanti and Sparks and Gutierrez and a couple

of those ballpark girls—you all went up to the apartment. Do you remember?"

"I remember. Who you been talking to?"

"Never mind. I just need to know what Gutierrez had on his mind. Did he talk about anything that might be hooked up to his death?"

"Randy was crazy those last weeks," Carpenter said. "Maybe his motor was running extra hard that night, I don't remember. I went to bed early, but Gutierrez, he had some strange raps." Carpenter laughed, then shook his head. "Listen, I thought you were going to keep the drug stuff out of it. That doesn't need to be in the papers."

"One minute you guys swear Randy Gutierrez was straight, the next minute drugs were ruining his life. It can't be both ways, and there's no sense in trying to protect him now that he's dead. To tell you the truth, this stuff about the snowflakes in Buffalo, it's not really what I'm after. I'm trying to figure out who killed Gutierrez. I need to know what he was talking about those last days."

"After Randy wound himself up, he said a lot of things. They're hard to remember. He was paranoid. He would tell a hundred stories, and everybody in every one of them was out to get him. Sometimes I wonder about it, maybe there was something buried in his talk that made sense, but back then I had to turn him off. I just stopped paying attention."

"Did he ever mention arson?"

"Arson?" Carpenter scowled. He seemed uncomfortable with the turn in the conversation, and he was no good at concealing it.

"From what I understand," Lofton said, "Gutierrez was spinning pretty hard that night at the apartment when he was talking to Amanti. Sparks was there. You two were roommates; you can't tell me Sparks didn't mention it to you. . . . Did Gutierrez ever talk to you about arson?"

"He talked to me about it," Carpenter said, though he didn't like saying it, and turned to stare out at the ballfield, as if something out there might help him out of the conversation.

"Did Gutierrez say Golden was involved?"

Carpenter sighed heavily. "Yeah, he said that, but he said a lot of things. I remember once he thought everybody on the team was out to get him. He even suspected me. . . . You aren't going to use this stuff in the paper, are you?"

"No," said Lofton. "I'm just trying to figure out why Gutierrez is dead."

Carpenter shook his head. He didn't know anything else. It was a mystery to him, he said, as spooky as the man in the moon. And that story about the arson, he'd kept it to himself until now. He didn't believe it, not really. He hadn't even told anyone on the team.

"What about Sparks? Did he believe it?"

"You'll have to ask him yourself," Carpenter said, his tone shifting. "I haven't learned to read minds yet."

Practice ended, and the game began, the Redwings whirling the ball one last time around the horn. Lofton wanted to talk to Sparks, but the pitcher still had not materialized. He was back in the training room, getting his arm worked over; at least that's what they'd told him at the clubhouse door.

Lofton felt someone tap him on the arm. It was the kid with the Redwings cap. The boy's eyes darted around, and his voice stammered hard—his right hand moving, touching his face—as he gave Lofton the message.

"Someone wants to talk to you. Up by the candy stand."

Lofton noticed burn marks down the kid's arm. The scars were mottled and brown, as if the kid had scratched at the skin before it could heal.

The kid close by his side, Lofton headed toward the concession. Amanti stood waiting. She wore sunglasses, so he could not tell if she watched him as he approached. She turned her back when Lofton reached the stand, but she did not walk away. Her hair was tied back with a thin black ribbon.

Lofton ordered a Coke from the girl in the concession.

"Didn't expect to see you here," he said to Amanti.

"I was worried. . . ."

The boy stared up at them; his hand moved nervously about, almost shaking.

"Kid gets around," Lofton said. "I see him all over."

"Yes, he does things for the team. Runs down to the store, grabs sandwiches. Retrieves fouls. Things like that."

The kid smiled at Amanti, enraptured. Amanti reached into her purse, counting out quarters. She handed the kid his

money, and he took off, hurtling away from the concession,
down to where some boys played flip, tossing their knives at a
circle scratched in the dirt.

"He's awfully young to be so nervous," Lofton said.

"I don't know what's wrong, but he's a smart kid, you can
see that sometimes. Once in a while he gets mixed up. They'll
send him down to get one of the players and he'll come back
with somebody else, or he'll go off down to some strange place
or the other. Most of the time he's fine, but he doesn't have
any parents. He lives in a halfway house, and one of the counselors says they think he was beat up a lot when he was little."

Lofton was surprised by the compassion she expressed; he
had not seen it in her before. He stood there with her, watching the kid. After a few minutes she said that she wanted to
talk to him, but not here. She asked him to meet her outside
the right field gate.

Lofton sipped at his Coke and headed slowly, casually toward the third base bleachers. Amanti had made her way past
the press box and was working her way through the opposite
grandstand. Lofton decided to go out the main gate and circle
around the ballpark to his meeting place with Amanti. Ahead
of him, Dick Golden leaned over the third base fence, watching the action. The visiting Lynn Sailors had scored two runs
in the top of the first. Now Holyoke had one run in, two men
on, and nobody out.

"Gonna be a wild one," said Golden. He smiled, friendly.
He did not seem like a murderer, an arsonist, but it was an
easy thing to lean over a baseball fence and lose your identity,
to forget about what twist of luck, good or bad, had conspired
to make you what you were. The foul lines touched at home
plate, then angled away from one another, the space between
them growing greater the closer they came to the outfield
wall, and growing still greater, infinite, if you imagined the
lines continuing past the boundaries of the park. You could
lose yourself in that space, there was nothing but the ball
game, there was no other world. Once inside it, Lofton didn't
know how to ask Golden about the fires. Instead, he stood
with the former pitcher and watched Elvin Banks wally-loop
a slow curve down the right field line, a ball that hit fair,
bounced first right then left, then over the charging outfielder's head and into the deep grass.

* * *

"Kill the whole business. Drop the story. The more I think about Gutiérrez's death, the more frightened I become. Brunner knows I've been talking to you, at least I think he does. It's time to stop."

Amanti walked beside him, her heels clicking on the broken pavement. Her reversal didn't surprise him, not completely. He could understand her fear of Brunner, but when trouble came, he knew, it would come in his own direction, not hers. Brunner would move against the outsider, not wanting to admit that the real trouble originated down home, in his own bed. Lofton knew he should be afraid, but the fear was not enough to chase him away. Partly it was because he was almost invisible on the Holyoke streets. No one knew him here; he had no identity. So if he happened to die, it would almost be as if nobody had died. Though he didn't like the idea of being nobody, there was a certain freedom in the idea, too, and it kept the fear down to a minimum, to a cold gray wave in the chest. A second later he abandoned this whole line of thinking. It was nonsense. He was scared to death.

"Why did you bother with Brunner in the first place? That's what I can't figure. It doesn't seem that you like him, let alone love him. His money and that apartment—those can't mean that much. I mean, you could just marry someone, some halfway decent guy with a little cash, and get the same thing. You could probably even sleep around if you wanted."

Amanti's face flushed. He could see that she did not like the way he was talking. At the moment Lofton didn't much care. She was backing off the story, abandoning what she had started, and he felt he could say pretty much what he pleased.

"What's it to you how I live?" she asked.

"It's nothing to me."

There was anger in her voice, anger in the staccato clicking of her heels. Her arms swung loosely, but her hands were rigid, tense; she flexed her fingertips, over and over, in and out of her palm. All around them the evening light was soft and red. Amanti's eyes welled for a second with a surge of anger and self-pity, and then it was just anger. It was the sort of anger that comes when someone touches a nerve close to the truth. The touch makes you want to talk, to be touched again, to feel the electric flashes as the truth becomes speech and then disappears into the air.

"Listen, you don't know anything," she said. "You don't have any idea."

"I'm not paid to have ideas. I just write things down. Other people have the ideas."

"Bullshit," she said. "Fuck yourself."

Across the street some schoolgirls walked along, dressed in their Catholic school outfits, white blouses and green plaid skirts. A small brown-skinned girl shuffled sloppily along behind the others, unconcerned, lost in her own reverie.

"That girl is me; that's what I was," Amanti said. Lofton couldn't see it. It wasn't how he had pictured her.

"You don't know what it's like," she said. "This place is cold as death all winter, then nothing but heat in the summer. There's hardly anything in between, just a few days in spring when everything bursts to life, so thick it could strangle you, and then a blaze of color in the fall—a blaze that comes after the heat and sinks straight into winter. There's no mild seasons, no transitions, nothing you can live in."

Lofton hadn't heard her talk like this before. The words burst out as if they'd been inside a long time, phrasing themselves over and over, and now they rang sharply, incongruently, in the evening air. Still, he understood what she meant. His last year in Massachusetts, after the breakup with his first wife, the winter had been so cold it had seemed to settle deep in his bones, in his heart, as if the flame that kept his body alive had been receding, dying with the weather. Then it was spring, and the flame roared back, and he could no longer stand being in the town where he and Nancy had lived together. So he moved back to the Santa Clara Valley in California, where the seasons were mild and the sky was blue and perpetually sunny.

"I hated my uncle Liuzza, I hated his money and everything about him, but when he offered my mother to pay for my college in Boston, I grabbed it, glad as hell to get out."

"Why didn't you stay in Boston?"

"You don't want to know that story." She spat the words out, not bothering to look at him, but then she told him the story anyway, caught up in her own anger. She told him how she had fallen in love when she was a student in Boston. She didn't mention Kelley's name—she was on the verge, but she held it back; her anger hadn't taken her quite that far, not yet —but she told him about the affair, how the man had been engaged to be married when they met and how Uncle Liuzza had found out and done his best to kill the whole thing. Then he'd taken up with Brunner, she said, to get her lover jealous. It worked for a while, but not well enough. So she went back to Brunner. And the other man came back again. Even now it was going on, she said, the same stupid dance, the same back and forth.

"What's the other man's name?" Lofton asked.

Amanti turned and took Lofton by the wrist. She gave him a look—her eyes wide and impossibly blue—that was so earnest it took him by surprise.

"Don't work on this story. It's time to drop it. You'll never get Brunner."

"So you need his money, is that it? Afraid to go out into the world on your own?"

She was shaken, he thought, but doing her best not to show it. She went on looking at him in the same way. He wondered what was going on beneath the surface.

"If you're dependent on Brunner," he asked, "why did you try to get me to go after him in the first place?"

"I'm not after Brunner."

"Then who are you after?"

"No one," she said.

They separated at the field, and he watched the rest of the game alone. Both starting pitchers were already gone. The whole relief staff paraded to the mound. But Holyoke held on, won, 16–13, the difference Banks's three-run homer in the eighth. Two wins in a row for Holyoke. The team had scrambled out of the cellar.

After her talk with Lofton, Amanti drove home. The undergrowth was dense close to the road, covering the guardrails. In places the undergrowth gave way to vistas that, during the day, would have revealed farmlands and suburbs reaching to the rolling hills. Now the same vistas offered only an expanse of darkness broken by the scattered lights of houses and roads. Despite the general darkness, the landscape seemed palpable, as if it were not simple scenery, a backdrop, but instead possessed a consciousness of its own. The consciousness was not great enough to understand itself, only to express itself—in the chirring crickets, the barking of a stray dog, the turning of gravel under the wheel, sounds whose meaning was poignant yet still unclear. At times, through the canopies of trees over the winding road, Amanti caught glimpses of the stars that punctuated the black sky overhead.

Kelley, of course, had put her up to talking to Lofton. She had done as Kelley had asked: She'd told Lofton to drop the story. Now she and Kelley planned to go away together for a few days to a cabin in the New Hampshire countryside. They'd been to the cabin once before, a few years ago, when Kelley had been making plans to leave his wife.

Tonight Kelley was supposed to meet her at her apartment. When she reached home, Kelley hadn't yet arrived. She took a shower, washed off the heat and dirt, then changed into some fresh clothes. She put on a new skirt, a white linen material that wasn't quite thin enough to see through but that was cool and loose around her legs. The skirt was very much like one she used to wear on the warm evenings when she and Kelley had first gotten together. When she had finished changing, she fixed herself a drink and sat down at the kitchen table. She sat with her legs crossed, swinging the top one back and forth, studying her fingers, sipping at her drink, and listening for his car in the drive.

She finished her drink, made another, and Kelley still didn't come. Kelley was always late. The feeling she had now, the excitement alternating with anxiety, was very similar to the feeling she used to have when she lived in Boston and would wait for him in her apartment. Except now the excitement and the anxiety were no longer new, but instead a kind of repetition that was more wearying than exhilarating. She remembered waiting until it was time to meet Kelley, then walking alone through the back streets of Italian and Irish neighborhoods. When they walked together, it was always away from the rush of the main avenues, where someone might recognize him. Eventually, though, they would have to walk down the busy street that led to her building. They would step into the street, into the sudden jostling of the crowd and the stream of lights. Once inside her building, Kelley would clutch her skirt in his fist while she reached up and touched his white skin, his black hair.

She had felt a similar excitement walking the Holyoke streets with Lofton; only the danger of discovery seemed more real, more dangerous, because there was always the image of the dead shortstop, and of Brunner, and the feeling, stronger than ever, that things were no longer under control. She had done what Kelley had asked, basically, but Kelley had not meant for her to tell Lofton the story of their love affair. She had almost come out with Kelley's name. In fact, she had almost told Lofton everything. At the last minute, as he was turning to go, she had almost grabbed him by the wrist and said, "I'll show you. I'll help you."

Kelley still did not call. She made herself another drink. She sat on the floor beneath the wall phone and put her hand on her white skirt. She knew now that he wasn't coming, that the phone would ring and she would hear his voice explaining that there were things he had to do in Boston. While he explained, she imagined, he would be in the apartment of his new mistress, and while Amanti listened to his voice, distant over the wire, the mistress would be hearing the same voice from the darkness of her bedroom, in the same way Amanti herself had heard it often enough when Kelley used to visit her and call home to his wife. Only this time Kelley didn't call. The phone didn't ring. He's tight in her embrace, Amanti thought, and she buried her fingers in the folds of her skirt.

The clerk reached into the dark bank of cubbyholes and pulled out a pair of envelopes for Lofton. All week there had been nothing; now two letters at once, one from Maureen, the other an unstamped envelope with Lofton's name written on the front in the clerk's crabbed handwriting. It was the clerk's method for passing on messages, phone calls, or the weekly bill. Lofton guessed it was the latter. He took both envelopes upstairs and put them down in his room, on the Formica table with the rest of his papers. He stared out across the rooftops; he could smell the roof tar sweating in the evening damp and heat.

The clerk, Lofton remembered, would not be giving him this week's bill until Monday. So the envelope held a message.

He lit a cigarette before he tore the envelope open. The note inside told him to call Tony Liuzza.

Liuzza. Lofton wondered what Amanti's cousin wanted. Maybe he didn't like the story Lofton had written about Gutierrez's death. Bad publicity, tasteless. Lofton agreed. Murder stories were almost always that way. He imagined the black-framed print of Gutierrez the *Dispatch* planned to run with his next piece, and he tried to guess which of the quotes Kirpatzke would pull out and block, to draw attention to the story. "I see him sometimes in the back of the bus out of the corner of my eye." And Lofton thought how it really made no difference who wrote this story. He had written pieces like it a hundred times, read them a thousand, shaking his head just like the man in the street, imagining that the dead man was himself, glad that he wasn't. Maybe Amanti was right. Drop the arson story. Pursuing it would do more harm than good.

That's what he'd decided back in California, too. He'd been working as a reporter for the *San Jose Star,* footlegging through the downtown pornos, gathering information for a grim color piece on Mexican cruisers, drunks, and adult arcades. He'd soon found out what almost every other reporter already knew: that the drug trade and other illicit business that went on there were part of a statewide ring, sanctioned from on high. What bothered Lofton was that although the corruption was common knowledge, he could find no way to break the story. His editor told him to back off, that it had nothing to do with the real issues. Nonetheless, Lofton hung around the seedy bars, drank himself silly tracing the story, ignoring his regular beat.

Then, one day, he'd gotten that call from Senator Hansen, offering him a chance to leave the paper to work as his press secretary. Lofton had thought about that phone call often enough since: how pleased he'd been, how flattered, and how he'd ignored the voice whispering in the back of his head that told him something was wrong. He heard the voice again, several months later. He was in Sacramento and had just finished a press briefing for the local hacks when a reporter he knew from the *Star* approached him. The man was a drunk, Lofton remembered, but a pretty good reporter. The drunk mentioned the story Lofton had been working on before he left the paper.

"Rumor is you were coming pretty close on that one—
before your new boss here bought you out."

Lofton ignored the crack. Jealousy, he thought, drunken
slander. I'm getting a good salary, but I deserve it. I've
worked hard. Even so, he did some checking around, slowly,
surely, and over the next few months, between briefings and
churning out press memos, he figured it out. His boss, the
good politician, whom Lofton admired . . . well, the Honor-
able Senator Hansen was in on it, too. He was in it for all the
right reasons—to protect his power base, for political sur-
vival, so he could go on pushing his progressive programs—
but he was still in on it.

Lofton worked for a few weeks more, telling himself that's
the way the world worked, the lesser of evils was what it came
down to, and though that was practical, and that was what he
believed, he stood up at his desk one day and said fuck it. He
drove to San Jose, gave the story to his friend the drunk
reporter, and left the state. Only the drunk reporter never
wrote the story either.

Lofton got his severance pay in the mail, forwarded to Colorado, plus a bonus he hadn't asked for or expected. There
was also a friendly note from one of Hansen's aides that for-
mally regretted his departure, thanked him for his services.

That was the last Lofton heard about it until a few weeks
after he'd married Maureen. His old editor at the *Star* had
called up to give Lofton the sweet news that if he were thinking about it, he shouldn't bother to come back to the West
Coast because both he and the drunk reporter had been unof-
ficially blacklisted by the California papers.

"Rumor is that you and your friend buried a few files for a
slice of the take," the editor said, his voice a strange mixture
of satisfaction and bitterness, "and all this time I'd thought
you were just a bumbling, honest Joe. But tell me, how much
did they give you?"

"Good joke," Lofton said, then hung up.

It didn't bother him that he'd taken Hansen's money. The
final paycheck, the bonus—he'd used the money, but he
hadn't asked for it; he could have gone ahead and written the
story regardless. It hadn't been a payoff, he told himself; he
wasn't obligated to anyone. Still, he wondered why he hadn't
gone ahead and written the story. Perhaps it was because in

the end he'd believed that Hansen, no matter his corruption, was better than the people who wanted to push him out. Or perhaps it was because the story had seemed like just too much trouble. He was simply lazy. Despite the business about the blacklisting, no one else had ever written the story either, at least not as far as Lofton knew. Lofton couldn't help wondering if Hansen's people had paid off his friend the drunk reporter or if the man had pushed things too hard and then simply disappeared, found himself buried in Mexico, mouth full of dirt, like all good California reporters. *I should've written the story,* Lofton told himself; *I should've fucked them.*

Now, sitting in his hotel room in Holyoke, Lofton opened the letter Maureen had sent him. "I need those papers signed," she wrote, "and your doctor called. He wants to talk to you."

He's calling to get me in there, to take the X rays, but there's nothing wrong with me. The doctor knows it; I know it. It was just a game, an excuse to get out of town. He thought back to what he had told Maureen, that first day they'd met, when she had asked him what he wanted in Colorado. "A clean shot," he had said—a ridiculous phrase, he thought now, and suddenly he remembered himself standing at home plate, back in his college days. It had been the last day of the season, his team was out of the pennant race, playing a Connecticut team that won the championship year after year. That season the Connecticut team had needed a victory to clinch the division title again. In the last inning Lofton had held his bat cocked as the pitcher reared back; then he had watched the ball come in, seeing it more clearly than he had seen any ball that season. He swung and knocked a clean hit between first and second. His team had won. Though the win had done his team no good in the standings, it had felt good to be the spoiler, to knock the perennial winner out of contention, at least for a while.

Tony Liuzza lived in a renovated house in an older section of Northampton behind Smith College. The house was painted a flawless beige, all except the elaborate cupolas, which were stained a darker brown, the color of wood.

Liuzza himself came to the door. He had light brown hair, just starting to gray, and hazel eyes. He seemed more relaxed

than he had that day at the press box when Lofton had first
met him. His smile carried only a trace of that painful awkwardness it had had at the park, and the awkwardness, quick
and boyish, made you want to like Liuzza. He seemed open,
honest, maybe even a bit naïve. As they shook hands, Lofton
looked for the other Liuzza beneath the surface, for the moment when the smile hurt and the man, however briefly, let
himself show. The moment did not come.

The office Liuzza led him into was lined with books. Law
and politics, even some literature. Liuzza's law degree hung
on the wall, alongside a framed letter from Richard Sarafis,
the liberal Democrat whose gubernatorial campaign Liuzza
had recently joined. Liuzza collected photos of himself. In one
he was standing with some Boston politicians; in another he
posed with a woman and two children; still another showed
him at MacKenzie Field with Brunner. Lofton's attention was
drawn to a wall near the desk. He noticed a family portrait of
some kind. Amanti was in it. There were lots of folks in the
shot—an older couple, Tony Liuzza, a woman in a floral print
dress—but Amanti stood out from the others. She stood next
to an older woman whom Lofton guessed to be her mother.
The picture was three, maybe four years old, judging from the
style of Amanti's hair, her clothes, and the careless way she
stood. A young couple was at the edge of the photograph.
When Lofton glanced up, he saw that Liuzza had been studying him, watching him as he looked at the picture.

"Jack Brunner took that photo one weekend, when we were
all out at my father's house."

"Who's this?" Lofton asked, pointing at the young couple.

"That's David Kelley, the state senator from Holyoke. He
and I used to work together. At a small law firm back after I
first graduated."

Although Lofton doubted he would have recognized Kelley
on his own, he could see it now; this was the same man whose
picture he had run across during his research in the library.
Lofton looked at Amanti again, then at the woman in the
floral print dress on Kelley's other side. The woman wore a
beleaguered expression.

"This his wife?"

"Yes." Liuzza spoke emphatically, as if pleased Lofton had
deduced the relationship. "Her father is Jim Harrison."

Lofton nodded. Of course he'd heard of Harrison. Harrison was a powerful man. U.S. senator for decades. Lieutenant governor a long time back. Served on all kinds of presidential commissions. So Kelley had married well.

"I won't beat around with it, Frank." Liuzza said Lofton's first name tentatively, studying Lofton's face, as if to see if it was all right to establish that intimacy. "I have a proposition to make, something I've been meaning to talk to you about. But first . . . I'll just say what I have to say."

Lofton opened his notebook.

"No." Liuzza frowned. "This is off the record. Can you go with that?"

"What is it that you want?"

Liuzza frowned, looking thoughtful, but there was no sign of anything else, any hidden intention.

"You've been seeing Gina Amanti, my cousin?"

"What are you getting at?"

Liuzza shook his head. "No. I'm not trying to interfere. I'd been meaning to talk to you anyway. About the political campaign . . . What business do you have with Gina? Something to do with the newspaper?" Liuzza controlled the tone of his question well, as if he were simply curious.

"How do you know I've been seeing her?"

"The ballpark's a small place, word gets around. . . . But I wouldn't worry about it," Liuzza went on. "People always talk, and it's natural, though I have to admit I get concerned at times."

There was a long silence now. Liuzza studied the top of the desk. Lofton looked at a picture of Liuzza's family. A very ordinary picture. The wife was good-looking but not beautiful. One of the children had his father's smile.

"My concern is for Gina—that you know how delicate the situation is, how delicate she is. I'm her cousin, but I'm closer than just that. Her brother died when she was young. Then, not too long after, her father died. My parents took her mother in, and they tried to help Gina get through school. Gina's like a sister to me. Though we don't always get along, I have a lot of loyalty to her."

Liuzza's eyes were clear; they even had a certain sparkle. He was a different person here in his own office, away from Brunner and the ballpark. Lofton thought how good he would be in the education post he wanted. People would believe Liuzza, they would trust him, and he would do anything, Lofton thought, to get what the position demanded. The only thing he had to do was learn to control his smile, the sudden look of pain. With practice he could probably learn to use it to his advantage.

"Anyway, I realize that you're a reporter and that you have a job to do, but Gina's had some unhealthy things happen to her, and—"

"I'm not writing a story about Gina. If that's what you're worried about. She's not quite headline news."

"No, no."

"I'm not fucking her either. If that's what you're worried about."

Liuzza retained his composure. There was no trace of the smile, nothing. His eyes were the same merry blanks.

"All right," Liuzza said. His tone implied, however, that it was not all right, but that he had other things to say, and those things, once said, would set matters straight. "That's between you two, and it's beside the point. Not at all why I contacted you. As I said, I've been meaning to talk to you for quite some time, before any of this came up. I called the people down at the *Dispatch*—the papers know me, as you can guess—and I asked around. I need somebody to help us with some political writing."

Lofton still did not understand.

"An editor there, Kirpatzke, he suggested you."

"Me?" said Lofton. "I'm crime, sports, only sometimes politics. I don't know what's going on locally."

"Sometimes that's even better. Gives a new perspective. Besides, Kirpatzke said you had experience with this kind of thing, back in California. That you were a press secretary. What do you think?"

Lofton thought it was hilarious, though it was not the kind of hilarious that made you feel like laughing. It gave him the same feeling he'd had as a teenager looking into one of those fun house mirrors and remembering how a few years before, when he'd been even younger, just a snot-nose kid with a dead mother, those mirrors had made him laugh; only looking into the mirrors again, when he was a grown-up kid, almost a man, he'd found the reflection wasn't quite so funny anymore.

It was the same way now. Here he was in Holyoke, tracing a
story that someone didn't want him to trace, just as he had
done in California. Here again was the man-behind-the-desk
with the promise of money and a better job, maybe even a
dog's share of power. Only now, the second time around, he
felt no excitement, as if it weren't just the mirror that was
warped and cheap.

"What do I have to do?"

"Write a few speeches, focused to the local interests, that's
all."

"What issues?"

"We don't need anything yet, not for a few weeks. Meantime, we'll give you a retainer and be in touch."

Liuzza handed him a check. A thousand dollars. In a way,
he was insulted; it really wasn't that much money, a mere spit
in the ocean of the Liuzza family wealth.

"Lot more than I'd make for a story."

"I don't want you working on any stories for a while. This
is more important," said Liuzza. "This is the future of Massachusetts."

"Wouldn't Jack Brunner disagree? From what I understand, he's not on the same side as you and Kelley, at least not
this time. Doesn't he think his future is with the other candidate?"

"I've been working on Jack. I think he's going to come
around to our side."

Lofton glanced again at the picture of Amanti. He listened
vaguely while Liuzza bantered about the good things that
were going to happen to the state when Richard Sarafis got
back into office. Liuzza explained that Brunner and himself
and Kelley had known each other for a while, and though
Jack disagreed sometimes on policy, he basically shared their
sensibility. Brunner would come around soon, Liuzza was
sure. Out in the hall, when Lofton turned to shake Liuzza's
hand, he saw that Liuzza's hair, somehow, had gotten mussed
during their conversation. The man's voice shifted, becoming
higher, slightly out of control.

"You know, you're right, though; there are some nasty rumors going around the ballpark. Somebody even said you
were working on a story to embarrass the team."

"That's ridiculous," Lofton said. "I love baseball."

"I know, I know. Kirpatzke said you're good as gold."

Lofton looked hard at Liuzza's face, trying to catch the mask when it dropped. No mask. The man's eyes were honest as corn on the way to market. There was only the smile, the thin red line across the face, to betray him.

On the way back to Holyoke Lofton drummed the conversation around in his head. Last night Amanti had tried to beg him off the story. And now Liuzza had given him this check. One thing seemed clear: He'd been given the money to drop what he'd been working on. His first thought was that Brunner had somehow found out he was on to the fires. Brunner got Liuzza to try to buy me off, Lofton thought, but then he wasn't so sure. It didn't quite fit. The two men weren't exactly cozy these days. He remembered the picture of Kelley on Liuzza's wall, the strange voice on Amanti's telephone, the trouble he'd had getting through to the senator's office in Boston. Lofton felt one of those chills people talk about, the kind you get when some truth is suddenly revealed, only you don't know quite what it is, and you feel the iceman's fingers dancing on your spine. Then the feeling was gone, and he could not figure what he had missed.

That night there were more sirens. The fire trucks drove down Lofton's street; their wailing and crying woke him up. No sooner had one truck turned the corner—its siren's echo fading, whipping, and whirling through some distant alley—than yet another truck left the station. It had to be a big fire this time, but Lofton did not get up. He did not even remember the sirens until the next morning when he was walking by the ballpark, near a senior citizens' home. A cloud of white smoke rose steadily into the air at the end of the block. A single fire truck stood parked in front of a large lot where a building had been burned. Not much stood, not even the shell, of what had been an empty apartment building. Though the fire seemed under control, two lines of fire fighters remained, dousing the wreckage with water from their big hoses. The water curled into steam when it hit the brick. Across the way a group of old men and women stood in front of their building and watched. Their lobby windows had been blown out by the heat explosion. The paint on the cars out front was blistered.

"You from the paper?" called an old man with a grotesque, mottled face that appeared to have been scarred from birth. The man leered up at Lofton. "I found the fire. I was the first one. Somebody set it, three places. I saw the flames. By the time I called the fire department it was too late."

"Anybody die?" Lofton asked.

The old man's eyes lit up. "Maybe so. Usually there's somebody squatting in these buildings. They move out when it catches fire, then come back with their mattresses when it cools down. But nobody'll move back into this one."

The old man did not want to let Lofton go. At one point he even grabbed on to his elbow; his fingers were bony; his grip was fierce and determined.

"Let me go," Lofton shouted, suddenly hysterical. The old man looked hurt. Lofton was embarrassed. To satisfy the old man, he wrote down his name as if it would be in the paper.

Later that day Lofton mentioned the fire to Kirpatzke at the *Dispatch*.

"Got it covered," said the editor. "You work on your own business."

6

The heat wave broke. The wind blew in from the north, the temperature dropped, and clouds gathered over the hills. At MacKenzie Field the talk in the press box revolved around the weather, and around Sparks. Coach Barker, after watching Sparks warm up, had yanked him out of the starting rotation. Golden came to the box to tell Tenace to change his scorecard.

"What's the story?" asked Rhiner.

"No story," said Golden. He did not look at the reporter, or at Lofton, only at Tenace. "Barker just wants to try Hammer as a starter."

Golden left as soon as he had given Tenace Hammer's stats. Lofton watched him amble down the right field line. He couldn't help liking Golden; at least he was intrigued by the man. He had mixed feelings about writing a story that would drag him lower. Given Amanti's sudden reluctance, he had mixed feelings about writing the story at all. For a moment he felt the same lethargy he'd felt in California during those weeks between the time he'd found out about Hansen and the time he'd quit his job; he felt the inability to do anything that made any sense, the itch to leave.

"That's the trouble with this team," Rhiner complained.

"Nobody tells you anything. Act like everything's a goddamn secret."

"No secret," said Tenace. "He's been drinking."

"Sparks?"

"Nah, Golden. You could smell it all over him. Who knows what Sparks has been doing."

Rhiner scowled. "I didn't smell anything."

Lofton watched Golden cross the field. The general manager had his head bowed, as if deep in thought or brooding. He did not walk as if he were drunk.

"Sparks had himself a bad case of red eye this morning, too. Doesn't look like he's been sleeping much. He's speeding, you ask me."

"You think everyone's on drugs."

"They all are," said Tenace. "Don't you read the papers?"

"Haven't you ever heard of high-strung? That's what Sparks is. High-strung." Rhiner lowered his voice, sighing. "Almost took my head off when I asked him how his arm's been feeling."

"Either way, he's losing out, and he knows it." Tenace nodded with satisfaction. "The Blues'll never take him up now."

"It's just temporary. His arm needs rest."

"Should've rested him months ago," said Tenace.

Lofton stood up. Golden was headed down the right field line. He decided to catch up to him, even though the idea frightened him a little. It might be risky to broach the subject of the arsons directly.

"Talk about high-strung," said Tenace, "look at this bastard here."

Rhiner agreed. "Yeah, you look real tired."

"Don't worry, he always looks like that. Been out cavorting. Leading the good life, huh?"

"The perfect life," Lofton said, and headed out after Golden.

He caught up with Golden in the ballpark men's room, a small brick outbuilding beyond the first base bleachers. Golden stood over the trough, pissing. He did not look up when Lofton walked in.

Lofton washed his hands in the sink and looked at himself in the mirror. He did look tired. His eyes were red, a little crusted, and his cheeks gaunt. He threw water on his face and called over to Golden.

"So no Sparks, huh?" Lofton heard his own voice quaver.

Golden looked over at him dimly, as if peering out of the darkness, up from the bottom of some deep well.

"No. No Sparks. He's been working his arm too hard; we want to get him into a more normal rotation." Golden came to the basin next to Lofton. The two men regarded each other in the mirror. Golden nodded. Lofton thought of Golden's crippled wife and the man's shattered career. He caught a glimpse of Golden's profile and saw there was softness to the man's face, as if he were a compassionate person, but when Lofton glanced back up into the mirror and saw the man's full face reflected back to him, he noticed Golden's mouth was twisted into a grimace—as if reacting to a joke more cruel than funny.

"How long you been in Holyoke?" Lofton asked.

"A few years." Golden combed his hair and wet his face, then dried himself with a towel from the dispenser. Lofton did the same. The rough brown paper felt good against his skin, and the feel of the towel made him think again of Golden's crippled wife. Did Golden wash her face?

"Have there always been so many fires in this town?" Lofton asked. His approach wasn't exactly subtle, he realized.

Golden ran the towel over his face again; the towel hid his expression, for an instant, and muffled his voice. "That's more up your alley, I think. Don't newspapers keep track of those things?" Golden chucked the paper towel in the garbage.

"I hear it's arson."

Golden stood a few feet behind Lofton, off to the side. Lofton studied Golden's face in the mirror, and Golden studied Lofton's.

"Don't believe everything you hear," Golden said. His face was passive, cold. When Lofton turned to look at the man directly, Golden had turned away. All he saw was the back of Golden's head as he pushed out the door.

Lofton studied himself in the mirror. He was losing hair—*have been for years*—and when he stepped back to get a longer look, he thought he might be losing weight, too. *I still don't know about Golden.* He stuck his fist under his belt. The pants seemed looser at the waist than they had once been—*I haven't*

been eating, the heat—and then he cursed himself. He was
fine; his health, perfect. He remembered a story he had heard,
about a pitcher who woke up in the middle of the night, always worried about his arm, swinging it in the air above him
to make sure it was all right, no muscles torn, no ruined
career. Until one night, waking in a strange bed on the road,
he swung his hand into the wall and broke his wrist.

Outside, he saw Golden leaning over the fence, half watching the game, half staring at the ground. The kid with the
Redwings' cap twisted backward on his head stood calmly by
Golden's side. The kid had taken to following Golden lately
and seemed happy just to be near the former major leaguer.
Lofton knew he should ride Golden harder on his arson routine, but he decided not now. He would do it when the kid
wasn't around.

Standing in the first base bleachers, Lofton looked across
the field at Sparks. Sparks stood in the dugout at the end of
the bench, holding his cap in his hand. He didn't have his arm
in the ice as he usually did. He was pacing nervously. He
would sit down, then stand up again a second later, clutch at
the dugout screen, and scan the stands near Lofton—where
Brunner and Amanti would be sitting if they were here. When
the sides changed, Sparks left the dugout, paced down the
line, and stood watching Hammer, the new pitcher, throw.
Then he paced back again, all the while holding the sore muscles above his elbow and surveying the crowd.

Sparks's anxiety, Lofton thought, might not have anything
to do with Brunner, or Amanti, or Gutierrez, or any of that
business. There might be a more innocent explanation. The
team was doing well without him. Hammer lacked grace, but
he got the ball over. A lanky young man, with a shock of
curly black hair that stuck out wildly from beneath his cap, he
held the Lynn Sailors down another inning. The fans applauded.

Sparks stood on the sidelines, watching Holyoke break it
open, a long rally loading the bases once, then again, after
Elvin Banks had cleaned them with a triple. The inning went
on, the temperature dropped, and the breeze stiffened. The
night was surprisingly cool after the long heat, a little too cool
to be pleasant. Lofton went back to the press box, where the

lywood at least cut the wind. He could catch up with Sparks after the game.

A couple of reporters, men who worked the city beat for the Springfield paper, had come by to catch the game. A hawker was taking their orders, then barking them through the screen to a boy who hurried off to the concession. The reporters grumbled about the sudden switch in the weather. Dead heat all day, now too cold for a beer. The hawker stuck around, smirking, watching the press.

The reporters had just returned from a mayoral press conference on the downtown renovation plans. They were full of nervous energy, and full of names, exchanging information like kids trading baseball cards, or like sportswriters trading statistics.

"Mayor Rafferty knew this was going to happen months ago. Don't know why he's making such a deal out of it now," said the smaller of the two men. He also appeared to be the older.

"Months ago? They knew from the goddamn fucking beginning. Since when's that Boston gang going to let loose money for Holyoke. Some joke," said the younger one. He spoke loudly and looked around at the others in the box. He was not so disheveled as his friend; his clothes were cleaner, in better taste, not so worn.

The older reporter spat through the wire and lit himself a cigarette. "Same thing that always happens," he said. "State budget comes out of committee, kills the Holyoke project, gives more money to Boston. The mayor calls a press conference to cry about it."

"Not so many votes out this way. Boston won't care how hard Mayor Rafferty cries," said the younger one.

His friend ignored him. He turned to Lofton. "Didn't the guy who owns this team buy an old mill down by the canal?"

"That's what I heard."

"Small fucking world."

"Not small, incestuous," said the younger man. "But Bruner's getting the dick on this one. No fed money to renovate his building now. Wonder what he's going to do with the turkey?"

"Burn it," said the hawker—as if he had been waiting to get out this one remark—and there was laughter in the box.

After a while the boy came with food for the press crew, the
hot dogs and pizza and ice cream that passed for a late lunch
The older reporter asked the hawker to go back and get him a
beer.

"Ain't allowed to get you guys a beer. A Coke, okay, but
you have to pay for beer."

"Brunner's a cheap bastard," said the reporter.

"He just doesn't want you guys getting drunk up here and
screwing up your job," said Tenace, then went back to his
food, eating greedily, happily, not in the least bit self-conscious.

"No. Brunner's cheap," said the hawker.

"He's going to be a lot cheaper soon, considering the way
he's going to lose out on that mill. Can't figure out why he
bought that mill anyway. Supposed to make it into lots of
little shops, some wonderful, charming little thing. But the
Hillside Mall is his baby, too, and I know he gets a cut out
there. What's the point of competing with yourself?"

Lofton thought about it. Jack Brunner's big piece of prop
erty, American Paper, was going to be worth a lot less now
Without the guarantee of federal renovation money, the insur
ance companies would devalue the property. That meant the
insurance payoff, if the building happened to burn, would be a
fraction of what it might have been before. He wondered what
Brunner was going to do now. He guessed Brunner was won
dering the same thing.

The game went slowly; it was only the bottom of the sev
enth. Holyoke loaded the bases again. The Sailors' pitcher, a
tall redheaded boy, was wild as a March wind. Hammer
Holyoke's pitcher, stood at the plate, ready to bat.

"This Hammer kid shows some promise," said Rhiner, who
said little while the others talked politics, just eyed them occa
sionally, suspiciously. He was not as surly as he had been the
last time Lofton had seen him, but he was still guarded, say
ing little, as if afraid he might let another news story slip out
between his lips and then be unable to recover it.

The redhead ran the count to three balls and no strikes
One more bad pitch would walk in a run. An embarrassment
for one pitcher to walk another. The Lynn catcher went to the
mound. The Sailors' manager stayed on the bench, letting his
catcher handle the youngster.

The redhead gave the next pitch his all, a hard strike at the fat heart of the plate. Hammer got hold of it, knocked the ball high to the left field fence. The Sailors' outfielder backed up a few steps, then kept backing, all the way to the wall. The ball arced away, a high fly that started to come down, then, caught in the wind, kept on going, over the fence and into the street. Hammer had iced it for himself, made his first start in Holyoke something to remember. Rhiner stood on his feet and screamed. The Redwings came out to congratulate the newcomer as he touched home.

"Imagine that," said the older reporter.

"He must feel good," said the younger one.

"Yeah, I betcha Sparks feels pretty good, too," said Tenace. "Punk from nowhere pitches a great game, then knocks himself a homer. I'm sure it makes Sparks feel like a prince."

After the game Lofton looked for Sparks. He couldn't find him. The pitcher was not out congratulating Hammer. He was not in the bullpen. He was not in the clubhouse. Lofton asked the old gatekeeper if he had seen which way Sparks had gone.

"No," the man said. "And it wouldn't be my business if I had."

He could be one of two places, Lofton thought, getting drunk or finding someone to console him. Amanti had said that Sparks had a girlfriend, one of the ballpark girls. Lofton figured he could find them if he wanted, but the whole idea of tracking Sparks and the girl down, or rooting Sparks out of some local bar, gave him a cold, sinking feeling in the stomach. Why do I bother? he thought. Liuzza's check, uncashed, was still in his pocket. He went back to the hotel, to his car, and drove over the Notch to Amherst.

The neighborhood was quiet, the houses dark. Coming up the walkway, Lofton thought he saw a light shining in Amanti's apartment. Maybe only a reflection; it was hard to tell. He pressed his nose against the kitchen window. The light came from farther back inside the apartment, from the bedroom.

He knocked and waited. The beam of light inside trembled, disappeared, then grew wider, as if coming from behind a door that somebody had pulled shut and then let drift open again. He knocked a little harder. Still Amanti did not come.

He sucked in his breath. The night was chilly, like the nights in California. He went to the window and studied the slant of light coming from the rear of the apartment. He saw the light blackened by a shadow, and he stepped back to the door. He stood under the porch light, wondering if Amanti stood on the other side, looking at him through the fisheye. When the door still did not open, he imagined Brunner on the other side, a scene like in the old movies: Brunner firing a gun through the door; Lofton grabbing his stomach, twisting, falling, dying in the yellow light. He reached to knock again. Just as he did so, the door opened. Amanti peered at him through the darkness. She wore a cotton robe. She held the collar closed with one hand; the other hand held the robe closed at her waist.

"Come in." She sounded sleepy. He followed her back to her bedroom. The thin white robe wrinkled against her back, shining a little in the darkness.

She said nothing. He could not read her silence. A woman's silence always held him captive. Maureen, though, never had that power over him; she rushed in to fill a silence with her trilling, musical happiness. He had never thought of her voice that way before, or at least not for a while.

"I talked to your cousin today."

"I thought we were going to drop this."

"He's a sharp guy. No wonder your mother liked him."

Amanti laughed, a sound that seemed to rise from somewhere deep in her throat and then was cut off immediately, so it sounded shrill.

"Your cousin expressed a lot of concern for you. He said you were delicate. And then, later, he offered me a job as a speech writer. He gave me money. A retainer."

"Oh." Her voice was noncommittal, polite, the same way she had been on the phone that one time, pretending that Lofton had called about the air-conditioning. Lofton remembered the man's voice, harsh and sleepy, that had originally answered the phone that day.

"Why did Tony Liuzza give me that money? What do you think he was after?"

Amanti shrugged. Lofton grabbed her hand. Her gown opened at the collar, and he could see the pale white of her breasts.

"Was he bribing me? Trying to get me off this story, away from you? And you, how come you're backing off?" Lofton thought of the group picture on Liuzza's wall. It wasn't simply familial love that had prompted the young lawyer to hang that particular picture. Every photograph, except that of Liuzza's wife and daughters, had some politician in it. That group shot was no exception.

"You didn't tell me you knew Senator Kelley."

Amanti's face became needle-sharp, panicky, an expression that was replaced instantly by the same wide-cheeked innocence he had seen the other day outside the park. Lofton felt the cold fingers on his spine again, but this time the associations clicked. The gruff voice on Amanti's telephone. The picture of Kelley and the china-faced woman on Liuzza's wall. Amanti's long, unhappy story about the man who would not leave his wife.

"Kelley . . ." he said, then just let it hang.

"What did my cousin tell you?"

He could see Amanti was upset, starting to cry, though there seemed to be something studied about her tears, something theatrical, as if she didn't quite believe the tears herself. He sat down next to her on the bed. She let the gown stay open. This whole business was more tangled than he'd expected. He wondered again if he should abandon this situation, forget his big story, forget Holyoke. Despite himself, he felt an enormous sympathy for Amanti.

He took her chin in his hand, ran his fingers over her lightly pocked skin, touching the blemish. She reached up, to take his fingers away, he thought, but instead, she gripped his hand and held it tight. He waited for her to say something, but she didn't. She seemed calm now, almost indifferent. He moved, thinking he meant to pull himself up off the bed, to ask her some questions and get the story straight, but instead, he found his hand touching her waist. Her eyes opened wider at his touch, surprised, maybe, or pretending surprise.

"Kelley . . ." he said again, trying to pursue the business, but she moved deliberately toward him. Her lips were warm, but the depths of her mouth, her tongue were cool, as if she had been drinking something cold, sucking on ice. Her robe, too, was cool, damp with perspiration. They slid back together onto the white sheets, their legs intertwining. Her fin-

gertips reached in to pull out his shirttails. Then he felt her
stomach against his, and Amanti's breathing, hot inside his
ear, was like the noise of the ocean inside an old shell, only
crazier, and he saw the jungle all around him, exotic red
plants, all blooming wildly inside his chest, Amanti's elaborate, teasing tongue, her fingers flat and tense against his skin,
her eyes half-open. He raised his head. As he did so, the
phone at the top of the bed rang. It startled him, and he
pulled away. Amanti did not try to answer it. She lay on the
bed, holding her robe at the throat.

"That's him. I'm not answering the phone."

"Who?" Lofton asked.

"Kelley."

Lofton sat down on the edge of the bed. The room seemed
filled with a blue haze. The phone stopped ringing, and the
night was very quiet. For a while they sat listening, as if
maybe there were some great secret out in the darkness.

"How do you know it's Kelley? It could be Brunner,
maybe, or someone else."

"Kelley was supposed to call me the other night, but he
didn't. The phone's been ringing all day. I know it's him."

She sat up in the bed, her fingers still holding the collar of
her robe, waiting, it seemed, for him to ask another question.
But she lost her patience, just as she had that day when they
had been walking out on the street, and the words came out in
a gush, quick and rapid, telling him about her long affair with
Kelley, about Kelley and Brunner's rivalry, and finally about
Kelley's plan to use Brunner's arson scheme against him. This
time she told him the names; she told him just about everything. Lofton had to admit Kelley's plan made a certain sense.
Use Amanti as bait. Get the reporter interested. When the
reporter got close, and Brunner got nervous, then pull Amanti
off the hook. Replace her with cash. Let Liuzza string the
lure. That way Kelley's own hands stayed clean—no dirty fish
smell. He could walk up to Brunner and say: Listen, old
friend, I've heard some rumors, and if you'd like to go ahead
with your scheme, switch your money and influence over to
my candidate, then I can help get rid of this reporter; otherwise, your renovation money . . . well, we can throw that
fish to the dogs.

"Okay, but why me? Why does he think I'll go along?"

"He checked into your background. He found out something in California—"

Lofton held up his hand. He didn't need to hear the rest. He could see Kelley's idea as clearly as if he had a box seat inside the guy's brain. "And what's your payoff?" he asked Amanti. "What do you get?"

Amanti looked at the floor. She swung her foot back and forth, but the effect was not what it had been the day he talked to her at the Little Puerto Rico Café. It no longer made you wonder about the girl beneath the woman's surface but instead made you realize that the girl was long gone, that the only thing to remind you she had once existed was something about the way the woman swung her leg.

"Are you still in love with Kelley?"

The foot stopped swinging. When Amanti looked up at him, her eyes seemed to glimmer a little, moist in the darkness.

"Tell me, what are you going to do? Are you going to take the money and back off the story? Or are you going to write it?"

"That business, a few minutes ago, when we were wrestling on the bed, were you doing that for yourself, because you wanted to, or were you doing it for Kelley—a little sweetening to get me on your side, to make sure I don't nail both of you away?"

Amanti flared. "That didn't mean anything. It was just an action, movement, and don't let anybody tell you different. If there's one thing I've learned, that's it. You can move any which way you want, and it doesn't make any difference. You know that, don't you? Didn't they pay you pretty well just to walk out of that office in California? All you had to do was a little movement, right, just put one foot in front of the other."

"That's not the way it happened. Kelley got it wrong."

"Are you going to write the story?"

"Right now," Lofton said, "I don't have a story. There's no evidence that Brunner is burning anything. All we have is Gutierrez's word, and Gutierrez is dead. And even if we could resurrect him, all we'd get is a coke-smeared blur. When you get down to it, I'm surprised Kelley would rig together this elaborate business for blackmailing Brunner on just this small bit of evidence. There must be something else you have on Brunner. What is it? Tell me, and I'll write the story."

Lofton leaned against the bedroom wall, watching her, waiting to see what she would say. She had some more information, he could tell, but she was holding it back because if she told him, it would give Lofton the real evidence—and even Kelley didn't want things to go that far. Kelley wanted only to humiliate Brunner, to make him switch sides. Though Lofton was angry with Amanti, he could see her dilemma. The only way she could keep Kelley's interest, even now, was by betraying him, but she had to be careful it wasn't a big enough betrayal to ruin everything.

Amanti came up close to him. Her robe was gathered loosely, and the light in the room was faint. He could smell the warmth of her body, and at the same time he could feel a very slight, cooling breeze coming through the window. She stepped forward, pressed her body against his, and kissed him hard. She hooked her thumb into his pants pocket; the fingers of the same hand arched against his thigh, held stiff and tense as she'd held them on the tabletop that first day he'd met her. He touched her robe, feeling the cloth in his hand, then pulled her closer. For a while they tried the impossible stunt of fucking against the wall—at least it had always been impossible for him, the white robe open all the way, her mouth just out of reach, his hands on her breasts, her head tilted up, eyes away. He pulled her hard down to him, and they rolled over again. She was underneath him, her back against the carpet. She put her fingers on his shirt collar and kept them wrapped there tightly, pulling him closer, and for a second all the rest of the world was gone—the business with Brunner and Kelley and the arson—and she pulled him tighter yet, her fingers still touching his collar, his legs flat against hers, and when he lifted his head, he could see outside to the stars, and for a brief instant it was as if the two of them were outside under those stars, and he were lifting his head above the line of the high grass, gazing, searching, and the breeze were cool in his face. But then Amanti pulled him back, her fingers still clutching at the shirt, and he fell into her rhythm.

Sunday was Dazzy Vance Day. The white-haired Hall of Famer showed up at MacKenzie Field, wearing plaid golf pants, an alligator shirt, and an old Brooklyn Dodgers' cap. Dazzy Vance made a living traveling the minor league parks, talking about the old days and throwing a few pitches from the mound, tossing them to old-timers and Little Leaguers. Afterward he wandered through the stands behind an advance man who sold black-and-white glossies.

The reporters asked the old ballplayer questions. The same ones, Lofton guessed, Dazzy heard in every town. A gaggle of kids hung nearby, looking for a chance to get an autograph. Dick Golden had also joined the crowd around Dazzy. Golden's mood seemed to have darkened. He glared bullishly at the ground, turning his head from side to side, glowering at the press.

"Sure the old hitters were great," Dazzy Vance was saying, "but there are some good ones around now, too. When I was young, just starting out, people said the same: The great days, the great players, all those times are over. And it's the same thing now. When these players here are my age, God forbid, when they're dead, people will look back and say they were the great ones. But really, no one is great. It's the game that's great."

Lofton wondered. Was Dazzy sincere? Smart or dumb, ballplayers tended to be sincere.

"Even the Redwings, are they winners?" shouted one of the kids, his voice lilting.

"The Redwings?" Dazzy said, confused, as if he no longer remembered what town he was in, what field he was working. There was a pause; Dazzy raised his eyebrows; then there was strained laughter from the onlookers. It was a joke; of course Dazzy knew where he was. He grinned, the shy smile of a huckster caught off guard.

Soon the television crew arrived. They upstaged the print journalists, with their polished clothes and smooth voices, the cameramen calling people out of the crowd, kids mostly, positioning them in the background.

"Television pushing you shoddy guys around," Dazzy said to the newspaper people. "Same thing used to happen to me whenever Johnny McGraw's Giants crossed the river from New York."

Lofton backed away, scanning the stands. Amanti had told him she would be at this game with Brunner and her cousin.

Last night, in the darkened room, he had told her about his encounters with Lou Mendoza. Mendoza seemed to want publicity, the same sort of publicity the dead Latino leader had gotten, not because it would do him any good, really, but simply because he wanted it. She listened carefully, especially when Lofton described the rival gang leader, Angelo, the dead Latino whose picture Lofton had seen in an old paper. Dark, full lips. Wild black hair. Smashed nose. He'd told her how Angelo had been speaking on street corners, criticizing the police, using his following as a patrol force, rebuilding houses. He'd told her about the City Council meeting when the Latinos showed up in battle gear and Angelo said he knew who was setting the fires.

"The Latinos say Mendoza's the one whose been setting the fires. At least that's the word on the streets. Could he be the one Gutierrez was talking about? The one hooked up with Golden?"

Amanti had shaken her head. She didn't know. He still wondered if she had anything else on Brunner, something he could actually put in the story—some hard, substantial proof. Einstein, Lofton realized, must have been faced with the same dilemma. The reporter had figured things out more or less, but he had only the word of the street gang as proof; Amanti's stories, too, were hardly reliable, when you got down to it, just as entangled in personal conflict and rivalry as the accusations of the Latinos. There had been a moment last night, just as he left her apartment, when she'd seemed on the verge of revealing something more, but his intuition could have been wrong, nothing more than the romantic cast of light on her face or the feeling that you get at such moments, walking away from a woman's house into the dark alone, that there is something unexpressed, something under the surface of things which you have missed.

Lofton looked up at the stands again, then over at Dazzy Vance. For a moment he was envious of the old ballplayer. His was a simple scam, driving from park to park, the long, anonymous gray of the highway broken only every few days, then only for a few hours, while you gladhanded children and told stories you'd told so many times that it was as if the stories were things in themselves and had nothing to do with you. And then it was back into the cab of the truck, where you were no one at all, or practically no one—just a stack of pictures headed for the next motel room. Lofton was thinking of this, of the sweet emptiness of the road, when suddenly he felt his heart jump. Someone jostled him gently from behind. Then a hand touched his waist, his arm. Amanti.

"What are you doing here?" he said. Although he'd known she would be here, he hadn't expected her to approach him. Regardless of her motivation, it did not seem a good idea for them to be seen together.

"Have you seen this?" She held today's paper, the one with his story on Gutierrez.

No, he had not seen it. Though Lofton still clipped his stories for his files, he rarely read them until much later. Either way, he was not much interested now. Lofton noticed that today she did not look well. Her complexion had gone pale; her hair was mussed; her blouse loose and untucked. He guided her by the arm to the other side of the press box, away from the flurry of activity, out of the sight of the crowd in the bleachers. He pointed at the paper in her hand.

"What's with that? Did I write something I shouldn't have?"

"I'm not talking about that; I'm talking about this piece, here, on the front page."

Lofton took the paper. The story was the one he had heard from the Springfield reporters: how the state legislature had canceled Holyoke's renovation project. Lofton scanned the lead paragraph, a quick summary of things he already knew. "So?"

"Kelley's behind this," she said. "He's trying to put pressure on Brunner. That's why he wanted to get you involved, like I told you, and that's why he got the committee to vote against the Holyoke project. He'll get the committee to swing back if Brunner switches."

She pointed to a paragraph well inside the article, on an inside page. City officials were concerned, the article said, because—as the result of the state's decision—several large insurance companies planned to devaluate the property downtown. They had threatened to cancel all insurance contracts in the core area immediately. "If they cancel the contracts, Brunner can burn all he wants, but he won't collect anything. Don't you see what Kelley's doing? It's blackmail."

"All right, but this article doesn't prove anything. It doesn't prove Brunner is behind those fires. What about the big building, American Paper? It's almost too late for him to burn that, especially if the insurance companies are reassessing. And besides, Brunner didn't own any of the buildings that went down this summer. He wouldn't have gained anything by burning those."

"Yes, he would. And I can get you proof. I can get papers that tell you everything."

Lofton didn't know what to think. He had suspected she was holding something back. Now that she offered to give it to him, he wondered about her motivation. She was angry at Kelley, he knew that, or at least she seemed to be. But she could have talked to Kelley since last night; things could have changed. He glanced around the corner of the box. The only person looking this way was Tenace. He was talking to Golden, but the general manager was looking the other way. The scorer gave a friendly wave, and Lofton turned back to her.

"How will you get these papers?"

"Never mind. I'll take care of that."

"I'll go with you. It could be dangerous."

"No. It will be better if I'm alone." Amanti shook her head and looked wearily down at her shoes. "Come by my house, Wednesday. I'll have everything then. . . . Brunner and Liuzza are in the stands. They're going to be wondering where I am. I'd better get back."

"You should be careful," Lofton said. He thought of going with her, but she smiled so suddenly, so sadly and awkwardly that he was disarmed. He put his hand on her shoulder and urged her away. She reached up, touched a thin curl of hair at the back of his neck, then hurried back into the crowd. Kelley put her up to this, he thought; the man wants me involved, he wants more pressure on Brunner. That might be the way it was. Or it might be that Amanti was tired of Brunner and Kelley, that she was acting on her own. There was no way for Lofton to be sure. He could not see into the darkness; he could not read her thoughts. When he walked around the back side of the press box, he saw Tenace standing with Golden. They both were watching him now; then the general manager stalked off into the bleachers. Golden was on one of his downswings, or maybe he was worried, afraid of getting caught.

Sitting in the press box, Lofton flipped through the paper to his postmortem on Gutierrez. His editor, Kirpatzke, had come up with three photos to accent the piece: an action shot of Gutierrez pivoting at short; a shot of him in street clothes, standing in front of the clubhouse; and a third, final picture, this one showing his casket as it was wheeled onto the airplane at Bradley International. The effect was maudlin, but it would get the reaction Kirpatzke wanted. People would read it. They would ponder the random violence, wanting to draw the conclusion that Gutierrez had done something for this to happen to him. But the link wasn't quite there; there was no apparent cause and effect. They would ponder awhile longer.

"Reading your own work?"

Tenace stood grinning. Lofton was embarrassed. He closed the newspaper.

"You're getting to be pretty hot shit, huh?"

"Dead shortstops bring out the best in me."

"I guess you're getting the angle on this place pretty good. You going to make us all famous?"

"Sure, you'll be the star."

Tenace grimaced, then forced out a laugh. Lofton turned to the field. Holyoke was up, 5–0. The team had come around in the last few weeks. With the slip-sliding going on at the top of the division, the good clubs losing momentum, Holyoke, impossible as it seemed, had a long shot at the division crown.

"We should get together, have a few beers," said Tenace.

"Sure. Anytime."

Lofton did not take the offer too seriously. He thought instead about what Amanti had told him. He knew Brunner owned several square blocks downtown, including the old American Paper Company, once the second-largest mill in New England, now boarded up and closed. Brunner planned to renovate the building, to put in polished floors and cordon the rooms off into small boutiques. Such projects had met with success in large cities like San Francisco and Denver. But Holyoke was not a large city. And there was another reason the project didn't quite make sense. He remembered what the reporters had said the other day, that Brunner's construction company, Bruconn, owned a percentage of the Hillside Mall.

Why would Brunner create another shopping area to compete with himself? Maybe I should go down to American, Lofton thought, and take a look around.

"How about after the game?" Tenace persisted. "We could knock a few down then."

Lofton squinted. Before he could answer, the public-address man reannounced Dazzy Vance's presence. A few people hissed—a few always did, no matter what was announced —but most cheered.

"And next weekend," the PA man went on, his voice echoing across the field, "MacKenzie Field will host another distinguished visitor: Democratic candidate for governor, Richard Sarafis."

There were more hisses and boos now, and a good deal of laughter. The announcer went on. "After a rally at the Hillside Mall, Richard Sarafis will be on hand here to throw out the game ball and answer questions from local citizens."

"He should go to Amherst," said Tenace. "Go there and talk to the college kids about the bottle bill and nuclear power."

"What's he doing out at Hillside anyway?" said Lofton. "I thought Brunner supported Ed Wells, the incumbent. Why is he letting Sarafis have a rally on his property?" Even as he asked the question, Lofton thought of an answer: Kelley's pressure worked; Jack Brunner was making ready to switch sides in the Democratic race.

"Beats me. It's a free country. I don't like any of them." The scorer moved closer. "I was serious about those beers. Besides, I've got something you should hear, something important."

"Sure."

"No, I'm serious."

Lofton heard an unusual urgency in Tenace's voice. The man's lonely, he guessed. "All right, let's get together for a beer."

"Tonight?"

"No, I've got something else going."

Lofton thought of American Paper, the building in the darkness, outlined by the moon. He wanted to go there, to see the old mill. "Tomorrow night," Lofton said, "I'll meet you at

Barena's." Then Lofton hurried away; he did not want to talk
with Tenace, not now.

He paused at the top of the stands. Dazzy Vance wandered
through the crowd below. It was a warm day, the tempera-
tures rising again, though not so high as before. The sun felt
good; the crowd was larger than usual, and healthier-looking.
Parents from the suburbs had brought their children to see
the Hall of Famer. Even so, MacKenzie Field still seemed a
seedy place. Young couples sat in the sparse grass beyond the
bleachers, smoking pot and drinking beer. Long-haired young
men sat cross-legged and shirtless in the dirt; next to them
their wives or girlfriends—or old ladies, as the men called
them—sighed under the weight of the children who played in
the laps of their print skirts. Teenagers scuttled hard after foul
balls. A white boy fell on his face when a Puerto Rican
pushed him from behind.

A dozen rows below Lofton, Amanti sat between Brunner
and her cousin. Brunner touched her to call attention to some
action on the field, and she smiled, nodding and touching him
back.

No smoke poured from the tall stacks of the abandoned
paper mill; its dock was empty. On the other side of the street,
which dead-ended at the canal, National Paper was still going
despite the late hour. The night shift workers leaned against
cars, eating sandwiches and listening to rock 'n' roll. In one
car a man sat behind the wheel, his head tilted against a
headrest. From a distance Lofton thought he looked asleep.
Then he saw the red-orange glow of a cigarette raised to the
man's lips. Coming closer, he saw the man pass the cigarette
out the window to one friend, then another. They cupped and
hid the glow as he passed.

Not all the men were on break. While some rested, others
worked, wheeling barrels of fiber onto the docks, pausing to
catcall to the men who lazed against the cars. Lofton crossed
the street toward the darkness of American Paper. The road
had worn through in places; the asphalt, thin and peeling,
showed the old brick cobbles and trolley tracks beneath. A
high chain-link fence separated American's dock from the
street.

As he approached the corner, he saw the dark waters of the

canal. A street ran parallel to the canal, and a cruiser turned the corner: a Puerto Rican cop riding shotgun, an Anglo behind the wheel. They stared glassy-eyed at Lofton, as if they really did not see him—but he knew they must have—and then drove past the workers, up toward the river.

He walked down the street, the canal on one side, American Paper on the other. The same cyclone fence, barbed wire at the top, surrounded the building. Up ahead, between the building and the fence, lay a large lot littered with broken concrete and scraps of wood. Several bulldozers and Caterpillars were parked in the lot, and a chained gate spanned the driveway. The space between the bottom of the gate and the asphalt seemed almost big enough for a man to crawl through.

Yellow signs with black letters hung on the gate. NO TRESPASSING. BEWARE OF DOGS. GUARDS ON DUTY. The signs were a bluff. Lofton had seen no evidence of dogs, no guards. Maybe Pinkertons patrolled the place, driving by a few times a night, shining their high beams on the buildings. But the old mill seemed too desolate to be worth much protection. Still, he wished he had brought something with him other than the small penlight and his pocket camera, both of which he carried in his shirt pocket. Maybe a lead pipe, something he could use on the dogs if there happened to be any.

According to what he had read in the library, American Paper had bailed out because the State Building Official had told the owners to get the building into shape. The old support system had rotted. The place was unsafe. But rather than fix it up and maintain a break-even operation simply to support the workers, American Paper had abandoned the building. Brunner had picked it up cheap. How much money he needed to bring it up to code was another matter. Lofton wanted to see what shape the building was really in and how much work Brunner had really done.

He glanced down the street. Nobody. He got flat on his stomach and crawled under the gate. The gravel crushed against his face. The bar at the bottom of the fence scraped on his tailbone. "Fat-ass," he whispered to himself, and scrambled through. He hurried to the building. He felt safe in its dark shadow, near the heavy equipment, the Cats and the dozers. Now he had to find a way inside.

The logical way, of course, was through one of the doors. He tried the sliding dock porticoes, where the huge sheets of paper, bundled and stacked, had once been loaded onto trucks. He tried the heavy steel office doors. These, as he expected, were drawn shut and locked. A bank of windows ran in a low line around the building. Most were boarded over; the others were made of thick, fogged glass that let in light but through which he could not see. The panes were small, bordered by steel bars. To squeeze in, he would have to smash out the panes, then somehow pry the bars away. In the corner of each window someone had placed a small decal: "Protected by AACO." American Alarm Company. Dummies, he guessed, distributed by the police force to help stop burglaries.

Checking the boarded windows one by one, he looked for a board that had not been nailed quite right, one he could pry loose with his hands or with a two-by-four from the parking lot debris. He chose a window a different size from the others, thinking it might not have the same small panes behind the boards. He pulled and twisted—there was a sticker here, too, pasted on the wood—then pried the board free from the crumbling brick. Behind the boards, he saw glass, clear stuff, not like the fogged panes. The steel bars were not there either.

Suddenly a car rumbled by on the road between the building and the canal. Lofton jumped into the shadow of a dozer. The car did not stop. Probably just teenagers out driving, he thought, but he stayed hidden until it was well past. For a second, crouching there idly, he contemplated starting the dozer. He knew how to do it. He and his brother, Joe, when they were kids in California, used to sneak out to the sites and climb on the machinery. Once, they'd gotten a dozer started, driven it through the half-finished streets of a new subdivision, and abandoned it in a ditch. Another time, they'd made a dummy out of newspaper and old clothes, then hurled it into the street, waiting for a passing car to stop, for someone to investigate the body. *A deaf policeman heard the noise and came to kill the two dead boys.* He had not thought of the old childhood rhyme—they used to recite it together, laughing secretly in their bedroom, after being punished—nor had he thought of their childhood adventures, not in years.

Lofton looked inside the dozer's cab. There, over the ignition, was another yellow sticker. Surely the stickers were a sham. He imagined one of Brunner's crew lumbering through the yard, sticking the things everywhere, avoiding the heavy work.

He went back and shone his light around the edges of the window, looking for the tiny wires of an alarm system. He looked at the top of the windowsill for the clips that sometimes held the wires together, triggering the alarm once the connection had broken. He saw neither wires nor clips. Possibly the place was wired some other way, or—even less likely —there was a hidden camera, knee-high, that hit an alarm when you walked across its eye. But he could see no evidence of that, or of any alarm system.

Lofton picked up a brick and smashed the window. He expected the glass to sparkle, to catch the blue light as it broke. Instead, the brick went through with a clean snap, and there was only a clearer, darker hole where the window had broken. He picked the glass from the frame, smashed out the jagged edges, and climbed inside.

The mill was all but empty. All the factory equipment was gone. The place still smelled like pulp and resin, wood and chemicals. Renovations had not begun.

He examined the support posts. The wood had rotted badly. He tore small, wet pieces from the posts with his fingers. He took his camera and photographed debris that had been pushed up around the supports in places, almost like kindling stacked under a fire. It might be coincidence; it might just be the natural thing to do with the junk before clearing it out, to push it into piles. Then he walked around the warehouse and took pictures of everything, all the floor space. There was nothing valuable here, except maybe the building itself, and the more he looked at it, the more of a wreck it seemed to be, hardly worth restoring. If I owned it, Lofton thought as he climbed to the second floor, I would burn it, too. In the meantime, though, I would have it patrolled, at least often enough to make it look as if I were protecting my property.

As soon as he reached the second floor, he saw light coming from outside. He went to the window. A Pinkerton car, motor running, was parked outside the gate. Lofton was sorry he had stayed so long. But if he had left a moment earlier, he would have been out in the lot just now, and the Pinkerton would have caught him. He watched the private cop get out and unlock the gate.

His first impulse was to hide somewhere in the building. *Fuck no, they'll shoot me.* So he hurried downstairs, counting on the fact that the Pinkerton, afraid for himself, would not enter the building until the real cops came. Besides, there was no way for him to know exactly when the window had been broken. It could have been hours ago; the intruder could have come and gone.

He heard the Pinkerton's car churning gravel out in the lot. He hurried around the debris on the cement floors, past the rotting timbers. He wanted to find a way out on the side of the building opposite the Pinkerton. He tried one door, then another, but they were locked as well. He ran through the building. He found himself in a large room with several steel porticoes and doors to the outside. He went to a window but could not see out. The glass had been painted black. He pushed against a door, expecting it to be locked, but it swung noisily open.

He found himself on American's dock, looking across at National Paper, where some of the workers still lounged by their cars. Several sat on the National dock, smoking cigarettes. One man pointed at him, and the others looked. None of them spoke.

Lofton looked up at the high fence. Barbed wire lined the top slanting away at an angle toward the street, designed to make it impossible for someone climbing in from the outside. It would not be much easier from his direction. Either way, he had no choice. He did not want to wait around for the cruisers, sweeping the fence with floodlights. He put his camera in his back pocket and started up. Meanwhile, the workers watched from across the way.

When Lofton reached the top, he got crossed up. He tried to throw one leg over the three stands of wire, thinking—insofar as it was possible for him to think—that he could sit sidesaddle, never mind the barbs, then throw his other leg over, hang from the wire by his hands, and, finally, drop. It did not work that way. His right leg slipped between the wires before he could turn around. *If my brother could see me now.* He struggled to get his left leg between the same two wires.

Maureen's probably sitting in his kitchen. The barbs tore at hi
palms and at his legs, digging into his thigh as he tried to eas
himself down. His back scraped against the fence. He lost hi
grip. A barb ripped up his pants leg, catching his pants nea
the groin. He hung in midair for an impossible second—al
the time conscious of the millworkers across the way, starin
silently up at him—and then he hit the ground.

He got up quickly. His hip hurt where he'd landed. Had h
heard the camera break? He hurried away, touching himsel
as he limped, feeling his balls first. The millworkers stil
watched; he could feel their gaze on his back as he disap
peared into the darkness. Then he touched his face, his legs
his arms. His fingers came away bloody.

On the other side of the canal Lofton felt safe. He coul
still see the lights at National. He could see into the lot a
American Paper where the Pinkerton had been. The Pinker
ton's car was gone. No bright glare. No humming radios. N
cops from downtown. He thought it unlikely the cops ha
come and gone. They would make a production out of it
walking around the building, flashing lights all over, talkin
back and forth on their intercoms. He peered into the dark
ness across the canal, but he still could not see the Pinkerton'
car. It wasn't there. Maybe the rent-a-cop had not seen th
broken window. Maybe he had seen it and not cared. Mayb
he had just been lazy. Or maybe, Lofton thought, touchin
the gash in his palm, I'm just luckier than I think.

The next morning he went to call the paper. The story o
Gutierrez's funeral had run its course, and he wanted a nev
assignment. He thought he would feel out the *Dispatch* on th
questions of the arson, to see if the paper might want him t
pick up where Einstein had left off. McCullough seemed to b
pushing him in that direction anyway, and it might be time t
bring the story out of the closet. He got Kirpatzke on th
phone. Before he had a chance to say what was on his mind
Kirpatzke told him that Einstein was dead.

"They found his body a few weeks back," Kirpatzke said
"in a gutted building down on High Street. The old Taylo
Arms. The place had been torched. The coroner said Ein
stein's skull was pretty smashed up. Whoever did it probabl

killed him somewhere else, then dragged him into the building; Einstein was already dead when they set the place off."

"If he's been dead for weeks, how come you're just telling me about it now?"

"I just found out myself. All the police had was a bag of bones down in the morgue—no name, no wallet. It all had been burned in the fire."

"Then how did they identify him?"

"His mother. Einstein was from New York, and he used to take the milk train down to see her every couple of weeks. When he didn't show, she started calling here. I told her to call the police. They tried to cool her off, telling her he had probably just gone to Bermuda or someplace. Then somebody down in the morgue got the bright idea of checking dental records. Took 'em awhile. Quite a few squatters die in those fires."

"So what happened?"

"So Einstein's mother got the dental records and sent them. Identification positive."

"Are you going to run a story on it?"

"No. I don't see the point."

"What? One of your reporters dies on an investigation and you're just going to let it fly? Where's his notebook? What was in it?"

"As far as I know, Einstein's notebook burned with him. I don't have any idea what it contained."

"But when McCullough asked me to interview Mendoza, you asked him if he had gotten the name from Einstein's notebook. I was standing right there. You started arguing about the notebook and over whether I should do the story."

"Mac is an idiot. He had no idea of what he was giving you. He couldn't put two and two together with a fork."

"Einstein was investigating the fires. You know it, and I know it. The Latinos had told him they knew who was setting them. Then, next thing, that man Angelo is dead, and so is Einstein. So what am I supposed to think? That Mendoza's name came from nowhere, like magic, out of a hat."

There was a huge silence on the other end. "Mendoza's the torch, isn't he?" Lofton said. "That wasn't just one of the Latinos' crazy stories. And you knew it all along, didn't you?

You figured it from Einstein's notes. How come you tried to keep me off this story?"

"Mac knows where the center of power is in this city." Kirpatzke sounded weary now, as if he had been through this one too many times, with other reporters, on other stories. "He knows how these investigations turn out, but he doesn't care. He doesn't think things through. I don't want to see another reporter dead."

"Is that why you got fired up at the *Post,* because you cared too much for your writers? Or was it because you were suppressing information? Who pays your salary anyway?"

"From what I understand, Lofton, you're not Mr. Purity yourself—"

Lofton hung up. The conversation confirmed what he'd already put together: Mendoza was the torch, the one who burned the buildings, who received Brunner's money, probably by way of Golden. He didn't need proof positive to know the Latinos, during their brief conversation, had led him in the right direction. He could feel it in his bones, as surely as Einstein had felt it in his.

7

When Lofton walked into Barena's the following night, Tenace was there, waiting. He sat alone in a Naugahyde booth, watching the Red Sox game on television, a half-empty pitcher of beer on the table in front of him. Already slightly drunk, he waved Lofton over.

"So you think the Redwings can make a run at the play-offs?" Lofton asked him.

"No chance. If they get close"—Tenace pointed at the ceiling with his thumb—"everybody will get called up. Cowboy's taking Kubachek this week, and Sparks ain't worth shit any-way, anywhere."

"He's taking Kubachek?"

Tenace nodded and looked at the game. Lofton looked, too. The TV's color was bad, the picture a blurry green, and the players seemed to be playing underwater. Zeke Strom, the famous slugger, was at bat. Boston was losing. Once again the team had gone into its late-season skid, slowly sinking in the standings, losing ground on Milwaukee, Baltimore, New York, Detroit. It was a problem that had haunted the team for over a decade, some said even longer; the town had good teams that started out fast and faded inexplicably in the stretch. Even those precious years when the Red Sox didn't fade, they still lost the big game, muffed the big play. Nevertheless the fans hoped each year that this would be the year Boston broke its jinx. "We've got the talent but not the luck," they'd tell each other on the all-night talk shows, "and luck will change, it always does." They might be right, Lofton thought, but not this year, not yet. The television announcer, having little else to talk about, focused on Zeke Strom. Strom was a timeless player, the announcer said. His was a name synonymous with baseball. With Boston. A great competitor. The reddest of the Red Sox. Strom knew, the man went on, better than any one of these high-paid youngsters, how to swing a sizzling stick, how to knock the white ball over the Green Monster, Fenway's famous left field wall.

The truth, Lofton knew, was that Strom was a bore. Lofton knew writers who had interviewed Zeke Strom. The man had nothing to say. His was dullness, without cause or explanation, that made it impossible for him to have a slump, to suffer psychological doubts, or have a bad day, no matter how the team played around him. Even now, trapped in the underwater haze of the barroom's television, Strom connected. He rapped the ball into short right and ran slowly—huffing and puffing, a lumbering giant in an unhappy dream—to first base.

"I hate the fuckin' Red Sox," said Tenace.

Lofton attempted the kind of comradely laugh he guessed Tenace wanted.

"I guess you're wondering why the fuck I wanted to talk to you," the scorer went on. Despite his loathing for the Red Sox, Tenace's eyes were still on the game. "I wanted to tell you to watch yourself." He reached across the table and patted Lofton on the shoulder. "You got me, pal?"

"No." Lofton felt a churning in his stomach, like glass.

"Okay, I'll say it clearer. Stay away from the slut." Tenace's eyes filled with a sharp, vicarious pleasure. "I seen you with her the other day. It's not smart. They're tight, all of them."

"All of who?"

"Amanti. Brunner. Liuzza. They been together a long time. You know those guineas. Fuck each other, screw each other, but don't *you* do it. Kinda like *West Side Story*. Man, woman, knife, cock—as long as it's in the family, as long as it's one guinea to another."

"Give me a break. You've been reading too many junk magazines."

"Suit yourself. Fuck her until you're silly in the head, for all I care."

"I'm going to see her tomorrow. I'll mention your suggestion."

Tenace smirked. "You're stupid."

"Why?" Lofton had a feeling he had just made a mistake, but he wasn't sure how. The uncertainty made him dizzy, as if the blood were leaving his head. He reached over for one of Tenace's cigarettes. Still smirking, Tenace turned back to the game.

"They called that one wrong. It's not a hit; it's an error."

"What were you and Golden talking about yesterday, down at the field, before you asked for this little meeting?" He remembered how Golden had looked, gloomy and sulking, ready to detonate.

"Golden confides in me. About his sex life." Tenace laughed, pleased with himself. Lofton didn't respond; sometimes Tenace just wasn't funny. "You're really something, Lofton, you know that." The scorer chuckled again. He stared at the table, at the beer glass in front of him. "Really something."

"Who sent you?" Lofton asked. Tenace stared at his glass. Lofton realized how drunk Tenace was; the scorer had got himself punched good to play this routine.

"I'm just warning you. You won't be the first guy who thought he could ride himself a piece of Italian ass to the gates of heaven. But let me tell you something: That ass'll trick you, they always do, and there ain't no heaven."

"Is this a friendly warning or a threat? Tell me who sent you to talk to me."

"Some big shot. I don't remember his name. . . .You could help yourself pretty damn good, Lofton, you know, by minding your own business."

"Why are you telling me this?" he asked again. When Tenace did not respond, Lofton reached across the table, hitting Tenace's shoulder. "Huh, pal, why the favor?"

Tenace clicked his head up. He no longer looked drunk. "You wanna know the truth, I don't give a goddamn. I'm fattening up my wallet. Gonna make it fat as a dago prick."

"You talk filth. How long since you been laid?"

"Forty years. And you want to know the truth, I'd like to see you stick it to him, stick it to him good."

"Stick it to who?" Lofton asked, but Tenace was wound up, and he kept going, ignoring the question.

"But it ain't gonna happen. I seen what's going on, I see it all. Guys like you, they think someone like me's a loser, but I know my situation, I know when to grab and when to duck. I want to go to Spain, you know, I had some good luck with the broads there back when I was in the service. But I'm too old for the service now, too fat. So, if I want to go there, if I want to do anything, I have to write my own ticket. I'm not going to spend the rest of my life working for somebody else, ticking away my life like a watch in that bastard's crotch pocket."

"Who's got you in his crotch pocket? Brunner?"

Tenace winced, as if he feared that the conversation had let something loose that was supposed to stay secret. But he could not keep himself from talking; it was just his nature. So he tried to correct his mistake.

"Back off. I done my job. Maybe I didn't tell it to you subtle, maybe I didn't whisper it to you one pal to another, but this is the message: Back off or your head's smashed." Tenace smiled, almost friendly; his grip was tight around his glass. "Okay?"

"Okay, but who's going to do it, you?"

"Sure, me. Why not me?"

"Thanks."

"No problem. My wallet's already getting fatter. My ass's floating right off the ground."

Tenace sighed as if relieved, as if he had just finished an unpleasant task. The scorer turned back to the television. At the plate Tony Ramas, whom the Red Sox had bought for big money, took a called third strike on the outside corner.

"Blind bastard," said Tenace. "Even Babe Ruth's corpse would've swung at that."

The walls were gray in the morning light, and the air was hot. Overnight, the heat had returned, and Lofton had not slept. At every sound in the hall or scuttle in the street, he started up. *Mendoza,* he thought, *the Latinos.* He chain-smoked through the night, worried that this investigation would lead him the same place it had led Einstein: into the middle of the warring street gangs. Einstein's investigations had gotten him near the truth, and Kirpatzke—well, he wasn't exactly a hard-nosed editor, snorting up the truth like a hog after truffles. It seemed the editor preferred leaving the dirt pretty much as it lay. Einstein had kept scratching anyway, and eventually he had scratched too close. When McCullough had sent Lofton down the same path, Kirpatzke had tried to steer him away from the story. Whom was Kirpatzke covering for? Despite everything, Lofton still had nothing proving that Brunner gained anything by the fires. It was possible that Brunner was just a businessman, interested in politics and baseball, who happened to choose a mistress that wanted to use him back, to get at her old lover. It could be the whole story was an elaborate scheme of Kelley's, a way of getting at his old rival. Or maybe Randy Gutierrez's stories were simply the ravings of a man who had done too much coke and found himself too far from home.

He almost wished that one of these explanations were true, that the arson conspiracy were nothing but a baroque invention and the fires had somehow started entirely spontaneously, for no reason at all. As in other stories he'd worked on, his notebook was full of names, written increasingly illegibly, lines drawn between them in an attempt to figure out connections, then crossed out and drawn in again, until finally he discovered that in an idle moment he had sketched his own name in among the others, as if in some mysterious way he were as guilty as everyone else, guilty as Golden, who acted as the go-between, and guilty as Brunner, who worked behind the scenes to keep the city burning, and guilty as Kelley, who tried to play the fires to his own advantage. By asking around for Gutierrez, Lofton thought, I brought him attention. I helped grease the trigger.

He wondered about Tenace. Someone had sent the scorer to talk to him, to warn him out of town—probably Brunner. It seemed Brunner knew Lofton was on the case now, too, and was beginning his own efforts to scare him off. Lofton doubted Tenace was Brunner's errand boy on any kind of permanent basis. The scorer's manner was too clumsy, unprofessional. He guessed that Brunner—or one of Brunner's people—had given the scorer a few bucks to pass along the message as a friendly warning, one buddy to the next. Tenace had botched it: He'd been too transparent; Brunner's hand was visible behind the scenes. Still, it might be well to heed the scorer's warning. The next person Brunner sent might not bother to keep his fists under glass.

As soon as business hours started, Lofton went to a quick-photo place and got back the pictures he had left there to be developed, the shots he had taken while rummaging in the old mill. Though his camera had broken when he fell from the fence, the film had survived. The pictures were foggy, all orange light and darkness, but you could still make out the debris pushed into deliberate piles. He wasn't sure what the pictures proved, other than the fact that Brunner really hadn't gotten too far with renovations. He pulled out his trunk and put the pictures in with his other papers. He gathered up Gutierrez's letters and the other things he had taken from the shortstop's apartment. He still hadn't managed to get the letters translated; they'd been no help to him so far. He bent over the trunk. His body was sore and scratched; he still hurt from his fall at the warehouse. His blood tingled with nicotine.

I have my mother's cancer.

The thought gave him a funny pleasure, like rubbing a sore spot or picking a scab. He thought of Maureen and the shining blue Colorado sky; he thought of his son in Vermont. I should see the boy, he thought, I should get going. I should take Tenace's advice and leave. Kirpatzke had given him the same warning. And Liuzza, with his check for a grand, asking for nothing, really, in return, had given him the means. He flipped through his clipbooks, his collection of old articles and headlines that he still carried with him from place to place: WOMAN LIVES WITH CANCER; DOG WEEPS ON MASTER'S GRAVE; BOY WITH NO ARM SURVIVES FIRE; HOMOSEXUAL MAYOR BOOTED; GIRL, FAMILY DIE IN FATHER'S SUICIDAL RAGE.

He had written these stories back when he started, back after he'd broken up with Nancy, traveling from one dusty weekly to another, working his way up to those rural California towns where enough people placed want ads for a daily to survive.

"He never loved his children."

"He lost his testicles during the war."

"She cursed the family on her deathbed. We fought over the old man's money all our lives."

Secrets. He scrawled them in the margins of his notebooks. Not the stuff of local papers. Better saved for himself and—he could not help imagining this, though who would ever be interested enough to struggle with his handwriting?—the person who rummaged through his papers when he was dead. "Fame is a killer," a local TV personality once told him. "Covers your whole life with dirt." Like everyone else, Lofton thought, I want my bit, too, just like Mendoza, in his drug-charged dementia, wants his name scratched in the dust. Then something else occurred to Lofton: If I keep on with this arson story, I might be killed. I won't die, sweet and slow, in a hospital, with time to think it over. I'll die on the street. Maybe that's better, but I'll never see my son.

Kenner, Vermont, was about two hours off the interstate highway, a small New England crossroads that did not have the upkeep and blush of towns more on the tourist trail. The white Congregationalist church was freshly painted, but the town's two main streets, and the buildings clustered around their intersection, were old and battered: a rusting breakfast diner; a G&Y grocery; an American Legion hall with two bronzed cannons on the lawn; and an old people's home, painted a dull green, where a solitary woman sat rocking on the porch.

Lofton drove through the village and took the road north out of town. Driving these roads that twisted and wound through the low hills, he began to feel drowsy, as if he were reading a book and his life were a distant concern. He began to see why Nancy stayed in this part of the country, although he always thought she'd hate to be so isolated. Nancy could have aborted the baby, she could have killed it, he thought, but she hadn't. That's why he'd driven up here, twelve years ago, to get her back. That's why he had thought she still loved him.

Lofton made the last turn, onto a dirt track road. He saw a boy playing in a field behind the trees, and imagined the boy throwing down the bat, running to meet his father—*to meet me*—and then Lofton turned the car again, plummeting down a dirt road that wound through the trees to his first wife's house.

The house was in the open sun, except for trees shading it in the back. There was a car in the driveway, a small foreign model with a hatch. He guessed that if Nancy were here, she had heard his car come in and was probably looking at him now. He wondered if her husband, Davenport, was here, too. Back when Lofton had known him, Davenport was just starting out as a contractor, redesigning old houses. Lofton had no idea if Davenport was still in the same business, if he had succeeded, or, for that matter, if Nancy and he were still married. Stepping out of the car, in the sun, he found it amazing that the house was still here, that Davenport's name was still on the mailbox. He walked a little more slowly, wondering if they watched him coming up the walk, if they recognized him and asked themselves why he had come. For a second he thought he saw someone watching him from behind the screen. As he walked closer, he was no longer sure. The image seemed nothing more than a phantom, sunlight and shadow rippling on the wire mesh.

When Lofton reached the door, he could see a man inside the house, sitting in the living room, his back to the door. Lofton knocked, full of foreboding. For a crazy second, as the man raised and turned himself in the shadows, Lofton thought the man was not Davenport at all but Brunner.

Of course he was wrong. His imagination had simply crosscircuited, confused the past with the present. Davenport had aged. He was no longer young and ambitious, fresh out of college, but a man close to forty, just a few years older than Lofton.

"I've come to talk to Nancy."

Davenport studied him. "Sure," he said, and disappeared into the house. He didn't recognize me, Lofton thought; he just thinks I'm a salesman or somebody from town whose face he's forgotten.

Lofton waited on the porch. The trees were thick and green nearby; mosquitoes gathered around his head. Tempted to leave, to forget the whole thing, he looked back at the car.

When he turned, he saw Nancy at the open door. She looked him up and down. Her face expressed neither surprise nor fear, nor any particular joy.

Lofton could think of nothing to say. He had not seen her in twelve years. Her hair had grown gray in a few places; she had not dyed it. She might be a little heavier, too, now that he looked closely. She looked good, he thought.

"What are you doing here?" she asked. Lofton shrugged. He saw her odd, crooked smile—he had forgotten about that —and then he shrugged again.

"I work at a paper down the road."

"How far?" she asked.

"Over the border." Lofton laughed.

Her smile softened, and Lofton stepped closer.

"What do you want?"

Lofton felt the sharpness in his chest and the sun on his back. He stared into her wide-cheeked face another moment, still not answering. He wondered if her husband was watching.

"Nancy." Lofton started to speak; then he heard the soft, childlike tone in his voice and felt his mouth fall open, heavy like a stone. *I have cancer.* He could not say the words. They seemed absurd, melodramatic, and they were probably not even true.

"What do you want from me?" Her voice lilted, loud enough for Davenport to hear.

He closed his eyes. He remembered the long conversations with her on the phone and the long pauses, the silence over the dark wires. She put her hands on her hips, a defiant gesture he had always found attractive.

"I want to see my son."

"Bullshit."

Lofton pursed his lips, a tight smile. She was probably right. When he imagined the boy, he imagined old pictures of himself, the black-and-white photos, ragged white edges, the boy posing—as Lofton had once posed—leaning against a stone wall, wearing baggy trousers and a striped T-shirt.

"Your son's away. He's at camp."

"Which camp?"

She would not answer; instead, she looked him over again, up and down. For a moment the world—the bushes, the trees, the hot summer air—seemed to be tight around them.

"Should we go for a walk?" he asked.

She nodded and led the way, starting down a path into the

forest. Along the way he thought of things to ask her—*Are you happy with Davenport?*—and he answered the questions for the most part on his own, guessing the answers from the movement of her body, the way the sun shimmered off her blouse, and allowing the surface talk between them, the one-sentence exchanges—*Do you walk down here often?*—to disappear into the hum and chatter of the afternoon.

They came to a clearing, and in that clearing was a cracked cement foundation, walls all but gone at the edges, a stone hearth at the center, still intact but crumbling, rising into the air like an old tree. The hearth was filled with twigs and leaves.

"The birds nest there in spring," she said. They stood watching each other, far from her husband.

"There's a root cellar over here." She pointed at a hatch, half-decayed, broken, that opened into the floor. Lofton thought he heard an animal scuttling below.

"Type of place you like to go when you're a kid," he said.

"Maybe." She turned and looked up the path they had come.

"John," he said, saying his son's name out loud for the first time in years. "Can I see him sometime?"

She faced him, her arms folded across her chest. There was a glimmer in Nancy's eyes, a great sadness, and she stepped a bit closer. He tried to read her eyes, and suddenly a horrible thought occurred to him. His son was dead. He looked at her and tried to read her, and the sun was bright overhead, spinning, a large, ominous ball whirling out of control. He could feel tears coming into his eyes. She stood a little closer.

"No," she said. "It doesn't make sense. I understand what you want, but he doesn't know you. His father is up there. There's no point. . . . Come on, before these bugs are all over us."

They stood there for a long second, the mosquitoes singing high and crazy in the trees.

"I just wanted to be sure he was all right," said Lofton.

"Of course," she said. He followed her up the path. He stopped at his car, waiting to say good-bye, but she kept walking, on up to the house.

* * *

After Lofton had left Nancy, he drove back to Holyoke. It wasn't until he was within sight of the city, and saw the church spires and mill stacks against the early-evening sky, that he remembered the meeting he'd set up with Amanti the last time he'd seen her, when they'd ducked behind the press box while Dazzy Vance worked the Sunday crowd. He was still unsure of her motivation, whether she was working for Kelley or against him; it could even be that she'd changed her mind again by now.

When he reached Amherst, it was almost dark. Amanti was waiting for him, Brunner's papers spread out on the table before her.

"I told you I'd get them," she said.

Amanti wore a white, sleeveless blouse and smoked hard on her cigarette. She had been drinking, and she flicked her ashes carelessly, but otherwise, there was little sign of drunkenness. If anything, she seemed sharper, more engaged than usual.

Since the last time she'd seen Lofton, Amanti had been busy. She had gone back to the secluded office to which Brunner had taken her on the day he revealed his involvement with the arsons. This time she had gone alone. There were two keys to the place, one for the alarm system and the other for the door. She'd remembered Brunner's gathering up the keys. She'd found them in the same place, unmarked, lying loose in a steel drawer in the bottom of his desk in the Redwings' office.

She had gotten the keys Sunday at the park and had already returned them. But in between she had gone to the other office, in the wetlands near Station Road, outside Amherst. Once inside she thumbed through the Rolodex on the desk until she found a listing scrawled in Brunner's hand: "Big Time Carnival." She had watched Brunner do the same thing, that time when he had been drunk and shown her the papers. As he talked, he'd looked up at her the way a more normal lover might when he revealed some personality flaw, knowing the revelation would come back to haunt him, that he'd made himself vulnerable, and that she would repeat it back to him, somewhat nastily, in such an everyday place as the grocery line. Brunner, however, did not reveal such ordi-

nary flaws. Instead, he had fumbled for this listing in front of
her.

Beside the listing, as Amanti expected, she found the combination to the safe. As she took out the papers, she felt a rush
of exhilaration, a satisfaction, but she also had in front of her
the image of Brunner's face: the slightly drunken twist to his
lips and glare to the eyes that had told her that he expected
her to betray him, that he did not know how or why or when,
or that it would even have anything to do with the papers, but
that he knew it would happen. The memory of the inevitabil-
ity in Brunner's glance filled her with a kind of dread.

Why am I doing this? she wondered. Taking the papers and
giving them to Lofton would ultimately hurt Brunner more
than Kelley, though it would hurt Kelley, too; the senator
could not pressure Brunner by threatening to reveal a scandal
that was already public knowledge. Kelley's plan would be
ruined. Amanti thought of the hours she spent alone in her
apartment. The hours seemed to her to have been spent in
darkness, a time in which she was in hibernation, a kind of
windup doll, an object among other objects. By coming to the
office and taking the papers, she had put herself into action; if
the end result was to destroy the world she knew, then at least
she knew how Brunner felt when he was planning his arson or
Kelley felt in making plans against Brunner. She could envi-
sion the ruined lives with an eerie satisfaction; at the same
time she could tell herself she had done the right thing. Then
she thought how she couldn't know what the results of her
actions would be, or if anything would change. She couldn't
even tell if her actions were truly her own, or if, instead, they
were the result of an impetus from the outside, the spring
inside the doll uncoiling, moving her feet across the floor,
raising her hands, opening the safe. In the end, however, she
knew the reasons made no difference. She was already in motion. She was doing what she was doing.

Now the papers sat on the table in front of her. She had
spent time studying the papers and thought she had it figured
out. She poured some scotch—it wasn't her drink, but it was
all that was left in the house—and started explaining things to
Lofton. In this folder, she told him, there are photocopies of
insurance contracts that had been issued to different people
and companies, all for property with Holyoke addresses.

Brunner's been running an arson ring—a big one. Some of those are proxy owners; some of them are real. Either way, Brunner gets a cut when the building burns."

"How do you know they're proxies?" he asked. She was getting ahead of him, showing him the papers faster than he could take them in.

"Here, look at these."

She handed him another folder. Inside, he found more legal documents, these concerning ownership rights and payment transfers for much of the same property covered by the insurance contracts. He could not tell much at a first glance, but Amanti seemed to be right. Substantial parts of the insurance money found its way into Brunner's hands; much of the rest went to people with Boston addresses. He noticed that the law firm handling the contracts, Nassau & Associates, also had a Boston address.

"I thought your cousin was Brunner's lawyer. How come Liuzza didn't draw up these papers?"

"I've wondered about that myself. Maybe Brunner didn't want him to know what he was up to."

Amanti gave him more to look at. First, there was a packet of papers, full of receipts for supplies and work down at the mill, American Paper. The work hadn't been done, Lofton knew, but that didn't mean Brunner wouldn't include it in his insurance claim when the time was right.

She handed him a small green ledger book. Each entry contained several items: the name of the hotel, a date, and then a dollar-and-cents number, the figure ranging from anywhere between a thousand dollars and fifteen thousand. Each page, down at the bottom, bore Dick Golden's signature. While Lofton turned the pages, she explained the book. It contained the names of the buildings that had burned so far, the date Golden contacted the torch, the amount of money Golden passed along, and the amount he kept for himself. Brunner made Golden sign the entries, she guessed. That way Golden was implicated, too; he stayed under Brunner's control.

"You've spent a lot of time with these papers," Lofton said. "You've got this pretty well figured out."

"No, I didn't have to think too hard. Jack Brunner's a smart man, he doesn't trust too many people, but he has one problem: He wants people to know he's smart. In that enve-

lope, the brown one, there are copies of canceled checks, con
tributions supposedly, to half the politicians in Boston. Kel
ley's father-in-law, Jim Harrison, is one of them. Brunner'
tied a lot of people into this scheme. It's his protection. If h
falls, they fall, too, and they aren't going to let that happen
He's proud of himself; it all shows how smart he is. Onl
there aren't too many people he can tell."

"So he tells you."

"You'd be surprised what people say late at night. The
think it's all forgotten in the morning," Amanti said, swinging
her foot, somewhat surprised at herself. The bedroom wasn'
the place Brunner had told her, but it felt that way. It was a
good as the truth.

Lofton looked over the papers. There was a lot of informa
tion here. Enough to prove that Brunner was running ar
arson ring and that a lot of prominent businessmen and politi
cians were getting a share. A good public prosecutor coulc
ruin a lot of careers. A good defense lawyer, however, coulc
confuse the information, introduce document after document
keep the proceedings long and dreary and confusing, so tha
much later, maybe even years—when the jury finally sat dowr
to make a decision—the real evidence would be so buried, sc
muddled, no one could tell who was guilty. It was a standarc
defense tactic in cases like this. Lofton had known reporter
who had covered similar court cases, sitting on hard benche
day after day, month after month, until finally even the pres
lost interest and wished only for a verdict, any verdict.

"Even if all this does protect him, Brunner's not going to b
happy. Your friend Kelley killed the Holyoke project in com
mittee. That leaves Brunner with one big building, Americar
Paper, that he can't collect on. The insurance companies ar
already moving to devalue the property, and if he burns i
now, that will look pretty suspicious."

"He'll figure something out," Amanti said. "He'll burn tha
building, and he'll get his insurance payoff. He never intendec
to renovate anything. The only reason he bought it in the firs
place was to prevent competition with the Hillside Mall. He
as good as told me. Even with the federal money it would cos
him too much, and he could make more burning it. He wants
Holyoke to stay the way it is."

Lofton went over to the curtains and stared out at the eve

ing. A car door opened and slammed. A man sat on the
oop across the street. The faint noise of children, playing in
ome backyard after dark, rose and fell in the darkness. It was
ll very domestic, very normal.

"Stay away from the window," she said. "You're making
ourself nervous."

"Won't Brunner get upset when he finds out these papers
re missing?"

"He won't know I took them, but even if he guesses, I
on't be the one he'll hurt. It'll be you."

Lofton didn't like the sound of that, but she was probably
ght. Even so, her voice quavered. She took another drink.

"For somebody that's not nervous, you're sure drinking a
ot."

"I haven't been able to sleep. It relaxes me."

Amanti crossed her legs. Though at times she stammered,
esitated, and looked at the world blurrily, she was still pretty
harp. He glanced at the glass in her hand. "Why don't you
e down and rest while I go through this stuff?" he said. "It's
oing to take awhile."

Amanti leaned back a little, watching him go through the
apers. He had to admit the alcohol didn't seem to have much
ffect on him either; at least it hadn't dulled his nervousness.
le went to the window every few minutes. She assured him
nat Brunner did not pay her unexpected visits, that it was an
nwritten rule between them, but Lofton still could not shake
ne overriding feeling of the man's presence. Maybe it was just
ne papers. Maybe they smelled of the man. Also, despite
verything, he wondered if pilfering the papers had really
een Amanti's idea; he still suspected Kelley's involvement.

"What made you change your mind? Why are you giving
ne all this stuff?"

Amanti hesitated. She had an answer, somewhere inside
er, but she couldn't call it forth. After the night she'd made
ove to Lofton, she'd called Kelley. When she finally got hold
f him, his reassurances had been the same as always; after-
vard she'd been angry and tired. No matter what she did,
othing changed. She couldn't get over the feeling that her life
vas buried, somewhere beneath the surface, a secret obscure
ven to herself. The events that happened—the scheme she'd
een helping Kelley act out—were only a reflection of her life,

not the thing itself, and she was trapped in the reflection. Sh
tried to express this to Lofton, and to express, too, the thing
she'd been thinking while standing in Brunner's office, th
papers in her hand, but she only stammered. The alcohol wa
suddenly catching up with her, a sleepy darkness, and she fel
her reasoning, her motivations, slip into that darkness.

"Kelley's two-timing me in Boston," she said. "He's go
another mistress."

Lofton questioned her mathematics, but he said nothing
When Kelley slept with Amanti, he was two-timing his wife
sure, but Lofton didn't know the arithmetic for what Kelle
was doing to Amanti or—for that matter—what Amanti wa
doing back. The only thing that seemed clear was that she wa
jealous, and the jealousy was strong enough, at least for now
to motivate her to drive down to Brunner's office, grab uj
these papers, and give them to him. How she would feel to
morrow, Lofton couldn't guess, but it didn't matter now. H
studied the papers. When he looked up from them, Amant
was still watching, but her eyes were half-closed. Later, whet
he looked back again, she was lying on her stomach, asleep.

Lofton looked out at the street again. The man who hac
been sitting on the porch across the way was no longer there
the noise of the children was gone, the same cars stood parkee
by the curb. Everything seemed quiet, safe. Still, he wonderec
about the wisdom of studying the papers here. Despite Aman
ti's assurances, somebody might happen along. He shoulc
take the papers back to Holyoke, maybe run off copies, then
have Amanti return the originals. Otherwise, Brunner migh
find out the papers were missing, and there was no sense ir
inviting trouble. Meanwhile, he would be better off studying
the papers back in his hotel in Holyoke. Better yet, he woulc
get his things, check into a new hotel, and study the paper:
there.

Amanti lay on the couch, her legs splayed apart, face to the
wall. Her black slacks were tight, the collar of her blouse wa:
turned up in back, one of her sandals hung off her foot. For a
moment Lofton did not want to leave. Something about the
whole scene—the scattered papers, the empty glasses, Amant
prone and vulnerable on the couch—stirred his desire. Taker
from the outside, without any idea of context, the scene coulc
be a domestic one, the woman lying there could be his wife

the papers could have to do with their business or their taxes. He might touch her gently and help her into the bedroom. Things weren't that way, of course, and because they weren't, he felt his desire even more keenly, in a way that, if this really were a domestic scene, he would probably not even feel at all. If this were the scene he imagined it to be, he would not yearn for the woman on the couch but for someone else, a stranger.

He gathered the papers into a pile, then searched the room for anything he might have missed. On the trunk in the corner he found Amanti's photo album. It lay open, as if she had been looking at it recently. He flipped through the pictures: Amanti as a child, then in college, her lips pursed in a cashmere pout, and then the shots of her and Kelley.

He placed the book back where he'd found it and walked over to say good-bye to her. Amanti was lying on her back, the top of her blouse undone, her face soft with sleep. She moaned groggily. He touched her on the stomach, felt the elastic band of her black slacks, and then went into the kitchen. After getting a brown paper bag from under the sink, he gathered Brunner's papers into the sack and left.

Lofton took the back highway to Holyoke. He wanted to think, to avoid the main roads. Another car took the same turn—he watched for a while in his rearview mirror—but the car stayed well behind.

He passed a small, lighted corner in South Amherst, a convenience store on one side of the street, a gas station on the other. Once he was past here, it would be darkness until he was over the Notch. He looked down at the stack of papers beside him on the seat. Now that he was away from Amanti's apartment he felt more comfortable. He looked forward to getting out of his old hotel and into a new one, someplace bright and cheap along the expressway, where he could take his time with the papers.

Lofton started mulling things over. It seemed he had the evidence he needed now, proof that Brunner was working behind the scenes, putting the touch on the Boston politicians. Brunner had hidden the arsons pretty cleverly, Lofton admitted, so that when American Paper finally went—it was the prize, the biggest, the multimillion-dollar bonus baby—then its burning would seem the culmination of a spree, of the violence and self-destruction that victimized everyone in the city, usually the poor. At the last minute, however, Kelley had found out about the arsons, decided to play politics with what he knew, and tied up Brunner's plan. The big one wouldn't burn; Brunner couldn't collect. He wondered what Brunner planned on doing now, how he would set up the burn.

The car behind him gained ground, its lights coming up quickly in the rearview mirror. Lofton panicked, but then the car slowed down, maintaining its distance. *A drunk, that's all.* Then the car rushed back up on him again.

Lofton's station wagon sputtered on the hill. The car was on his bumper now; its headlights flashed off and on. "Bastard," Lofton hissed, "just get around me." He edged over to the shoulder, giving the car room to pass. The car stayed on his tail, looming in his rearview mirror, a steel dark shadow. Lofton glimpsed the man's silhouette through the headlights' glare, and he imagined the man in the other car, the brightly lit dashboard, the car surging beneath his feet. The lights on his own dashboard were burned out, the upholstery was torn, patched with duct tape. The car behind him swerved into the oncoming lane, then swerved back.

When they reached the Notch, a flat hollow of land cradled between the sharp peaks of these low hills, the driver leaned on his horn. He pulled up close to Lofton, backed away, pulled close again, flashing his lights off and on, his horn blaring through the darkness. The road crested and headed downhill. In his old boat of a car Lofton did not dare drive much faster. He would lose control. The car came up close, and Lofton tried a trick he had learned on the California freeways to keep tailgaters at a distance. He touched his brake pedal lightly. On a car like this, with its brakes worn, you could often trigger the brake lights before engaging the brakes themselves. The trick worked. The man behind him hit his brakes; his car wrenched to the side, spun, lost ground, but then came down on Lofton again, faster than before. Lofton tried the trick again; but the car came down on him hard and fast—*right up my ass*—and Lofton swerved onto the gravel shoulder. He felt himself floating, weightless, behind the wheel, felt the dizzy rush of the darkness around him. The wagon spun and crashed, and the world disappeared into a

crosshatch of fear, an ugly black wave that washed over him
and then away, leaving Lofton sideways on the seat, broken
glass lying scattered over him. He touched himself for blood
but could not find any.

He struggled to get up, trying to unlatch the seat belt. Outside the car he heard a quick scuffle of gravel. He heard a
motor running. A passing car swished by on the road—he
could see its lights—but it did not stop. The gravel crunched
closer to the car. Footsteps.

The door on the driver's side opened, and he saw a man, a
stocking pulled over his head, holding a gun. The man
climbed into the car. Lofton closed his eyes. He was trapped.
Suddenly he saw himself back in the library looking at Einstein's by-line, at the picture of the Latino leader up above.
"They are burning our city; they are being paid." Like Einstein, maybe even better than Einstein, he'd figured it all out.
The only thing he didn't know was the name of this man in
the stocking cap, kneeling over him, getting ready, Lofton
thought, to answer all my questions forever.

"Bastard."

The man's voice was unnaturally high, choked with emotion. He put the gun to Lofton's head. Lofton thought of how
his death would look in the paper. REPORTER SHOT TO
DEATH. He wondered how Kirpatzke would play it, if he
would play it at all.

The man pushed his knee into Lofton's groin and bent over;
Lofton stared into the stockinged face.

"Bastard."

His breath smelled like whiskey. *He's not a good killer.*
Raising himself up, the man gathered force, then brought the
butt end of the revolver down toward Lofton's head. Lofton
squirmed, and the blow glanced off. The gun slipped from the
man's fingers, but Lofton could not reach it. The man
pounded him in the face, over and over, with a vengeance that
was not mercenary but personal.

Then the beating stopped. Lofton felt him reaching for the
gun but could do nothing to stop him.

"Bastard."

Why doesn't he just kill me?

"Bastard. Bastard. Bastard."

Grabbing Lofton by the collar, the man pushed his knee

deeper into Lofton's groin and touched the gun to his head. Lofton's skull hurt from the beating, his vision blurred, but he could still see the man; he still waited for the shot. Leaning over Lofton, backing the gun away then bringing it closer, the man began—suddenly, horribly—to sob. The man was close, and Lofton could see the features through the mask. And, finally, he recognized the voice.

"Golden," Lofton said.

There was a pause. Golden sat up. He was no longer crying. He stared at Lofton a long moment and then began to hit the reporter, again and again, and with each blow Lofton watched the darkness burst into light, until finally there was only one pure light, indistinguishable from the darkness.

The old man would not leave him be. "It happened in a split second," he said, leering up at Lofton, grabbing on to his sleeve. The old man pointed at the building. Lofton saw shadows moving up on railings, then a small light, like a candle or someone striking a match. The old man pulled Lofton closer; his face was mottled, ugly. "I saw a small flame, then a larger one, and I knew what it was." The man's breath was dank. The night smelled like gasoline. "I knew I had to call for help, but I knew it couldn't get here in time. The fire was in three places; then it was everywhere."

"All right, all right," cried Lofton, "all right," but the man held on. His face twisted and became uglier. The fire spread over the wooden porches, the railings, the window frames, the gutters—a glowing filigree. "The whole building in three minutes, just blown up and gone, just a shell, a corpse." Lofton felt himself sweating. He tried to pull away. The old man grabbed him by the collar; his grip was unshakable. "The explosion is white," the old man hissed. A main exploded, the heat blistered out, the walls of the empty rooms were gold and red. A man disappeared down an alley five blocks away. Then came the second explosion, brighter than the one before. Lofton couldn't breathe. "This is what it all comes to," the old man said. "Somebody sets a fire, and your soul's got three minutes to get out." Then there was one last explosion, a weariness in Lofton's chest. . . .

8

Lofton woke up in the hospital. His dream of the old man and the fire was far away; his head hurt, and he drifted in and out of consciousness. He had been drugged hard, so he kept falling back to sleep, the pain ringing in his bones—his skull, his cheeks, his jaw—each time he woke. When he touched his face, he found a bandage there, and beneath the bandage a tight, aching pain he could not escape, not even in sleep.

He forced himself to sit up, but a nurse came and forced him back down. He slept some more, his sleep no longer black and seamless but filled with dreams, fragments acted by a kaleidoscope of interchangeable players. Tenace lumbered in bed with Amanti; Maureen and Brunner went off together.

Finally, he pulled himself up again—the pain was fading—and he saw the nurse, a brisk older woman who took his pulse with a professional, almost distasteful air. He asked her what day it was.

"Go back to sleep. You have a concussion."

Lofton was in a large room. There were other beds nearby, and he could hear, aside from the footsteps of his nurse, hard breathing and moaning. A cop sat on a stool by the entrance.

"Officer," he called, but it was a weak cry. The policeman

did not come. Lofton felt dizzy. The car spun. Golden raised his fist. The room turned bright, then black.

The nurse was adjusting his IV. He was in a different room now, a private room: television set, empty bed beside him, no policeman at the door.

The nurse left, and he dozed. When she came back—hours later or a few minutes; it was impossible for him to tell—she showed in a small, seedy man dressed in a light beige suit and black tie.

"Frank Lofton?"

The man extended his hand as he walked across the room, as if to shake Lofton's hand from a distance. The man had a thin, snakelike smile. He held his hand palm upward as if expecting something to be placed in it. When Lofton reached over to shake it, the man's hand went limp. The nurse leaned against the door, watching.

"My name's Ray Nassau. Jack's lawyer."

"Jack?"

"Yes, Jack Brunner. He asked me to handle your problem." Nassau held out his hand again.

"We already shook."

Nassau smiled. "Yes, you're right."

"What do you want? I thought Liuzza was Brunner's lawyer."

"Different lawyers have different specialties. Jack Brunner got you this room. See, when they pick someone off the street —out-of-state ID, accident, no insurance card, junky car, that kind of thing—they don't give you the best treatment. Put you in the ward with the crooks and the drunks."

"I don't want anything from Brunner."

"No?"

"No." Lofton raised his voice. "Nurse, I don't want this man here. He's making my head hurt."

"Are you in pain, Mr. Lofton? Should I call the doctor?" The nurse did not move from the door.

Nassau bent over, whispering—hissing really—at the bedside. "The little shortstop is a sympathetic figure, you know. The jury will be hard on you."

"What are you talking about?"

"Murder. An accomplice at least. Leaving the scene. Suppressing evidence." Nassau pursed his lips and shook his head. "Bad stuff. You'd think a reporter would be above such things. Playing rough stuff with a Mexican over a few nosefuls of cocaine."

"He was from Nicaragua," Lofton said. "And I didn't kill him."

"That's what they all say. And I believe you all, of course. It's a common problem: an innocent man caught in the wrong place, at the wrong time, holding a bloody sword. Still, I wouldn't expect a man like you to get so tied up in this, so complicated. You might go to jail. Unless you have a good lawyer. Or a good friend."

"Fuck off."

"Fine. Nurse, could you show in Officer Ryan?" Nassau gleamed. "I think you'll find this interesting."

A policeman came into the room, a short man, blond hair, small, tight curls. He joined Nassau at the bedside, and Nassau sent the nurse away.

"You are going to see my poetic side, Mr. Lofton, something few people see. . . . Let's think back. Let's remember the summer. Let's remember a day, one of those grimy, awful days, when the air was full of pig sweat and fat, when old men were dying of strokes and young men dying of boredom. Let's think back. . . ."

"Get to the point," said Lofton, but he was afraid of the cop. What were these two trying to pull off?

"Let's think back to a hot and ugly night. The ambulance lights are flashing. A dead man lays on the floor—a *Mexican* —his skull blown to tiny pieces. Outside, there's static. A reporter sits in a squad car, waiting, thinking, plotting, scheming." Nassau paused. "Can you see it, Lofton? Can you imagine the reporter? Can you see him at the scene of the crime, hours earlier, studying the dead body? The question is, Why would he conceal such a thing? Why wouldn't he call the police?"

"Fuck off."

"You said that already. . . . Now imagine the hardworking policeman, coming back down from the crime to the squad car." Nassau pointed to Ryan. "The hardworking, honest policeman, the man on the beat." Lofton remembered.

The detective came down the driveway. He spoke in the intercom. He looked through the cage at Lofton in the back seat.

Nassau turned to Ryan and gestured at Lofton. "Do you remember this man, Officer Ryan? Have you seen this reporter before?"

Ryan peered at Lofton. His eyes were gray slits.

"Should I remember him?" Ryan asked.

"Should he remember you, Lofton? Should he?" Nassau smiled.

"What do you want from me?" Lofton asked.

"Want, want, want. All this talk of want. Of need. Of desire. Would men have ever climbed from the slime, would Christ have ever died on the cross, if all we thought of was our own paltry *wants,* our own paltry *lust*?" Nassau's face was twisted and happy. The lawyer was in ecstasy.

"Officer Ryan, tell us what the police found in Mr. Lofton's car when they arrived at the accident."

"A medallion, some letters written in Spanish—the personal effects of Randy Guitierrez, the murdered ballplayer."

"Those things weren't in my car," Lofton said. He was telling the truth. The letters, the medallion, he'd left all that stuff back in his hotel room.

"What else did the police find in Mr. Lofton's car?"

"Cocaine. A dozen ounces, not very pure. Cut with milk sugar, Benzedrine, just about everything under the kitchen sink. Same as the drugs found at the ballplayer's apartment, a perfect match."

"That's a lie," Lofton said. "If that was in my car, then someone else put it there—"

"Officer Ryan, what's your position in the department?"

"Detective, homicide."

"If somebody asked you to speculate, what would you infer from the evidence in Mr. Lofton's car?"

"I would guess that he killed the shortstop and stole the cocaine. That he was getting ready to leave town when he lost control of the car."

"That's ridiculous," Lofton said. "I was on my way back into town when one of Brunner's men, Dick Golden, forced me off the road. I was investigating the arsons—"

Lofton had directed his appeal at the cop, but he broke it off. He could see it was hopeless. Ryan stared at the hospital ed, not seeming to see Lofton, not seeming to see anything. Brunner had had the cop bought off, clear and simple.

"On the other hand, Detective Ryan, if nobody said anything to you, if nobody asked you to speculate on the meaning of this evidence, what would you do then?"

"Not much," Ryan said. His face was deadpan—nothing, no emotion, not even a flicker.

"Good, good," the lawyer said. "I'm happy to hear it, and I bet Frank is happy, too."

Nassau dismissed Ryan. The policeman left Lofton and the lawyer alone together.

"Get the picture?" said Nassau.

Lofton said nothing. He understood Nassau's message: Keep out of Brunner's business or we'll turn this whole thing around on you; you'll find yourself on the line for Gutierrez's murder.

"I've warned you. Jump out of this." Nassau's voice was iron. The fun and games were over; he'd finished his routine, and he wanted Lofton to know he was serious. "We'll pay the bills on this room. We know the meaning of generosity. You stay here as long as you need. Weeks. Years. Decades. Just leave town when your nose stops bleeding."

Nassau put his checkbook down on the table and filled out one of the yellow sheets. He stuck the check under Lofton's pillow.

"Et cum spiritu tuo," he said, and left the room.

Afterward Lofton talked to his doctor. The man was friendly, short, and balding, thick around the middle. It was obvious, from his friendly, innocent manner that he knew nothing about what was happening. "We did X rays all over," the doctor said, serious now. "The abdomen, the chest cavity, we checked it all." Lofton took a breath. It hurt. "You're a lucky man. Not even a broken rib."

"Nothing wrong internally?"

"Not a thing," said the doctor, and he gave Lofton a generous smile.

LA CASA DE EMPEÑOS. PISTOLAS. JOYAS. CÁMARAS FOTOGRÁFICAS. Lofton stared at his bandaged face in the pawnshop window. Underneath the Spanish the same words had been written again in English—in the same gold Gothic

lettering, only smaller. THE HOUSE OF PERSISTENCE. GUNS.
JEWELRY. CAMERAS. The window was plated silver, its reflection blue and warped by the cheapness of the glass. Lofton
tore the bandage from his face. Bruises blackened the skin
beneath his eyes; his eyes were streaked red; his nose was
bashed and sore. "The bone's broken in one place, cracked in
two others, very difficult to set," the doctor had told him
while changing the bandage. He gave Lofton prescriptions for
codeine and antibiotics. "The bandages will help hold things a
little firmer." The doctor laughed. "But mostly they'll keep
you from looking so ugly." Lofton pressed the bandage back
on and headed down the street.

"Señor, quiere algo?"

Lofton wheeled. The pawnbroker, a small, fat man with
eyes the color of asphalt, stood in his doorway. "Are you
looking for a pistol? Something small?"

"No," Lofton called. "Not right now."

Lofton went into a tavern on the corner, not far from his
hotel. He needed to make a decision. He took one of the
doctor's painkillers, ordered a beer, and lit a cigarette. *No
internal injuries. Not even a broken rib. Lucky bastard.* Nassau's cheek was in his pocket. Twenty-five hundred dollars.
He still hadn't cashed Liuzza's check, the note for a grand
that Amanti's cousin had given him that day in his Northampton home. All things considered, he hadn't made out too
badly. True, now that Brunner had gotten his papers back, the
story was pretty well ruined, or at least difficult to document.
But Lofton was alive, he had some money, he hadn't lost
everything. Still, something nagged at him: Somehow Dick
Golden had known exactly where to find him. Certainly the
general manager had not followed him all the way to Vermont. Golden must have known he was going to be at Amanti's that night, then waited for him there, finally catching up
to him on the dark, open road.

He felt a confused surge of hatred for Golden, not at all the
pure hatred you should feel for a man who had beaten you
senseless. Somebody had told Golden where to find him, he
was convinced, but who? He had a suspicion he didn't like.

He went over to the phone and dialed Amanti. There was
no answer. He was worried, despite himself and his suspicions. He slammed the phone into its cradle.

"Easy," the barkeep called out to him. "We only got one phone here."

Lofton flipped through the phone book. Golden. A street in the Point District, a mile or so beyond MacKenzie Field. He dialed the number to make sure. A woman answered, her voice slurred, barely audible. That was the handicapped woman, Golden's wife. Lofton hung up harder than he had the first time. He winced, drawing his shoulders tight, realizing what he had done. This time the bartender said nothing.

He walked back to his hotel and checked his messages. The clerk was not there, and nothing was in his box. He started up the stairs, but then the clerk appeared. He shouted at Lofton in Spanish. He blocked the staircase, his arms outstretched, one palm flat against each wall. He told Lofton he could not go up to his room until he paid for the damage. If Lofton did not pay, he would call the police.

"I almost lose my job because of you," the clerk said in English. "The room has been destroyed by some one of your hoodlum friends. Five hundred dollars' worth."

"I'll pay," he said, though he had no intention of doing so. "Just let me get my things out of here."

The clerk looked at him warily. Lofton walked steadily forward, until he was face-to-face with the man.

"I said I'd pay," Lofton said. He could feel the clerk's breath in his face. He imagined his own face in the man's eyes. It was an ugly face, distorted. The clerk backed off, and Lofton brushed by.

"You move nothing before you pay," the clerk yelled after him. Lofton could hear the man following behind him, muttering in Spanish.

Lofton's door had been kicked in, and the room thrown into shambles: cupboards and refrigerator cleared; drawers and closet emptied; food, paper, laundry, and glass—all scattered on the floor. The mattress had been stripped of its sheets, turned over and slashed, as if the intruder had expected to find something inside the mattress. Tiny bits of foam rubber lay everywhere. His clippings and his notebooks were gone, his trunk all but empty.

He gathered up his clothes, clean and dirty, and stuck them in an old duffel bag he had taken around the country with him. He put what was left of his papers and correspondence into the bag, everything except the most worthless scraps of paper. The pictures he had taken in the warehouse were gone, his camera, too, even his fountain pen. They had taken it all.

"Five hundred dollars," the clerk shouted. "Or you take nothing. I call the police now."

"You call the police?" Lofton yelled. "I'm the one who is going to call the police! I leave my room and come back to find it destroyed. What kind of place is this? And what do you mean, five hundred dollars? For the door? The mattress? This whole fucking hotel isn't worth five hundred dollars."

The blood rushed to Lofton's face. He clenched his fist. The clerk clenched his fists, too, but he backed up as Lofton came forward. Lofton could see the man was afraid of him. He imagined how he must look to the clerk: the bloodstained, dirty bandage; the rumpled clothes from the night of the attack; the half-drugged, glinting eyes. He enjoyed the fear he inspired and took a menacing step toward the clerk. For a second he thought he might grab the man and hit him; but the clerk had a scrappiness about him, and Lofton did not really want to fight. Instead, he pulled out his wallet.

"Paid, you want to be paid?" He took out a Redwings' schedule that had small, mugged pictures of the owners and a ticket office phone number.

"You want your money, you call this man." Lofton pointed a finger at Brunner's name. "You tell him one of his pigs tore up this room. You call the police on him."

Lofton pushed past the clerk, feeling a real flush of anger, a good feeling, a powerful swagger in his step, a happy rage he could barely contain as he brushed past the people in the hall who had come out, attracted by the noise.

Outside, the daylight made him wince. He squinted down the sidewalk at streets, his sack of clothes and paper slung over his back. The anger had not left, but now he felt foolish. The clerk was no enemy, not really. He was just an easy target. He thought, again, how the intruder had even taken the old silver fountain pen, tarnish and all, that his brother had given him.

"Gutless," he hissed out loud, not at the clerk but at himself, as he walked past a drunk on the street. "Taking it out on the smallest, the weakest you can find. You want to smash Brunner, you want to smash Golden, but you're afraid. Fool."

His heart beat raggedly in his chest and he reached first for another cigarette, then for another painkiller. Who is it that you really hate? he thought, and looked down at his gnarled hands.

He stood still on the street. He wasn't going to give up on it this easily. He pushed open the pawnbroker's door.

"Una pistola?" asked the pawnbroker.

"Sí," said Lofton. *"Una pistola."*

The clerk showed him a cheap one, an H&R .32, something small that could kill from across the room.

Golden lived in a neighborhood south of MacKenzie Field, away from the tenements. The houses were small but clean, at least for the most part, and the yards well trimmed, the bushes flowering, the sidewalks free of garbage. The neighborhood reminded Lofton of the one he had grown up in, tucked between the business district of San Jose and that city's rail-yards, back before the city had boomed, the orchards had disappeared, and the suburbs had grown. Here, as there, you did not have to walk the streets long to see how modest the neighborhood really was, how thin the prosperity. On each block a few houses needed paint, their yards were overgrown, and if you looked closely, you could see that many of the houses, built without real foundations, had sunk and shifted with the earth. He touched the gun he carried in his suit coat pocket. The practical reason for coming here, Lofton told himself, was to see if Golden still had Brunner's papers.

Golden's door was open. Lofton stood on the porch step and looked through the screen. The television was on in the far corner of the living room. He could see the back of a wheelchair and a woman's head tilted to the side. He rapped on the screen door, pulled the handle, and stepped in.

The wheelchair's motor whirred, and the chair turned. Mrs. Golden looked up at him. A thin-faced, blond-haired woman, she wore a brightly colored blouse, slightly faded, drawn at the collar, the kind hippie girls used to wear in California. She controlled the chair by pressing her palm against a small disk on its arm.

"I'm a reporter," Lofton said. He smiled—an old habit, an interviewer's trick. "I'm looking for your husband."

"Yes," the woman said. Her head was still tilted, and her

hand had slipped off the control disk. Footsteps came from the hall. He touched the gun in his pocket, thought of taking it out, but changed his mind. No, not in front of the woman.

A second later Golden appeared. He did not seem surprised to see Lofton; he looked him over carefully, studying the way he held his hand in his pocket.

"I think we should talk," Lofton said.

Golden looked to his wife. Lofton looked, too.

"All right. In the front yard."

"No," said Lofton. "In the back."

Golden sighed. He was not the same man he had been the other night. His anger seemed to be gone. "All right."

Golden walked to his wife. He straightened her head, put his cheek against hers, and pushed her back to the television. Then Lofton followed Golden into the backyard. They walked past a small garden and stood behind the shed.

"What are you doing at my house?" asked Golden. His anger was suddenly back, his cheeks red and shiny. "And what have you got there in your pocket?"

"I want back what you took from my room."

"I don't know what you're talking about."

Lofton looked up at Golden. He was a good-looking man, eyes gray like the ocean—the sort of man whom you did not believe would do anything wrong unless backed into a corner. His hand was bandaged.

"Hurt your hand the other night?"

"No worse than you hurt your face."

Despite himself, Lofton laughed.

"Nothing's funny, Lofton. And you might as well take your hand our of your pocket. That gun's not going to do you any good."

Golden said the words coolly. Then his eyes watered, his lips turned downward, and Lofton remembered the bizarre look of Golden's face through the mask. His anger then, his frustration had seemed too personal to be mercenary. Now the man regarded him dispassionately, as if Lofton were of no importance, just another cog in the deaf-and-dumb, thoughtless universe. Lofton feared, however, that Golden's emotions might swing the other way again. What will I do if he rushes me? Lofton thought, and then realized he was holding the gun tight, pressing the barrel against the fabric of his pocket, like a thug in a movie. *Did I come here to kill him?*

"I've got all the evidence I need. The police and the newspapers are on my side." Lofton bluffed. He was talking nonsense, he knew, but he went on with it. "If you talk, if you say what you know, the justice system will go easier on you. People know your situation. They'll have compassion."

"You're a blood-fucking-fool."

Even so, Lofton thought he sensed a hesitation in Golden, a willingness to let go of everything he knew, to get it off his conscience and hope for the best. Before that could happen, he needed to get Golden's trust. He decided to take a chance. If Golden were going to kill him, he would have done it the other night.

"I'm going to put this gun on the ground." Lofton took the gun out of his pocket. He held it by the barrel.

"Suit yourself," said Golden.

He laid the gun on the dirt. Golden looked at it for a long moment, then walked over and picked it up. Lofton felt his heart leap crazily. *I made a mistake.*

"Anything that's happened, I won't use it against you. We'll work together. I'm not out to get you."

"Who else has been snooping around the ballpark lately? Gutierrez?" Golden sneered. "Felipe Alou? Jesus of Nazareth?"

Golden pointed the gun at him, pulled his finger tighter on the trigger. Lofton thought of the woman inside. Golden took care of her—*how could the same man kill me?* Then Golden raised the gun over his head. He fired straight up, into the sky.

"I should have killed you the other night. But I lost my guts. I couldn't do it. I waited for you outside the woman's house. I waited for hours, and somehow the whole time I knew I would lose it, that I would fail."

"I don't understand."

"Join the human race," said Golden. "Join the fucking human race. I have a crippled wife. A bum job. And once I was every-goddamn-thing. The world sang when I shat. Who Jesus-hiding-in-the-wall understands anything? I don't even know what I'm doing staring at your ugly face."

"Do you know why you picked me to beat on? You must

have some idea about that. And how did you know where to find me? You were waiting outside Amanti's in your car; then you tailed me up the hill. How did you know where I was going to be that night, that I was even planning to go anywhere near Amanti's?"

Lofton wanted the answer to that last question. He could see Golden was thinking it over, wondering if he should answer. Though Golden seemed calmer now, more reasonable, it was partly only because he could afford to be; he was the one holding the gun.

"Listen, it didn't take too much brains to see you were up to something at the ballpark, not just writing about fly balls. Then I got word you were trying to put this whole business on me, Gutierrez's death, everything. I'm not a murderer." His voice was insistent now. "If I was, I would've killed you."

"Who told you where to find me that night?"

"Give it up. I'm not going to tell you. You should just give this up. There's no way you can beat them."

"Beat who?"

"Shut up."

They were quiet for a moment. Lofton could hear kids playing in the yards nearby. They yelled and played in English; it sounded strange almost, with all the Spanish he'd been hearing. Golden sat down on an old tree stump. His eyes were wet, luminous, and he studied the revolver.

"That was clever, trashing my room and planting Gutierrez's things in my car. Trying to make it look like I was the murderer. Was that your idea or Brunner's?"

"I didn't trash your room. I don't know what you're talking about."

"Did you give the papers back to Brunner? Or do you still have them? I'd like to take a look."

"What papers? I don't know what you're talking about. And I didn't go anywhere near your room. The only thing I wanted was to scare you off. Now get out of here," said Golden. He raised the tip of the revolver.

"There's no point playing stupid. I've figured things out."

"If you're so smart, why am I holding the gun?"

"A lot of people died in those fires. Your best way free of this is to let me see the papers."

"Get the fuck out." Golden did not shout; his voice was calm, miserable.

"Tell me what you know about the fires."

"I don't know what you're talking about. Leave me alone." Golden pointed the gun at Lofton's head.

"All right," said Lofton. "All right."

He left Golden sitting on the stump. Mrs. Golden had gotten her wheelchair through the back door, somehow, and onto the porch. She did not look at Lofton. She stared out at her husband. Tears ran down her cheeks; they left furrows, or seemed to, like rain across the infield dirt.

Brunner's house stood on the other side of the Connecticut River. A picture window ran the length of Brunner's den, overlooking the river. At the moment Kelley stood by the window, looking toward Holyoke. Amanti sat in a thickly cushioned chair across from Brunner. On the desk between them were the papers she had taken from his office.

"How did the reporter happen to have these?" Brunner asked.

Amanti shifted uncomfortably. Kelley approached her. He walked in a way that at first glance made him seem at ease despite the situation. However, his eyes, always chameleon in nature, were brighter than usual, melancholy, and his skin seemed coldly, sadly beautiful, the color of marble in famous statues. He touched her on the shoulder while Brunner watched.

"Listen, Jack," Kelley said. His voice was as bright, as sad, as his eyes. "You've got this whole thing wrong. That reporter's been calling my office. He has this thing in his head about arson, and he wants a little cash to keep his mouth quiet. I only told you about it because I was concerned."

He was lying, of course. The reason for the lie, Amanti guessed, was that Kelley's plan to pressure Brunner had gone wrong. She didn't know the details, but she had known something was wrong earlier that day, the instant she had heard Kelley's voice on the telephone telling her to meet him at Brunner's in South Hadley. When she'd walked into Brunner's study and seen the papers stacked on the desk, her heart had sunk. She hadn't seen or heard from Lofton for days, since she'd given him the papers, and now here were the pa-

pers again, back in Brunner's possession, sitting on his
desktop.

"I don't know how you got the idea I was trying to use the
reporter against you. Maybe in the heat of the moment it
sounded that way, but I was concerned," Kelley was saying
now.

Brunner cut him short. "Save it. You thought you had me
by the balls."

"No. I told you. The thing with the Holyoke project, the
way the committee went, I couldn't control them. I wasn't
trying to put pressure on you. I know better than that."

When Amanti glanced over at Kelley, she could see that he
smiled with one corner of his mouth upturned, the look he
had when he'd said something open to interpretation, to be-
fuddle or belittle the person he was talking to or to show his
own cleverness. Only now it was obvious that smile was just
there by reflex, or to entertain himself, because he hadn't said
anything clever, and Brunner wasn't paying any attention.

"How did the reporter get these papers?" Brunner asked
her again. He drummed his fingers on top of the stack, played
with the edge of one of the papers. He looked at her in a way
that was charged with anger but also, oddly, with sexual energy, too, as if he were not touching the papers at all but the
buttons of her blouse. Kelley shifted on his feet.

"I don't know why you persist in this, Jack. She doesn't
know, and I don't know either. It must've been inside work.
Somebody in your organization; somebody you don't suspect."

"That's nonsense," Brunner said. He looked to Amanti for
confirmation. She felt trapped. It occurred to her that it made
no difference what she said. The two men were playing a
game with her, a battle that was a mere sideline to the one
that had already taken place before she had come. Brunner
had spoiled Kelley's plan, Lofton had lost the papers, everything was back to where it had always been.

"I gave Lofton those papers," she said suddenly. "I did it
on my own. I was sleeping with the reporter."

Both men were silent. They exchanged glances. Kelley's
eyes were very empty, very blue; Brunner smiled faintly.
Then, as if from a point high up, removed from her body, she
watched herself get up and leave the room. She abandoned the

two men to their awkward glances. She did not realize, until she had closed the front door behind her and taken her first breath of the dim, sultry air, that she had left her purse, and her car keys, inside the house.

The big door locked behind her; she could not get back inside even if she wanted. She walked into the heat, then back into the shade of the porch, before deciding to walk to town, to catch a taxi home. Just as she started, however, Kelley opened the door behind her. He held her purse in one hand, her car keys in the other.

"It's a good thing you forgot these. I want to talk to you."

Kelley did not give her time to argue. He handed her the car keys. "Just drive—I don't care where."

"What about your car?"

"We'll come back for it. I've got to talk to you."

She was anxious to get away, so she did as he asked. They drove along awhile in silence, Amanti taking the back roads that wound up into wooded hills. Though the hills were low, they were rugged, deceptively so, and the road switched back many times to circumvent the old, crumbling cliffs and twisting streams. Kelley put his hand on her leg. She gave the hand a deliberate look of contempt but let it stay.

"Why did you give those papers to the reporter?" he asked.

"I'd think you could figure that one out on your own. I'm tired of this game between you and Brunner. I want it over."

Kelley sighed, then put his head down between his hands. "I'm tired, too," he said, and for a second his composure and his coolness were gone, and she saw the real weariness underneath, though you could never tell with Kelley, because that might also be an act. She remembered one time, back when Kelley's father-in-law had discovered their affair. At that time Kelley had confessed to Amanti that he couldn't break up his marriage, not for political reasons or for fear of the old man but because he loved his wife, as much as he loved Amanti. It was just a simple, confusing fact of life, he had said. He had been close to tears, it seemed, utter disintegration. A second later, though, Kelley had been smiling.

She spotted a gravel pullout on the roadside ahead. She drove in and killed the engine. Through the trees and some hollyhock gone wild she could see a small valley, a pasture full of high brown weeds. In the middle of the pasture an old tractor sat sinking into the mud. Kelley raised his head. His eyes were red, weary-looking, but there was no sign of tears.

"I'm sorry about the papers. I didn't mean to ruin everything," she said, though of course it wasn't true. She touched his cheek where it was flushed. She hoped things were ruined even more than they seemed, that Kelley would give up politics, his wife. At the same time she knew it was an idle hope, that his involvement in that other world was what attracted her to him, besides.

"You didn't ruin anything," Kelley said. "Brunner had a way out all along. He was just lying low, studying his cards."

"What happened? The last you told me Brunner was getting ready to switch sides; at least it looked that way."

"He's got Harrison."

"What do you mean?"

"I mean he's got Harrison, or Harrison's got him, damn it! I had no idea they were hooked up."

"He's involved with your father-in-law? How could that be so?"

"Forget the specifics. The old man called me this morning. He told me to stop playing games. He told me I had to knuckle under to Brunner." As Kelley spoke, he made his own knuckles into a fist and placed the fist on the dashboard. He looked down into the valley, at the sinking tractor, and swore.

"Maybe you can pressure Harrison, too," Amanti offered.

"That's a joke." Kelley made a noise resembling a laugh. "Nobody in Massachusetts pressures Harrison. It isn't just this state either; presidents run to wipe his nose when he sneezes."

"I thought Harrison supported Sarafis."

"He does, in his own way. He mumbles the right words in public, keeps the liberals happy, and it's what he believes, too. He explained it all to me, gave me a little lecture on democracy. 'When you get down to it,' he told me, 'there are things more important than one man, one election. There are many men, a system, and it has to run smoothly, my personal opinions aside.'" Kelley laughed, then went on, his voice no longer imitating his father-in-law's. "In other words, Brunner's got the grease. Harrison and his friends've got the palms. A perfect match. And I didn't even know about it."

Kelley seemed genuinely upset. Whether it was because his schemes had gone for nothing, or because he was wearied by the corruption—both his own and that of others—or because he simply didn't like losing, Amanti didn't know. His eyes were watering now, and he made no attempt to hide it. She reached to touch his lips with her finger; his lips were soft, like those of a child, and she felt a sharp pain when she kissed him, a pain that she imagined to be his pain as well. She pulled him closer, so both their pains would disappear. When they pulled apart, Kelley's mouth was red from lipstick; for a brief, crazy second she thought the lipstick was blood.

"The old man told me if I didn't go along with Brunner, I'd never be anything but a two-bit representative to the state legislature," Kelley said. "If it weren't for his daughter, he'd burn me at the stake himself."

Amanti sighed. She reached for the ignition, but Kelley grabbed her hand.

"You have to help me get rid of the reporter. Brunner wants him off the case. So does Harrison." Kelley spoke rapidly, urgently, all trace of weakness gone. "Brunner had one of his people give Lofton some money to get lost, but my guess is that he'll want more. He checked out of the hospital today, and you're his best connection to us. He'll be by your house, I'd be willing to bet on it."

Amanti thought of telling Kelley he was wrong. Lofton wasn't interested in the money, or at least she didn't think he was. "If you don't help out," Kelley said, "Brunner's not going to be happy, with me . . . or with you."

She started the ignition. She didn't like the idea of dealing with Brunner when he was angry, but she was pretty sure he wouldn't do anything to hurt her. When things settled down, he would come see her at the apartment. His touch would be a little fiercer than before, for a while; he would hold her in the way you held someone who had almost left you, but hadn't, because you were the one who orchestrated the leaving, and the coming back, and the other one could do nothing without you. That's the way it would feel for him, except every once in a while there would be the look of dead rage because he suspected she wasn't paying attention but instead was thinking about Kelley.

As Amanti drove down the hill, back the same road she

had come, Kelley explained what he wanted her to do. When Lofton came to see her, she was to tell Lofton to go to Brunner's house. Brunner would pay him off and at the same time ask Lofton to write one more story: a piece about the rally that was going to take place the following afternoon at the Hillside Mall.

"Why doesn't Brunner just give him the money and let him go?"

"You know Brunner. He likes to get something for his money," Kelley said. When they reached the bottom of the hill, Kelley handed her a piece of paper. She saw two lines written in Brunner's hard, narrow script:

The old railroad depot.
Conch Street. 8:00 P.M.

"You're going to come to the rally with us, but afterward that's where you meet Lofton. At the old depot. After the rally. I don't care how you do it, but make sure he meets you. Then leave town. When you've got him far away from here, in a month or two you can come back. I'll take care of you."

"That's sweet," Amanti said, but she didn't buy it. The whole thing was too canned, too detailed. If they wanted her and Lofton to leave town together, there was no sense in arranging every detail so precisely, down to the place and the time. And there was no reason to keep her occupied every minute until it was time to meet him. Unless they had other things planned.

"You're not going to let me meet him at the depot," she said. "That's not why you want him there. You're going to kill him, aren't you?"

Kelley shook his head. He told her no, Lofton wasn't going to die, but as he spoke, she sensed the weariness in him, the weariness in herself, and knew that he was lying.

Lofton took his duffel into the stands and watched the practice. After talking to Golden, he had bought a small bottle of women's makeup. He had removed his bandages, then put the makeup on thickly, clumsily. The makeup had become dry and crusted on his skin, but at least he would not call quite so much attention to his bruises.

The Redwings looked tired. They had been on the road
nce the last time he'd seen them, the day Dazzy Vance had
een in town, and they had played ten games in the last week.
Jow they were back home, under a grizzled sky that blew
usts of infield dirt across the playing field. The breeze sent
hirlwinds of trash skittering across the field—an erratic, jig-
ke dance of beer cups and paper wrappers.

The Redwings had played well on the road, winning seven
ut of ten and pulling within four games of first-place West
Iaven, but only five games remained in the season. The Red-
ings would have to sweep this series against West Haven,
hen beat the Sailors twice in Lynn, all the while hoping that
West Haven would lose again in its last game at home. The
cenario seemed unlikely, but at least the team had a chance,
nd that had not seemed possible a month before.

He walked to the outfield fence, where Sparks paced the
arning track. Sparks had been around the night Gutierrez
old Amanti about the arsons, and Lofton still had not talked
o him about it.

Sparks saw him coming, spat in the outfield grass, and
alked briskly the other way. Lofton followed. He knew that
lot of players, particularly pitchers, were superstitious about
alking before a game, especially to a reporter. Lofton, how-
ver, wondered if something other than superstition lay be-
eath Spark's reluctance.

Lofton caught up, but Sparks was in no mood to talk. He
ept his eyes to the ground and kept pacing, chewing his
obacco and spitting every few steps, ignoring Lofton beside
im. Lofton started out talking baseball.

"Pitching rotation's a lot stronger now, what with you and
Kubachek and that new kid up from A ball. That must make
ou feel pretty good."

Sparks sighed as if he realized the question were a ruse.
Kubachek's gone," he said, and kept walking.

"Gone?"

"Yeah, gone. Cowboy pulled him back to California for the
lues' big pennant drive. What's the matter, don't you read
he papers?" Sparks started to brush Lofton away. Then he
aught sight of the reporter's face.

"What are you made up for? Halloween?"

Lofton touched his face. The makeup came off in small

flakes. "No, I got in an accident. The makeup looks bette
than the bruises."

Sparks shook his head. "Yeah," he said, and resumed pac
ing.

"You think you guys can do it without him?"

"Without who?"

"Kubachek."

"Doesn't matter. We would be where we are with him o
without. And that's in a hole. We haven't won five in a row al
season, let alone against these guys. They've clobbered us al
year. And if by some chance we slip them now, they'll be ou
to fuck us in the play-offs. . . . So you got what you need
You got your quote. Now let me pace. Alone."

"I need to talk to you about something else."

"Surprise."

"It's about Gutierrez."

"Forget it."

"I need more information."

"He's dead. What else is there to know?"

"Listen, this is serious stuff, Sparks." Lofton heard the an
ger in his voice. "I'm trying to figure out what happened. Yo
knew him. Tell me, flat out: What was Gutierrez fooling with
Why was he killed?"

"No sé, señor."

"Don't crap me, Sparks. Or is that just the way it goes
Gutierrez is your friend for a while, up to a limit, then yo
worry about yourself?"

"Back off. No wonder you got bruises."

"You were there, with Amanti, when he told her about th
fires, about Golden."

"I wasn't in the room." Sparks curled his lip. "I was ou
driving my car, I think. Or maybe I was asleep."

"Sure. Dreaming about Los Angeles."

"Screw yourself, Lofton. I been here three years, and
don't want to be here any longer. I want my chance. I can'
help what Gutierrez got himself mixed up in. This town wa
here before I came, and it will be here when I'm gone. I'm no
around to give some reporter his big break. I got my ow
breaks to worry about."

While Sparks talked, Lofton felt himself getting angrier, th
same sort of anger, maybe, that Golden had felt. He decide

to push Sparks, to find out if there was something the pitcher was hiding. "You want to hear how I got it figured?" he asked.

Sparks didn't answer. The pitcher was getting angry, too, his face red. When they reached the left field foul line, Sparks spun on his heels and headed back the other way. Lofton kept pace. Then Coach Barker appeared on the field. He started out toward them in a huff. Lofton knew he didn't have much time.

"This is how I put it together: Amanti confided in you, and you went straight to Brunner. You told him about Gutierrez; you told him I was on the story. Later, after Gutierrez was fixed, you talked to Golden and set me up for this bruising—a little something to get me out of the picture."

Sparks hesitated. He was vacillating, it seemed, torn between answering Lofton's accusations and lashing back. He clenched his right fist, but he had enough control over himself to realize that if he struck out at Lofton, he might hurt his own hand as well, and that would hurt his performance on the mound.

"What are you saying?"

"You set Gutierrez up. You told Brunner. You're the reason he's dead."

Sparks's eyes widened. Losing his restraint, he grabbed Lofton by the collar.

"Hey, what's going on here?" Coach Barker shouted. Barker was almost on them now. He waved his hands. Sparks loosened his grip, but he did not let go.

"You stool to Brunner, your friend dies, and you get your shot at the majors. Big cock on the block."

Sparks pulled back his fist now, as if he were ready to hit Lofton. Nonetheless, he hesitated again, deliberately, it seemed, giving Coach Barker time to push between them.

"What are you two doing?" Coach Barker turned to Sparks. "Do you want to pitch tonight or should I send you to an early shower?"

"He called me a murderer," Sparks said.

Coach Barker, gumming up his chaw of tobacco, spat in the direction of Lofton's feet. He shook his head at Lofton. "You out of your mind? Get away from my pitcher, goddamn you. Are you trying to lose me a game?"

"I'm a Redwings' fan," Lofton said. "I wouldn't do anything to make you lose."

Sparks put on another show of temper. "Keep this bastard away from me, will you? He's trying to ruin my game."

"Shut up, Sparks," said Coach Barker. "And you, Lofton, it's time to get lost. If you're not off the playing field in two seconds, I'm calling security."

When the game started, Sparks was almost unhittable. If anything, the angry conversation had helped more than it had hurt. He struck out five of the first nine batters. Only one man reached base, and that was on a Japanese liner, a cheap squib over Carpenter's outstretched glove. Behind Sparks, the team played cleanly and crisply. They scored two runs, scrabbling and clawing: in the first, Tim Carpenter walked, stole second, scoring on Elvin Banks's single; then, in the next inning, Singleton doubled, advanced on a grounder, and raced home when Lumpy sacrificed to the warning track. It was baseball with a razor edge, and Lofton—despite everything else that had been happening—enjoyed it.

In the fourth Sparks weakened. He was never meant to be a starter, Lofton thought. A reliever, yes. A couple of quick innings and out. Surely Coach Barker must realize this as well. Sparks was good through three innings, mediocre through five, horrible after that. Chances were, however, that the Blues' management would see only the combined stats, unless someone bothered to point out the distinctions. If that had happened, if the Blues were going to call him up, even if it was just for a cup of coffee, it would have to happen soon.

Sparks loaded the bases with one out. The next man hit the ball weakly, too weakly, and Carpenter, charging hard—twirling, stumbling, throwing: all in one motion—got the runner at second. But the relay for the double play was late, and a run crossed home.

Sparks came into the next batter hard, hard as he could. The batter hit it deep. Coming to its feet, making a low, collective gasp, the crowd watched as the ball arced down and the Redwings' left fielder, turning, gathered it in at the warning track. The inning was over, the damage minimal; Holyoke still led.

In the Holyoke fourth Elvin Banks was brushed back. A

high fastball sent him diving at the ground. Banks got up, screaming.

"I been beaned!"

The ump said no. The Holyoke fans yelled encouragement. "Come on, Elvin. . . . Go clobber 'em. . . . Go kill 'em."

But Banks watched strike three rush by on the outside corner. The West Haven players jeered and laughed. Banks, the bat still in his hand, turned glowering toward the West Haven bench. Nothing happened. The field changed hands. It was past twilight now, and the clouds were very thick.

Since his fastball had lost its zip, Sparks grew cautious and started throwing his curve. He trailed four pitches too far from the corner, and the leadoff hitter took first.

Pull him, Lofton thought.

Coach Barker did not move. Sitting placidly on the bench, one hand on his stomach, he looked like a small, fat Buddha. Lightning flashed in the sky overhead, and a solitary, fat drop of rain fell on Lofton's sleeve.

A shallow pop, another walk, and there were runners at first and second, one out. The rain came down harder. If Sparks could somehow hold the score and kill the rally before the downpour began—and the umps called the game—Holyoke could walk away with a win.

Sparks played it coy, loping curve after curve, half of them missing the strike zone, half edging over. Finally, he had to come in with the fastball. The West Haven catcher tagged it, a short, powerful swing that sent the ball ricocheting toward the outfield fence. At first Banks seemed to have misjudged the ball. He backpedaled; then, slipping on the wet grass, he changed field, snaked out his glove hand, and came down diving. He held the ball in his glove. The runners returned. There were two outs now, Holyoke still leading by a run, and the West Haven pitcher was coming to bat. He was the same man who had brushed back Banks the inning before, sending a pitch in close to his head. Sparks stepped off the mound, yelled out an insult, and came in with a fastball, tight at the wrist. The pitcher jumped back. He complained to the umpire. Some West Haven players yelled from the dugout, screaming that Sparks was trying to hurt their pitcher.

Sparks ignored them, turning his back and staring out at

center field. Then Sparks threw his fastball again. The West Haven pitcher tried to duck, but he could not get away. The ball bounced off his helmet and caromed toward the dugout as the West Haven pitcher fell to the ground. Both benches cleared.

The players ran from all directions toward the mound, the West Haven players leaping toward Sparks, the Redwings jumping to protect their pitcher, bodies slipping helter-skelter on the wet grass, punches flying, hitting, missing, arms flailing in the rain. Barker walked toward the melee, still calm, his arms still folded over his stomach. Around him, in the increasing downpour, the ump tried to settle the players. A group of Redwings grabbed Sparks, trying to pull him out of the fight. Some West Haven players tried to do the same with their pitcher. But just as things seemed to calm down, a West Haven man broke loose, hurtled over the others, and threw a punch at Sparks. The brawl broke out again, the umpires in the middle, Coach Barker milling at the edges. A photographer jumped the fence, and some teenagers followed. Then came the crew from the halfway house. The security guards followed, one hand waving the nightstick, the other on the holster. Somehow they managed to chase away the crowd. Soon it was only a few players fighting. Then it was only Sparks and the West Haven pitcher, rolling in the mud on the mound.

Barker stood over them, arms crossed. On the ground beneath him the two pitchers continued to struggle, though not so fiercely now, until finally Barker reached in and pulled Sparks away. The umpire pointed his finger at Sparks, raised his thumb in the air, crossed his chest, and threw him out of the game. The West Haven pitcher took first base. After Barker had sent Hammer in in relief, the game went to its last out, the bases loaded now, Holyoke still clinging to its lead.

Jimmy Jefferson, West Haven's leadoff hitter—on his way to the As in Oakland at the end of the week—went after the first pitch. He hit a grounder that the Redwings' first baseman, Lynch, had a hard time grabbing. The wet ball slipped from his hands, but it did not matter. Jefferson slipped coming out of the box, and Lynch, fumbling and stumbling, beat him to the bag. Holyoke had sloshed out a victory in the rain.

* * *

The rain came down harder, but Lofton took his time. He was on his way to Barena's. He felt the rain slick his hair, soak through his shirt. There was no hurry; he was already wet clean through. You were safe in a hard rain, he thought. At the top of the hill Barena's neon flashed off and on, casting an orange shadow on the brick. Once inside, he called Amanti. Again she didn't answer. So he got himself something to eat, then sat by the window, where he could watch the rain coming down against the darkening sky.

Who had told Golden where to find him? From Lofton's conversation with Sparks, he was still no wiser. The pitcher had blown up when Lofton suggested he was involved with Brunner. That could just be an act, but chances were that Sparks was just what he seemed: a guy who wanted his chance, who would push hard to get it but would stay away from anything that looked like real trouble.

Lofton heard someone call his name. He looked up and saw the woman who worked the bar, a beer in one hand, the telephone in the other. She seemed to have lost her patience after barking his name out just once and was now ready to hang up if someone didn't come quickly. Lofton identified himself and took the phone. He was taken aback. It was Golden on the other end, and he wanted Lofton to meet him at the clubhouse. "In half an hour. When this place is good and cleared out and I don't have to worry about somebody coming back because he forgot his shoes," Golden said, and hung up. So Lofton had no choice but to go back and sit down at his table and stare at the orange shadow of Barena's neon on the sidewalk rippled by the rain. When twenty minutes had passed, he left. He walked down to the main gate at MacKenzie Field. The stands were dark and empty in the rain. Ahead of him the clubhouse door was open, but the lights inside were off. Lofton stepped in quietly. He found Golden in the next room, straddling a bench that ran in front of a row of lockers.

"I saw you walking up the hill after the game. I figured you were on your way to Barena's," Golden said. "I'm taking a chance talking to you." The room smelled of cigarette smoke and steam and sweat and dirty clothes. An ashtray sat on the bench beside Golden. The general manager wore a Redwings'

cap on his head. "I talked to Brunner today. You were right
about the papers in your car. They were there, but I didn't
know it, I had no idea. The police gave them back to Brunner.
. . . I think Brunner's going to have you killed."

Lofton could think of nothing to say. His silence seemed to
agitate Golden.

"Look, I'm trying to do you a favor. This has gotten way
out of control. I had no idea things were going to get like this.
When I went after you, I was frustrated, I was cracking. You
should be careful. Brunner has friends on the force."

"What about you, you his friend, too?"

"Listen." Golden gave him a dim look, then went on. "The
bastard set me up. He has buildings all over town, most of
them garbage. Going to turn them into parking lots, I don't
know, I didn't ask. He gave me money, five, ten grand sometimes, to pay one of the community people there, to sort of
spread the money around and get the rest of the Ricans out
before the building was demolished. That's all that I thought I
was doing: helping clear out the buildings. But this last time
the fucking building burned with people still inside. Five people died. That's when I started thinking about what was really
going on."

Golden lit another cigarette. Seemingly he was calm, but
there was always the look about him as if he could snap any
moment. He would move his hands suddenly, cast a black
glance at the concrete floor, his voice rising as he talked. Then
he would look at Lofton, his face as calm as the water of the
Dead Sea.

"Have you been paying the torch?" Lofton asked.

"I didn't put it together. I didn't know what I was doing."
Golden studied the locker beside him. It belonged to one of
the ballplayers and was decorated with pictures of the guy's
family, a bunch of blondes in front of a ranch home in the dry
hills of what was probably California. "Buildings go up all the
time. Coincidence, I thought. I didn't know I was paying the
torch. I didn't know he was a torch."

"Who did you think you were paying?"

"Community people, that's what Brunner called them.
They were supposed to pass the money around, help vacate
buildings, stuff like that."

"What community people?"

"Okay, gang leaders. Whatever word you like. You're the writer. I really didn't know what was going on. Or I told myself I didn't know. I need the money. Disease is expensive."

"Mendoza, is he one of the men?" Lofton asked.

Golden nodded. And so the circle closed on itself again. At least for the moment the names connected, intertwined, but when you tried to prove it, when you reached out and grabbed, your hand got snarled, you pulled in people you didn't expect, ruined their lives, and missed whom you were after.

"What happened with Gutierrez? Did you lose your temper with him, too?"

Golden gave him a reckless look, the dark flash of anger. He didn't like Lofton's question, but he was snarled up in guilt, trying to escape, so he answered it anyway.

"Gutierrez was a coke freak. He put things together somehow, but he didn't talk to me about it. He went to the Wanderers and tried to put some pressure on Mendoza, thinking he could pick up some more coke. That's another thing Mendoza's people are into. They used the payoff money to buy coke and sell it, trying to move themselves up in the world. When Gutierrez fooled with him, they blew him away."

"How do you know that?"

"Mendoza told me. He seemed pretty proud, like he had done us a favor."

"It wasn't Brunner behind the murder?"

"No. He was mad as hell when he found out about it. He was afraid it would somehow come back on him. He got in touch with his friends at the police and did what he could to kill the investigation."

Lofton listened to the rain. It still fell pretty hard outside, but there was the sound of water dripping inside, too, back in the shower room. A faucet, maybe, or a leak in the roof. "Tell me one more thing," Lofton said. "If you didn't know I had Brunner's papers, why did you bother to follow me? How was it you knew I was going to be at Amanti's that night?"

"I didn't know about the papers, but I knew you were investigating me. I wanted you to stop. I still do, but I'm not so worried. You'll never get to them—or to me."

"How did you know where to find me?" he asked again.

"Let's just say I put a nickel in the jukebox, and the jukebox sang all night. I didn't call you to get other people involved. You don't need to know anything else. I'm just trying to warn you. Forget your story. Just get out, and get out now."

"What about you? Are you out?"

"I've got one more errand to run. Then that's it. Then I'm free. I'm finished with Brunner."

"Do you really believe that?"

Golden didn't answer. He lit another cigarette while the old one still burned in the ashtray and straightened the cap on his head.

"How are they planning on killing me?" Lofton asked.

"I don't know the details," Golden said. "And it wouldn't be safe for me to tell you if I did. I'm not trying to be noble. I'm just giving you fair warning."

Lofton was wet, cold to the bone. He imagined how he must look—drenched clothes, sunglasses, bruised cheeks—but the cabbie said nothing. It was a good, long fare to Amherst. He still had not been able to get in touch with Amanti; he did not know if he should be worried about her safety or suspicious about what she might be up to now. In the meantime, he wanted to let his thoughts rest in the silence, fade to nothing in the blackness of the cab. Only it wouldn't happen. His chest tightened again, and the darkness was veined with small streaks of red, impressions of blood-colored light left lingering on his retina from passing cars. Lofton found himself sorting through the last few days. Car chases. Hospitals. Revolvers. When the cab reached Amherst, he had the driver let him off at the end of Amanti's street. He paid and walked toward her apartment. The rain had stopped, the asphalt was wet and shining, lights glowed in the houses. He could hear voices drifting out from the porches. He guessed that while he had been standing in the rain at MacKenzie Field, these same people had heard the rain from inside their houses, listened to it thrum on their rooftops, and thought that the world was good. If he had stayed back with Maureen, back in Colorado, then it could have been the same way for him. The world could be good.

Her place was dark except for the light in the bedroom. He knocked and waited. She did not come. After several more tries he walked to the back of the building and looked through the bedroom window. The bed was made, but there was no one there.

"Gina," he called through the screen. He went to the front of the house again, tried knocking, then returned to the sliding door in the rear. He called her name again, but she did not answer. He decided to go inside. He would look through her papers, and he would see if he found anything unexpected, maybe some clue to her whereabouts. He jimmied the sliding door—an old trick he had learned in high school—turned on a light, and started rummaging.

There was a noise behind him. He turned. Amanti stood in her nightgown, blocking the doorway. *More revolvers.* Lofton laughed. She held a gun pointed at his chest.

9

Lofton took a deep breath. Amanti stood half in the darkness, half out. The light from the hall lit one side of her face and at the same time illuminated her figure from behind, making her nightgown seem bright, fringed with light. She stood very quiet and very still. She held the gun waist-high.

"What are you doing?" he asked.

She didn't say anything. Lofton glanced down at the papers he had taken from her drawer.

"Where did you get the gun?"

"I was sleeping." Amanti stepped out of the light, so now he could not see her face at all. She lowered the gun, pointing it at the carpet. "I woke up and heard some noise."

He toyed with the papers between his fingers and took another step toward her. With the sound of her voice, his fear had started to pass, but he was not sure, not completely, that he should let it. He sat down in the chair and switched on the light nearby. Her face was that of someone who had just woken up.

"Why are you going through my things?" Amanti held the fingers of her free hand pressed against her thigh, just as she had held them on his first visit here.

"Why don't you put the gun away?"

"You know, I might've shot you; you shouldn't sneak around."

"I knocked a dozen times. I came around back and looked in your bedroom. It was empty."

"I was in the extra bedroom, up front. When I heard noise, I got up to check."

"Who did you think it was?" Lofton motioned toward her gun. Amanti shrugged. She sat on the couch and placed the revolver on the light stand. Well out of my reach, Lofton noticed.

"I was just with Golden. He's the one who smashed my face. Caught up to me in his car after the last time I was here. Or hadn't you heard?"

"What are you getting at?" Amanti looked at the papers he still held in his fingers. "I don't appreciate this."

"How did Golden know to find me here?"

"I don't have any idea about that."

Amanti moved her hands sharply, in the motion of someone pushing someone else away, refusing to move. The gesture was unconscious, until the last minute, when she realized the effect she was creating. Earlier that evening, until the time she had fallen asleep, she had debated whether to help Lofton or to go along with what Kelley wanted her to do. She had come to no decision. Then she had woken up, heard the voice calling, the screen rattling, and had pulled the gun from its blue towel in the drawer. She had not been sure who it was. If Lofton had moved suddenly when she first saw him, or if the light had been different, then maybe she would have shot him. As it was, he didn't seem to realize she was telling him the truth: She didn't know why Golden had shown up out on the highway when he did. All she knew was that Brunner had his papers back. "Why would I give you the papers, then arrange for Golden to beat you up, and risk the police finding everything? That doesn't make sense."

Lofton agreed. It didn't make sense. But that didn't mean it hadn't happened that way. He had the brief sensation that in some important way he was blind, that there was an easy passage out of this thing, one foot in front of the other, as Amanti had said, but instead, he groped along.

"Your face, it looks terrible," Amanti said.

Lofton touched his eyes; his makeup had smeared badly.

"Do you have any more of this cream?"

Lofton watched Amanti go down the hallway. He picked up the gun off the light stand. The safety was on. When Amanti came back, she glanced at it in his hands, but she said nothing. As she sat down next to him, opening her bottle, he put the gun back on the table.

"Let me see your face."

She ran her fingertips over his bruises, rubbing off the makeup that was already there. "Does this hurt?"

"A little, but not much. My face is drugged."

Pursing her lips, she studied his face intently, with the same look Lofton had seen on other women—Maureen, Nancy, his mother—when they were concentrating on their own faces in the mirror. She obviously enjoyed the task.

Amanti's face was very close to his own, but he still couldn't read her; he still didn't know what was under the surface, what she was telling him and what she was keeping to herself. She held her tongue between her teeth while she studied his bruises. He felt her knee against his thigh.

"Brunner wants to talk to you."

Amanti reached for the cream on the table behind him, but Lofton, thinking of the gun, pushed her hand away. She held her lips tight together now, her fingertips pressed against the cushion beside him. She shook her head unhappily. The scar on her cheek seemed larger, more visible, now that her face was flushed.

"Brunner and Kelley are working together. They want you to drop the story. They're sure you'll do it if I ask—and if they slice the pie a little larger. . . . Will you calm down and let me finish your face?"

Her blue eyes were large and wet. He pulled himself up from the couch and lit a cigarette. The smoke hurt his chest, and his face, too, was beginning to hurt. The pills were wearing off.

"Brunner's going to ask you to cover a political rally, to write a whitewash for him, something to cover up what's going on with the fires. I'm supposed to tell you to take the money, do what they say, meet me, and get out of town. That's what they want me to do, lead you out of town."

"Where do we go?"

"That's your choice. Either way, no matter what you do,

I'm not leaving as easy as they would like. I stay here. I'm safest when I'm close, where I can watch." She made the same sharp gesture again, quick, defensive, though this time she did not seem to realize it. For a second, something about her—the way she raised her head, maybe, or the way her eyes looked not at him but at the floor—reminded him of those Mexican girls in San Jose who traveled the streets alone, in stark heels and black skirts, and who, when they saw groups of men wandering the streets, white men, usually, and drunk, would follow packs like that through the streets, the stores, the arcades, keeping the group in sight until it had moved out of their territory. A girl would follow not because she wanted them but because the men were dangerous together, like young dogs. It was best to stay in the open, to keep them in sight. But later, if one of the men should approach a girl alone, when the others had scattered, then it was a different story.

"Go along with what Brunner wants you to do," she said. "Or let him think you are. Take the money; do everything he asks. Then, at the last minute, do it the way you want."

Her composure left her. He felt a long shudder run through her body. He watched her face, waiting for the tears. They didn't come.

"I don't have much to base my story on, not without Brunner's papers," he said. "Losing those, that hurts things. But I can piece some kind of story together."

He thought of insisting that she go into hiding, a motel in Chicopee or Hartford, someplace where she would be safe until the story was written, not the way Brunner wanted, of course, but the way he wanted. He wondered how things would be if they loved each other, but he dismissed the question as soon as it came to him—like a breath taken quickly and then let go—because there just wasn't any way to answer.

Amanti felt herself vacillating. She was entertaining the same question she'd been entertaining all night, not the details of it, of course, but the question itself, the gut answer. She could finish setting Lofton up, the way Kelley wanted, or she could say nothing and simply let him go. The conversation could still go either way; it just needed the right ending, the right twist. Whatever she did, she should watch out for herself.

"Maybe it's not such a good idea for me to stay here," she said, listening to herself, to the dip and catch in her voice. "Maybe I should meet you after you talk to Brunner. It might be better." She thought of the paper Kelley had handed her with Brunner's handwriting: "The railroad depot. 8:00 P.M."

"It's up to you," Lofton said. "Where do you want to meet?"

"Barena's," she said suddenly. "After the game. Tomorrow."

Lofton heard the change in her voice and wondered what it meant. Through his half-shut eyes he could see her revolver, a black smear on the white tabletop. *Can I trust her?* He studied the gun until she was done with his face and her fingers glided over his cheek, moving downward, touching the soft hair on the back of his neck.

The morning was hot. "The hottest one yet, you ask me," the cabbie told Lofton as they drove down Brunner's street in South Hadley. Lofton put on his sunglasses and loosened his collar. These clothes—a faded pink shirt, a black tie, a rumpled suit jacket—seemed to make it even hotter, but there was not much else in his old duffel. Maybe the outfit would help give Brunner the impression of someone transient and shabby, someone who would take his money and leave. The cabbie pulled over, and Lofton paid him. He went to Brunner's door and knocked.

"I heard you wanted to talk to me," he said when Brunner came to the door. Brunner looked Lofton over as if a circus con man had just shown up on his stoop. Up close the man's face seemed tremendously large, the features exaggerated.

"Come in."

He guided Lofton across the thick carpeting to a room in the back, a study. Here a picture window looked across Brunner's yard to the Connecticut River, drained, this time of year, by upriver mills and tobacco farms. Lofton looked across the river to Holyoke, the church spires, the tenements, the redbrick mills, all tinted green, cooler, more serene, through his sunglasses. He could feel Brunner's gray eyes on his neck; the idea of Brunner behind him made him nervous, but he did not want to show it. In the backyard a handsome older woman, with silver-gray hair—Brunner's wife, he

uessed—appeared, wandering toward the rose hedge. She
ore a blue day robe of a shining, almost elegant material.
ofton watched her until she disappeared around the hedge.

"Looks like you've gotten yourself into a bit of trouble,"
runner said. He sat down behind his desk and motioned for
ofton to sit as well. Lofton hesitated. Finally, he sat, and
hen he did, Brunner stood up. Holding his hands behind his
ack, Brunner headed toward the window, then continued
round the back of Lofton's chair, talking as he walked.

"I've heard a little about you, Lofton, and I admire your
itelligence. Or maybe I should say cleverness. I'm not sure,
et, how smart you really are." Brunner's voice was dull, flat,
ɔ devoid of depth, so calm that Lofton was not sure of the
arcasm. "Obviously, as a writer, you're much sharper than
aany of those I have to deal with."

Brunner appeared from behind Lofton, still circling. He
ave Lofton a hard look, which Lofton returned. The sun-
lasses, Lofton thought, give me an advantage. Brunner can't
ee my eyes; he can't read me.

Brunner stopped, put his hand on the desk, and picked up
n envelope.

"Wasn't Randy Gutierrez sharp enough for you?" Lofton
sked. "Or Einstein? How about him?"

"Don't distract me." Brunner's voice was cold, irritated.
Ie shook his head. "I would like to settle this matter. And I
ould like to do it easily, painlessly. But if we can't do it that
ay, then it will be settled another way. Everything is always
ettled."

"Sure, let's settle," Lofton said. "Go ahead. Shoot."

"You talked to Ray Nassau, my representative, when you
ere in the hospital, so you know I am a generous man."
Brunner smiled, the first smile Lofton had seen from him. He
apped the envelope against his palm as he spoke. "Murder.
Leaving the scene of a crime. Withholding information."

"Prove it."

"A vial of pills. Randy Gutierrez's letters. A medallion.
Vhy were these in your apartment? Where did you get them?
Officer Ryan, homicide, will find you suspicious, Lofton."

"I've heard this story. But how did you get these things,
his evidence, from my room? Who did you hire? Or maybe I

shouldn't be asking you? Maybe Kelley pulls the string here?"

A small glint flowered in Brunner's eyes, like the glimme on his wife's robe, and then was gone.

"No one works for Kelley; they work for me. Don't foo yourself, Lofton. Be clever."

He could tell the suggestion that Kelley might be in contro irked Brunner, however momentarily. But then Brunner eye him, calm again as a hog in a wallow, and Lofton felt himse sweating profusely despite the air-conditioning.

"Now, being clever, you probably have noticed this enve lope in my hand. And being clever, you probably think yo know what's in it." Brunner stood directly in front of hin "You probably think I am going to hand this to you. Yo probably think I am going to say, 'Take it, my compliment: leave town, best wishes.' "

Brunner extended the envelope toward Lofton. Then, jus as Lofton moved, almost imperceptibly—as if he were goin to reach out and take it—Brunner pulled back and restarte his circling.

"The intelligent man, of course, would wait a bit more pa tiently. Down in the little dark part of his heart, he woul wonder what small favor he could do for me. This man, h might think: What are my skills? What could I do?"

"You want me to write a story," Lofton said.

"Oh, good. We are not merely clever."

Brunner held out the envelope, and Lofton took it. Inside he found a check for ten thousand dollars. He held the chec between two fingers and touched it to his cheek. The stake were going up.

"The clever man, my friend, would take that check, cash i and leave town. He would say to himself, 'Brunner won' bother, Brunner won't follow.' And the clever man might b right. But the intelligent man, he would make the extra effor The intelligent man would repay the favor."

"A feature?" Lofton asked. "The man who loves Holyoke Who struggles to bring baseball, business, and progress to thi town that burns all around him?"

"There's a rally at Hillside this afternoon, and a game to night. I want something sweet in tomorrow's *Dispatch*. The leave Holyoke, Mr. Lofton. Go back to your wife in Colo

rado." Brunner stopped. He smiled. "Or if you have somebody else in mind, take her. Take the money and go."

Lofton swallowed. His face hurt, and so did his chest. So
far Brunner had done everything the way Amanti had said he
would: offered him money; asked him to write a story; promised him an easy way out of town. And now that he had done
so, there was for an odd moment the look of the patriarch
about him, a sort of gentleness that implied that the rest of
what he had done had been a stern act, for Lofton's benefit,
but that Lofton had better pay attention. In another instant,
though, the gentleness was gone.

"A hack feature? That's all you want?"

"Timing," Brunner said. "It's all timing. You're a baseball
fan, you know that. I want it in the *Dispatch* tomorrow."

"Why trust me?" Lofton asked. "Arson is great copy. So's
bribery. Maybe I'd hang you."

"You'd hang yourself. The people at the *Dispatch* are my
friends. And Kirpatzke, he's had a hard life. He's sympathetic
to me. We're buddies, you might say."

"I knew Kirpatzke had to be friends with somebody, might
as well be you. But I have other contacts. I know other editors."

"So do I."

Brunner smacked his hands together. Lifting his sunglasses,
Lofton took a closer look at the check, then threw it back on
the desk. "I've already written out the real story, the truth,"
he lied. "Anything happens to me, and the story's printed, no
questions asked."

"If you believe that, good."

"I want more money."

Brunner circled out from behind Lofton. He gave the reporter a long, brutish look which Lofton did not quite believe.

"Maybe the amount needs adjusting," Brunner said. He
reached for his checkbook and drew up another draft. The
check was for fifteen thousand dollars.

Lofton held the check in his hand. "Maybe it's not a question of money?"

"Tell me, Mr. Lofton, is it a bad thing to give money to be
distributed to the poor, money which—if not helping them
find a better place to live—gives them a little food? Is it bad to
destroy the slums; is it bad to give landlords the money to tear

down their buildings, to rebuild; is it bad to give a beaten man a chance, to help him take care of his dying wife? And if the government does none of these things, is it bad to do it our own way?"

There was the slightest trace of a whine in Brunner's voice, a misery that the man himself did not recognize.

"But people died in those fires," said Lofton.

"That couldn't be foreseen."

"What about Gutierrez, did he have to die? And is Mendoza really giving that money to the poor, or is he keeping it for himself? From what I hear, he's using it to buy drugs and push them around town. I don't see the saintliness in that."

"The minor players, the bit actors, cannot always be controlled. They have visions of their own. I would like to know your vision, Mr. Lofton?"

"My vision is cash."

Brunner smiled now. "Ah, a pragmatist. But I am a pragmatist, too. I like to keep these checks. They act as receipts later, you know, in case I need a record of your involvement, for whatever reason."

"Considering everything . . ." Lofton added slowly, smiling, "considering the moral dilemma . . . this still isn't enough money."

"There are limits."

"Yes, but aren't you up against one yourself? How long can you wait to burn American Paper? Aren't the insurance companies ready to pull out? Isn't that why you want me to write a sweet story about you now, something to deflect the attention away from the buildings you're about to burn?"

"The story's just icing. I don't need you that much. Don't get too convinced of your own importance."

"No." Lofton drummed his fingers on the table. He stalled a bit longer, smiling faintly, deliberately to himself, then put the check in his pocket. "I'm intelligent, remember. And reasonable. I'll take what I have here."

"Good."

Lofton felt his sweat growing cold now on his skin, in the air-conditioned room. Even so, he was pleased with himself. Brunner believes he bought me, Lofton thought; I acted the thing well.

"I'll call the bank and tell them to cash that draft for you.

No waiting. No questions. They'll cash Nassau's check, too. That way I get my receipts, you get your cash." Brunner opened the door. Lofton stood, and the two men looked at each other.

"Kelley found out about your arson scheme, didn't he? He tried to use me to put pressure on you to switch sides in the primary. Did it work? Are you going to switch sides?"

Brunner glowered; his pupils were ice white, it seemed, and his neck was red. The anger was genuine. "No," Brunner said. Lofton decided to go on, to press whatever advantage he had while Brunner was angry. "All right, I'll write the story in a way that makes you look good. But there's one thing I want to know. For a while someone's been on my tail. Someone contacted Golden, got him all worked up, and told him where to find me. And somebody trashed my room. I want to know who that person is."

"You're talking too much, Mr. Lofton, and asking too many questions. It makes me doubt your sincerity."

"No, like I said, this is something personal." Lofton gestured at his face. "I want to know who set me up for this bruising."

"I can't help you with it."

Getting up, saying nothing, Brunner walked behind him and opened the door. Though he knew Brunner was telling him it was time to go, Lofton stood there for a few stubborn seconds. Then he followed Brunner down the hall. Mrs. Brunner stood on the front stoop, perspiration dampening her silver hair.

"Mr. Lofton, this is my wife, Helen. She always enjoys meeting young men on their way up."

The woman smiled demurely. She was tall, handsome, bigboned. "Are you in construction, too, Mr. Lofton?"

"Yes. I'm working on something for your husband."

"Profitable, I hope."

"Yes, I think so."

Brunner laughed. "But I'm afraid Mr. Lofton's going to make his killing and leave us. Back to Colorado. He was just telling me how the simple life is the best."

Lofton looked at Brunner for a sign of sarcasm, of mockery. He could not find it. He headed down the walkway. Halfway down the street he turned and looked back. Brunner

stood in his front yard with his wife, the two of them bending
over, tending to some late-summer flowers.

The old steel bridge over the Connecticut River vibrated all
around him, rumbling and wailing as the cars rushed over its
grating. Toward the Holyoke side of the river, water spilled
over the milling dam and rushed southward through the
weeds. On the South Hadley side, not far from Brunner's, a
wider, shallow channel swept around the dam, or appeared to
from this angle, carrying the water not needed for the mills.
The center of the river was dry, an island of gray rock,
mostly, river grass, and rusting metal. Lofton walked toward
the Holyoke side, studying the line of the city. Upriver were
the flat roofs, tenements—gray, brown, and dirt-colored
buildings, porches streaming with laundry—which had
housed Holyoke's immigrant families since before the turn
of the century. Closer by, new steel and concrete apartments
—the projects—towered over the mills. Already graffiti covered the new buildings.

Lofton reached the edge of the bridge. He looked back toward South Hadley and the houses along the other bank:
weeping willows, wide green lawns, picture windows. He kept
walking, taking a road that wound along one of the old
canals. There were more canals, he knew—or so he had heard
—underneath the city, a system of tunnels and gates that
moved the water from place to place.

He watched a band of kids disappear into the weeds behind
an old warehouse and thought of the Latinos. He had not seen
them since the day they confronted him on the street in front
of his hotel. No doubt they were still searching out Mendoza;
the street war was continuing. If he wandered around the
streets of Holyoke long enough, he could find the Latinos.
This was their territory. He did not know if he wanted to find
them. Even if by some chance they could help with the story,
the gang was still dangerous. Lofton also wondered how
much real chance he had of getting his story into the *Dispatch*. Was Kirkpatzke really in Brunner's debt? If so, Lofton
might have to forget the Holyoke paper altogether and go see
his old friend Warner at the *Globe*. When you got down to it,
he thought, what real difference did it make if he wrote the

ry? Who cared if Holyoke burned, if Brunner made money
stroying buildings that no one should live in anyway?
Brunner is right, Lofton thought, I should go home.

He went into Brunner's bank to cash the checks. It was
lfare day, and people were lined up at the windows for food
mps: old men who spat on the bank floor; women with too
any children; young men, who stared at the well-dressed
lers with glazed eyes.

"I was told you would cash these for me," Lofton said. He
nded the teller both checks: the one Brunner had given him
d the one he had gotten a few days back, in the hospital,
m Nassau. For good measure, he handed her a third check
o, the one Liuzza had written in Northampton. "Ask your
anager if there's a problem."

The woman came back after a minute or two. She said
re was no problem. She counted out the money in big bills,
housand at a flip.

"Break one of these up for me," Lofton said. "And put the
st in an envelope."

Lofton put the small bills in his wallet. He tucked the enve-
pe with the big bills into his inside jacket pocket and left the
nk. The rally up at the Hillside Mall, the one Brunner
anted him to see, was scheduled for three-thirty. He had
me time, so he walked over to the small park in the center
town. Across the street from the park a fireman sat in front
the station, arms folded, waiting for a call. An old man
zed on one of the green benches, and pigeons skittered
ong the hot concrete.

The Hillside Mall was brightly lit, full of color, its windows
corated with back-to-school displays, manikins in plaids
d sweaters. Out in the white stone corridors, teenagers clus-
ed in groups, drinking Cokes, smoking cigarettes, and star-
g sullenly at the passersby.

At the center of the mall three tiers of shops came together.
fton stood on the top tier, staring down at a platform
ich had been set up at ground level and decorated with
lloons and crepe paper. An awning was stenciled:

RICHARD SARAFIS AND THE HOLYOKE REDWINGS
MAKING HITS IN WESTERN MASS

He walked down the concrete spiral. At the bottom of t
platform, arranged at angles, were glossy black-and-wh
photos: Richard Sarafis and Senator Kelley and Tony Luiz:
all standing together, grinning; Mayor Rafferty throwing c
the first ball; a panorama of MacKenzie Field, a mill sta
rising in the background.

He went back up to the second tier and waited. The T
crew arrived, including the young woman reporter who h
been at MacKenzie Field interviewing Dazzy Vance, the c
Hall of Famer. A young white girl wearing a baseball cap a
a Sarafis sweat shirt handed Lofton a leaflet. A Puerto Ric
boy followed behind her. Very dark-skinned, cleanly dresse
loose-hipped, he reminded Lofton of those young men w
hung around in the squares in Mexico waiting to meet Ame
can women. He looked at Lofton with piercing eyes, as
Lofton were trash.

A crowd started to gather below. Lofton saw a repor
from the *Springfield Post* milling with the shoppers. A m
employee drummed his fingers against the stage microphor

Not too long after, no longer than it took to smoke anoth
cigarette, Brunner & Co. appeared at the platform. Amar
was there, dressed in a straight skirt and a high-collar
blouse that might have seemed demure on another woma
She wore the collar open and the sleeves rolled high. Senat
Kelley walked beside her. Except in photographs, Loft
hadn't seen the senator before. He was smaller than Loft
expected, just slightly taller than Amanti, a surprisingly fa
skinned man with a smile that seemed shy, at least in tl
crowd, today, and disarming eyes, even from a distanc
Walking just behind was Brunner, not quite the malevole
presence he had seemed earlier but simply a tall, heavys
man, obviously in the circles of power. Glancing from Amar
to Kelley to Brunner, you could feel the tension among t
three; it was a kind of electricity that the crowd felt, tc
Lofton thought; at least they drew the crowd's attention mc
completely than Richard Sarafis, the gubernatorial candida
who walked a little farther back, alongside Tony Liuzza.

Rickey Sparks and Kirpatzke followed the others. Spar
was awkward, out of place in his baseball uniform; Kirpatz
dressed like one of the politicians—blue suit, white shirt, tie
but somehow a little shabbier, a little seedy. In a few minut

ey all were on the stage, except Kirpatzke, who drifted into
e crowd. The loudspeaker played "Take Me Out to the Ball-
me."

Last night at her apartment Amanti had told Lofton that
e was going to be at this rally, that Kelley and Brunner had
inted her to be here. After the rally, she had told him, she
is supposed to go to dinner with them, then over to Mac-
enzie Field, where there was a special promotional night
inned: The Hollywood Chicken was scheduled to be at the
ld, entertaining the kids, doing handstands and stunts along
e sidelines.

"I don't understand," he'd said. "If they want me to run off
th you—if that's their whole plan, to get rid of me—how
me they're keeping you so tied up?"

Amanti had not given him an answer. Lofton didn't like it.
seemed Brunner and Kelley had every minute of her time
counted for, down to the time they had scheduled her to
get him. Meanwhile, they kept him busy with this story,
mething any number of paid hacks could take care of easy
ough. Part of the reason, Lofton guessed, was that Brunner
ed control; he liked to have his hand on your head, your
ce underwater, a firm grip that let you know he'd let you up,
at all, when he pleased. Lofton doubted, however, that he
d such tight control over Amanti. Brunner might want
ch control, Kelley might want it, too, but neither had it.
e played her part in all this; no matter what she said or how
e pointed at grim fate, she still played. None of what had
ppened, or whatever might happen, would be possible with-
t her. Brunner, Kelley, both knew that. They were depend-
g on her to help escort him out of town, but Lofton
ondered if they really meant to let him get away, and just
iat Amanti's part would be.

While Lofton headed down into the crowd to talk to
irpatzke, someone in a chicken suit bounded onstage and
etended to struggle with the man at the microphone. The
ds pushed and cheered at the front of the crowd.

"What a surprise," Kirpatzke said when he saw Lofton.
is voice held the same flat tone as always.

"I'm sure you're thrilled."

On the platform Amanti was seated between Brunner ar
Kelley. The PA boomed, loud and scratchy: "Nope, folks, th
is not the Hollywood Chicken." The kids groaned. The a
nouncer came back quickly. "Nope, this is the Hillsi‹
Chicklet." The Chicklet looked up, surprised, grabbed himse
in the stomach as if he'd been shot, then bounced up, wavii
his pennant.

"Listen," Lofton said to Kirpatzke, "I talked to Brunner

"Another thrill." Kirpatzke stared straight ahead. F
chewed gum and would not look at Lofton.

"The Chicklet was sent ahead by the Hollywood Chick‹
to tell you he'll be at MacKenzie Field, tonight, along wi
these gentlemen on the bandstand. . . ."

"What does Brunner have on you?"

"Not a thing." Kirpatzke continued staring at the platforr

"First, we have to punish you by making you listen to son
of our politicians."

"Damn right you're punishing us," a teenager yelled fro
the back. The crowd snortled and laughed.

"Come on, Kirpatzke. Brunner as much as told me. If
give you the real story, will you print it? Or is the whitewa;
the only thing you'll take?"

"What piece, what whitewash?"

"The one Brunner wants me to write and you to publis
You know what I'm talking about."

"Maybe I do. So what?"

"Be patient. Hold your breath while the politicians let o
theirs, and pretty soon we'll meet Holyoke's star pitcher ar
soon-to-be major leaguer, Rickey Sparks."

"Let me give you some advice." Kirpatzke turned to hir
"Get lost. Forget the story. Don't fuck yourself."

Onstage Senator Kelley stepped toward the mike. H
whole scheme had been squelched, but here he was at tl
rally, taking the stage, going at the crowd. There were sever
women onstage behind him, campaign workers and a few f
male representatives from the Holyoke City Council. Amar
was the only one among them who did not smile brightly; sl
stood at an angle back from the others, much the way she hz
stood when Lofton first saw her, that day at the ballpark, h
weight resting back on one leg, somehow aloof from tl
scene, disengaged, though at the same time she was the or

who seemed to know something the others didn't, the girl with a secret. She knew Brunner, she knew Kelley, she knew what the two men wanted—Brunner to own the team, the town, the players, and Kelley to hear the crowd's shouts and cries—but it amounted to the same thing: Each wanted to be the dog on top, the one with the sharp teeth and the big dick who nobody screwed with unless he was crazy, and then that poor fucker got what he asked for all right, every time. Or that's the way it seemed, for a moment, as Lofton looked at Amanti, and he guessed, even if he had known nothing about her at all, that she would be the one onstage who drew his attention.

"One big happy family up there. Gives me a warm feeling inside," Kirpatzke said. The corners of his mouth turned up in a small smile. He put his hand on Lofton's shoulder. His tone changed, suddenly friendly, intimate. "You're a sap," he said, and edged forward into the crowd.

Lofton edged closer, too. He wanted to catch Amanti's attention. He saw the way Amanti seemed to be watching Kelley from behind; he saw how Brunner in turn watched Amanti and how Kelley, at the last second, turned to look at them both before, finally, directing his full attention to the crowd.

Kelley was a small man, and he seemed even smaller, standing in front of the crowd alone. He had lithe movements and black hair, black like the hair of Italian girls in the movies. He took the microphone in a manner that was faintly silly but aware of its silliness, deliberate, charming; he grabbed it between his two hands, more like a singer than a politician.

"This isn't a political rally," he said, speaking softly in the accent of the Irish North End. He gestured at the balloons and streamers, as if to call attention to how their presence contradicted his words. The combined effect of the gesture and Kelley's soft, insistent voice made you wonder for a second if perhaps there was something obvious you had missed, if perhaps all the politicians were gathered on the decorated platform for some purpose beyond the ordinary.

"I know a lot of you are tired, a lot of you are cynical. You've seen too many times how things come down in Boston, how the big boys"—he turned and looked at the men behind him—"how the big boys ignore the people out here in western Massachusetts."

Kelley paused, surveying the crowd. The security men surveyed, too. Amanti looked up at Kelley, her lips parted, eyes blue and radiant, her face in the same ironic pout he remembered seeing once before: in those pictures, taken beneath the trees, when she was a college girl in Boston.

"But I tell you, this is a day we can celebrate the bipartisan spirit. Just yesterday, as I sat in committee—yes, in one of those long rooms with the long tables—the big boys lifted their sleeping heads, awakened by your shouts, by your pleas." Kelley raised his voice now for a moment, then lowered it again, softer than ever. The crowd was quiet. "Yes, those statesmen—supporters of Wells and Sarafis alike—decided to reconvene, to rebudget. . . . Holyoke will get its funding. Holyoke will get its new downtown."

There was a long hush in the mall. Then suddenly it seemed to sink in. The minicams were rolling. The reporters scrawled their excitement. The crowd seemed subdued, confused. Brunner sat smiling. The money for Holyoke's downtown had been allocated after all. Brunner's property held its value, at least until the next committee meeting, after the election. If Brunner acted now, he could burn and collect.

Brunner had not switched sides in the campaign. Kelley had lost; his plan to pressure Brunner had failed. After his failure he must have done some last-minute maneuvering to get the committee to reverse the funding decision, to give the go-ahead for the project. Now he stood in front of the crowd, claiming a spiritual victory, and for a brief second—though Lofton knew better—it seemed almost true. "Don't think this doesn't mean that we won't be back at our squabbles tomorrow, that we won't be fighting for what we think is right." Kelley gestured at the men behind him. "But because we fight, it proves our passion for what is good, just as this one pure moment, today, proves how we can work together."

Lofton watched Amanti, the serene way in which she stood there, not quite immersed in the scene. She was suspended above it, remote but still enmeshed. He knew that if a person wanted, he could dream up all kinds of explanations for why she kept herself locked between Brunner and Kelley. You could make like a front-porch psychologist, stir your stick around in the mud and come up with all kinds of things: a dead brother; squabbling parents; the sheer force of circumstance and accident. But in the end, nothing washed clean, you had no explanations; all you had was a stick and a lot of mud. Lofton thought of the moment Amanti had described to him, when she had first met Brunner and Kelley around her uncle's table. He looked up at the stage, trying to catch the connection between that moment and now, but then suddenly Amanti looked in his direction. He forgot what was on his mind, instead trying to read what he should do, if he really should meet her at Barena's, but her eyes skimmed over his, not seeming to see him. Her glance told him that for a brief instant Amanti was not distracted; she had felt the rush of the crowd in Kelley's voice, the holy moment of victory in the electric air of the mall, but now the feeling was already fading. Kelley's words were disappointing, ordinary. ". . . soon there will be a new Holyoke, one steeped in the past, one steeped in the sweat and toil of the Irish, the Portuguese, the French, the thousands upon thousands who have worked the mills. . . ."

It was an odd business. Lofton watched the reporters taking down notes. Though he had felt the exhilaration, and knew the other reporters had, too, he also could guess what they were thinking because he had thought such things often enough himself: It made little difference who won the election. One guy might put in a new road to encourage business along a suburban strip. The other guy might construct a drive-in window for handing out money to the poor. In the end, the only difference would be the shape of the buildings along the side of the road and whose friends got the contracts to build them. To pretend anything else was arrogance, but you did it anyway, because that's the way things were.

Amanti was seated now, blocked from his view, so he turned and walked away from the stage while Kelley's voice echoed around him, down the long corridors of the Hillside Mall.

When Richard Sarafis's limousine pulled away from the mall, Amanti was in the back seat between Tony Liuzza and Sarafis himself. Kelley was in the front, his arm draped over the seat. Despite the ebullience of the rally, there was a hard, bitter silence in the car.

"We can still beat them at the polls," Sarafis said. "It's a close race—even without Brunner's money."

The silence continued. A smile was fixed on Tony Liuzza's face, his knife-sharp, painful smile. Her cousin was not happy, Amanti knew. This had been his first political move on his own—with his father's money, but against his father's advice —and it had turned out badly. The secretary of education post was distant now, a castle in somebody else's sky.

"This is the last week of the primary campaign, and we need the television push. Our campaign chest is empty," Sarafis said. No one responded. The others acted as if they had not heard. "Tomorrow I'll say the Wells people plan on canceling the Holyoke funding as soon as the election comes through their way. That'll get us on the air, at least around here. I'll need your help on this, Senator Kelley."

"No," Kelley said. "I can't play politics with this issue."

While on the platform, Amanti had caught a glimpse of Lofton staring up at the stage. If she'd had any intention of actually going with him, that would have been the moment to do it—when the security guards were intent on the crowd, when Kelley was speaking and Brunner was flush in his glory —but that moment had passed. Brunner and Kelley had no intention of letting her get away from them; she had been right about that. The instant the rally was over, they had led her to this limousine. One of Brunner's security agents had been keeping a close eye on her. If she made an attempt to leave, to catch up with Lofton, then they would follow. So everything was better if she just went along, went out to dinner, offered no resistance.

Lofton, of course, would not show up at the depot. She had changed the time of the meeting as well as the place. "Barena's," she had said at her apartment. "Meet me there after the game." She wanted to think that the change had been a deliberate act on her part. She couldn't be sure. It may have just been a slip of the tongue, a moment of hesitation and panic in which some other part of her took over. Still, she had done it.

"You know, we might win this race yet. Massachusetts politics are quirky. It's closer than people think." Sarafis had the

tone of a loser, of a man hoping the front-runner would slip
and fall. Soon he would be dragging out old clippings of
Dewey's projected presidential landslide to prove that anything might happen, that he might win, too, just like the un-
derdog Truman, despite the pollsters.

Amanti leaned her head back against the seat. She wished
somehow that it would be possible for both Sarafis and his
opponent to lose, for them all to go down together. The feeling brought back a memory. It was after her brother had died,
and she had stood with her mother and Aunt Liuzza in the
kitchen. There was snow on the ground, a dirty, ragged yellow snow that had been lying around too long. Her mother,
with hair the color of that snow, was in one of her moods,
tortured by grief over her dead son, Amanti's brother.

"It's all right for you," she said to her sister. "You have
your son, and you have your husband. They do things, they
succeed in this world. But me, my son is dead, and my husband is nothing."

"You're wrong," Aunt Liuzza said, with a bitterness that
was surprising. "I have nothing."

"What do you mean, you have nothing? Your husband has
power, you have power."

"The only power I ever had is to spread my legs," her aunt
said, giving her young niece a meaningful glance, as if letting
her in on a small bit of gossip. "And that isn't any power at
all."

Now the limousine pulled up to the restaurant. She noticed
the way Kelley ignored Sarafis. Kelley had his own reelection
bid coming up; he was already separating himself from the
loser. She remembered how Kelley had told her that someday
he would run for governor himself. With Sarafis losing this
time, Kelley's chance might come in four years, with the next
gubernatorial election. Sarafis's defeat could work to his advantage. He's probably already considered that, she thought.
He'll try for that governorship, he'll get his father-in-law's
support for that. As she got out of the car, she caught Brunner's glance, the turn to his smile. What if Lofton writes his
story? she thought. That might disrupt things for a while, like
a stone thrown at the spokes of a turning wheel, but the wheel
would keep on turning, spinning, careening. If she wanted to
escape her situation, it would have to be by leaving, by be-

coming someone else and forgetting Regina Amanti, just as you forgot a dead woman. She would do that, she thought; then a second later she knew that she wouldn't. She thought of the stage, the brief elation and the emptiness afterward, and guessed she would be up there again.

For Chicken Night at MacKenzie Field, fans were supposed to wear outlandish costumes. Ordinarily Lofton didn't participate in such events; he only watched. Tonight, though, was different. He was uncertain about Brunner's intentions, just as he was uncertain about the scheduled meeting with Amanti at Barena's. There were several hours between now and then; he did not want one of Brunner's thugs to recognize him at the game. He decided the best way to hide in the crowd would be to disguise himself.

He went to a secondhand store in the basement of the Iglesia del Cristo, an old church in the canal district. He always enjoyed such places, rummaging through the clothes bins, immersed in the texture and smell of other people's clothing, other people's lives. *Arthur Stewart, age 62, died Tuesday after a long illness. . . .*

He found a green jersey, the number 13 stenciled on the front, the name Bonzie on the back. Digging through a sack of discarded hats, he came across a plastic batting helmet, the type Little Leaguers sometimes wore, with bright orange flaps hanging over the ears. He tore out the Styrofoam padding and placed the helmet on his head. The thing fit.

After rummaging a little longer, he salvaged some white, baggy pants, grease-stained at the knees, and a pair of old tennis shoes. He looked at himself in the mirror of the tiny, unlit changing room. The pants hung low, but the effect was right. He looked like an over-grown kid on his way to play sandlot ball, wearing a uniform fashioned from hand-me-overs and backyard trash. He smiled, pleased. He would look ridiculous on the street, but at the ballpark he would be just another idiot fan, someone dressed for the occasion, goofy and dead serious at the same time.

"A costume party," he told the lady at the register. She did not smile. Behind him a young man carried an overstuffed bra and a very short velvet skirt.

* * *

At the park Lofton sat in the bleachers, away from the
ress box. It was a big crowd: families from the Longmeadow
uburbs; the Holyoke regulars; all kinds of local clubs; even a
roup—sitting not far away—from the state mental institu-
on in Belchertown. A man pounded over and over on an
pturned can. Children shouted. The ballpark kid Lofton had
een all over town, who ran messages back and forth for the
eam, stood not far away, looking about distractedly, his Red-
vings' cap twisted, as always, backward on his head. The boy
at down near him, his chin cradled between his dirty, mot-
led fists. He did not look happy, though; his eyes were
lazed, teary, and his mouth was open.

Lofton scanned the crowd. Amanti, Brunner, Liuzza,
arafis, Kelley, the whole entourage, even the security agents
rom the mall—all sat behind the first base dugout. Sparks did
ot seem to be with them; he was not on the field either.

The Hollywood Chicken did not emerge from his trailer
ntil the end of the second inning, when the Redwings were
lready down, 2–0. Two bodyguards escorted the Chicken.
)ne man cleared the way, the other walked behind, and chil-
ren streamed all around, trying to touch the Chicken's
lumes. The Chicken ran through the gate into the midst of
he Holyoke players as they retook the field. After looking at
he scoreboard, the bright yellow bird somersaulted clumsily
own the third base line and attacked the umpire.

Lofton had seen the Chicken do the same routine before, at
3ees Stadium in San Jose, but the stunt did not have much
unch tonight. Even so, the kids enjoyed it, screaming louder,
naking more noise than they had at any time earlier in the
ame.

"Some Chicken," said the kid with the baseball cap. He had
noved lower in the stands, closer to Lofton, and spoke qui-
tly, nervously, as if attempting to exchange secrets. The two,
.ofton and the kid, exchanged a long glance, and Lofton real-
zed the boy saw through his disguise; in fact, he did not even
otice it. Lofton remembered what Amanti had told him
bout the boy: how sometimes the kid mixed up faces and
imes, forgot where he was, and how other times he noticed
hings most people did not see.

Below him the game was looking bad. Holyoke needed to

win tonight, and the next night, too, if it wanted to stay in th
pennant race, but Hammer, the young fastballer, was begin
ning to lose control. He walked the first batter, then threw
fastball to the next—a sweet white flash. Too sweet. The Wes
Haven batter socked it away, a hard liner that arced an
twisted, skipping past Porter into the right field corner.

The batter now stood on third, pleased, clapping his hand
and the Chicken went into a fit. He grabbed his heart and fe
backward onto the ground. The crowd hooted and screamec
Later in the inning, when the opposing player scored, th
crowd got excited again. It gave them another chance to se
the Chicken's antics: a flip and a handstand on the third bas
sidelines. A man near Lofton hoisted his little boy into the ai
trying to give him a better vantage point. But the Chicken'
gymnastics were poor, and the man's wife complained. "
that the big deal? They do better on TV."

"What do you expect? It's just minor league ball. They gc
a minor league Chicken."

"No, it's the Hollywood Chicken," their son protested.

"I don't understand," said the mother, shaking her head.

Lofton did not understand either. He had met the Chicke
once. The Chicken played parks all over the country, an
Lofton had interviewed him in San Jose. The Chicken,
sandy-haired young man, had described how he started out a
Los Angeles football games, coming to the gate in his home
made suit, buying a ticket like everyone else, then racin
through the aisles, leading the crowd in cheers. "One day th
game was close, and I wanted to lead the crowd, everyone.
raced out onto the ledge in front of the scoreboard." Stadiun
management was angry. It evicted him and told him not t
come back. But the fans objected, the papers made a storm
and the team reneged. They put the Chicken on salary. Nov
he had a national career, so many engagements he coul
barely keep up with them all. "That first night, when I cam
back to work and the fans applauded, thousands of people i
that big stadium, all applauding for me, it was the experienc
of my life. I cried inside my chicken suit."

Though it was a ridiculous story, Lofton had believed th
man's emotion. He'd seen the Chicken perform again, year
later, in Denver. That time, also, the performance had beer
far better than tonight. Maybe the man had lost enthusiasm

lost heart. Something had happened. This was not the same Chicken.

The Chicken retired to his trailer, the crowd seemed to lose track of the game, the Redwings fell farther behind, and the PA man announced the presence of Richard Sarafis. Sarafis stood, and a crush of gray-suited agents hurried to form a circle around him; they looked as if they had not expected the announcement.

"They shoulda run Sparks for governor," said the kid. Lofton had forgotten all about him. The kid seemed unnaturally excited and looked at him, eyes wide, as if he wanted to talk but did not know how to begin. "You seen Sparks?" he asked.

"No," Lofton said. He noticed the irritation in his voice, the anger, and immediately was sorry. The kid flinched but went on talking, scrutinizing Lofton as if ready to jump, to run.

"Well, yeah, he's probably back in the clubhouse, soaking his arm, always back there these days," the kid said in his stumbling nasal voice. Lofton turned back to the field. Holyoke batted—down one, two, three—then retook the field. The team showed no real enthusiasm. The deadly grace of their winning streak had vanished. The kid elbowed Lofton.

"You friends with the girl?" The kid smiled oddly. He touched his cheek in the place where Amanti's cheek was scarred. "The pretty girl?" he said. Lofton looked around, checking the gates, the crowd. "Did they beat you, too?" the kid asked.

"Did who beat me?"

The kid couldn't answer the question. After struggling with it for a second, he looked up at Lofton as if all sense had left his head. The kid was shaking. A bad case, this kid, Lofton thought, and wondered what had happened to the kid when he was younger, what the kid's parents—or the people who took care of him now—had done to make him this way.

"Pay attention to the game," Lofton said, and touched the kid on the shoulder.

"You sound like Barker. He wouldn't talk to me either, he just shouted me away. And he tells me everything before the games."

Lofton had seen the kid hanging around during practices, leaning over the fence, asking the players, and sometimes

Barker, questions that they sometimes answered and sometimes didn't, tossing off flip cracks instead and laughing among themselves.

The kid made an overhand motion with his arm, like a pitcher throwing a baseball. "Yes, Spark 'em right by 'em, strike 'em out. Then we'd win." The kid had suddenly calmed. He seemed normal, like any kid anywhere. Too normal, Lofton thought.

Lofton fell silent, staring out at the field. The kid fell silent, too, imitating him, staring seriously. Then, as the West Haven shortstop lined a single to right, the kid elbowed him again. He wished the kid would go. He longed for the spiteful silence of the press box.

"See," the kid said, "they got that guy standing out front the clubhouse door so anybody just can't go in."

He ignored the kid, and the kid repeated himself.

"I tried to go in, down in West Haven, just wanted to say hello to old Rickey, but they wouldn't let me. The guard made a goon face and pushed me away. But then Golden came along and yelled at the guard. He let me in special. Golden let me talk to Rickey."

The kid elbowed Lofton again. Lofton, irritated despite himself, elbowed him back; the kid smiled shyly, frightened, but he moved closer. Lofton remembered Golden's brusque manner with the kid, how the kid dogged him everywhere anyway. Down below, West Haven's runners stood at first and second, the cleanup batter at the plate. The Sox hitter smacked a double off the center field wall.

"Bastard," Lofton said.

The kid stood up and screamed at the field, "Give us Sparks, bastards!" Then he sat down, turning to Lofton. "Yup, I'm his best fan, and I saw him in Waterbury, too."

"That right?"

"I went down there every night, and it was the same thing, except for the night he pitched. 'Rickey's in the clubhouse, soaking his arm,' that's what he told me. That same one down there. He doesn't like letting me in."

Lofton arched around toward the clubhouse. A ballpark cop stood by the door, pacing first one way, then another.

"But it didn't matter. Golden let me in down in Waterbury, too."

"You go to the Waterbury games?"

"Sometimes the counselors take us down there." The kid's ⸱ce had changed strangely. "But you know something, I ⸱on't think Golden will let me in anymore."

"Why not?"

"He's dead," the kid said, without smiling, his eyes black ⸱nd glassy. Lofton winced.

"No, that's not true. I saw him just the other night. I talked ⸱ him in the clubhouse."

The kid was not listening.

"Dead, like Gutierrez, all dead and bloody." The kid let ⸱ut a squirrellike cry; tears welled in his eyes. Lofton grabbed ⸱e kid's hands, trying to calm him; then, looking down, he ⸱oticed again the kid's scars—burn marks, perhaps from the ⸱buse he'd suffered as a child—which covered his arms and ⸱rearms.

"Dead. Dead. Dead," the kid cried out, louder now. "I saw ⸱e Latinos kill him."

"The Latinos?" Lofton asked. The kid nodded, frightened. ⸱ofton was not sure what the nod meant. The kid wandered ⸱ll over town, almost everyone knew him and teased him and ⸱sed him for errands, and maybe he'd run into the Latinos.

"Yes, yes! The Latinos!" the kid yelled at the top of his ⸱ngs.

"Shh," Lofton said. "Shh. Shh." Grabbing the kid by the ⸱rms again, he tried to calm him. The kid babbled on, not so ⸱ud as before, but shaking furiously, as if on the verge of ⸱ome sort of fit. "I followed Golden on the street and down to ⸱he tunnel, to the tracks, and the Latinos waited in the tunnel ⸱nd talked, and I couldn't understand. Golden came up in the ⸱unnel, and they wrestled him. I saw his face full of blood. ⸱hen they saw me and started to run to get me, to chase me to ⸱he ballfield. And I ran, and they jumped on Golden. They ⸱ook money from his pockets and threw it into the air. They ⸱illed him!"

The kid was yelling again. His cap had fallen off, and his ⸱ower lip shook visibly. Lofton watched the boy, waiting until ⸱e quieted.

"What tunnel, where? Was it Golden that you saw, are you ⸱ure?" Lofton asked, but the kid said nothing. Lofton waited, ⸱hen asked again, and again. The kid wouldn't talk. His features were twisted, his eyes were glazed, and Lofton could see it was hopeless.

The seventh-inning stretch was starting. A new set of sirens wailed in the distance, and Lofton set out into the stands. Somebody should stay with the kid, he thought; somebody should help him. But Lofton went off alone to find Amanti.

He spotted her at the concession, near the top of the stands, on the first base side. She was standing behind Kelley. Lofton pushed through the crowd. It became denser the closer he got to the top, not so much because of the concession but because of the sirens. People wanted to see the fire.

Finally he reached her. He took her by the elbow, gently, and waited for her to turn and recognize him.

"It's me. Lofton."

Her lips parted. She glanced nervously back at Kelley—the man still had not turned—and she gestured toward the rear of the concession, indicating she would meet him there.

Lofton backed away. The sirens rushed by again on the streets outside MacKenzie; a group of teenagers, bored with the game, with the Chicken, with waiting in line, bolted away.

"It's a fire, a big one," said a girl nearby.

"So?" said her friend, but they went off together, toward the top of the bleachers, for a better look.

When Amanti came, Lofton grabbed her hand, pulling her closer, deeper into the bleachers. They stood inches apart. Her skin seemed dark now, wonderfully dark, set off by her soft white blouse and her glistening jewelry. She smelled of perfume.

"Your kid, the one who runs errands around here, he just told me he saw the Latinos kill Golden."

Amanti looked confused. "The boy's hysterical. You know how the kid is. He mixes everything up; he tells stories."

"I have to find out what's going on, and I might not get back in time to meet when we planned. I'll have to meet you later."

Amanti did not respond. They stood quietly together; the crowd pressed toward the fire. He touched her waist. She was an odd woman: putting him on to the arsons, trying to clamp the lid on Kelley and Brunner, but never leaving, not com-

etely, the circles of power in which she was enmeshed and
hich she wanted to destroy.

"Listen, I shouldn't be talking to you," she said. "I never
anned on meeting you anyway. Just take the money Brun-
r gave you. Go. Leave town. Write the story or don't. It
oesn't matter. If you run, I'm safe, I got rid of you like they
anted. If you write the story—if you do it right—then they
on't dare touch me. I'll be all right."

"Don't kid yourself," Lofton said.

"I think you're wrong. One way or the other—"

"One way or the other they'll control you forever. I'll meet
ou as soon as I'm done and help you get out."

Amanti looked at the ground. "Listen, don't play saint. Get
t of town."

"Oh, but I am a saint." He pulled Amanti through the
owd, to the top of the stands. There were more sirens in the
reets, smoke plumes rising over the Flats. He whirled her
ound and grabbed her by the collar.

"Tell me what the fuck is going on."

She held her lips open, slightly, and seemed to look at him
t not to see him, like a face inside a photograph, one that
ou study for a long time. The people nearby muttered to
emselves. They saw how he held her collar in his fist, and
ey backed away.

"I was supposed to set you up," Amanti said. "Brunner
d Kelley arranged everything just like I told you the other
ght, only they had no intention of letting me meet you.
hey were going to have you killed."

"At Barena's?" Lofton asked.

"No, I was supposed to tell you to meet me at the old
ilroad depot at eight o'clock, about an hour ago. I told you
e wrong place and the wrong time. I did it on purpose."

Lofton let go of her collar. He could see flames, bright and
ange, leaping up over the factory district, down toward
merican Paper. There was screaming and whooping in the
reets.

"Don't you understand? When they found out how much
ou knew, how much I had told you, they figured a way out—
set you up. I was supposed to tell you to meet me, that we
ould leave town together. As far as Brunner and Kelley
ow, I did everything they asked. It's not my fault if you

decided not to meet me, if, on your own, you take the mon
and run."

"Why didn't you let me in on this?"

"I couldn't take the chance. I didn't want them to thir
that I was deliberately fouling their plans." Amanti paus
and looked out over the city toward the flames. "I had no id
they were going to start the fires again so soon."

"Are you sure you don't want to get out of here—just
escape, leave them all behind?"

"Write your story, or don't, it's up to you. I did what
could," she said. "Now I have to watch out for myself. Tʰ
rest is yours."

She twisted away into the crowd. He started to follow b
saw the security agent waiting, watching her descend tʰ
stairs. Lofton ducked away, behind the concession stan
Amanti and Kelley were together now, arm in arm. Brunn
approached them, smiling. He closed his fingers arour
Gina's other arm.

Lofton hurried to the exit. On the way he passed the Chic
en's trailer. Through the trailer window he caught a glimp
of the young man, half in his suit, half out, the costume heʲ
on the chair beside him. The man's head was glistening wiʳ
sweat, Lofton noticed, and his cheeks were wet and shininℊ

The streets were always unpredictable, sometimes quiℯ
stretching out long and empty, the buildings seemingly dℯ
serted; other times whole blocks were seething, people rushⁱⁿ
back and forth, shouting at one another, pushing, shovⁱⁿ
Now the air overhead was filled with smoke, the engines crʸ
ing, wailing, whistling, and the sky was lit by the crazy glaʳ
of American Paper burning at the bottom of the hill, acroℱ
the canal. People left their tenements to watch, to get cloₑ
enough to see the reflection of the fire in the water, and kiℒ
ran up High Street, pulling alarms, smashing glass, grabbⁱⁿ
cassette decks, cameras, anything from the shattered displaʸ
windows. Lofton turned down the railroad tracks and hurriℯ
toward the river. In the tenements beyond High Street, moℯ
fires had broken out, set—Lofton guessed—by looters to crℯ
ate distractions, to keep the police busy, or simply for the fⁱ
of it.

He followed the trestle across the canal. He stood wheℯ

Penn Central tracks ended, not far from the river, near the
dge where he had found himself earlier that day. A large
sted turbine lay in the weeds nearby. The breaking glass,
e alarms—all seemed distant now, like something in a
eam, except for the fact that he could turn his head and see
e smoke and glare of American Paper. The lights of the
er houses shone pale and yellow from the other side of the
nnecticut. People must be watching from their back
rches, Lofton thought, and he imagined Brunner's wife, her
e robe shimmering as she worked her way through the
llows to the riverbank. When he asked himself why he
nted to catch up with the Latinos, he could find no answer.
e wanted to see the story through to the end, that was all.
e kid at the ballpark had told him he had seen the Latinos
l someone in one of the underground tunnels; Amanti had
d that Brunner and Kelley had planned out Lofton's own
ath, down near the old depot. These were the two stories
'd been tracing all along—Brunner's intrigues on one hand;
e gang warfare on the other—and now at last he was ap-
oaching the place where the stories converged. The tunnels
re somewhere nearby, down near the railroad tracks and
e canals.

He remembered he still had the money with him, and he
cided he'd better get rid of it for now. He put the envelope
neath a railroad tie. Then he heard footsteps. He turned. A
an stood about twenty yards away, just in front of an old
umpster. He was thin, and he wore a white T-shirt that
od out against the darkness.

"*¿Quién es?*" the man said. His voice was soft. Lofton did
t know whether to answer. He considered running, but he
dn't think he could outrun the man. He was too close. Then
ofton glanced back and saw two more men behind him.
ey stood like the other one, shoulders arched, feet spread,
nds loose and ready. The Latinos. He had stepped into the
ddle of them again.

The men walked around Lofton in a circle, always facing
m, the circle growing smaller, tighter, with each revolution.
ey called back and forth to each other in Spanish. It was
o dark for Lofton to tell if these were the same gang mem-
rs he had encountered on the street.

"*¿El reportero?*"

"No sé."

"Un pendejo mas."

The men laughed, all except the one in the white T-shir He seemed to be in charge, and he did not take his eyes o Lofton. Lofton raised his arms above his head to show he ha no weapons.

"I'm not looking for trouble," he said. "I'm looking help."

For a moment he imagined the scene as it might look fro above. The three young men circling and himself in the mi dle, his hands in the air, the trainyard spiraling away, the ci flaming. He was frightened, but the scene was melodramati funny. He laughed.

"¡Vamos!"

The men rushed him. Lofton turned one way, then t other; he felt his arms pulled back; he caught a glimpse steel. The men pinned him to the gravel, face down; the m in the T-shirt held a knife under his throat.

"No. Don't kill him. *Es el reportero.*" The Latino went in Spanish, explaining something to the others. Loft coughed into the dirt.

One of the men searched him, running his hands along t inside of Lofton's thigh. Satisfied, the Latinos pulled Loft to his feet. Up close, Lofton recognized the tall one in t white T-shirt; he had been the one who did the talking th day out on the street in front of Lofton's hotel. The other tw however, did not look familiar. They looked him up a down, amused at his clothes, at the bright orange helmet still wore on his head; one of the men, laughing as he did tugged at Lofton's jersey.

"What are you doing here?" the tall one asked. Loft stammered over an explanation. He did not want to menti the kid because he did not want them to think he had co here looking for Golden's murderers; the Latinos might n appreciate such curiosity. The young man in front of hi however, did not wait for an answer to his question. He r membered Lofton from that day on the street. "We have Me doza," he said proudly, self-satisfied.

"Let me talk to him," Lofton said. "I need to do that."

The three men led him toward the river. They took him a concrete tunnel, built into the riverbank, that seemed to back toward town, toward the main canal. A bleeder tunnel, he guessed, used as a safety valve if the canals got too full too quickly. He remembered what the kid, in his hysteria, had told him: how the Latinos had dragged Golden into the tunnel and beaten him, shouting as they pulled money from his pockets. Golden had always paid Mendoza before, Lofton thought, and most likely he'd been on his way to make the payoff again. Except this time the Latinos, persistent in their tracking of Mendoza, happened to have the place staked.

One man led the way, and the other two followed behind Lofton, their shoes splashing in the seepage that flowed along the bottom of the tunnel. A moaning sound came from deeper in the tunnel—voices, Lofton realized, echoing and vibrating against the old concrete. A light flickered ahead. Soon they stood with other gang members. Lofton listened as they talked in Spanish, apparently deciding what to do with him.

In another moment they'd made up their minds. They shone a flashlight in Lofton's face. Somebody grabbed him by the arm and pulled him forward. Mendoza lay at his feet. Mendoza was alive, but he was bleeding from the mouth and asking to be let go. When Lofton looked up, he saw a Latino he hadn't seen before, the gang's headman evidently, the one who had been trying to hold the gang in place since Angelo's death.

"Es el hombre del fuego. The arsonist," the leader said, pointing at Mendoza. "He's paid by the Mafia."

Lofton laughed, his quick chortle. It was a funny idea. The Mafia. People liked to think there was a group of men behind the corruption in the world, overweight thugs in movie suits, and that you could shoot a few, put a few in jail, and solve everything. The truth was that the Mafia was not a single group of people or an organization, at least not anymore, so much as it was a system, a method of operation, one that a lot of people used.

"How do you know it's the Mafia?"

"That's what he says."

They kicked Mendoza in the legs.

"¿Quién te pagó?"

They kicked him again.

"¿Quién te mandó?"

"The Mafia."

"See." The young man turned to Lofton. "They're burning our town. Go ahead, ask him what you want. When you're finished, get out, write it for the paper."

Lofton knelt over Mendoza. Then he turned to the Latinos. "All right. But tell me, what do you plan on doing when you're finished beating on him? It won't do any good to kill him."

The Latinos did not answer. The tunnel was silent, the only noise Mendoza's sharp, irregular breathing.

"You know what they're going to do," Mendoza hissed. "One of your people was here earlier. A white man. Ask what they have done to him. Ask."

The Latinos stood quietly. One man turned a flashlight on Mendoza, so Mendoza's eyes shone in the darkness, small, yellow, like a candle flame about to go out.

"Ask," Mendoza said again, his voice still hissing, still defiant.

Lofton hesitated. He thought of the ballpark kid trembling in this tunnel while the Latinos collared Golden. *"I have one more errand to run for Brunner; then I'm finished."* He imagined the man's screams. He thought of Golden's wife in the wheelchair. He did not like thinking that Golden was dead.

Mendoza breathed heavily. The Latinos were silent, watching, waiting. They could still turn against me, Lofton thought, and a simple idea occurred to him, one that he'd had before but that seemed more important now: The Latinos were fighting for vengeance, for blood. Nothing he said would persuade these men to let Mendoza go. Whatever ideals Angelo had expressed, those were shattered now. Down here, below the city—just as above, in City Hall—what was good, what was evil, the line between them was all murky. If the Latinos had killed Golden, Lofton didn't want to hear about it, not here, not now. Because if the Latinos guessed that he suspected they were murderers, then they might not let him go.

Mendoza raised his head. The Latino's leader shot out a command in Spanish. One of the men kicked Mendoza in the stomach.

The tunnel was silent again except for Mendoza's gasping, trying to regain his breath in the dank air. Lofton could feel the Latinos behind him. Mendoza rolled over. He peered at Lofton, struggled to regain his focus. He looked around him

n the dark, and for the first time he seemed afraid, like a child
waking up from a bad dream. He reached a hand toward
Lofton.

"I'll tell you everything, just get me out of here. Get me
away from them. To the police. I'll tell you everything."

Mendoza held on to Lofton's shirt pocket. Lofton looked
back at the Latinos. The leader said nothing, he did not move
his head, there was no sign of assent.

"All right," Lofton lied. "You'll be safe."

Mendoza's eyes flickered back and forth. For a moment
they held a flash of the same defiance.

"Mentiroso," he scoffed. "You're a liar." He let out a loud
laugh. A Latino kicked him in the face.

Mendoza moaned and rolled over again. Blood came from
his nose, his mouth, his teeth. Slowly he struggled up to his
elbows.

"Gutierrez," Lofton asked. "Who killed him?"

Mendoza smiled; there was no focus in his eyes. "One of
my men, he told me not to come get the money by myself. He
had a bad feeling. But I wanted the money in my own hands.
I made a mistake."

"Do you know who Golden was working for? Who paid
him the money he gave you?" Lofton felt the Latinos bristle
at the mention of Golden's name, but he shot out the questions, trying to get answers while Mendoza was still coherent.
He knew, of course, that Brunner was behind it all, but he
wanted to hear it from Mendoza, to have some confirmation
besides his own and the papers that had been taken away from
him when the police found him on the side of the road. Mendoza, though, was quiet again, his eyes vacant.

Lofton grew impatient. He took Mendoza by the collar.
One of the Latinos laughed.

"What happened to Gutierrez?"

"Yourself—you are lucky you didn't come to the depot.
Your boss wanted us to use your corpse for kindling, to help
light the fire. The same thing we did to the other reporter.
When you didn't show up, it was a bad sign. My men told me
it was a bad sign, but I said, 'Go ahead, to burn the building.
I'll go alone for the money. You burn, I'll go alone.' "

Lofton listened as Mendoza's voice drifted off. Mendoza
started to repeat himself, but Lofton grabbed him a little

tighter by the collar and asked his question again. "What happened to Gutierrez?"

"You were supposed to die tonight, not me." Mendoza paused to catch his breath. He struggled awhile before answering Lofton's question. "Your Mr. Shortstop, the big baseball player, he came to me. He said he knew about the fires. He said if I gave him money, or maybe cocaine, he'd be quiet. . . ."

And there was that funny smile again, like the one Mendoza had given him in the church pew. It was a smile Lofton had heard about from other reporters and even seen a few times himself; in jails, in asylums, in the faces of men fighting guerrilla wars.

"I had to do to him what these men are going to do to me."

Lofton headed out of the tunnel alone. The lights went dim behind him. He heard voices murmuring, he heard a thick, thudding sound, over and over in the darkness, but he did not hear Mendoza cry out. Outside, the smoke from American Paper had drifted over the railyard, a thick gray pall that covered the bit of sky overhead and made it impossible to see the stars.

He hurried along the railroad tracks. The Flats burned down below, not all of the houses, of course, but enough so that you could not count them, so that the sky seemed to flicker and turn bright, the darkness creased with the beautiful flames.

Lofton left the tracks and ran across Andersonville—a small outcrop of shacks, part of the city, a neighborhood of dark-skinned children, houses with corrugated roofs, tomato gardens, and narrow alleys. A hill beyond the neighborhood rose up to a highway that snaked along the ridge out to the suburbs. The streets here were dark, the fires had not spread this far, but Lofton, as he ran down a street, looking for a way up the hill, thought he could feel the people in the neighborhood—old men, women, children—staring at him from their porches. There was no road up to the ridge, but he found a path into the trees. It was dark, and he had a hard time seeing, but he hurried on. Something rattled in the bushes ahead of him: a dog maybe. Lofton swerved off in another direction, off the path. He took off the orange batting helmet,

hrew it into the bushes, and struggled upward. He heard
'oung voices calling to each other in Spanish down below. He
ushed on, found himself tangled in the bushes, very close to
he top. A vine ensnared his foot and he fell, and then he
eard more rattling nearby—*my imagination*—and he felt a
udden, crazy panic, his heart palpitating unevenly, and he
urst through the bushes. He stood on the street, on the side-
valk of a four-lane highway. He walked along more slowly
ow, catching his breath. He decided he would go to the *Dis-
atch* and take his chances with Kirpatzke. He worried about
Kirpatzke, of course. He wondered, again, who it was that
ad followed him to the library, who it was that had told
Golden where to find him, that he was investigating the fires,
nd who it was that had trashed his room. He doubted it was
Kirpatzke. It didn't seem his style. Kirpatzke might kill my
tory, Lofton thought, Brunner might have that much power
ver him, but I don't think Kirpatzke would do anything
lirect.

He worked his way through the streets until finally he was
t the *Dispatch,* pushing through the glass doors and standing
n the cool air-conditioned building.

There were a few reporters here, more than usual for this
ime of night, but not so many as he expected. An older man,
younger woman each sat at their desks, absorbed in the
omputer screen. Three young reporters stood gathered
around Kirpatzke's desk.

"We need someone on the official end . . . fire chief,
nayor, insurance companies. We need someone to talk to the
nerchants downtown. And someone on the human interest
. . burn victims, relatives of the dead. . . ."

Kirpatzke talked sadly, laconically, his lips twisted in a half
mile. Lofton stepped forward into the circle of younger re-
orters. He could feel the men bristle.

"What do you want?" asked Kirpatzke. He looked Lofton
ip and down, and Lofton remembered how he was dressed:
green baseball jersey, sagging pants, makeup on his face.

"I have a story about the fire," Lofton said.

"Thanks. But I think we got it covered."

"I've got the arson angle," said Lofton. "I didn't hear you
nention that."

Kirpatzke sighed.

A reporter turned to Lofton. "They don't know it's arson yet. They can't start to investigate until the fire cools down.'

"Just hold off, Lofton. We got it covered," said Kirpatzke

Lofton turned away. He headed to the proofreaders' ghetto He worked on his story there. Kirpatzke ignored him.

Several hours later, when the darkness outside had started to lift, Lofton was still working. He had gone to the *Dispatch's* files for Einstein's fire stories; he had patched some of the other reporter's work into his own piece for background. Because Lofton's own notes had been taken while he was in the hospital, he had to rely on his memory for the stuff he had dug out on his own. Inevitably that meant some of the quotes were not quite right, words transposed, sentences forgotten But that didn't bother him too much; that sort of thing happened in every story, though most reporters wouldn't admit it. Still, there were other weak points. He did not want to mention Amanti by name; it could be dangerous for her. That strained the story, and so did the fact that he could not prove he'd seen Brunner's papers. The story was weak on figures Still, it had to be that way. If Amanti wanted to come forward later and make some kind of on-the-record statement, then she could do that. As for the rest of them, whatever they had said to him and whatever bits of it he could remember, he used. Except for Golden. He was not quite sure why, but he refrained from mentioning his name either. He had a dogheaded loyalty to the man that he himself did not quite understand. Perhaps it was because Golden had been a big leaguer once, or because Lofton didn't want to believe Golden was dead, or because if the man was alive, he wanted to give him a chance to come forward on his own, to leave town forever, to do whatever he had to do.

By the time he had finished the story, the other reporters had gone. Kirpatzke, however, still mused at his desk. Lofton read over what he had written.

Investigations begun earlier this summer indicate that a statewide arson ring may lie behind the fire that devastated Holyoke's mill district last night.

The alleged conspiracy involved people from all ranks of society, ranging from the members of local street gangs to those at the highest levels of state government. The conspiracy reportedly involves such figures as Holyoke businessman John C. Brunner, Senator David Kelley (D.-Holyoke), and retired U.S. Senator James Harrison.

Last night's blaze, which lit up the evening sky for miles and spurred looting in the neighborhood near the canals, was the largest in a series of fires that have plagued the town all summer. Though local residents have often expressed the belief that an organized ring lies behind the fires, reports by the city's fire officials have repeatedly cited negligence and random vandalism as prime causes.

"The fire officials are lying. Somebody is buying them off. We know who's behind the fires. . . . The police, the white businessmen, they're the ones who gain," said the leader of the Latinos, a local street gang, in an interview with *Dispatch* reporter Dennis Einstein earlier this summer.

The leader, known only as Angelo, was killed shortly afterward in a street clash with a rival gang. According to members of the Latinos, Angelo was killed by the Wanderers, an opposition gang that was paid to set the fires and that used the payoff money to finance a drug operation.

Einstein's investigations into the fires stopped abruptly in early July, when the reporter disappeared without explanation. His charred body was finally identified last week after having been discovered sometime earlier in the ruins of an apartment building on High Street.

A third person, Randy Gutierrez, was shot to death just hours before a scheduled newspaper interview in which he was to discuss the arson. Gutierrez, a shortstop for the Holyoke Redwings at the time of his death, reportedly had information linking the team's front office to the arsons. The team is co-owned by John C. Brunner and Anthony Liuzza, Jr.

"Randy Gutierrez was really scared. He told me he knew who was behind the arsons, and he was afraid they would kill him," said one source who talked to

Gutierrez before his death. The source, who asked not to be identified, claimed that Gutierrez believed a member of the Redwings' management was delivering money to the arsonists, acting as a go-between for someone higher in the Redwings' organization.

Gutierrez apparently told the same story to several of his teammates, including second baseman Tim Carpenter and pitcher Rickey Sparks. "I didn't know what to believe; Randy was pretty wired up those days," said Carpenter. Sparks refused comment.

Material evidence apparently indicates that a majority of the buildings which burned were owned not by Brunner himself but by proxy owners who then forwarded the largest percentage of the insurance premiums to Brunner via Nassau & Associates, a Boston-based law firm. The only building directly in Brunner's name was American Paper, which was engulfed in fire last night and which should continue to burn for several days.

"Is it wrong to destroy the slums or to give landlords money to rebuild? And if the government doesn't help, maybe we should do it our own way," Brunner said yesterday afternoon before the fires, when questioned about his role in the arsons. Brunner stands to collect upwards of $10 million in insurance from last night's blaze.

The arson scheme apparently took on political overtones when it was uncovered by Senator Kelley, Holyoke's representative in the state legislature. According to one source, Kelley threatened to reveal the scheme if Brunner did not use a percentage of the arson money to help finance challenger Richard Sarafis's election campaign. Kelley reportedly reneged on his threat when he discovered his father-in-law, Senator Harrison, had received large sums of money from Brunner in the past.

Last night, when the fire started, both Brunner and Kelley were in attendance at MacKenzie Field. While they watched the game, members of the Latinos had caught up with the head of the rival gang, Lou Mendoza, in an underground tunnel near the city's railyard.

Lofton stopped reading here. He pictured again the damp
:wer, Mendoza's gleaming eyes, the Latino lighting a ciga-
:tte. Brunner's plan had gone awry. He hadn't figured on
.manti's refusing to send me to the depot, Lofton thought,
nd he hadn't figured on the Latinos catching up with Men-
oza when they did, and he couldn't know that the kid would
umble by and call me to the scene.

He looked over his story again. It didn't have all the facts it
ould have. The story relied in places on supposition, it attrib-
ted important information to unnamed sources; but it was
ie best he could do with what he had available, and it wasn't
ad. If the story somehow made its way into print, then that
i itself would help. Its mere presence in the paper, cast in
/pe on newspaper rag, would get other reporters working,
ould force official investigations, and would start something
:rious. Maybe. Anyway, he had seen such things happen
efore, and he'd seen it happen the other way, too, when a
ory seemed to make no impact at all, or not enough to
aatter. Lofton scanned the story again, saved it in the com-
uter's files, and hit the button for hard copy.

"What are you being so diligent about?"

Kirpatzke stood over him. He looked as disheveled as ever;
is eyes were red-rimmed, and his shirttail was out. His skin
as the same worn color.

"I told you. I've got a story."

"Yeah, the whole world's got a story. Isn't that the schlock
iece for Brunner and the Redwings, the end-of-the-year
romo? Something to make the powerful citizens look good in
ie midst of confusion? Pro like you should be able to whack
iat off in a minute."

There was bitterness in Kirpatzke's voice, as if the idea of
ofton's writing the lie for Brunner had made him sick. Lof-
in had almost forgotten all about it: how he had promised
runner a well-timed whitewash for today's paper. Still,
.irpatzke seemed ready to publish the lie. He did not even
)ok at the screen.

"What kind of outfit is that you have on there?" asked
.irpatzke. "You joining a baseball team?"

"You know the story behind that fire, don't you? You've
nown all along," said Lofton.

"I know, and so does everyone in town. Keep your mouth

shut, and keep your money. Just do what Brunner paid you t
do."

"Read my story; it's on the screen." Lofton walked to th
printer and tore out the printed copy. He folded it and put
into his back pocket. Kirpatzke's eyes opened as he read. H
smiled, at first, then chuckled out loud. His pupils were sma
and black.

"Are you out of your mind?"

"Print it," said Lofton.

"Hearsay, circumstantial, libel, the stuff of lawsuits."

"The story's true."

"Doesn't matter."

"No? What does Brunner have on you?"

Across the building the front door opened, a couple of th
proofreaders arriving for work.

"It won't fly. It's not my problem," hissed Kirpatzke. "It
tough luck. Now get out of here."

"Everybody knows you're nothing, not even a goo
hack . . . . How much does Brunner pay the paper to kee
you on here?"

"Listen"—Kirpatzke kept his voice low—"you're dam
lucky I don't run this. He'd have your ass. You're damn luck
I don't take this over to him right now. You'd never stick you
dick in a newspaper office again. The only thing you'd b
screwing is the dirt in your grave."

"You won't tell Brunner," Lofton said. One of the proo
readers walked closer; he could hear her footsteps behin
him. "You don't have any guts. You're a fuckin' first-clas
loser."

"And so who do you think you are, Willie Mays?" sai
Kirpatzke. He glanced down at the screen.

"I have other places to take this." Lofton started away. H
almost bumped into the woman. She kept her eyes on th
floor.

"They won't print it either," said Kirpatzke. He stood wit
his back stiff, eyes to the screen, his long fingers on the term
nal keyboard. And Lofton left, hoping that he was right abou
Kirpatzke, hoping the man was too much a half ass, a play-i
as-it-goes, to turn him in to Brunner.

0

s only chance was to get the story into a paper, and his best
ot, as far as he could see, was with his old friend Warner
wn at the *Globe.* So he drove a rented car through the
orning twilight, over the blue-gray stretch of turnpike
aded east to Boston, where he phoned Warner from a booth
the side of the road. Warner's voice, normally slick and
ofessional, was groggy and surprised. He agreed, reluc-
ntly, to meet Lofton at the Carson Wall in South Boston.

The Carson Wall was a retaining wall, three feet high, dull
d gray, stretching along between the ocean and the street.
hind Lofton, across the beach, the ocean washed up over
e ankles of the morning bathers and covered the sand with a
rty filigree of foam. In front of Lofton, across the lanes of
affic and exhaust, stood the offices of the *Boston Globe,* a
one building that had a large window so passersby could
atch the presses hammering out the daily news.

Leaning against the wall and closing his eyes, Lofton lis-
ned to the screeching of the gulls and the thrumming of the
ean. He could smell the peculiar mix of ocean smells: the
w-tide stench, the crisp salt air, the pork-fried rice grizzling
the Ocean Kai. He thought of old times, when he and
arner had walked the streets of Cambridge, talking about

women and writing and the future. "I'll make it," Loft
remembered himself saying. The memory was vivid, Warne
young, glowing face in front of him, the traffic hammering b
the air filled with the shuffling of feet. Just as suddenly, ho
ever, the memory was gone. He's not coming, Lofton though
and his chest filled with dread. But he was wrong. He open
his eyes, and there was Warner, working his way up the stre
to where Lofton leaned against the wall.

Warner looked good. His sandy brown hair had recede
but his cheeks were ruddy, and he was thin, healthy-lookin
despite the pace—the long, sedentary hours of waiting, th
the heart rush to deadline—that he must keep at the newsp
per. He wore glasses with tinted lenses to hide his eyes, som
thing he had done since college because of the dope
smoked, a habit, Lofton guessed, he had not given up.

"You look horrible," Warner said.

"Thanks. Glad to hear it."

Lofton knew what Warner said was true. He was slum
shouldered, the hospital had short-cropped his hair, he had
bruised face. He had changed his clothes, for the most pa
but he still wore the green baseball jersey underneath h
jacket. Nonetheless, the moment was good, a wry exchang

"So what's so important that you had to get me up a
down here on my day off? You still married to that woma
out in Colorado?"

"I've got a story."

Warner raised an eyebrow. For a second he looked li
Kirpatzke, the same seen-it-all glare.

"It's about Holyoke."

"Holyoke? You mean, the fire? I think we've got that co
ered."

"It's more than Holyoke. It's bigger."

"Bigger? Than Holyoke?" Warner laughed. "All right. B
why don't you tell me what's been going on first? You shou
get some sleep or something. You been walking into lam
posts?"

"No, they been walking into me. Will you read this?"

"In a minute. Tell me the story first."

Lofton was not sure he liked the way Warner was treati
him. He remembered doing the same thing when dealing wi
free-lancers over the telephone. Tell me the story first. A

ow, as Lofton started talking, Warner glanced around the
vall, watching the traffic, the women walking by. When Lof-
on got going too fast or too loud, Warner would whisper,
Hush, buddy, slow down." Lofton did not like the way his
riend was acting, but he told him the story anyway: about
ow Amanti had approached him; about Gutierrez's death;
bout how slowly the names and tangle of Holyoke sur-
ounded him until it became clear that Brunner was using
Dick Golden, the Redwings' general manager as a go-be-
ween, a payoff man who fed the head of an old street gang
noney to burn the city. Everything had been going smoothly
or Brunner, Lofton explained, until Senator Kelley discov-
red the scheme and tried to use it against him. When Lofton
vas done talking, he took the story and handed it to Warner.

"Will you read it?"

Warner took the story and held it between his fists. He
ooked at it for a while, turning the pages, his lips parted, just
arely, as he read.

"Well," Warner said, handing the pages back to Lofton, "so
his is how come you look like a goon battered by his own
sts?"

"Can you print it?"

"No."

Lofton didn't ask why. He felt the muscles below his eyes
haking. He looked out beyond his friend to the ocean.

"I think you're too involved. Too close."

Lofton turned his back, looked out at the traffic. He con-
emplated walking away.

"I told you, Frank, we can't print this. It's subjective, it's
bel, and you don't have any proof. And who are these peo-
le? Brunner? Mendoza? The Latinos? This is small-town gos-
ip, twenty-five-cent melodrama. You know that. Inside, you
now it."

Lofton looked at the sea.

"Frank," Warner said, "I know this is tough, but maybe I
an work something out. A kill fee, give you a couple hun-
red, as if I'd commissioned the story, and you get yourself a
tart out of here."

Lofton said nothing.

"It's tough, I know." Warner's tone was sympathetic.

"Don't give me this crap about how tough it is."

"Listen, Lofton, don't you give me crap either, this naïv
and holy shit. What do you expect? I haven't seen or hear
from you in years, and now you come up to me, looking lik
something out of a carnival, and act as if you've just writte
the next Pulitzer. You want to indict half the politicians in th
state on the basis of what some street punk says in som
gutter tunnel? Give me a break. Now come on, over to m
office, and I'll see what I can do about a kill fee."

"Nah, I'll stay out here and get some sun."

Warner sighed and leaned against the wall. The two ol
friends looked out toward the ocean. Warner pointed to Co
lumbia Point, a government housing project that overlooke
the water.

"The old folks, they like to say that on a clear day you ca
see Ireland over the ocean," Warner said. "But all they reall
see is Columbia Point. The slums. And they hate it."

"So?" said Lofton.

"Would they cry if it burned? Would it really be so bad?"

Sleeplessness and motion. Exhaust and rubber. The stretch
ing gray asphalt, and gray steel guardrails, and pluming gra
exhaust. *Too much hearsay.* Lofton swore and tried to kee
pace with the traffic but found himself going either too slo
or too fast. One minute he would feel overpowered, su
rounded by a crush of cars, a huge truck bearing down on hir
from the rear. *Goddamn Warner.* In another minute—or wha
seemed like a minute—he would be gliding fast over the roa
the rented car smooth and powerful beneath him, but n
quite under his control, rolling so easy that he had to swerv
lanes to avoid the traffic ahead of him. He dug through th
ashtray, looking for a good-size butt.

Outside Boston the scenery was green and lush. Some c
the trees, though, up in their highest branches, were changin
colors early, as often happened in New England, their leave
bursting into orange.

So Warner didn't take the story. So I don't have all th
loose ends. So what? Things don't always work out tha
neatly. You can't always dance through the convolutions c
the plot, the twistings and turnings, elaborating on them i
some baroque counterpoint, and then tie everything togethe
at the end. A lot of times people die before their big momen

before everything makes sense. He turned on the radio and let it crackle. Maybe Warner had been right.

He kept driving, but he did not know where he was headed, where he would stop. These gently rolling hills could be anywhere in America: Iowa maybe, or Wisconsin, or upstate California, or Oregon. And the highway was always the same; in fact, the road had a way of dominating the scenery, so that he could be approaching any American city. He could be driving into Denver, back to Maureen and his brother.

He thought of Maureen, the white cotton gown she slept in, her head against the pillow. A sign read POINTS NORTH: NEW HAMPSHIRE, VERMONT. On the radio there was news of Holyoke, the fire, the looting. Nothing he had not heard, nothing he hadn't seen firsthand while running along the railroad tracks.

The money! Suddenly Lofton remembered. He had taken the envelope from his pocket, down at the railyards, and hidden it under the tracks. Did he want the money? Would it be safe to try to find it? And what would he do once he had it? He passed another sign: HOLYOKE: NEXT 3 EXITS.

On the radio the announcer finished the local news, then patched in a national sports broadcast, a pregame show, the Boston Red Sox playing the California Blues. The station faded out as the road climbed, then came in louder than before.

"Yesterday, in a move to bolster their pitching staff for the stretch drive in the American League West, the California Blues called up pitcher Rickey Sparks from their Double A club in Holyoke. Not long after Sparks stepped off the plane, however, the Blues brass handed him his walking papers.

"In an unusual late-season shuffle involving four players and three teams, the Blues dropped Sparks after Yankee veteran Tommy Sands was unexpectedly placed on waivers by a disgruntled George Steinbrenner. Sparks now finds himself on waivers, without a team, and Tommy Sands in California, occupying Sparks's place on the roster. The Blues also announced that they will be sending two minor league players to Cleveland as compensation for slugger Billy Reames, whom the Blues had signed away from the Indians earlier in the year. Meanwhile, a spokesman for the Royals in Kansas City

criticized the Blues' last-minute dealing as being in violation
of league trading deadlines. . . ."

Lofton listened for more about Sparks, but the sportscaster
went on to talk about other games, other players, other cities.
If Sparks had done any special favors for Brunner, this was a
funny way to get repaid. He had been brought to the brink of
the big show, but then that was it, party over. There was
nothing for Sparks to do but play the hope some other team
would lift him off waivers.

"Not with his stats," Lofton muttered. "Not a chance in
the world."

The last exit came, and he swung the car into Holyoke.
Part of him did not believe that Golden was really dead, that
the city had really burned. He wanted to take a last look, to
see the place in the daylight. Also, down in the railyards, the
money was waiting. He could use it. He could go and take it,
make the long drive back to Maureen, to Denver.

He followed Dwight Street into the city. Close in, the traffic
thickened more than usual; in the neighborhoods close to
downtown, where the fires and looting had been worst, people
wandered the streets. There were a lot of people, in from the
suburbs, coming to look at the burned mill. The town had a
strange, festive atmosphere. Smoke still plumed up from the
ruins. On one corner a fire fighter stood in heavy gear. Children rode their bicycles in the streets, blocking traffic. Lofton
turned the corner toward Barena's. He would get a closer
look later.

He considered calling Amanti, but he could not see much
point. She had made herself pretty clear the last time he'd
seen her: She'd done as much as she could, and now she'd
wait it out, caught between Brunner and Kelley, just as always. He couldn't expect her to do much else.

The operator's twangy Colorado voice made Lofton home-
sick. Maureen caught the phone on the fifth ring, when Lofton was about to give up. She was out of breath. After she had
recognized his voice, there was a long silence. While waiting
for her to speak, he imagined her on the phone in the kitchen
of the old house, leaning against the counter in one of those
wide skirts she wore to teach in.

"Have you done your story?"

"Almost," he said. "They're giving me a kill fee. The *Globe* is. The story's too hot to print."

"You fuck anyone yet?"

He said nothing. There was another silence on the other end of the phone.

"I need you to sign some papers, to finalize the divorce."

"I'm leaving here," Lofton said.

Maureen was quiet. He listened to her breathing, imagined her turning, looking out the window. He thought of getting the money, of going home.

"Another one of the cats died," she said. "It was Merle; he got sick all of a sudden."

"How's my brother? You seen him lately?"

"No. Didn't you hear me? I told you Merle died."

"I heard you. I said I'm leaving Massachusetts."

"Don't you care about the cat?"

"Of course. Have you sold the house?"

"No. I decided not to. I was reacting to the divorce, but the house is mine. I want to keep it."

"Good."

Though he wasn't quite sure why, Lofton felt a surge of anger, of jealousy. What was she trying to tell him?

"Your doctor called," she said.

"What did he want?"

"Money, I guess. He didn't say."

"I have one last thing left to do here in Massachusetts; then I'm leaving."

She said nothing, and then they began to talk of small things: her job; the weather; a hailstorm so bad it killed a small child in a Colorado parking lot. The longer they talked, the more Lofton began to feel as if he'd hardly known Maureen, as if his time with her had been something that had happened to someone else, something he'd read in a book. He was about to tell her the feeling, how the sudden remoteness was bothering him, when she switched the subject.

"Legally we're still married. If you don't sign the papers I sent, I'll have to file for desertion."

"The papers are lost."

She sighed, exasperated.

"It wasn't my fault. Someone ransacked my room."

He listened to the empty sound of the long-distance wires

and wondered if he should tell her about the money. The idea of taking the money, and building his life with it, suddenly filled him with disgust—as if he really had accepted Brunner's bribe.

"I have a boyfriend," Maureen said.

"Fantastic," he said, and hung up the phone fast, without thinking. He stared at the receiver a long time before realizing it wouldn't ring back.

Lofton drove his car to Golden's house and parked in the street. He did not get out. Golden's car was not in the driveway. From his place on the street he could see Mrs. Golden's head at the front window. Though he thought of going to her, of asking if her husband had been in, he still didn't move. She was looking out at the street, Lofton could see that. He imagined how he must look to her: the long car; his head behind the steering wheel; a shadow in the smoke gray windshield. My husband's murderer, she would think, and perhaps she would be afraid for herself. It had been a long, weary night. She could not move. She could not defend herself, but this was not unusual for her. Fear was an everyday thing. At first brutish, slow, overpowering, but after a while it settled, and you got to know it well, meaningless, shapeless, like a gray fog in your lungs.

Lofton drove away. He wondered what to do with the money. After what had happened in the tunnel, he was not going to give it to the Latinos; they were as bad as Mendoza, as bad as Brunner. And Amanti had fended for herself so far; he was sure she would manage. He could always give the money to Mrs. Golden.

It took him awhile to work his way across town. After crossing the canal into the warehouse district, he drove down Commercial, parallel to the white business district just the other side of the tracks; down here English names were scattered among the Spanish. LOS PESCADORES FISH MARKET. MEDINA PACKAGE. THE GOLDENHORSE. LA JUSTICE PRINTING. JUBINVILLE PACKAGE. RAMERIZ 5 & 10. The street had a changing face to it: one building restored, the next crumbling, the next a pile of ash and cinder. Sometimes a single building would have a new glass storefront, scrubbed red bricks; to the side, the same brick would be half-scrubbed, alternating colors in dirty disarray; up above, the brick would be crumbling, the top stories boarded up, abandoned.

The streets smelled like smoke. He could see American Paper again, closer now. The building's frame had fallen in on itself. What still stood was blackened and soot-covered. Fire fighters formed in long lines around the building, holding the hoses and streaming water onto the fallen bricks. Steam gushed into the air. The bricks would be hot for days, and nothing could be salvaged. The men kept pouring, sweating, alternating places on the line. Some workers dug trenches; others sandbagged the perimeters. All around him people wandered in the streets, shouting and laughing, the men and women flirting with each other, as always: the men standing with their forearms exposed, shirts torn at the sleeves, and the women gathering in groups, their skirts tight, their blouses bright and colorful as blood.

Finally Lofton made it to the old depot, down where the Connecticut River fed the Lower Canal. A dirt road ran into the railyard. When he stopped the car, the dust raised around him in the heat. The cops were here, coming back from the tunnel where Lofton had been last night. Two of them carried a stretcher, a figure draped in a white sheet. Mendoza, Lofton thought, or Golden. Either way, it didn't seem a good time for him to go down there looking for the money. Instead, he drove up to MacKenzie Field.

In the lot behind the stadium, not far from a big pile of gravel and soot from some buildings that had been torn down a few weeks before, he found Golden's car. Its windows were open. There was a ticket under the wipers.

OVERNIGHT PARKING NOT ALLOWED.
$15.00 FINE PER NIGHT.
CAR TOWED AFTER 48 HOURS.

The ticket had been dated, the time initialed: August 28, 2:30 A.M. So Golden had left his car here and walked to the dropoff, Lofton guessed, and the kid had followed him.

Lofton walked over to MacKenzie Field. Though the gates were unlocked, no one was here yet; practice had not started. He walked back to his car and curled up in the driver's seat.

Closing his eyes, he had an image of Golden back in his glory days, young and tall, standing out on the mound and feeling all the power the world had to offer right there in his hand, where his fingertips touched the ball. He imagined Golden scanning the stands as he went into his windup, catching a glimpse of his wife, the flaming blur of her dress, as he let loose and threw, hard as he could, toward home.

Maybe Golden will still show up, Lofton thought. Maybe all the evidence is wrong. Maybe he's still alive. Maybe the car's battery is dead, and Golden's at home. Maybe he'll be at the park later. Then Lofton, knowing it wasn't true, knowing he'd better leave town himself, nodded off into a sweet black sleep with no dreams at all.

It was twilight, and the lights were on over MacKenzie Field. A gang of kids hung out near the right field gate, the same kids who had hung out there all year, fighting with one another and jiving the ticket taker.

The security guard, an old black man, asked Lofton for his ticket. Lofton flashed his press pass. The black man nodded, his yellow eyes flickering, then went back to talking with the kids. The guard had to know, Lofton guessed, that while these kids distracted him, their friends sneaked in behind the bleachers.

Lofton had gotten about four hours' sleep. He felt tired, sore, but no worse, physically, than he had felt for weeks, and his head was clear. When he had woken up, Golden's car had still been there, the ticket still under the wiper. He imagined Golden inside the stadium, wandering the stands, counting the gate, staring out at the field. Lofton thought of Golden's dedication: The man had taken a stand against the war; he had stayed with his wife despite her disease. But was it commitment that had inspired Golden, or cowardice? He remembered how Golden was, friendly one minute, surly the next. The second he walked into the park, Lofton scanned the seats for Amanti.

Her seat was empty; Brunner was not there either. The crowd was small. The scoreboard read 3–0, Holyoke trailing in the third. The Carib took the mound for West Haven. He threw hard. He looked better, if possible, than the time Lofton had first seen him, the night after Gutierrez's death.

When Lofton reached the other side of the field, he ap-
roached the old gateman who worked the glass booth near
ie clubhouse.

"I'm wondering, by any chance, if you've seen Dick Golden
round here today."

"Nope, he ain't come in yet," said the old man, his expres-
on unreadable as stone.

Golden's dead, Lofton thought, convinced, though he did
ot want to be. He did not want to let it drop. It still bothered
im; he still hoped maybe the kid had been wrong about
'hom he'd seen in the tunnel. There was also the money
nder the railroad tracks. He questioned whether he could
ive the money to Golden's wife, even if he wanted to. It
ould be complicated: retrieving the money, taking it to her
ouse, maybe even helping her get it into the bank. Worse,
omething told him she would not even take it. The thought
voked a dull resentment against her.

The people in the stands did not seem to be paying much
ttention to the game: Holyoke had lost last night, there was
o chance for the play-offs, and besides, this was the last
ome game of the season. The diehards chattered constantly,
1any would not see each other again until next season, and
1ere was a lot to talk about now—the fire mostly. His heart
uickened. A dark-haired woman, wearing a white blouse,
:ood not far away toward the press box. Amanti. No, she was
)ined a second later by another woman, a blonde, who car-
ied a baseball bat under her arm. The brunette turned. She
/as not Amanti. She was much younger. As Lofton passed,
eaded a last time for the press box, the blonde gave him a
mile.

"Jesus Christ, the fucking devil himself," said Tenace. He
urned toward Lofton, and as he did so, he made a clumsy
1ovement with his hand, taking something off the yellow
ench board, next to his scorer's pad, and maneuvering it into
is back pocket. Lofton did not catch what it was, but he
idn't ask; Tenace was always playing games.

"Where do you think our friend here's been?" Tenace said
) Rhiner, the Springfield reporter.

"I been in Bermuda," Lofton said.

"Playing hero, huh?"

"Yeah, that's right. You seen Golden around here?" He

asked the question again, though he knew it was hopeless
stupid. Tenace shook his head. Rhiner gave Lofton a dim
silly look. The Carib went to his windup, a strangling over
hand that dropped and whipped at the last moment, a move
ment more like cracking a whip than throwing a ball. Thi
young black pitcher was the best player Lofton had see
down here; no doubt Oakland would lift him up before long

"I was talking to some guys from the *Dispatch.* I hea
they're real shook up down there," said Rhiner.

"What do you mean?"

"About your story. It's causing trouble. The police bee
down, all hot. Something about the Gutierrez murde
They're saying you were involved."

Lofton looked at Rhiner, into the man's milk blue eyes, an
grabbed the *Dispatch.* There, on the first page, was his story
the one he had given Kirpatzke the night before.

"Kirpatzke ran it!"

"Yeah, now he's gone. Nobody can find him. He ble
town."

Lofton laughed.

"Lawyers been calling. They're going to make it tough o
you, on the paper. McCullough's wording a retraction."

"So Brunner's putting the pressure on Mac now, huh?
asked Lofton. Behind him a bat cracked against one of th
Carib's pitches.

"Rumor is they're going after you. The police, the court
the paper. Everybody."

Tenace shook his head. Rhiner, who had been animated a
he spoke, stared at the ground. Lofton was excited. He kne
he should leave—*will they extradite me?*—but it was such
triumph, Kirpatzke going with the story. *Will Brunner ki
me?*

"Shame what they did to Sparks."

Lofton turned. He had a sudden, unexplainable fear. "Is h
dead?"

Tenace looked at him in disbelief. "No, he's in Los Angele
near Disneyland; people don't die there. . . . Didn't yo
hear? They flew him out yesterday afternoon, and he got ther
in time for the second half of a twin bill, a night game. The
gave him a big-league uniform, let him sit on the bench. Hi
picture is in the paper—standin' around with some majo

gue hams. Today they pull it out from under. Cut him off
the knees."

Sparks had played it careful. He had pitched hard, played
to Brunner early on, when he thought it could still help,
d, when things got dangerous, he had kept his mouth shut.
ine of it had done him any good. Chances were Sparks had
en a good kid all along. Self-obsessed but still good. If
arks had been working for Brunner, and if Brunner's influ-
ice did extend upward into Cowboy's California office,
iere the Blues decided whom to cut and whom to save, then
seemed the Blues would have at least let Sparks sit the
ison out on the bench, rather than cut him so completely.
), it didn't make sense. The only answer was that the Blues
d brought him up on their own impetus, then let him go the
me way. The more Lofton thought about his own interview
th Sparks, the less likely it seemed that the pitcher was
irking for Brunner.

"Lucky for Tim Carpenter, though," Tenace went on.
jetting out of here, up to Cleveland. They're taking him up
e beginning of next season."

"The Indians?"

"It's the major leagues, the big show. The women"—Ten-
e raised his eyebrows—"have bigger vaginas."

"They traded Tim Carpenter to Cleveland? I didn't know
at."

So Carpenter had made it. Lofton liked the idea. He felt a
dden boyish burst of enthusiasm, partly for Carpenter, but
ire for himself—pleased that the story had appeared, that
his work hadn't been for nothing. Brunner must be angry
hell, he thought, and the idea pleased him even more. He
indered what Kirpatzke was doing, where the former editor
d run to.

"Sparks may not know it," said Tenace, "but he's a lucky
stard to get out of this hole. His arm's shot, but he's had a
od time. At least part of his body's done okay. Ask the girl
wn there; she knows about a good time."

Tenace pointed to two girls who sat behind the Holyoke
gout. They were the ones Lofton had seen earlier in the
ind, sixteen, maybe seventeen years old, the blonde one
all and slender, the other small and dark. Both girls wore
:ir jeans and blouses tight, and the blonde wore so much

makeup on her high-boned cheeks that her face looked like
mask. One of the girls held a baseball bat, some sort of souv
nir, Lofton guessed; she rested it on her shoulders. "Spar
was making it with blondie there, the one with the bat. Sh
heartbroken. You and I can help ease her pain after t
game."

"Last time I saw you, Tenace, you wanted to kick my face

"Nah, you don't need me. You fuck yourself just fine."

Hammer was pitching now, Holyoke in the field. Hamm
threw a floater, and the West Haven batter smashed it back
him. The ball bounced off his glove, over second and in
center.

"Another loser," said Tenace.

"Barker's working him like he worked Sparks," Rhin
protested. "It's not the kid's fault. There's something wro
with management here."

"Yeah, but he's not the real stuff. Take a look at the Car
there. Lotsa poise. Not a hit against him today, not even
walk. Little sucker's on his way to a perfect game. He's g
what you need, the beautiful stuff. The other guy, he's j
your regular slob."

Amanti's seat was still empty, of course; she wasn't goi
to show up. He remembered his last image of her vividly no
descending the bleachers into the brutal, carnivallike crow
fire sirens piercing the air, Kelley on one side, smiling, Bru
ner on the other, his hand clamped around her wrist.
wondered what effect his story would have on her, how ang
Brunner would be. She might have changed her mind abo
staying close to them now, he thought; she might want to ru
Last night, though, it seemed she had considered that event
ality. She would stay regardless.

"Why don't we give the girls a try, you and me, after t
game?"

The girls stood in the stands behind the Holyoke dugo
Beyond them were some kids playing a flip game; one of t
boys was the kid Lofton had talked to last night in the stand
The kid seemed to have calmed down, nothing on his mi
but the game he was playing with the other teenagers. Loft
stood up. He could give the kid a note for Amanti and fi
out what was happening, if she needed his help, if she need
the money.

"Where you going now?" Tenace asked.

"The Grapefruit League."

"No, come on. Where you going?"

Lofton said nothing. Tenace looked around. Rhiner studied them both.

"Take my advice, man, go far, get lost, do it."

"A second ago you wanted me to stay, help you with girls. What is it?"

"My heart wants you to leave," whispered Tenace, pointing to his chest, "but my wallet says stay."

The scorer gave him a cryptic smile. Though Lofton knew there was something he was missing in Tenace's crack, he didn't take the time to figure it out. The man had warned him out of town once before, and apparently he'd been paid to do it—by Brunner, he guessed—but Lofton did not know what the scorer was getting at now. I'll ask him when I get back, he thought, and went on toward the kids playing flip. The two girls were nearby. Lofton's head felt as if it were floating away, the same way it had felt after Gutierrez's murder, when he had wandered back to the dead man's apartment. *A stupid thing to do.* The image of his own hotel room came to him: mattress slashed, papers and clothes strewn all over.

Though Hammer could not get out of the inning, Coach Barker showed no signs of helping him; there were no relief pitchers out in the bullpen, no one warming up. The girls were watching Hammer, giggling. The blonde still held the bat under her arm. The teenagers silently flipped their knives in the dirt. Lofton's kid no longer wore his Redwings' cap; the kid placed a handful of quarters down in the dirt in front of him. He was losing his money to the others.

Reaching for his pocket, taking out a cheap plastic pen and a small pad of paper, Lofton stood watching the kids, trying to decide whether he really should send Amanti a note and what exactly he would say if he did. Then he remembered this was the last home game of the season. In all likelihood Amanti wouldn't be down here again; even if Lofton could decide what to write, the kid would not be able to deliver the note. Lofton doubted he should risk searching her out on his own; he had no delusions about leaving town with her. Instead, he imagined her sitting in her apartment, the hectic phone calls from Brunner and Kelley after the story hit, and

then the long silence, as the men did what they could do to
put things straight, and she sat there, waiting. She was probably right, he thought. They wouldn't hurt her, at least not in
any way you could write up and put in the paper, nothing
physical, no bruises, no bloodstained carpet. She'll leave
sooner or later, he thought, maybe not today or tomorrow
but she'll leave, she'll just walk out. He wondered if that was
true.

"What are you writing?"

Lofton turned. It was the blonde who had asked the question. She looked at him coyly. "I haven't seen you here before."

"One of the players give you that?" Lofton pointed to the
bat.

The blonde looked him up and down. "Yeah, Elvin Banks.
Gave it to me a couple nights back. Right after he fouled
out," said the blonde. "Why, you wanna *hold* it?"

"Sure."

The brunette stared off. She wore an initial pin, a silver *J*,
clipped to her blouse.

"You a scout?" asked the blonde.

"Yeah," Lofton said. "I'm a scout."

"You wanna sign my bat?"

Glancing over his shoulder, Lofton saw that Tenace was
looking at him, staring back. Closer by, a few yards away, the
kids were getting loud in the dirt. Lofton's kid lost another
quarter.

Lofton turned the bat in his hands. The girl had been collecting signatures. There was Sparks's. Large, looping letters.
Apparently the girl had gotten his signature before he left
town. Most of the other players had signed, too. Banks.
Barker. Lynch. Carpenter. He studied the last one longest,
staring at the letters.

"He's going to the majors next season, you know; maybe it
will be worth something," the girl said.

As he turned, Lofton saw the kid lose again. Though the
kid didn't seem to mind, it bothered Lofton. He remembered
how he'd abandoned the kid last night, when he was shaking
in the stands, and now he was trying to get the kid involved
again, sending him off with another note. He became very

nscious of the bat in his hands, the good feel of the wood
ain against his palms.

"Can I have this for a minute?" he asked.

"Why?" The girl was suspicious now.

"I want to show it to the boy over there. He'd get a kick out
it."

The blonde looked sidelong at her friend. Suddenly she
oke to the brunette in Spanish. Lofton was surprised. The
rls laughed. The blonde went up on her toes and whispered
Lofton's ear. She touched the front of his shirt, clutching it
htly with two fingers. "Okay, but there's something I have
show you, too," she whispered, and then backed away. The
onde laughed again. The brunette turned away.

"Doesn't she speak English?"

"Not to *scouts,*" said the blonde, and she twirled away,
llowing her friend. "Bring us our bat back soon." She gave
ofton a long, silly backward glance—the look of a teenager
asing an adult. He wondered, again, if he should bother
ying to contact Amanti. He looked to the outfield. It was
lm there; things made sense. The fielders stood in their posi-
ons, hands on knees, feeling the good sun on their necks.
hey waited for the batter to swing.

Glancing back to the press box, he saw that Tenace was no
nger there. Odd, he had never known Tenace to leave the
x, not till the end of the game. He had to keep track of
lls, strikes, hits—all for the record, no matter the score.
ow only Rhiner sat in the box, a solitary figure behind the
re mesh.

The kids paid no attention to the field but went on playing
eir game. Still holding the girls' bat, intending to show it to
e kid, he watched while the boy lost the last of his quarters.
eaching into his pocket, Lofton took out five dollars and
elt down with the kids.

"What do you want with us, man?" asked one of the kids.

"I'm going to stake your friend here."

"That's not smart."

Lofton put his hands on the kid's shoulders, and the kid
niled. Lofton slapped his money on the dirt. From the cor-
r of his eyes, he saw Tenace coming out of the clubhouse.
hat's he been up to in there? Lofton had a sick feeling. On
s way out, Tenace jostled up against the two girls, pretend-

ing it was an accident. Holding his hands to his head, makin
some joke, then laughing, Tenace was trying to strike up
conversation with the girls. He didn't appear to be su
ceeding. Lofton heard a siren in the distance. One of the teen
agers playing flip heard it, too.

"More fires." The teenager smirked.

"Nah, it's a cop car, not an engine," another one said.

After listening a moment, Lofton realized the second k
was right. Holyoke's fire trucks sounded a siren that rose an
then died and then rose again, a piercing and falling cry,
the engine rushed down the streets. This noise was not lik
that. This noise was that of a police car: a steady, insisten
wail. The car seemed to be coming in their general directio
toward MacKenzie Field.

After turning his head and saying one last thing to the gir
Tenace shrugged his shoulders and headed over to Lofton.

"How come you're not up in the box? You got Rhiner keep
ing score?"

"I just had to run an errand." Tenace winked. "Wanted
check out those girls you been talking to. Look like sluts
me."

"Didn't look like they thought much of you either."

Outside, the siren was closer. At the last minute, though,
the noise got closer, it suddenly stopped. Trouble a few stree
over, Lofton guessed. Looking up at Tenace, he saw that th
other man's face was red, embarrassed.

"No, they liked me fine, Lofton. It's just those girls, to te
you the truth, I just don't think they're your style."

Below him, Lofton's kid flipped and missed. The othe
shuffled quarters up out of the dirt, into their pockets. The
closer than before, just over the outfield wall, the siren waile
again, a brief, anxious bleat, as if the cop were testing his sir
or snapping it for fun. Tenace glanced nervously toward th
front gate. Lofton looked, too. *Leave,* he told himself. *Get o
of here now.*

"What are you up to?" Lofton asked.

"Nothing, pal." Smiling, pleased with himself again, or pr
tending to be, Tenace put a hand on his shoulder. "I got to g
back up there and do my job, but I tell you those girls aren
your type. You know, you need someone more intellectual-

ou know, like that girl down at the library, that little pale-
aced one."

Tenace patted him again, grinning hard, then turned to
eave.

"Hey," said Lofton, "I didn't know libraries were the kind
f place you spent—" Lofton cut himself short. Tenace had
valked only a few steps, and Lofton, glancing down at the
nan's ass, had seen—riding in the scorer's pocket, stuck half-
vay out—the fountain pen Lofton's own brother had given
im back in Colorado. He recognized it instantly, the black
ocket clip down the center of the tarnished silver, and he
unged toward Tenace, grabbing him by the back collar with
ne hand, forgetting that he still held the baseball bat in the
ther. "You bastard, you're the one who trashed my room.
ou been staking me out from the beginning, setting me up all
he way around." Tenace tried to pull himself free. He was a
ig man, and he pushed hard, so that Lofton lost his balance
nd his grip. Lofton reached out to grab him again, but the
corer gave him another shove and pulled away quickly, de-
pite his weight, and the kids behind them suddenly let out a
cream.

"The cops!" they yelled, and then they scattered, grabbing
or the money, Lofton's kid included. *Run,* Lofton thought,
ut he hesitated, taking a step after Tenace, then turning,
eeing the cops, watching the kids scamper and disappear.
)ne of the cops was Ryan, homicide. Glancing back, Lofton
aw Tenace was gone, working his fat ass up to the press box.
Meanwhile, the girls watched: the brunette in her pink blouse,
yes half shut, dim and sultry, and the other girl, who stood
wirling a strand of her honey-colored hair between her
ngers.

Detective Ryan sauntered toward him slowly. The cop was
mug; he was savoring the moment. Lofton gripped the bat
ighter in his hands. It must have been Tenace who told them
was here, Lofton thought, patting my back one minute, then
neaking off the next, calling the cops from the clubhouse.
enace. He wasn't the type who went down to the library to
alk over classics with the woman behind the desk. Tenace
ad been following him from the beginning, that was clear,
nd had trashed his room, taken the fountain pen. Everything
lse fell in place quickly, easily, behind those facts, so that

Lofton didn't have to think about the details: how Tenace had seen him with Amanti here at the park; how Tenace had taken him aside, that day at Barena's, the day before Golden tracked Lofton down; and how he himself—thinking Tenace nothing more than a deliveryman, clumsily spouting someone else's message—had mentioned that he was supposed to meet Amanti the next night. True, he had not said where he was going to meet her, or why, but Tenace must have passed the information along to Golden; then Golden had searched Lofton out on his own, waited outside Amanti's. *"Let's just say,"* Golden had said, *"that I put a nickel in the jukebox."* So Tenace had been the one gathering information, selling it back and forth, to Brunner, to Golden, to anyone who would pay.

Detective Ryan paused in front of Lofton. The cop's hands hung loosely at his side. His fists were closed.

"I think you made a mistake," Ryan said. "You're a murder suspect now. You should have done like you were asked."

"I guess you're right," said Lofton.

Ryan, as he moved to reach for his handcuffs, looked Lofton up and down. Another cop stood at the main gate, but the ballpark kids were taunting him from the street, distracting him just for fun. Lofton's best chance was across the field at the right field gate, where there was only that old security guard. It would be a long run across the outfield grass.

"You're a suck-ass, Ryan."

Ryan's face dropped. Lofton didn't hesitate. He came around with the baseball bat and hit Ryan hard in the face. Ryan, a bright burst of blood covering his eyes, dropped to the ground. The blonde's mouth fell open; the brunette was serene, passive. Lofton jumped the fence and starting running toward the right field gate.

The Carib, halfway into his windup, saw Lofton but did not stop. He followed through and fired at the plate. The bat cracked back, and Lofton got a glimpse of the ball arcing away from Banks's bat, headed for the left field wall. He saw Banks digging for first, and he could tell, by the crowd noise, that the hit had fallen in. They cheered because Banks had broken up the Carib's attempt at a no-hitter; then they cheered for Lofton as he ran. He headed toward the old black watchman, ahead at the gate. The guard, Lofton guessed, was dumbfounded, and for a minute Lofton felt good, knowing he

ad smashed Ryan good, written his story, done everything
hat it was in his power to do. The running exhilarated him,
is lungs felt good and clean, and he pushed himself, stretch-
ig his legs as far as they would reach. He thought he heard
he crack of the bat again, not once, but twice, three times,
npossibly loud, as if the noise had come from inside his
ones, his heart. That cop is shooting at me, he guessed; then,
efore he realized he'd been hit, he was hit again, his neck
napped backward, and the crowd went silent, watching, as
e fell against the outfield grass.